FOR
YOU
ALONE,

FABIO

PIRATE

by

Fabio

in collaboration with

Eugenia Riley

AVON BOOKS ◆ NEW YORK

PIRATE is an original publication of Avon Books. This work has never before appeared in book form. This work is a novel. Any similarity to actual persons or events is purely coincidental.

AVON BOOKS
A division of
The Hearst Corporation
1350 Avenue of the Americas
New York, New York 10019

Copyright © 1993 by Fabio Lanzoni
Photograph courtesy of Fabio
Published by arrangement with the author
Library of Congress Catalog Card Number: 93-90341
ISBN: 0-380-77046-6

First Avon Books Printing: November 1993

AVON TRADEMARK REG. U.S. PAT. OFF. AND IN OTHER COUNTRIES, MARCA REGISTRADA, HECHO EN U.S.A.

Printed in the U.S.A.

RA 10 9 8 7 6 5 4 3 2 1

In loving memory of my grandmother, Ines,
and supporting the American Cancer Society
in its efforts to help all mothers and grandmothers
win the war against cancer

I gratefully acknowledge the contribution of Eugenia Riley, without whom this book would not have been possible.

I would like to express my special appreciation to Peter Paul, my friend, partner and manager, who shared my vision and was the first to help me communicate my message of love and romance by making it possible for me to write my own romance novels;

To Robert Gottlieb, whose vision as a super literary agent enabled me to get my first publishing contract with Avon Books, and to his associate Mel Berger who has supervised this project;

To my friend and business partner Eric Ashenberg, whose support and counsel have been invaluable in helping advance my career;

To Ellen Edwards, my editor, and Liz Perl, Avon's publicity director, who have guided me through my new experience as a writer and member of the literary community, and have helped establish me in this new role;

To my mother and father, who have raised me and afforded me the opportunities and advantages that have uniquely prepared me for my career;

And especially to the millions of women who support the Romance publishing industry, and who have supported my career as a cover model, enabling me to step off the covers of their books to develop my career in publishing and entertainment.

ONE

Off the South Carolina Coast
September 1742

A FIRE BLAZED ON THE DISTANT ISLAND, ETCHING THE night sky with a haze of crimson as the sound of screams and the acrid smell of smoke filled the air.

With the sea breeze whipping about his tall, powerful body, Marco Glaviano stood on the quarterdeck of the brigantine *La Spada*. Spyglass raised, he watched the slaughter on Edisto Island half a league to port. While the wind whistled in the rigging and the ship's timbers groaned, he observed cottages and plantation homes ablaze, and Spanish pirates chasing the helpless English citizens—men, women, and children—with sabers cruelly slashing. The horrible mêlée seemed almost obscenely incongruous on such a mild September night, when the sea gleamed with tranquil splendor.

Marco's helmsman, Giuseppe, spoke up from his post at the wheel. "Carlos at work again, *capitano?*"

Marco nodded grimly. "I must assume our enemy is raiding the English cotton plantations in retaliation, after four of his company swung at Hangman's Point in Charles Town ten days past." He made a sound of contempt. "How I hate the Spanish."

Giuseppe chuckled. "That does not stop you from bedding Rosa."

Marco smiled wryly. "There is a vast difference between sporting with a Spanish woman and wanting to skewer her countrymen."

Giuseppe, a slightly built man with dark hair and eyes, threw back his head and laughed. "Perhaps not so subtle a difference, after all, *amico mio?* A mere distinction between a saber and a pike?"

Marco appeared far from amused by Giuseppe's bawdy humor as he again raised his spyglass and watched a Spanish pirate plunge his cutlass through the back of an Englishman, while another whoreson threw down a hysterical woman and slashed through her nightgown to bare her for his rape. He groaned and lowered the spyglass. How he abhorred the violence in this world that impelled him to respond in kind. He need not pray to *il Dio* to know what he should do here.

"Let us make for the island and see what damage we can do to our enemies. It does not sit well with me, women and children being raped and slaughtered in this manner."

With a mumbled "*Sì, capitano,*" Giuseppe turned the wheel to port. Marco shouted orders to his crew. While the seamen scrambled, hauling sails and trimming the yards, Marco smeared his face with soot, checked the load in his pistol and the edge of his cutlass. Remembering the carnage witnessed through his spyglass, he felt rage churn inside him as he recalled how the Spanish had tortured and killed his very own father.

Marco Glaviano had been born and raised in Venice. Four years ago, his father, the Venetian ambassador to Spain, had been accused of spying in that foreign land and had been turned over to the Inquisition to meet a horrible fate. After hearing of her husband's death, Marco's mother had wasted away from a broken heart. At the age of eighteen, Marco had become a man without a family, having lost his only sister, Bianca, to a fever years earlier. Anguished and embittered, he had taken to the seas as a pirate, with a crew gathered from amongst his own countrymen. He had become a man who shunned convention and the practice of formal religion. Eventually, he had arrived in the New World, where an offer from the British admiral at Charles Town had at last afforded him his opportunity for revenge. He had signed up as a privateer with the English in their war against Spain over colonies and the sea lanes.

As the hull of *La Spada* scraped the edge of a sandbar, Marco gave orders to strike the sails, drop anchor, and lower the longboat. Leaving his lieutenant in charge, he quickly chose seven of his trustiest men—including Claudio, his quartermaster, and Luigi, his boatswain—to accompany him on his mission of mercy. The eight clambered down the rope-and-cleat ladder into the longboat and quietly rowed for shore, with Marco uttering terse instructions for their mission.

The men beached their craft and crept through the marsh grasses, advancing stealthily toward the raging flames, the screams, and the carnage. Marco signaled to his party to spread out, while he himself sprinted off toward the Spaniard he had spotted raping the Englishwoman. The fat bastard was rutting on the frail, shrieking female like a bloody pig!

Marco leapt in to rescue the woman, yanking the villain off her. The startled man tottered on his feet for a moment before anger mobilized him. Without even bothering to button his gaping breeches, the

Spaniard drew out his cutlass and charged at Marco
with a howl of rage. Marco sidestepped the lunge
and engaged the man, deftly blocking blows while
responding with quick, aggressive strokes and nimble footwork. The two locked swords with a shrill
shriek, and Marco shoved the man back. He ducked
as his adversary sprang forward again, aiming a
mighty slice at his neck. Surging upward, Marco
felled the man with a thrust to his midsection.

Marco quickly turned to the woman. Staring com-
passionately at her distraught face—battered features
and haunted eyes—he leaned over, pulling down her
gown and helping her to her feet.

"Go hide in the fields, woman," he ordered gruffly.
"And remain there until the danger has passed."

She nodded convulsively and stumbled off.

Marco was watching her flee to safety when another corsair jumped out at him with cutlass flashing.
Marco swung his weapon, deflecting the stroke. For
several seconds, the air was rent by the sound of
steel striking steel as the two danced about deftly,
whacking and lunging at each other, dodging swings
and parrying blows. Marco drew first blood, slicing
his opponent across the forearm and enraging the
man to the point of carelessness. With a scream of
fury, his foe lunged forward for the kill, only to be
knocked unconscious by the flat side of Marco's well-
aimed cutlass.

Marco caught his breath. His blue eyes scanned the
landscape and he blinked at the stinging smoke.
Grimly, he watched several of his men engage the
other pirates. It was his nemesis, Carlos, he sought—
Carlos he so yearned to defeat, here on this battle-
ground, where any man was fair game, and not in
port, where the two men were required to walk as
equals. As the best privateers their respective countries had to offer, he and the notorious Spaniard had
clashed repeatedly throughout this bitter war.

Just as he spotted his towering enemy swinging his cutlass in the distance, his gaze was abruptly seized by a child in a nightgown and wrapper who emerged from a nearby cottage, one of the few remaining structures not ablaze. She was a striking creature, surely no more than twelve, tall and slender, her thick, light brown hair streaked by the sun and blowing in the breeze. Her face was lovely—long and angular, her mouth full, her chin strong, her upturned nose and large eyes perfect in every detail.

Two things at once struck him about her. She was the most beautiful child he had ever seen. And, unlike the others, she betrayed no fear. Indeed, she was staring at him quite boldly . . .

Christina Abbott had been sleeping when the smell of the smoke and the sounds of the horrible mêlée awakened her. She had just ventured out from her cottage when she spotted the giant of a pirate standing across from her on the beach. Now she stared at him, fascinated, mesmerized. He wore a leather vest with no shirt, and bandoliers sheathing pistols and daggers. The moonlight gleamed on his smooth, powerful shoulders and arms, the silvery light glinting off his single gold earring and the deadly cutlass he held in his hand. The wind rippled his Turkish trousers against his hard thigh muscles. With his blackened face, long blond hair, and blue eyes that seemed to burn out at her in the night, he appeared to Christina's childish imagination as the most glorious barbarian she had ever seen, like some mythical raider out of *The Arabian Nights*. Oddly, she felt no fear of the fierce conqueror, and was instead instantly captivated by his rugged beauty . . .

In the split second after his eyes had locked with the girl's, Marco watched a Spaniard make a dive for her. In the space of a heartbeat, he drew out his cutlass and leapt between them, engaging the man in fierce swordplay. Wielding his cutlass aggressively as

he advanced, Marco slayed his adversary quickly, lest
the ravager bring any harm to the girl.

As his opponent crumpled to the ground, Marco
turned back to the child, feeling astonished that she
revealed no trepidation at having watched him kill a
man—indeed, she still held his gaze raptly. Then he
again spotted his adversary Carlos in the distance,
steadily approaching them as he whacked away with
his cutlass.

Should he stay and fight, risk the possibility that
Carlos or one of his band of predators might grab
the girl? She appeared all alone, with no protector
in sight. Had her family already been lost in the
slaughter?

The Spaniards would rape her, he thought with revulsion. What some of Carlos's men would do with
this child would be much worse. The knowledge
filled him with a disgust bordering on physical
malaise.

Staring into her guileless eyes, Marco quickly
made a decision. Here was one prize that would not
be plundered this night.

He spoke to her, rapidly and urgently. "*Cara*, you
are not safe here. The Spanish pillagers will hurt you.
Will you come with me?"

She nodded and smiled.

Realizing the need to bear her to safety in haste, he
closed the distance between them, hooked an arm
around her slim waist, and heaved her over his
shoulder. She resisted him not at all, and she felt
light as a feather. An unaccustomed tenderness
choked his heart, and again he thought of Bianca, the
sister who had never gotten the chance to grow into
lovely womanhood.

This child would. He had not been able to save his
sister, but this precious life he would defend.

He glanced around them to reconnoiter the battle.
Carlos had slipped out of sight. His own men had

done what good they could, slaying several of the ransackers, and the other marauders were fleeing, manning their longboat. But Marco did not trust the *bastardi*—they would return later, when the danger had lessened, and rape and pillage at their leisure.

This child they would never touch.

Marco whistled a signal to the others to retreat, and strode off toward his longboat with the girl.

Yet before he had proceeded ten yards, a shrieking, bent crone in a nightgown and bed cap rushed at him and attacked his back with both fists flying.

Marco turned on his assailant with cutlass drawn, the girl still dangling over one shoulder. He scowled magnificently at the fierce little woman who confronted him with hands balled and bloodlust gleaming in her dark, beady eyes.

"Desist, woman, or meet your death!" Marco roared.

The woman did not back down an inch. "Release that child, you bloody heathen, or I shall see you in hell this very night!"

"Who is the child to you?" Marco demanded.

"I am her nurse."

Marco snorted contemptuously and started off toward the longboat. "As her nurse, you should be far more concerned with her safety. I shall not leave the girl here to be molested by the Spanish when they return later this night."

"And what do you propose doing with the child, my fine barbarian?" the nurse hissed as she raced alongside Marco.

"I propose taking her to a place of safety," he snapped.

"Then I shall be coming along with both of you!" the woman insisted.

By now they were striding through the surf toward the longboat. "Very well, woman," Marco said disgustedly. "But if you value your life, I should advise you to curb that loose tongue of yours."

The nurse was wisely silent as Marco placed the child into the longboat, handed the nurse in, then hopped aboard himself. As Luigi slipped in beside them, he glanced askance at the girl and the nurse, then quirked a brow at his captain.

"Have you resorted to carrying off children, boss?" he teased.

Marco glared at his boatswain. "I am saving the rest of this girl's childhood, and see that you curb your loose tongue, man."

The chastened Luigi fell silent, and once all had boarded, the other members of Marco's crew regarded the girl and her nurse with wary glances as they rowed back toward the brigantine. Meanwhile, *La Spada*'s cannon boomed out as Marco's gunners took aim at Carlos's sloop setting sail to the south of them. Marco cursed as he watched the shots explode harmlessly in the water, missing the out-of-range vessel as it made off into the night.

Across from Marco, her eyes wide as she took in the scene, Christina Abbott was filled with excitement over this great adventure on which she had just embarked. When she had first awakened tonight to the screams of the islanders, she had felt a momentary twinge of fear. But all her trepidation had fled the instant she had ventured outside and spotted her huge blond pirate. This giant who had saved her from the plunderers was truly the most magnificent man she had ever seen. She took a moment to admire his exquisitely chiseled face—the noble slant of his nose, his firm mouth and strong chin, his high cheekbones, his deep set eyes and broad brow. She watched the wind whip tendrils of his long blond hair about his noble face. She had never seen anyone like him before.

Now they were pulling alongside a large, two-masted brigantine whose lowered sails snapped and billowed in the breeze. The pirate easily lifted Christina onto the ladder, and she clambered up it and climbed onto the main deck of the ship. As the others joined her, she looked around at sprawling, cluttered decks, at cannon and ropes and rigging, at loose chickens and pigs scurrying about, at bearded crewmen in dark clothing and tricorn hats who regarded her and Hesper with open curiosity.

Their host barked out orders to weigh anchor, hoist sails, and come about to the south, and then he turned to Christina and the nurse. Nodding to both, he said simply, "You two, follow me."

Christina glanced at Hesper, and when the older woman nodded, the two of them wordlessly followed the towering man across the deck and down a companionway. The odors of bilge, decaying food, and animal excrement assaulted Christina's nostrils as the pirate ushered them through a narrow passageway and into a small cabin. Amid the soft glow of an oil lamp, Christina took in a rumpled bunk and a table cluttered with maps, a brass tankard, and a sextant.

Hesper at once charged their host verbally. "I insist, sir, that you return the child and myself to our rightful home immediately."

The pirate did not even blink as he picked up a cloth, wet it in a basin, and slowly began wiping the soot from his face. "That is out of the question, woman—leastwise, until all of us have a little chat." He nodded at the bunk. "Please, sit down."

Hesper faced down the pirate with fists clenched and eyes blazing. "If you are thinking to get one of us in your bunk, you are sadly mistaken, you bloody beast!"

Surprisingly, at Hesper's diatribe the man threw back his head and laughed. Christina watched him, enchanted by the flash of his perfect white teeth and the gleam of merriment in his beautiful blue eyes. Oh, he was such a divine creature, she mused, especially now that he had rubbed off the soot and she could so clearly see his sun-browned visage. His body appeared doubly magnificent with the soft light gleaming on hard muscles and bronzed skin.

"You delude yourself, woman," he said to Hesper, "if you think I am so desperate for female solace that I would seek out your company. I merely thought that you and the child might prefer not to stand."

Hurling a glare at the pirate, Hesper grabbed Christina's arm and backed them both up to the bunk. They sat down primly on its edge.

Marco gazed at the two observing him so intently—the nurse with her pinched mouth and glare of contempt, the girl with her innocent beauty and look of fascination. He could not resist winking at the little angel, and she grinned back, displaying beautiful small teeth and the most adorable dimples he had ever seen. It occurred to him suddenly what fun it might be to have this minx as a little sister—to tease her, spoil her rotten.

Then he froze at the gleam of promised retribution in the nurse's eyes. He hastily cleared his throat. "Your names, woman?"

The nurse snorted. "The girl is Christina Abbott, and I am her nurse, Hesper Bainbridge." Sarcastically, she finished, "And with whom do we have the honor of speaking, your lordship?"

Marco drawled lazily, "I am Marco Glaviano, in His Majesty's service as a privateer against the Spanish."

"A privateer!" Hesper spat. "Meaning you are no better than a bloody pirate!"

A smile pulled at Marco's sculpted mouth, but he did not comment directly. "What brought you and the girl to Edisto Island?"

Hesper's gaze narrowed. "The girl is an orphan,

her father and stepmother having drowned in a shipwreck off the North Carolina coast a year past. Her guardian in Charles Town has little patience with children, and thus he sent both of us to his cottage on the island. There, it has been my charge to rear and tutor the child."

Marco listened to these revelations with a fierce scowl. "What sort of imbecile is this guardian you speak of, madam? Is he not aware that England and Spain are at war, with sea islands such as Edisto frequently raided by Spanish privateers?"

Hesper bristled visibly at Marco's scolding. "It is not my charge, sir, to dictate to Christina's guardian what his decisions should be."

"Then you are a fool, woman," Marco retorted. Ignoring Hesper's outraged cry, he glanced at the child. "Since the girl has no kin and her guardian has woefully neglected his duty to provide for her safety, it occurs to me that she would be much better off at the Caribbean island base occupied by me and my men."

While the girl appeared highly intrigued by this suggestion, the nurse, wild-eyed, was enraged. "Why, you bloody heathen! I have heard of these odious dens of iniquity that your freebooting kind swarms all over in the Caribbean—drinking and debauching and committing Lord knows what other sin! I tell you, the girl and I will have none of it."

Marco fought a chuckle. "I assure you, woman, that you and the child will be safe from all harm and molestation. Do you actually think you would be better off back on Edisto than you would be with me in the Caribbean? I am well acquainted with Carlos, your tormentor tonight, and I assure you neither the child nor you will be safe from his savagery when he returns."

Hesper sucked in her breath and fell silent.

Marco glanced at the child. "Let the girl decide

what she wants." When Christina merely stared back
at him, he went to stand before her. A powerful emotion, something he could not quite name, tugged at
his heartstrings as he observed her gazing up at him
so intently. "You are very quiet, *cara*," he said gently.
"Tell me; are you frightened of buccaneers?"

She shook her head vehemently. "No. I think you
all are quite wonderful."

While the nurse emitted an outraged cry, Marco
had to smile. The child's voice was like music, so lyrical and sweet. "What do you want to do, then? Go
back to your island, or come with us to the Caribbean?"

Her smile was instant, and stunning in its radi-
ance. "I want to come live with you on your island."

As Hesper uttered her dismay, some paternal instinct made Marco reach down and tenderly touch
the child's soft cheek.

"It shall be as you wish, then, *cara*."

Hesper, meanwhile, again bared her wrath on
Marco. "Sir, I insist that you take us back to the island at once!"

Marco only shrugged. "The girl has made her
choice, but as for you, woman, nothing would please
me more than to give the order to come about and to
relieve myself of such a festering thorn in my side."

Hesper trembled in her anger. "If you think I shall
allow you to dump me, then take the girl off to do
heaven knows what with her on your godless island,
you have seaweed where your brains should be—
that you do!"

"Then the matter is settled," Marco drawled. "The
two of you may have the use of my cabin until we
return to Isola del Mare, and I shall see if some suitable clothing can be found for you." He stared kindly
at the girl. "Good night, *cara*."

"Good night, pirate," she whispered back.

Marco grinned as he slipped from the cabin.

Hesper turned on her charge and spoke in an angry undertone. "Why did you tell that beast of a man that you wanted to go off with him to his godforsaken Caribbean?"

Christina raised her chin defiantly. "Because he rescued us from the pillagers and because I like him."

Hesper snorted. "Will you like what he and his heathen kind will do to you?"

Christina faced down her nurse unflinchingly. "Marco will not harm us. He promised."

"So he is Marco to you now, is he, you saucy miss?" Hesper demanded with contempt. "And you believe the promise of this—this marauder?"

"He spoke the truth," Christina argued. "Uncle Charles was wrong to send us to the island. We were not safe there. The Spanish would have returned and slaughtered us."

"If you had only stayed in the cottage as you were supposed to, none of this would have happened."

"If I had stayed in the cottage, the brutes would have murdered us in our beds."

Hesper groaned and turned to straighten the rumpled bunk. "For now, we must get some rest," she mumbled wearily. "We shall figure out this muddle on the morrow."

Hesper snuffed the lamp, Christina removed her wrapper, and the two females climbed into the narrow bunk together. Christina could not sleep for all the excitement she felt. Ever since she had lost her beloved parents a year past, her life had been a prison, her only companion being her martinet of a nurse who spouted endless rules and lessons. But tonight, her gallant rescuer had come and taken her away on a grand adventure. She eagerly anticipated tomorrow's discoveries.

Marco. She liked the sound of his name. Endlessly she recalled the beauty of his tall, muscled body, the

laughter in his eyes, and the gentleness of his smile.
She remembered his strong, warm fingers brushing
her face, and the odd thrill that had coursed over her
at that moment. She knew she was not quite a
woman yet—and yet she also knew in her heart that
she already felt very drawn to the handsome prince
who had changed her life forever this night.

Next to the girl, Hesper found sleep elusive also,
but for a far different reason. Fear and rage churned
within her at the fate of herself and her charge—
being the helpless captives of these barbarian pirates.
The girl was a naive fool, thinking that they were
embarking on some magical journey, but Hesper
knew better. She trusted these foraging Italians no
more than she trusted the plundering Spanish.

Another worry plagued her. Although Christina
did not know it, she was heiress to a large fortune
her father, Richard Abbott, had left in trust for her
future husband. But never would Hesper Bainbridge
reveal to the freebooters the girl's true wealth, for
that would only be an open invitation to the scoundrels to ransom her . . .

Marco Glaviano stood on the quarterdeck as his
mighty brigantine plowed the silvery Atlantic. A bemused smile curved his lips. He had taken on the
protection of a child tonight, for reasons he did not
completely understand. On principle, he liked his life
unencumbered, as any man with a quest had to style
his own existence.

Not that the girl would present undue
difficulties—she had her nurse to care for her, and he
was hardly prepared to take on the role of father
once all of them returned to his island.

Perhaps it was his emotional reaction to the child
that troubled him. When she had stared at him so
bravely, he had become inundated with feelings alien

to him ever since he had lost his family—tenderness, protectiveness, and a welling joy at the very sight of her.

She was a glorious one, all right. If she remained on his island, there would be the very devil to pay when she matured into a ravishing young woman and all his men fell hopelessly in love with her.

In the meantime, he could ill afford the luxury of succumbing to brotherly feelings for this babe in arms! He was a man with a mission, a man who would not rest until all the Spanish miscreants were destroyed.

TWO

Four days later
The Caribbean

THE BRIGANTINE *LA SPADA* PLOWED THROUGH THE CRYS-
tal blue waters of the Caribbean. The mighty square-
rigger appeared glorious in her full suit of sails, her
bow dipping through the waves.

Marco stood near the helm, the crisp breeze tugging at his hair and clothing as he scanned the bright
horizon for the first sighting of his island. Gulls, a
sure sign of imminent land, swooped about midships, squawking stridently and diving for the crusts
of stale bread his men threw out.

Beside Marco stood Christina. Today she wore a
simple shift of white, sea-island cotton that her nurse
had hastily sewn after Marco had presented the
woman with a bolt of cloth, needles, and thread. The
loathsome shrew herself stood several paces behind
them, leaning against the bulwark, watching Marco

16

and her charge with arms akimbo and face screwed up in a perpetual scowl.

The child appeared totally caught up in their adventure, Marco mused with pride. She stood with her wide green eyes eagerly searching the horizon and her mane of sun-streaked, light brown hair curling in the wind. Over the past few days, she had followed him around the ship, much to the chagrin of her nurse. Marco, on the other hand, had found the girl to be a delightful companion—ever present with her sunny smile, but never demanding anything of him. She had appeared fascinated by the workings of his brigantine, and Marco had encouraged her to ask him questions, and patiently answered her every query. His men had also taken an interest in the girl. Patrizio, his carpenter, had taught her how to sound the pumps, while Francesco, his sailing master, had instructed her in handling the halyards and hoisting the jibs. He had chuckled the morning he had found her on deck with several of his men, cheerfully scrubbing the planks with a holystone. Only yesterday he had been compelled to pull the little monkey off the ratlines after he had caught her clambering up the ropes after two of his sailors who had gone aloft to tie down a mainsail that had broken loose in a gust. When she had scolded him for his caution, he had laughed at her spirit and courage.

Now she gently tugged on his hand, and he smiled down at her. "Yes, *cara?*"

"Will we soon reach Isola del Mare?" she asked solemnly.

She was a clever one, he thought. He had mentioned the name of his island to her only a couple of times. He ruffled her hair and replied, "*Sì, cara*. We should sight land very soon now."

She nodded. "What does the name of the island mean?"

"Isle of the sea," he replied.

"The name is Italian?"

"*Sì.*"

She smiled. "And you are Italian?"

"Actually, I am Venetian."

"What brought you to America?"

He hesitated. He rarely discussed his motives for being in the New World, and yet he trusted this guileless child, and found it easy to share with her. "I lost my parents, *cara*," he murmured tightly. "It was because of the Spanish."

Her eyes grew huge. She gripped his hand and regarded him earnestly. "How horrible! Tell me, please!"

Any adult who had pressed Marco for such details about his past would have met with instant, unholy retribution. Yet again he found himself totally disarmed by the innocence of this girl. Her hand in his felt so trusting.

He sighed. "My father was a very successful silk merchant in Venice. Almost five years ago, he was appointed Venetian ambassador to Spain. During his sojourns in that foreign land, he began to suspect that the Spanish Crown was withholding from the Pope the Church's share of the gold and silver treasure the Spanish galleons brought back from South America." A bitter line hardened his mouth. "On his final journey to Spain, my father planned to confirm his suspicions and then later contact Rome. However, before he could act, he was discovered, turned over to the Inquisition—and murdered."

"That is so very sad!" she cried, crestfallen. "What of the rest of your family?"

"My mother—she was lost without Papa. Within a year, she developed a bad cough and died soon afterward."

"I am so sorry. And have you any brothers or sisters?"

He regarded her with sudden tenderness. "Only an

older sister, Bianca, who took a fever at the age of sixteen and died while off at convent school."

She squeezed his hand. "Poor Marco. Then you are an orphan, just as I am?"

He nodded, finding to his surprise that he felt not at all put off by words he normally would have interpreted as indicating pity. "*Sì*, we have much in common. We are both lost lambs."

Her young face tightened. "My father and stepmother did not die because of the Spanish. It was a shipwreck."

"I know, *cara*," he murmured sympathetically.

"And now you fight the Spanish to avenge your parents' deaths?"

"For one so young, you are very wise."

"Do you capture their treasure to punish them for cheating the Pope?"

He fought a grin. "In a manner of speaking."

She frowned. "Hesper calls you a bloody pirate. But I think you are splendid." She stared up at him raptly. "And very beautiful."

At her open, childish adulation, Marco found himself, for the first time in his twenty-two years, actually blushing! He was not prepared for such hero worship from this trusting child. Her high esteem for him made him tempted to assume responsibilities for her life that he could ill afford to take on.

Glancing over his shoulder and grimacing at the nurse's murderous glare, he released Christina's hand and whispered conspiratorially, "Do not think me too wonderful, *cara*, else your nurse will no doubt murder me in my bed."

At once, her small hand touched his tanned forearm, and her solemn eyes met his. "Do not worry. I shall never allow that to happen. I will protect you."

Marco feigned amazement. "You would battle your nurse for me, *cara*?"

Christina glanced dispassionately at Hesper, then back at him. "I would cheerfully strangle her."

She looked so adorable then, the expression of determination on her precious face so fierce, that, had it not been for the nurse's blistering scrutiny, Marco would have pulled the child into his arms and swung her about, laughing his delight.

"There, *cara*, look."

Ten minutes later, Marco and Christina stood at the rail. He handed her his spyglass so she could catch her first glimpse of Isola del Mare. The large island was nestled among a chain of smaller islets. She viewed a vast curtain of lush greenery, gleaming white beaches, the sprawling roofline of a plantation house, and, in the distance, the gentle wooded rise of a volcanic slope. Scanning back toward the water's edge, she spotted beds of glistening coral, black rocks, and spray-tossed tide pools that gave way to white coral beaches. She watched a hermit crab zigzag along the beach in his shell, while a fat turtle plodded into the surf. To the far west stretched a salt marsh where stunning pink flamingos dug for shrimp.

She handed Marco back his spyglass. "It is most beautiful. That is your house I saw?"

"*Sì*. It used to be the home of English planters. After they left, the British Navy assigned me this island as my base."

"That is where we shall all live?"

"*Sì*."

Christina nodded happily as Marco strode off to attend to his duties. She gazed down at the ocean floor, studying in fascination the vivid sea grasses, beds of fingerlike coral, and a rainbow variety of fish. She sucked in her breath as a sleek dolphin swam by, sending the other fish into swarms of motion.

Marco joined Giuseppe at the wheel, and noted to

his chagrin that, far from minding his duties, the helmsman was staring at the child. When his order to bring the craft about brought no response from the Venetian, Marco shoved the man aside and grabbed the wheel, steering hard to starboard as he belted out orders to his men.

"Have you gone daft, man?" he demanded furiously of Giuseppe. "Are you blind to the coral reefs ahead? Do you intend to bring us into harbor or splinter us to smithereens on the reef?"

"I am sorry, *capitano*," Giuseppe replied hastily. He glanced at Christina. "I have discovered my future bride."

"The girl?" Marco inquired in disbelief as he maneuvered the wheel. "What depravity is this? She is a baby!"

Giuseppe shook his head solemnly. "Give her another two years, and she will be plenty enough woman for me." His dark eyes met Marco's earnestly. "Let me have her, boss, and I swear, she will be my queen. My first move will be to fetch a priest—even if I must go all the way to Havana to find one."

"You are serious!" Marco cried. "In two years, she will still be a baby. She must be given time to grow and mature. *La bambina* must be a child first, before she can be anyone's woman."

"My cousin Carmelina in the Old Country was married at fifteen," Giuseppe argued.

"I know," Marco replied, "but I think it is wrong. A female should not be required to care for a husband and children when she is still so young herself."

Yet Giuseppe disagreed. "Look around you, boss. All of your men have already noticed her. It will not take two years for all of them to start fighting over her—and thus I must get my claim in first."

In consternation, Marco glanced about him—at tall, slender Francesco staring at the girl as he braced the mains; at portly Patrizio blinking at her with his bleary-eyed stare as he manned the pumps; at swarthy Luigi slanting her a glance as he tightened the rigging. Good heavens, Marco thought, had he placed the child in even more peril through his rescue of her?

"Your claim is denied," he snapped at Giuseppe. "Furthermore, you will make it known to my crew that the girl is not to be harassed, that any man who harms her will answer to me. Is that clear?"

"*Sì, capitano,*" answered a clearly disappointed Giuseppe.

During the next few moments, Marco became busy maneuvering his craft into the deep-water cove where the harbor lay. At his orders, the sails were struck and the men climbed the yards to tie down the canvas. As *La Spada* glided up to the weathered wharf, Marco gave the order to drop anchor and tie up the ship. Once the craft was reasonably secured and the gangplank extended, Marco rejoined Christina and Hesper, escorting the two females down onto the pier.

They were met by a merry welcoming party of women and small children—dark-skinned, mostly Italian peasants in colorful garb who jubilantly embraced members of the crew. Christina smiled as a charming boy who appeared no more than four handed her a nosegay of exquisite, tiny pink flowers. She thanked the child and watched as he scampered off, screaming exultantly, "Papa!" A tug of emotion gripped her heart as she watched a laughing, bearded pirate heft the child into his arms and proudly kiss his cheek. Christina smiled and waved at the lad as he went off in his father's arms, with his mother by his side. In the meantime, the rest of the assemblage was dividing up into various family groups and heading off into the woods.

"Come, *cara*," Marco said.

As they approached the trail leading into the jungle, Christina glanced at the half-dozen cannon perched on stone buttresses around the harbor. Several seamen, with conch shells slung about their necks and muskets braced against their shoulders, were patrolling the area.

"You are expecting other pirates?" she asked Marco gravely.

"Not just pirates, but Indians," he explained. "When we first arrived at the island, we were impelled to run off a tribe of fierce Carib warriors."

"Bloody cannibals!" Hesper chimed in, and Marco shot the nurse a quelling glance.

"*Are* they cannibals?" Christina asked Marco, wide-eyed.

"Do not worry, *cara*," he replied gallantly. "My men and I will protect you. We have lookouts posted on the beaches as well."

Satisfied, Christina slipped her hand into Marco's, and the two of them, with a sullen Hesper following, strolled down a narrow trail into the lush forest. Looking upward, Christina was enchanted by sprays of light drifting through towering palm, gum, and chestnut trees. She was equally enthralled by the massive kaklin roots that dangled to the jungle floor. Night sage, honeysuckle, and bougainvillea spilled their fragrant blooms, and the scents of dew and greenery were heavy on the air. Watching two vivid-green parakeets flit about and shriek to each other, she knew she was going to be very happy here.

In due course, they emerged before a massive, raised, West Indian-style plantation house with a weathered facade and shutters askew. The appearance of the home was ramshackle, but Christina did not care—she might have been standing before the most enchanting European castle.

"This is where you live?" she asked Marco excitedly.

"*Sì.*" He led her up the worn steps, Hesper following with a disapproving frown.

"It is most beautiful."

Marco chuckled, and Hesper uttered a snort of contempt.

"Where do your men live?" Christina asked as they arrived on the sprawling porch.

"They have cottages all over the island."

"And the peasants we saw at the docks are their wives and children?"

Catching the look of savage condemnation in Hesper's eye, Marco coughed and hedged. "So to speak." He hastily swung open the rickety door and escorted the two females inside.

Christina blinked at the dimness of the corridor in which they stood, and wrinkled her nostrils at the unpleasant, musty smell. The hallway was wide, cluttered with several scarred tables and sagging chairs. A magnificent Renaissance tapestry hung at a precarious angle along one wall, and several other priceless treasures—bronze vases, gilded chests, and rock crystal pieces—sat dusty and abandoned on various pier tables or chiffoniers.

Hesper glanced haughtily at the disorderly salon opening off to their left and at the equally unkempt dining room on their right. "You live in a pigsty, sir," she spat at Marco.

"And your compliments warm the cockles of my heart as usual, woman," he drawled back.

Before Hesper could launch into another diatribe, a door at the end of the corridor creaked open, and a plump, attractive woman with black hair in a bun strode forward. She wore a long, plain gown and a stained white apron.

"So the lord of the manor has returned," she sneered to Marco.

He sighed. "I am not sure I can endure this hero's

welcome." He turned to Christina and Hesper. "This is my cook, Eunice."

Hesper at once assailed the woman. "Madam, you live in a pigsty."

The cook roared with derisive laughter and swiftly retaliated. "I am not the housekeeper but the cook, you witch. If you want this sty cleaned up, then I suggest that you make use of the broom you flew in on." She turned to Marco, and with a curt nod toward the newcomers, demanded, "Who are these fools?"

"Refugees from one of Carlos's raids," he explained. "They will be staying with us."

The cook issued an outraged cry and threw up her hands. "Two more mouths to feed?" She shook a finger at Marco. "It is bad enough that all your men are always showing up begging for a meal. Now this! I tell you, I must have an increase in wages."

"Very well," he conceded wearily. Watching her lumber off, he confided to Christina and Hesper, "Eunice is Greek and a very difficult woman."

Christina clutched Marco's arm possessively. "I shall protect you from her."

Spotting the vengeful look in the child's eyes, Marco chuckled. "Now, *cara*, do not forget that we need her quite badly. After all, we must all eat, must we not?"

She nodded, but her expression remained fierce.

Marco led them down a winding hallway to bedrooms in the western wing of the house. Hesper's expression was one of purest revulsion as she eyed the two adjoining rooms with their unkempt furnishings and moth-eaten draperies. Then, with a cry of outrage, she stormed over to the dresser and hastily flung a yellowed dresser scarf over a statuette of a naked Venus.

"And where do you sleep, your lordship?" she demanded of Marco.

"Across the hallway," he answered evenly.

Hesper balled her hands on her hips. " 'Tis inde-cent!" .

The line of Marco's jaw hardened. " 'Tis for the girl's own protection—and you will do well, woman, to remember that I am the one who rescued the child!"

Hesper uttered a derisive hoot. "And now you are claiming to protect her from your heathen crew?"

"*Sì*, woman. I will keep her safe."

Something about the look in Marco's eye must have given Hesper pause, for, though she har-rumphed, she said no more.

The awkwardness abruptly ended as the door to the hallway swung open further and a very dark cheetah cub, who appeared to be all paws and ears, sprinted inside and padded over to whine patheti-cally at Marco's feet.

Hesper sucked in her breath and recoiled in fear.

Christina tore across the room and scooped the cub up into her arms. "A kitty!"

"*Cara*, don't!" Marco cried, then froze.

Oh, *Dio mio*, he thought, why had he not remem-bered to warn Christina about the cub? Even now, it had been on the tip of his tongue to caution her that his new cheetah cub intensely disliked other females, but the girl had grabbed the cat before he could even speak—

Yet the cub was quickly disavowing his previous assumption as she purred in the girl's arms and stared up raptly at her face! He was utterly amazed!

Hesper spoke in a tense, murderous undertone. "Your lordship, what is this beast?"

Christina swung around to grin at Hesper. "Can you not see? It is a kitty!"

"She is a rare king cheetah," Marco corrected, star-ing at Christina with a flabbergasted grin.

"Get that filthy animal out of here!" Hesper cried, prompting the cub to direct a savage hiss her way.

"Careful, woman," Marco admonished the nurse. As she wisely fell silent, he turned his attention back to Christina. "*Cara*, I would advise you to put the cat down."

"Why?" The girl's expression was crestfallen. "The kitty likes me."

The cub demonstrated by licking Christina's face.

Marco was shaking his head and laughing. "It is truly remarkable. You are the first female the cub has taken to. Why, she took a bite out of my mis—out of a certain lady's ankle a few weeks ago."

"I cannot believe that!" Christina exclaimed stoutly. She stared into the cheetah's innocent gold eyes. "You would never bite anyone, would you, kitty?"

The cat nestled her head beneath Christina's chin and purred contentedly. Marco looked on with delight.

"Where did you get her?" Christina asked.

"Off a Spanish slaver that was returning to Havana from Africa a month past."

"But why did the Spanish have her?"

He shrugged. "I assume they captured her in Africa, hoping eventually to sell her to a circus or carnival back in Spain." He regarded the cub with pride. "She is quite exceptional, you know. Black cheetahs are almost unheard of."

"Yes, she is so beautifully dark," Christina agreed, studying the cub's dusky, spotted face and the exotic, near-black mane along her back. "What is her name?"

"I have not named her yet," he confessed.

Christina peered into the animal's eyes. "With her gold eyes and their black centers, she looks just like a yellow pansy."

"Pansy?" Marco repeated, outraged. "Is that a fitting name for the fastest hunting cat on earth?"

Christina threw him a beseeching glance, filled with childish longing.

He gestured in defeat. "Very well. Pansy she is." He crossed the room and gently retrieved the cub from the girl's arms. "Come along, Pansy." He nodded toward the still scowling nurse. "I shall allow you two to get settled in. Dinner will be served at sunset."

"Cursed barbarian!" Hesper spat at the closing door. "With wild animals living under his very roof amongst civilized folk!" She eyed their surroundings in exasperation. "Look at this sewer!"

Christina, heedless of Hesper's outburst, wandered over to the French doors. Opening them, she stared, fascinated, at the lush tropical jungle just beyond the courtyard. She gazed at a profusion of palms, banana trees, climbing bougainvillea, and blooming hibiscus. She watched a captivating emerald hummingbird buzz at the flowers. The breeze surged, rustling the heavy foliage as it would the many layers of a woman's skirts, and wafting the scent of the perfumed air across her.

A tremor of emotion coursed through her, a feeling of belonging she had not known since she had lost her dear parents and had been banished to Edisto by her guardian—

She wiped away an unexpected tear. For the first time in so many long months, she felt at home.

Marco sat in his study, completing the log of his journey and scratching the ears of the cheetah cub, who was curled up, purring, in his lap.

"So you are Pansy, are you?" he teased the cat. "The girl will turn you into a big spoiled baby yet." He chuckled. "She is a breath of fresh air, that one, isn't she? *Il Dio* smiles on us for rescuing her and bringing her here. Now you have a big sister to play with."

Pansy purred her agreement and gently chewed on Marco's fingers. He glanced up abstractedly as Luigi strode in through the opened doorway.

"You sent for me, *capitano?*" the man asked respectfully.

Marco nodded. "Please go to Rosa's cottage and tell her I have returned."

The boatswain smiled. "She was not at the docks?"

Marco shook his head. "She lives the life of a cat, that one, and does her roving at night."

Luigi grinned at the cheetah. "And does she mate like a cat, *capitano?*"

A rueful smile pulled at Marco's mouth, but he made no comment. "Please caution her that I am too busy to—um—entertain her until after the evening meal."

"She will not like that, boss."

Marco raised an eyebrow. "Then tell her that if she comes too early, she will be denied her treat."

Luigi howled with laughter. "Do not worry, boss. She will never risk forgoing that pleasure."

Marco was grinning as his boatswain left. But his smile swiftly faded to a thoughtful frown as he continued to stroke Pansy's ears. Already the child he had rescued was changing his life and his habits. Yet he could not have Rosa at his table tonight, for she would feast on him wantonly and rapaciously. Indeed, the wench was so brazen that she might well shamelessly mount him in front of the others. He grinned at the thought. Normally, he would be delighted.

Not that his mistress would not earn her keep tonight. He had not tasted a woman in weeks, and the night would definitely be reserved for vigorous sport, not slumber. Yet, for the child's sake, at least a modicum of decorum must be maintained.

Staring down at the newly christened cub, he found he minded this small intrusion of civilization not nearly as much as he would have thought.

At sunset, Marco, Luigi, and Giuseppe, along with Hesper and Christina, were all seated in the dining room. The evening was warm and balmy. Near the sideboard stood a peasant child pulling the chord that swung the huge punkah fan back and forth over the table. Pansy crouched near the child, lapping a bowl of goat's milk.

Christina admired her gallant rescuer, who sat flanking her at one end of the table, the candlelight sculpting his handsome features and dancing highlights in his thick hair. Hesper sat opposite Marco at the other end of the table; and the two crewmen, across from Christina.

The cook, Eunice, and her helper, a pretty young Spanish woman named Maria, brought in plates heaped with grilled sea trout and saffron rice. As the two women made their rounds serving the food, Marco winked at Christina and reached over to pick up her water goblet.

"Wine, *cara?*" he asked.

She beamed. "Oh, of course!"

Hesper quickly protested. "Spirits for a child? It is out of the question, sir."

Undaunted, Marco added some wine to Christina's goblet. "You English are far too thin of blood," he chided. "In Venice, as in many parts of Europe, we raise our children on watered wine. It makes them strong of heart and spirit."

"It makes them bleedin' sots!" Hesper spat. "Just like that dissolute husband of mine who was in his cups when the press gang got 'im and took 'im off to perish at sea with the scurvy."

Fighting a grin, Marco handed the goblet back to Christina. "We shall be ever mindful of the press gangs, then." Watching the child take a hearty gulp, he admonished, "Slowly, *cara*, or we shall be compelled to dilute your brew even more."

Christina nodded and turned her attention to the sea trout, which she found to be very tender and wonderfully flavored. Despite the cook's haughty manner, Christina agreed with Marco that she did serve her purpose.

Hesper was again glaring at Marco. "Well, now that you have us both here as your hostages, your lordship, what do you propose doing with us?"

"You are not a hostage, woman," Marco answered. "Indeed, you are free to go at any time."

"Hah!" Hesper said derisively. "And are we to swim back to South Carolina through the bloody shark-infested waters?"

He shrugged, yet his voice held a menacing edge. "You may do as you please, woman, but do not presume to decide for the child."

"Why, you savage brute!" Hesper railed. "The girl is in my charge and don't you ever forget it!"

Marco's fist slammed down on the table and his eyes gleamed with anger. "The girl is in no one's charge, woman! As long as she remains on this island, she is accountable only to herself."

"What kind of bleedin' anarchy is this?" Hesper cried. "Are you saying you propose to allow the child to do precisely as she pleases?"

Marco's smile was near frightening. "But, woman, that is what we are all about on this island. We all do *precisely* what pleases us—short of bringing harm to any of the others."

"The girl will be hopelessly corrupted! She will go primitive!"

He raised his wineglass. "Islands are primitive places, madam."

Hesper was stunned speechless. Christina was captivated by the exchange. For at the moment when

Marco had smiled so ruthlessly at Hesper, he had become all savage pirate—pure, uncompromising wickedness. As a child unaccustomed to having a champion, she had loved him at that moment, every bit as much as she had reveled in his defending her.

The tense silence was at last broken as the Spanish girl, Maria, flounced back into the room with a loaf of bread. As she passed Luigi's chair with a saucy swing of her hips, the dark pirate reached out and pinched her bottom. Maria shrieked with lusty laughter, sending her hot loaf sailing across the table. The missile narrowly missed Christina's head, then splashed into a cuspidor. While Christina watched, wide-eyed and fascinated, Luigi grabbed Maria around the waist, hauled her brazenly astride him on his chair, and buried his face in her bosom.

"Your lordship!" Hesper was literally purple with rage, and shrieking like a demon at Marco.

At the cry of the crone, Luigi looked up, grinning unrepentantly at all those assembled. Marco caught his man's eye and soberly shook his head. With a shrug, Luigi hefted himself to his feet, the buxom, laughing Maria still dangling in his arms, her skirts tousled and her legs wrapped tightly around his waist as he left the room.

Christina remained enthralled. Not twenty seconds after the two had gone, she could hear the sound of Maria's soft cries of pleasure coming from a distant room.

"Your lordship!" Hesper shrieked.

Marco nodded to Giuseppe, who dashed from the dining room. Seconds later, a door slammed and the bawdy sounds came no more.

Hesper surged to her feet, trembling in her outrage. "You bloody swine!" she screamed at Marco. "So you all do what you please on this island, do you? With no thought given to the girl's sensibilities?"

"I have told you, woman, that you and the child will not be molested!" Marco snapped.

"And I trust you about as far as I could throw the whole bleedin', fornicatin' lot of you!" Hesper shouted back.

She grabbed Christina's hand, yanked the girl up, and hauled her forcefully from the room. At the portal, Christina just managed to pivot and face Marco. She grinned at him, and her heart sang with joy when he winked back.

THREE

Soon after they returned to their rooms, Hesper demanded that Christina go to bed. But sleep proved elusive to her as she lay in the big tester bed with the mosquito netting drawn around her, listening to the sounds of frogs and owls, the pounding of the surf, and the rustling of tropical foliage. She watched the night breeze billow the curtains at the window, sending strange shadows dancing across the room.

At last Christina pulled back the netting and tiptoed over to her dresser, idly looking for a water pitcher and a glass. She touched a beautifully carved but tarnished brass urn, a chipped, dusty crystal dish. She pricked her finger on the ragged edge of the crystal and uttered a cry of dismay.

Grabbing her wrapper from the chair and licking her wounded finger, she ventured out into the darkened corridor, and saw a light under the doorway across from her. Certain this must be Marco's room, she skipped over and softly knocked.

She heard his deep voice command, "Come in," and she opened the door and stepped inside eagerly.

She spotted him on the rosewood bed, shirtless, in his breeches and hose. His blond hair hung about his shoulders, and he was sipping wine. Pansy lounged next to him, wetting her paws and washing her face.

At the sight of Christina, Marco set down his wine, a look of surprise and wariness etching his features. "*Cara*, you should not be here," he said sternly.

"I could not sleep." She held up her wounded finger and sniffed back her tears. "And I hurt myself."

"Oh, *cara*. Poor darling."

At once Marco sprang up, shrugged on his shirt, and crossed the room. Pansy followed, whining as she seemed to pick up her master's mood of concern.

"Let me see that," Marco said. He took Christina's hand and scowled at the tiny cut. "It is nothing, but then, we must be very careful. Even the tiniest wound can fester badly here in the tropics. Come with me."

With Pansy faithfully following, Marco led her to a washstand, wet a cloth, and wiped off the blood. Then he tore off a strip of clean cloth and wrapped the wound. He ruffled her hair and grinned. "All better now. See that you keep the finger clean and wrapped. It is important that you take good care of yourself."

"Aren't you forgetting something?" she asked.

"Am I?"

She held up the wounded finger. "You must kiss it and make it better."

He chuckled. "Oh, of course." He took her hand and solemnly kissed the bandage. "There, m'lady. Now it is off to bed with you, before that nurse of yours strings us both up from the nearest gibbet."

She raised her chin. "I am not afraid of her. I would die for you."

He stared at her quizzically for a moment, then

grinned. "Such devotion and bravery are commendable, but hardly necessary, I assure you. Come on
now. Mayhap I have a remedy for your restlessness."

He took her hand, picking up a lighted taper as he
led her out into the corridor. Pansy loped along behind them. They wended their way to the front of the
house, crossed over and turned into another wing. At
the end of the narrow passageway, he escorted her
inside a small room filled with several large chests.
Using the flame of the taper, he lit an oil lamp.

"What is all this?" she asked, glancing about.

"Plunder, *cara*," he said, throwing open the lid of
one of the chests.

Christina gasped in awe and delight as she viewed
the contents of the velvet-lined interior—fabulous
silks, gold and silver coin, bronze and pewter urns
and dishes, and jewelry of every description.

"Oh, how splendid!" she cried, her eyes alight
with wonder. She leaned over and scooped up the
cub. "There, Pansy, look at Marco's booty!"

Pansy emitted an appreciative purr, and Marco
chuckled.

"May I play with the treasures?" Christina asked.

He tweaked one of her ears. "But of course. That is
why I brought you here." Soberly, he added, "But it
must be our secret."

"Oh, yes!" she cried earnestly. Setting down the
cub, she crossed herself quickly and spoke with vehemence. "I cross my heart and hope to die if I tell
anyone!" She picked up a small gold coin, with
strange writing and an emblem of a ship. "What is
this?"

"A Danish ducat."

She held up a larger silver coin emblazoned with a
shield and a crest. "And this?"

"A Spanish piece of eight."

"But where did you get it?"

"When we raided a Spanish galleon near St. Augustine."

Christina's eyes were enormous, her expression fascinated. "Will you take me along the next time you raid the Spanish?"

"Sorry, *cara*, but I cannot. The sea is no life for a child."

"And why not?" she demanded indignantly. "Can I not climb the ratlines as well as any of your men?"

He struggled not to smile. "You would not like it nearly as much as you think."

"If you were there, I would love it!"

He chuckled, but his expression turned serious. "It is a hard life, *cara*. Sometimes we can be becalmed for weeks at a stretch, with naught but fetid water and maggoty bread, if we have rations at all. Besides, you would not be safe. My men and I are charged with attacking Spanish shipping, and often even the merchant ships do not strike their sails without a fight."

"Must you be very brave, then?" she asked earnestly.

"Oh, yes, very." His words were grave, but laughter danced in his blue eyes.

She turned petulant. "If you won't take me along, you must at least stay and tell me how you obtained every bit of this plunder."

"A demanding little minx, aren't you?"

"Oh, please!" she begged.

Staring down at her eager, angelic face, Marco was tempted, more than he ever would have dreamed, to while away several hours with this child, spinning yarns of his various exploits. But then, he could not linger tonight. Rosa was due in his room at any moment, and he was already on shaky ground with his mistress. If he spurned her again, she would go into one of her pouts and he would be denied the night of sport his body so badly craved.

"I cannot tonight, *cara*," he replied gently. "But I

will another time. In the meantime, as long as you are quiet and your nurse does not discover you, you are free to play here just as long as you please."

She grinned. "May Pansy stay, too?"

Marco stared down at Pansy, who whined plaintively. "Of course." Actually, he felt relieved that his cub would be kept occupied here, out of sight of Rosa, since his mistress and the cheetah detested each other.

Wearing a delighted grin, the girl again heaved the cub up into her arms. "Pansy, you get to stay!"

"Just be careful with her," Marco warned, watching the cub chew on the lacy collar of Christina's wrapper. "Sometimes she becomes overly enthusiastic with her teething."

"You mean she is not fully grown?"

He threw back his head and laughed. "She is a baby, like you."

"I am not a baby!" she declared irately.

He wisely did not argue. Nodding toward the cub, he said, "I had a devil of a time weaning her after I rescued her, half starved and seasick, from the Spanish. I had to feed her milk with my fingers."

"Poor Pansy." Christina cuddled the cub and regarded Marco with devoted eyes. "You are very kind to go around saving orphans, Marco."

The moment was becoming far too poignant, and Marco tried humor to lighten the mood. "Ah, but what a winsome couple of orphans the two of you are."

Christina set down the cub and began sifting her fingers through the various treasures. "May I keep some of these? And Pansy wants a treat, too, of course."

Marco shook his head. What a delightful and clever child she was. He would surely spoil her rotten in no time. "I tell you what, *cara*. You and Pansy

may take all you can carry in your own two hands,
or—er—paws. Is that fair?"

"Oh, yes!"

He turned to leave, then tarried as he heard her
chortle of glee. He pivoted to see her pick up a long
section of glittering gold chain and stare at it, captivated, beholding the light dancing over the links.
Pansy, meanwhile, was trying to climb up her wrapper. Giggling, Christina squatted to her haunches and
picked up the cub; then both of them toppled over,
Christina laughing as Pansy landed on her chest.
Marco stood in fascination as Christina wrapped the
chain about Pansy's neck and the cheetah cub affectionately licked her face. Again he felt that odd catch
of tender emotion tug at his heart, and he realized
that he longed to stay and watch this adorable child
cavort with the cub, to delight in her innocence and
joie de vivre. He thanked *il Dio* that here, she could
remain childlike and free, that she would be protected from the horrors that had long ago shattered
his own youth.

With reluctance, he tore himself away to go to
Rosa.

She was waiting for him. When he entered his
room, he spotted her lusty, plump body sprawled
across his bed. Her ebony hair hung down around
her shoulders, and her skirts were invitingly raised,
her bodice scandalously low. A smoldering expression sculpted her dark, exotic face and a full pout
curved her ruby lips. His manhood hardened to life
at the sight of her.

"*Gattina*," he murmured, and crossed the room to
her.

He knelt on the bed, but as he reached out to take
her in his arms, she shoved him away petulantly.
"Why did you not want me at your table tonight?"

Hoping to distract her, he reached for her again,
teasing, "Oh, I want you at my table, *gattina*. I shall

feast on you at my leisure. Indeed, spread your legs and allow me to demonstrate."

But again she pushed him away. "Not until you explain."

He stood and sighed, frowning at her sulky expression. Sometimes he wondered why he tolerated this hot-blooded Spanish piece. She could be such a bitch sometimes.

But then, she really knew how to sport. The very thought further heated his blood and sent a thrill of potent arousal through his manhood.

He strode off to the dresser to fetch her present. "How is the ankle?"

Rosa snorted as she stared down at the fading red bite marks. "Healing—no thanks to that monster cub of yours."

He laughed. "The two of you are too much alike—both female cats, and both jealous."

"Is that why you banned me from your table tonight?" she countered sullenly. "Were you afraid that the cub would take another chunk out of me—or that I would take a chunk out of the cub?"

At the dresser, he grinned, reaching for the velvet case that held her present. The ruby should help redeem him, he mused ruefully. "Actually, we had some guests for dinner. Some English we rescued from a Spanish assault on Edisto Island."

"And you were too ashamed to have me share your table?" she retorted indignantly.

"Of course not, *gattina*. I simply did not wish to scandalize our guests into apoplexy with the sight of you mounting me at our feast." He turned, winking at her lecherously. "At least, not on their first night here."

When Rosa roared with ribald laughter, literally holding her sides, Marco knew his troubles were over. He drew out the fabulous ruby pendant and grinned as Rosa's gaze became riveted on the dazzling necklace. Swinging it enticingly, he rasped, "Now, come here, you bad girl, before I lose all patience."

With a sensual purr and a sultry flash of her long lashes, Rosa rose and strutted over to stand before Marco. Jiggling her breasts wantonly, she stroked him brazenly through his trousers. "Ah, yes, I do so hunger for my treat, *corazón*."

He groaned and clasped the necklace about her throat. He was so aroused now, he feared he might burst in her fingers. His hand caressed a ripe breast. He was staring into her fiery dark eyes, about to lean over and kiss her, when, all at once, the door behind them flew open and he heard Christina's voice.

"Marco, are we not beautiful?"

Both of them whirled and leapt apart to face the child, who had burst in, leading Pansy by a long gold chain. Normally, Marco would have been furious to have his seduction of his mistress interrupted, but the sight of Christina with the cub was so delightful, so enthralling, that all lustful thought abruptly fled his mind.

She stood there like a young goddess, laughter gleaming in her eyes and enchantment shining on her beautiful face. Her body was swathed in shimmering jade-green silk. She wore a red velvet cape, a glittering diamond tiara, and more bracelets, necklaces, and rings than he could ever possibly count. Pansy, too, was absurdly and regally attired, for somehow Christina had managed to wrap gold chains around all four of the cub's huge paws and had tied a giant red silk bow around Pansy's neck.

"*Sì*, you both look beautiful, *cara*," he murmured, fighting laughter.

Then the girl spotted Rosa, and her smile instantly faded. Pansy hissed at the Spanish woman. Rosa herself appeared no less pleased by the intrusion of the child and the cub, regarding the girl with hostility, the cub with fear.

The tension stretched and crackled for another long moment; then Christina muttered to Marco, "Oh. I am sorry. I had not realized you were—busy."

"You should have knocked, *cara*," he admonished.

She lowered her head and he watched one frail shoulder sag. "I know. Again, I apologize."

Marco heard the tears in her voice, and felt instantly contrite. He crossed the room, took Christina's hand, and smiled at her. Relieved when she smiled back bravely instead of bursting into sobs, he led her back toward Rosa, scolding Pansy when the cub, whom Christina was tugging along, began to hiss and spit at the Spanish woman again.

Once Pansy was subdued, Marco said to Christina, "*Cara*, this is my friend, Rosa." To Rosa, he added, "This is Christina."

Christina regarded the woman resentfully. "How do you do?"

Rosa sniffed contemptuously. "Little girls like you should be in bed."

Christina's defiant eyes flashed up to Rosa's. "And what about big girls like you?"

Marco howled with laughter, while Rosa visibly seethed with indignation. Marco wisely and hastily led Christina and the cub to the door, whispering, "Go to bed, *cara*, before your nurse—"

"Strings us both up from the nearest gibbet?"

"*Sì.*"

Hurling the other woman a look of contempt, Christina exited the room with Pansy.

As soon as the door had closed, Rosa charged on Marco. "*That* is the English you rescued?"

He shrugged. "She and her nurse would have been raped and killed by our adversaries."

Rosa shook a finger at him. "And you claim she will be safe here with you and your men?"

"*Sí*. I have already laid down the law to my crew. I brought the girl here to protect her."

"To protect her? Are you blind, Marco? How can you say that with a straight face, you *bastardo!* Look at her!"

"Just what are you saying?"

"I am telling you to get rid of her!"

Now Marco was enraged, shaking a finger at the maddening wench. "Since when, woman, do you presume to tell me what to do?"

"If you want me in your bed, you will do it!" she spat.

He advanced on her, gesturing angrily. "Enough of this rebellion! Never have I allowed a woman to tell me my business, and you, Rosa, will not be the first one." He shoved her against the wall. "Do you know who I saved the child from?"

"Who?" she flung at him.

"Carlos."

Her eyes went wide and she gulped.

"What—no clever reply, my love?" he snarled.

Rosa had none. Indeed, her anger was fading into an electrifying mixture of fear and desire as Marco pinned her against the wall, his manhood rock-hard against her lower belly. Carlos, the Spanish pirate, had for a very long time been a sore subject between the two of them.

"Please, *mi corazón*," she pleaded, "just because he took my innocence so long ago does not mean—"

Marco silenced her with a kiss, knowing he had the upper hand now and loving it. Actually, he enjoyed their spats. The sparring matches aroused Rosa to a fever pitch ... and made his victory—and her surrender—so much sweeter.

"Have you been faithful to me while I've been gone?" he demanded. He raised her skirts and stroked her. He smiled at her gasp of tormented arousal.

"Ah, just as I like you," he murmured, nipping at her ear and slipping a finger inside her. "Hot, wet, and very tight."

Her fingers dug into his shoulders. She was trembling with desire, breathing in gasps, her eyes large and dilated. "Take me, *mi amor*. Please. Now."

"If I thought you still wanted him . . ." he growled.

"Oh, never!"

"I would strip you naked, hold you fast, and thrust into you until you screamed for mercy."

"Oh, please do it," she begged, her impatient fingers popping buttons on his shirt. "I do so hunger to feel your large hands on my backside."

He chuckled. *"Dio mio*, you are shameless."

She pressed her hand against his trousers. He heaved a mighty groan and ground his teeth.

"How could you think I could still want Carlos?" she purred. "Compared to you, my mighty stallion, he is like the most limp and scrawny bean pod."

Marco laughed heartily. "I almost feel sympathy for the bastard, to hear him so maligned."

As she began unbuttoning his trousers, he pulled away. She watched sullenly as he went to the dresser and put on a condom.

"Oh, *corazón*, please do not use one of those tonight," she begged. "I long for your big blond baby growing inside me."

Marco smiled as he returned to her. Doubtless Rosa would love to trap him with his seed in her belly. But Marco could ill afford to assume the burden of a wife and children at this point in his life, nor did he have any desire to die the agonizing death of syphilis, to which he had watched several of his crewmen succumb. Thus he took care with his dalliances, just as he respected and cared for his own body.

He embraced her again and chided, "It is either this, or I must pull away at the very moment of your pleasure. Choose, *gattina*."

She was still pouting. "You call her *cara*. You have never called me that."

He pressed her against the wall and unfastened her bodice. "But you are my kitten. You have claws."

"*Sì*, just like that nasty cub of yours." She demonstrated by digging her own "claws" into his shoulders.

Marco growled his pleasure and reached beneath her skirts. He gripped her bottom, raised her, and positioned himself, capturing the turgid peak of her breast with his lips and nipping gently.

She was gasping with desire. "Oh, *mi corazón*, give me all of yourself tonight. Take me hard and fast. Brand me with your love."

"You'll be sorry," he teased.

"I won't."

He chuckled. She never was. He sucked her breast deeply into his mouth and thrust hard, burying himself in her snug sheath. Her gasp of surrender brought another deep, ruthless parry, a soft cry of pleasure. When she sank herself onto him and wrapped her legs tightly around his waist, he lost all control, giving in to a rampage of devouring thrusts, and he was certain from her wild sobs that she would soon be sorry.

But then, she never was.

Across the hallway, lying on her bed and petting Pansy, Christina had a good idea what Marco and Rosa were doing behind closed doors. Her mouth tightened in anger and her heart burned with jealousy. They thought she was a mere child and did not understand. But she did.

Back when she had lived with her father and stepmother in Charles Town, they too had spent such time alone. Sometimes, she had even heard low sounds coming from their bedroom, and from this, she had gained her first intuition of the physical bond between a man and a woman.

Oh, why did she have to be a child? she asked herself in sudden despair. Why couldn't she be a woman—a woman Marco could love with all his heart?

A hard surge of possessiveness washed over her. Even though she still had not crossed the portal from childhood to womanhood, she knew she wanted this giant, golden pirate with his laughing eyes and beautiful smile. She knew she did not want to share him.

In time she would grow up. In time, he would be hers.

FOUR

It took Christina only a few days to make the happy discovery that she was her own boss on Isola del Mare. At first, Hesper tried to continue to rule her life with the same iron fist; yet Marco and the other pirates not only would not support Hesper in her bid to retain authority over her charge, they also openly undermined the nurse by indulging Christina's every whim and reinforcing her willfulness by constantly bringing her treats and presents. After making a run for supplies, Luigi brought her back bonbons and lace from the shops at Road Harbor. Patrizio whittled her a wooden doll and Francesco wove her a straw hat. She was allowed to roam the island at will and do precisely as she pleased.

When she perversely ran off to the beach rather than recite her sums to Hesper, Marco forbade the nurse to chase after her and threatened the woman with bodily harm if she so much as touched a hair on the girl's head. Hesper waved a fist at Marco, screaming, "The girl is becoming a bloody wastrel, your lordship, and one day this entire disaster will be heaped upon your head!" Marco laughed off Hesper's dire warning, and after a few more failed attempts at controlling Christina, the nurse relegated herself to taking charge of the household, and set about to restore order to the ramshackle abode with fanatical zeal, as if, after being thwarted in her attempts to control the child, she would instead wreak her vengeance on inanimate objects.

While she had no luck in ordering around the recalcitrant cook, or in persuading Marco to keep the "beast," Pansy, outside, Hesper was able to set the house itself to rights. Marco even engaged four peasant girls as laundresses and chambermaids just to silence the shrew's perpetual harangues. Yet as the days passed, he began to realize that it was rather nice to have clean clothing, sheets, and towels on a regular basis—and not to stumble over the rats or iguanas that normally scurried about in the darkness.

Christina became enthralled with the workings of the island itself, and she soon played with the peasant children along the verdant trails, drinking from crystal-pure streams, eating bananas, mangoes, and coconuts straight from the trees, even adopting her own parrot, Cicero, whose only fault was a determination to terrorize poor Pansy. Over all was a feeling of lazy ripeness and burgeoning life, from the tall sugarcane plants that waved and rustled in the fields, to the massive tangle of roots, plants, and wildlife forever encroaching on the jungle trails, to the babies growing large in the bellies of the expectant mothers.

While Hesper perpetually cursed what she called the "open fornication" of the pirates and their women, Christina found the way the families lived to be sweet, harmonious, even surprisingly innocent. Most of the pirates had mates and small children, with the exception of Marco and a few others who

sported with unattached and promiscuous females
such as Rosa. Each of the family units occupied a
small hut of thatch, wattle, and daub, and had a
small plot of land for farming. Christina was warmly
received at every household. More than once while
she was visiting with a mother and children outside
one of the cottages, the master of the house himself
would appear with a lusty grin, haul his woman up
into his arms, and carry her off inside. Laughter
would be heard, and within seconds, low moans of
pleasure would filter out through the chinked walls.
Christina made it her policy at such times to lead the
rest of the children a safe distance away from the
hut, to teach them songs and games until their pirate
father would reappear with a satisfied grin, kiss his
children, and swagger off happily. In this way,
Christina learned to think of the love act as something joyous and beautiful, without shame.

She noted that, though the men and their mates
were faithful to one another, a communal, coopera-
tive atmosphere did prevail. One group of women
worked together roasting a wild pig or preparing a
salmagundi stew for supper, while another watched
the children swim at the beach, and a third minded
huge boiling pots of laundry. The men busied themselves with the important task of tending the cane
fields in preparation for the coming harvest or scrap-
ing and refitting the careened *La Spada*.

Thus Christina was able to flit from one interesting
activity to another; her help was never requested but
always welcomed, and the jaunts became highly ed-
ucational as she learned to weave baskets, keep a col-
icky baby happy, or pound conch for the evening's
stew. She especially relished the steamy afternoons
when the other sun-browned, laughing children
would pull her out into the surf. Under the watchful
eyes of several of the mothers, the peasant children
taught Christina how to swim, and she was soon fol-

lowing them out to get a better view of the dazzling coral reefs and multicolored fish, being ever mindful not to venture too near the razor-sharp formations. Her body became trim and brown, her hair light as summer wheat.

After her afternoon swim, Christina often ventured farther down the white sands to the small cove where *La Spada* was beached. She watched the men scrape and caulk, repair sails and rigging. Marco and the others patiently answered her many questions regarding why the vessel had to be turned on its side in order to be repaired, why a number of planks had to be replaced due to the tunneling of the teredo worm, and how barnacles were removed from the hull. Demonstrations often accompanied their explanations.

Marco remained Christina's major fascination, and while he invariably treated her with kindness and good humor, she suffered from the dual disappointments that he continued his relationship with Rosa and that he seemed to think of her as "just one of the children." For the moment, she could not conjure how she could relieve him of his obsession with Rosa, and she felt her position was still too tenuous for her to risk an overthrow.

She did feel intensely grateful late one night when she heard, across the hallway, the sounds of a loud fight between Marco and his mistress. She smiled with vindictive pleasure at the sounds of enraged screams, glass breaking, even Pansy hissing and yowling. Then at last there was total silence.

Christina grabbed a favorite book she had found in the library and crossed the hallway, knocking on Marco's door.

"Come in!" he barked.

His tone of voice was so savage that Christina actually cringed, hesitating for a moment. Then she creaked open the door and tentatively slipped inside.

What she saw was most amusing and intriguing! Marco stood across from her, fully dressed but with his hair mussed, a thin red scratch marring his strong jaw, and several of his shirt buttons missing. He wore a murderous scowl—and he was sweeping the floor! Pansy, on the bed, looked none the worse for wear. The cub was intently watching Marco's every movement, but then her golden gaze flicked to Christina.

The girl could not restrain a giggle as she faced Marco. "What are you doing?"

"What does it look like?" he retorted.

"You can't be sweeping!" She started toward him eagerly.

"Hah! If I leave this mess till the morrow, I shall never hear the end of it from that witch who calls herself your nurse." Watching Christina advance, he held up a hand. "Oh, no, you don't. Not another step, or your feet will be sliced to ribbons." He pointed at a Campeche chair and muttered curtly, "Sit."

Stifling laughter, Christina quickly detoured to the chair, sat down, and tucked her feet beneath her. Setting her book on the table next to her, she made a clucking sound to Pansy, and the black cub at once bounded over, landing in her lap.

"What happened?" she asked Marco, petting the cub.

He rolled his eyes heavenward. "Didn't you hear? Rosa and I had a fight, Pansy got upset and bit her leg, and then the wench threw a bloody pitcher at both of us. Fortunately, she missed."

Christina fought a smirk and stared at the cheetah. "Pansy, you didn't bite Rosa, did you?"

Pansy buried her face guiltily beneath Christina's chin and purred loudly.

"Why did the two of you argue?" Christina asked Marco.

He glanced at her sharply.

"I'm sorry," she hastily added. "I know it is rude to pry."

He shrugged. "You may as well know. It was over you."

Christina was astonished. "Over me?"

His jaw tightened. "For some reason, my spitfire of a woman keeps insisting that you be cast from the island." Watching Christina go pale, he quickly said, "Do not worry on that account, *cara*. I do not exile children from Isola del Mare." He frowned in magnificent indignation. "Besides, the woman is being a bloody nag and telling me my business. That I will never abide."

Christina stared at him raptly. "You are so brave to fight her for me." Shifting the cub in her arms, she moved to stand up. "The mess is my fault, then. I must do the sweeping."

"With no shoes on?" he snapped, his expression outraged. "What have I told you about being careful not to cut yourself here? I have no desire to bury you, *cara*." He winked at her solemnly and teased, "You grow so lovely and brown, 'twould be a shame if you perished before reaching womanhood."

Christina beamed her happiness.

"There," Marco said, sweeping the remainder of the glass fragments into a corner. "The maids can gather up the shards on the morrow."

Setting aside the broom, he strode over to stand before her, managing a wry smile. "What brings you here tonight, *cara?*"

"I could not sleep."

He laughed and tousled her hair. "No wonder, with all the screaming." He glanced down at the book she had placed on the table. "What is that you brought?"

"A wonderful storybook," she replied. "Patrizio introduced me to your library."

"Ah, yes. The English planters who lived here before us left behind a number of books. Which one is that?"

"*The Arabian Nights.*"

An expression of great tenderness filled Marco's eyes. "My mother used to read me those stories when I was a small child."

"So did my father." She gazed at him expectantly. "Will you read to me, Marco?"

He stared at her for a moment, then nodded. "Of course."

She set Pansy down, and Marco took her hand and led her to the window seat, where the lamplight was amplified by the moonlight spilling in. He settled himself on the outer edge of the seat and she sat down beside him. Pansy eagerly leapt up to curl herself in Christina's lap and stared at the two of them expectantly.

Wrapping an arm around Christina's shoulders, Marco opened the book and smiled at an illustration of a Moorish ship. "You know, I have been to Arabia, *cara,*" he murmured.

"You have?" she asked eagerly.

"Before I came to America, my men and I briefly sailed the Eastern seas, and we once sacked an Indian ship belonging to the Great Mogul." He chuckled. "We caught a monster gale off the Cape coming back, however."

"Did you?" she asked, wide-eyed.

"We fought the seas for days and days, and the bloody tempest all but demasted us. But the voyage was well worth it. If memory serves, we still have some of the ivory and silk we plundered."

"May I see these treasures?"

"Of course."

Her expression turned wistful. "When you go on such long journeys, do you ever get lonely, Marco?"

He smiled. "Now, why would I be lonely?"

She petted the cheetah. "Oh, I do not know—

losing your family and all. Of course, you have your men and your battles to fight—but it is not the same, is it?"

Once again, Marco had to marvel at the child's perceptiveness. "Sometimes the world crowds in on me—all the responsibilities I alone must bear," he admitted. "It is then that I must find contentment within myself."

She tilted her earnest face up toward his. "I do not find such contentment. I get lonely."

He struggled not to chuckle at her unflinching honesty. "You will find your peace in time, *cara*," he advised. "You will seek that wellspring within yourself. We are much alike, you and I."

"Are we?"

"*Sì*." Feeling uncomfortable with the way the girl could so disarm him, he affected a stern visage. "Now, listen to your story, and then we must get you to bed. The hour grows late."

She nodded.

Marco read "Sinbad the Sailor," and Christina snuggled contentedly beside him, lulled by his deep, mesmerizing voice. She had not felt so secure since her father used to read to her back in Charles Town, during what seemed a lifetime ago.

Marco, too, found his mind drifting back to the long-ago nights of his childhood when his mother had read to him thus. Again, those tender emotions he feared assailed his heart.

After the story ended and the cub bounded off to go sleep on Marco's bed, he stared for a long time at the child sleeping so trustingly beside him. He remembered her touching question: *Do you ever get lonely, Marco?* How long had it been since he had allowed himself to feel loneliness, or to need anyone?

Blessed Mary, he could not give in to emotions this child inspired—the fierce yearnings to have, once again, a family of his own and a sense of belonging.

He was a wayfarer, a man without roots, and he must keep his life that way until he got his revenge against the Spanish. He could not afford these debilitating paternal feelings toward this girl, or the gnawing realization at the back of his mind that one day this glorious cherub would become a woman—heaven help them all!

He must keep matters in their proper perspective. He carried Christina back to her room.

The next morning, Marco was striding down the hallway when he heard a sob of pure frustration coming from Christina's room. He knocked on the door, and after he heard her annoyed "Come in!" he stepped inside.

Christina sat at her dressing table, struggling to yank a brush through her mussed hair and fighting tears.

"What is it, *cara?*"

"My hair!" she cried. "It is full of tangles, and Hesper warned me that if I don't get rid of the snarls, she will cut all my hair off while I sleep."

Marco was enraged. "I shall feed the witch to the sharks."

Christina tried not to smile, then hiccuped as new tears welled. "But she may be right this time! She says I am becoming a hopeless wastrel and a reprobate, like the rest of you."

Marco struggled to maintain a sober, sympathetic facade as he stared at the distraught child. "Do you even know what those words mean, *cara?*"

"No." She sniffed. "But I do know that cleanliness is next to godliness, and I don't want to rot in hell, as Hesper says I surely shall." She threw down her hairbrush and wailed, "What am I to do? My hair is in a dreadful state."

Studying the child, Marco had to agree. After weeks of shameful neglect, swimming and playing, she looked like a hoyden. Her long, thick mane of wheat-brown hair was hopelessly wild and snarled. "Bring the brush and come out on the porch, little sister," he murmured. "We shall see what can be done."

She beamed with happiness and brought him the brush.

Later, after spending almost two hours with Christina on the gallery, gently, patiently disentangling each snarled lock, Marco mused ironically that he was doing a splendid job of keeping things in their proper perspective. And yet his heart rang with joy each time he remembered Christina's glorious smile afterward, when she had looked at herself in the mirror, and how she had hugged his neck, loudly smacked his cheek, then danced off for a new day of adventure. He knew then that they were friends now, and she was a part of his life, whether he had wanted it that way or not.

Late that afternoon, Marco was enjoying his bath in a waist-deep island stream, scrubbing himself with lye soap and singing a Rossi aria. Pansy lounged nearby, chewing on her paws. His rich baritone voice had just boomed out a loud crescendo when he heard a childish giggle.

He whirled, mortified, to see Christina sitting on the bankside in the dappled light, staring at him, her splendid purple-and-green parrot, Cicero, perched on her forearm. He quickly thanked the saints that the waters shielded her innocent eyes from anything improper.

As the silence stretched between them, all at once Cicero began to flap his wings and scream like a banshee. Pansy's ears perked up and she regarded the parrot with fear. Cicero vaulted off Christina's arm, sailed into the air, and made a murderous nosedive for the cat. Pansy emitted a shrill whine and scampered off into the jungle. Cicero pursued the cub relentlessly, cat and bird shrieking and screeching as they disappeared into the foliage.

Stunned by the small drama, Marco could only shake his head. Unfortunately, he was in no position to go rescue the cub.

He turned his attention back to Christina, who seemed totally unconcerned as she continued to stare at him. He mused ironically that he would likely feel more comfortable confronting a war party of Carib cannibals than he felt being at this child's mercy.

"*Cara*," he scolded, "you should not be here."

She appeared not to hear him, trailing her fingers through her sun-bleached locks. "Is my hair not beautiful, Marco? You did such a splendid job of brushing it."

He held back a chuckle. The minx was so adorably, unabashedly vain. "Your locks are lovely, *cara*, but now you must run along. I do believe your bird is about to eat poor Pansy. Should you not rescue the cub and teach that naughty parrot some manners? Besides, it is not proper for you to be around a man who is bathing."

Still she did not budge. "Do you want me to scrub your back?" she asked helpfully.

"Certainly not!"

She shrugged and kept gazing at him, her expression solemn and wistful. "Marco, when I grow up, will you marry me?"

"What kind of question is that?" he cried, feeling more intensely ill at ease with each passing moment. "You must run along—"

She tilted her chin up proudly. "Not until you tell me if you'll marry me. That is, when I grow up," she hastily added.

He groaned his frustration as he stared at the determined, mischievous moppet across from him on the bank. He did not doubt for a moment that she would stubbornly remain there until hell froze over, or until he answered her question. *Dio*, what had he unleashed?

Thinking that she was a mere child and would soon forget, he grinned at her and replied, "Of course, *cara*."

Her smile was more radiant than any sunrise.

Marco heaved a sigh of relief as he watched the girl spring up and happily dance off into the jungle.

Christina, meanwhile, was exultant as she hurried down the verdant trail, calling for Pansy and Cicero. She knew what Marco thought. He assumed that she was a child, and that she would soon forget his promise.

He was wrong, she told herself fiercely, vehemently. In her heart she was already a woman, and she would *always* remember.

FIVE

May 1748

"Giuseppe, why will this parrot say only 'Bad girl'?" Christina asked.

"Because you are a very bad girl, little one," he replied with a chuckle.

In a clearing along one of the verdant trails of Isola del Mare, eighteen-year-old Christina Abbott stood across from Marco's helmsman, Giuseppe, as the two prepared to begin her daily self-defense lesson. Christina's parrot, Cicero, offered his squawky commentary from his perch high in a nearby mangrove tree. Marco had asked Giuseppe to teach Christina how to protect herself, following a disturbing incident several months earlier when a raiding party of fierce Carib Indians had entered the island by canoe. Before the warriors had been discovered and defeated, they had killed two of Marco's men, who had been weeding the newly sowed cane plants. Ever since, an atmosphere of tension had prevailed on the normally placid island, with the population forever watchful and wary. Marco and his lieutenants had even discussed moving their base elsewhere, but so far no concrete plans had been laid.

Thus, preparedness had become crucial, with additional sentries being posted on the beaches and even the field workers arming themselves to protect against a surprise attack. For this reason, Christina and Giuseppe now stood squared off in the dappled light, ready to tackle another "exercise."

Giuseppe stared at the young woman across from him, and wondered how he managed to retain the composure to teach her anything at all, so bedazzled was he by her beauty. At eighteen, Christina Abbott was tall, slender, and tanned, her long white shift accentuating her willowy curves and the tawny splendor of her skin. Her glorious wheat-colored hair spilled down almost to her waist, and she possessed a face to make the most glorious sea siren look like a shriveled hag. He admired the long, well-sculpted lines of her visage: the delicate, perfect nose and huge green eyes, the high cheekbones, wide mouth, and strong chin. He knew the girl to be determined, ruthless, spoiled, and willful—and a pure seductress at heart. He likely would have succumbed to her charms long ago, except that Marco would have strung him up from *La Spada*'s yardarm—

Besides, he well knew that he was not the one the girl truly wanted. All a man had to do was to observe her looking at Marco Glaviano just once, and it was quite clear where this little vixen's heart lay. Whether his boss was aware of it or not, the girl wanted Marco, and she always got what she wanted. Marco might be nearly twice her size, but Giuseppe feared his friend was in trouble. The girl was ripe— only she would be the one who would soon do the plucking. Giuseppe almost laughed aloud as he anticipated the coming drama. In some ways, the girl might prove more of a challenge than the Spanish Marco still battled.

"Are you ready to tackle me?" he now asked her with a grin.

"Are you ready to suffer grievous pain?" she teased back.

"Bad girl," Cicero called from his perch.

Giuseppe laughed. "You realize, of course, that it is not just the cannibals we must heed. At some point, Marco's enemies may still discover our base. Pretend that I am one of Carlos's confederates, determined to ravish your innocent body."

"Your defeat will be my pleasure," she replied.

Christina assumed an aggressive stance, bracing her feet apart and raising her fists, while Giuseppe lifted the blunt wooden knife they used for their exercises and prepared to make his leap. "Remember what I told you—all is balance. And be gentle with me, little one."

He vaulted for her, and she reacted with lightning speed, grabbing the arm that held his knife, whacking his forearm with her other fist, and sending the knife spinning off. She kneed him in the groin area— hard enough to extract a pained gasp from him, yet not hard enough to permanently maim—flipped him over her hip, and landed on top of him, grabbing the discarded knife and shoving the mock weapon against his throat.

"Did I do well, Giuseppe?" she teased, her eyes gleaming with pleasure.

He nodded convulsively.

"Bad girl," Cicero called out.

Both of them laughed.

"Will you let me up now, little one?" Giuseppe asked.

But Christina had turned reflective. "What if you truly were one of Carlos's men, intent on raping me? What would you have me do to such a villain?"

Giuseppe scowled fiercely. "I would advise you to cut the bastard's balls off."

Wearing a vindictive grin, she pulled back and drew the pretend knife lower. "You mean like this?"

"Bad girl," called the parrot.

Giuseppe had visibly paled. "Please, little one, we have no need to practice that particular procedure, do we?"

Christina chuckled and tossed the knife aside. In doing so, she caught a distant motion out of the corner of her eye—a glimpse of a tall, blond man coming slowly toward them through the ripe tropical foliage, a huge black cat ambling along beside him.

"Will you let me up now?" Giuseppe repeated.

"But we are not through with our practice," she murmured.

His eyes widened. "You can't mean—"

She flipped her hair and assumed a sultry pose. "You have taught me how to defend myself, Giuseppe, and now further lessons are both useless and boring. But there is something else I hunger to learn."

"What?" he croaked, staring raptly at the lovely goddess who so ruthlessly tormented him.

"Teach me how to kiss, Giuseppe."

Stunned, he shoved her aside and sat up. "You cannot be serious!"

"But I am." She licked her lips and stared at him earnestly. "Surely you must know by now how high I hold you in my esteem."

His voice vibrated with shock and excitement. "But I thought you wanted—"

She leaned toward him quickly, her sweet scent further inflaming his wayward senses. "Kiss me, Giuseppe—quickly, before we both lose our nerve!"

Giuseppe was no saint; indeed, he was leaning eagerly toward the hot-blooded siren, his lips a mere hairsbreadth above her own, when an outraged male voice stopped him cold.

"What is this?" Marco demanded.

The two jumped guiltily apart to see Marco standing at the edge of the clearing, muscular arms crossed over his chest and a massive scowl creasing his handsome face. Next to him stood the fully grown king cheetah, Pansy, now magnificent with her thick black mane and golden, predatory eyes.

"Boss!" Giuseppe cried, lurching to his feet. "I was merely teaching the girl, as you requested—"

"Teaching her *what*, pray tell?" Marco demanded.

Christina popped up, giggling. "Marco, I simply asked Giuseppe to teach me how to kiss."

"Bad girl," Cicero interjected.

Spotting the parrot, Pansy perked up her ears and crouched in place. A moment later, when Cicero began a menacing flap of his wings, Pansy whined loudly, then leaped off into the jungle.

Rolling his eyes at the cat's disgraceful retreat, Marco turned his frown back to the other two. "Leave us," he commanded Giuseppe with a curt nod.

His first mate dashed from the clearing.

Still glowering, Marco stepped closer to Christina. She watched him approach, feasting her eyes on his tall, muscular body, beautifully chiseled features, and deep set, vibrant blue eyes. His thick blond hair hung over his shoulders and caught the shimmering light. He wore his flowing white shirt half open, revealing the hard golden muscles of his chest; his dark breeches hugged his muscular thighs. She knew him to be twenty-eight years old now, and the vigorous glow of full manhood only added to his mesmerizing appeal.

She smiled a secret smile. She had waited six long years to stake her claim on him, and now the time was right.

Marco, in turn, was studying Christina—but much more warily, almost as if he were sizing up an opponent. He knew Christina at eighteen to be a spoiled beauty, and a perpetual tease with an earthy, sultry appeal that frequently made him rue the day he had rescued her. The girl dressed like a peasant and swam like a fish, and more than once he had found himself groaning as he caught sight of her lovely brown legs skipping down the beach, her white shift trailing behind her in the breeze. It highly disconcerted him that, now that she had fully matured, his feelings for her ceased to be brotherly or paternal and often hovered somewhere between gnawing attraction and raw lust. These were feelings Marco was determined to fight—for he wanted far better for this rare beauty than to see her share a pirate's bed. Over the years, he had tried to maintain his patience with her and continue their friendship, and yet her headstrong nature was now often at war with his own protective instincts—and torn feelings—toward her. Lately, they had been like wary strangers, the atmosphere between them constantly charged with emotional tension and sensual awareness.

He tried his best to feign a stern look—although, being this close to the little temptress, he found it very difficult. "Christina, what do you think you were doing just now?"

"Practicing," she replied with an eager smirk. "Are we not in danger of attack, Marco?"

Still struggling to maintain a sober facade, he stroked his jaw and replied ruefully, "I would say you were definitely in danger of attack—but not the type of assault I would have you preparing against."

She chuckled.

"Christina," he pressed, "why did you ask Giuseppe to kiss you?"

She shrugged. "Because it is high time for me to learn of such matters, don't you think?"

"I do not!" he retorted. "You cannot go around teasing grown men this way!"

Her chin came up. "And why not?"

"Because you have no idea what you are doing!" He threw up his hands. "Already half my crew are hopelessly in love with you. Francesco is like a love-sick lamb, Patrizio drools over you constantly when he is not drunk, and Luigi gives you such burning looks, I am surprised your clothing does not burst into flames."

"And what is so terrible about all that?"

He gestured angrily. "What is so terrible is that you seem blissfully unaware of the possible consequences of your careless flirting. Whether you are aware of it or not, grown men, when provoked by women, tend to be—er—very direct."

"Are they?" She grinned at him, and he glanced away and coughed in acute discomfort.

In the tense silence, Pansy, crouched low on her paws, began to creep back into the clearing toward Marco, warily eyeing Cicero in the mangrove tree. Cicero, meanwhile, spotted the cheetah approaching and began to screech and pound his wings like a ship caught in a gale. Pansy turned tail and streaked back into the jungle.

Marco shook his head.

Christina chuckled at the sight, then turned her attention back to Marco and their fascinating discussion. "Marco, I am eighteen now. My friend Isabel is seventeen, and already she has a mate and twin babies. Why, only yesterday I watched Paolo and Luisa suckle at their mother's breasts." She stared at him, a dreamy look coming over her. "I think I would like a baby, too."

Marco made a strangled sound as her words and the unconscious sensuality of her expression all but tore his resolve to ribbons. "You have no idea what you are saying, Christina. You cannot just decide you want a baby, and then—"

"And why not? That is what everyone else on this island does."

Marco's voice was rising. "You are different."

"What do you mean, I am different? Am I not allowed to choose a mate like everyone else?"

Marco was growing highly uncomfortable having such a provocative conversation with this ravishing, outspoken beauty. He drew his fingers through his hair. "No, you are not."

She tossed her curls and regarded him defiantly. "Then what are you going to do with me? Put me in a convent?"

Marco couldn't restrain a chuckle. "In truth, Christina, I'm not sure just what I should do with you."

"Bad girl," called the parrot.

"And you are a very bad girl, *cara*," he concurred wryly.

Her expression grew turbulent. "Why am I so bad?"

"You should not be asking Giuseppe to kiss you," he said sternly.

"Why shouldn't I?" she challenged. "You will certainly never kiss me. You won't even brush my hair anymore."

Marco groaned as he remembered the incident she referred to, which had occurred only last week. They had been sitting on the gallery together, and he had been patiently disentangling her long golden locks when an insane urge had come over him to pull this vision of sultry womanhood into his lap, bury his hands in that glorious mane of hair, and savage her lovely lips with his kisses.

Now he said to her just what he had said last week. "You are old enough to brush your own hair.

And besides, I should have taken the flat side of the brush to your bottom long ago."

"The fact remains that I am grown now," she told him recklessly. "And if I want to take a lover, I shall."

He grabbed her arm and spoke in exasperation. "You shall do no such thing! Besides, you are such an innocent. You don't even know what taking a lover means."

"Oh, yes, I do!" she retorted, batting her long eyelashes at him. "People are mating constantly all over this island."

Speechless with shock at her words, Marco released her arm.

"And they make such loud sounds," she continued with relish. "Sometimes they scream like scalded cats—louder than Pansy and Cicero when they fight." She touched the front of his shirt and stared at him boldly. "Tell me, is it terribly painful, this mating business?"

Marco remained speechless, his heartbeat and breathing quickening as Christina's scent filled his senses and the heat of her hand on his chest seemed to sear him clear through to his heart.

"How does it feel for a woman the first time?" she whispered.

Now Marco had to laugh as, at last, she caught him up in her seductive little game. "I don't know, cara. I am not a woman."

She edged closer and asked brazenly, "How does it feel for a man?"

He shoved her away. "Enough of this. You are a child!"

"I am a woman," she insisted.

"Not yet," he drawled meaningfully.

"Then perhaps you can remedy this lack in my education," she taunted remorselessly.

"Just what are you suggesting?" he demanded, his pulse roaring in his ears.

Her siren smile would have trapped the devil, and her voice was a sultry purr. "I am suggesting that, since you interrupted my session with Giuseppe, now you must teach me to kiss."

Oh, the little tease! Marco could not believe she was enticing him so relentlessly—any more than he could believe his manhood's turgid rise toward the ripe bait she dangled.

"Christina," he scolded, shaking a finger at her. "Behave yourself, or you will rue the consequences."

She tilted her impudent, lovely face up toward his. "You mean you don't want to kiss me?"

An ironic grin tugged at his lips. "That is not what I said."

She feigned a wounded expression. "Perhaps you are too preoccupied with your current concubine to kiss me. Who is it you bed these days? Rosa? Minerva? Giselle?"

She was brazen! "Not that it is any of your concern," he retorted, "but I have been only with Rosa for a long time now."

She strolled off to a mango tree, plucked a ripe red fruit, peeled it, and slowly began to eat it. "You sport much, Marco, but you do not father children."

Marco was going insane as he watched a thin trickle of mango juice trail down Christina's chin. How tempted he was to haul the vixen into his arms and lick clean that adorable, impertinent mouth and stubborn jaw. "Not every man feels comfortable about the prospect of fathering bastards," he drawled with a telltale quiver in his voice. "There are ways that conception can be prevented."

She took another slow, sensuous bite—watching him swallow hard and stare at her—then lazily licked her lips. "I am relieved to hear that you suffer from no impediment."

His gaze was riveted to that wet, delectable mouth. "Believe me, *cara*, I suffer from no impediment." He watched her perfect white teeth bite into the fruit again, and imagined her sinking those same sharp teeth into his shoulder.

"Because if you marry me," she went on recklessly, "I want many babies."

Marco's equilibrium was spinning. Determined to hide the devastating effect she was having on his senses, he shook a finger at her. "*Cara*, you are shameless. I never should have spoiled you so. All this baiting for a mere kiss?"

She turned petulant again, her eyes flashing with a defiant, determined light. "Very well. If you are such a coward, so afraid of one little, tiny kiss, I will go find Giuseppe or Luigi. I am certain one of them will be delighted to teach me."

"Over my dead body—and yours."

It was the sight of the full pout on those glorious lips, the gleam of rebellion in those large green eyes, that made Marco snap. He grabbed her arm, sending her half-eaten fruit flying as he hauled her hard against him and lowered his mouth to hers. Yet even as he would have thoroughly kissed her, she stretched upward to give him her mouth, her own fruit-flavored lips trustingly parted as they eagerly sought his.

Dio, she was teaching *him*, kissing him with innocent abandon! God in heaven, she was so sweet, her lips so soft and delicious on his! Desire consumed Marco, and his tongue plunged deep into her warm mouth, devouring the peachlike taste of her. She trembled and moaned, and he crushed her harder against him. Nothing in her resisted him! Indeed, her slim arms curled around his neck and her small breasts nestled sensuously into the heat of his hard chest. *Dio*, he felt as if she had been made for him. His blood roared in his veins at the sweetness of her surrender.

Christina felt equally enthralled by Marco's kiss.

She had waited for so many years to feel the heat of his lips on hers, and this moment was paradise, everything she had ever dreamed of. He felt so strong, so magnificent, as he crushed her in his arms, and he smelled so wonderful. When his tongue plunged audaciously into her mouth, she knew she had broken his restraint at last. Joy and passion welled in her, and the feeling of intimacy was riveting, electrifying. As his warm tongue stroked, teasing and parrying with hers, new, hot, and powerful yearnings built and twisted between her thighs, until she found herself arching her hips eagerly into his—and contacting something so tantalizing and hard—

It was at the very moment when her pelvis thrust brazenly into his that Marco was at last propelled to his senses. Somehow, he managed to shove her away, then felt as if a massive fist had just slammed into his gut when she stared up at him with so much desire, adoration, and trust.

"Now you are mine," she whispered fiercely.

Marco stared at her. Holy Mother, she really *meant* it! Mumbling a curse, he hastily took his leave.

SIX

"Pansy, what am I going to do about Marco?"

That evening, Christina sat on the beach with Pansy beside her, her expression wistful as she petted the cheetah, watched the spectacular Caribbean sunset, and thought of him. Beyond her, gulls dipped and soared along the pink-gold horizon of waves; the breeze was brisk, the sound of the surf crashing in her ears. High in a nearby palm tree, Cicero, after having been banished by Christina for scolding Pansy, watched the girl and cat resentfully, periodically flapping his wings or screaming, "Bad girl!"

Christina shivered with delight as she relived her and Marco's first kiss today. That glorious moment had been her first major victory in her battle to win over the heart of a man she had idolized as a child and now loved as a woman. But she could not delude herself. Marco Glaviano did not belong to her. His heart belonged to the sea, and during the torrid hours between dusk and dawn, his body belonged to a certain Spanish strumpet.

She frowned with fierce determination. She knew that, were she to conquer Marco's heart, she must first put a stop to his wenching. If the sounds coming from his bedroom each night were any indication, Marco was a man of very strong urges. Surely if she could just deprive him of female companionship for several weeks, he would become desperate enough to take her as his bride—

And she was absolutely determined to have him as her husband. Which meant that, somehow, she must drive off the whores he bedded. He claimed he was sleeping only with Rosa, but she suspected he sported with other women as well.

She was not certain, either, that she liked his periodic voyages to raid Spanish shipping. She worried herself sick over him while he was away, and all too frequently he returned wounded, with nicks from knife fights marring his beautiful body.

Her heart lurched painfully as she recalled an incident two years past, when he had returned to Isola del Mare after having sustained a severe gunshot wound to his left arm. For several days afterward, she had quietly gone insane watching him as he lay in bed, racked by fever and infection. At the time, she had felt terrified of losing him, for she had seen many others on the island die from injuries far less serious. With an anxious Pansy pacing nearby, she had mopped his brow and fretted over him endlessly. And for the first time in years, she had prayed, spending hours on her knees, humbly beseeching the heavens for his recovery. Even Pansy had crouched low beside her in an attitude of reverence, her doleful eyes forever fixed on her master.

During those desperate hours, Christina had first begun to realize how much Marco meant to her. Then, three nights later, when the loud sounds of his groans had awakened her in her room across the hallway, she had gone dashing off to his aid, distraught with fear that he might indeed be dying, only to stop in her tracks outside his door when she heard a woman's bawdy laughter and realized that he was again sporting with Rosa. He had recovered—the pig! In tears, she had retreated to her room and had prayed vehemently—this time, that the miserable reprobate would die and go straight to hell.

He had not, of course, and although she often yearned to strangle Marco Glaviano, in her heart she was fiercely grateful that he was still with her.

A dreamy expression came over her face as she again basked in memories of their incredible kiss—the strength of his massive body surrounding her, the male scent of him, the sensual heat and taste of his lips. At that moment he had stirred something primal and potent deep in her belly—a desire to truly be one with him, to have him inside her, loving her so deeply and fiercely, giving her his child.

He would be hers. She would see to it.

But how would she stop his womanizing?

She was frowning over this when she heard a rustling sound and turned to see a fat gray snake slither into the bushes. Pansy's ears perked up, and with a ferocious mien, the king cheetah leapt up and charged after her prey.

Christina sprang up as well. "Pansy, please don't eat the snake! I think I may need it!"

She tore off after the cat and the serpent, her mischievous laughter echoing across the pounding surf.

"Good evening, *corazón.*"

That night, Marco stepped inside his room to find Rosa waiting for him, her curvaceous body sprawled across the daybed. His mistress looked as appealing as ever lounging before him in her red, low-cut peasant dress, her sultry dark eyes focused on him and her lips sensuously red, wet, and ripe. But curiously, he found his manhood failed to respond to her presence with its usual vigor.

"Good evening, *gattina*," he drawled with a smile.

She flounced up and pranced over to stand before him. The scent of her perfume assailed him, yet the fragrance seemed cheap and tawdry tonight, rather than enticing. *Dio*, why was it he could not get out of his mind the image of an untried wench who was willowy-slim, who smelled of nectar and tasted of mangoes?

"I have missed you, big one," Rosa teased, pressing her fingers to his crotch. Then she uttered a cry of dismay. "What is this? I thought you hoisted your flag at the mere sighting of a feminine skirt, *corazón*."

His vanity smarting, Marco shoved her away. "Take off your clothes and get in bed. You will rue the day you so insulted my manhood."

Rosa merely grinned wickedly and licked her lips in brazen anticipation. "The day you can wear me out, *corazón*, is the day you will die a very young and exhausted stallion."

Marco threw back his head and roared with laughter. "That is quite true. You are insatiable, *gattina*—as well as shameless."

Rosa laughed ribaldly as she began to peel off her clothing. Yet even the sight of her full, ripe breasts failed to excite Marco. He found himself fantasizing about two small, firm, perfect mounds nestling against his chest, and reeling at the image of taking one of those tiny, delectable nipples between his teeth and nibbling slowly on the turgid peak until he drove Christina insane. At last an agonizing pang of arousal stabbed his loins—but at the thought of bedding a winsome virgin, not the seasoned whore who stood before him.

Frustration assailed him anew. "Get in the bed," he ordered hoarsely.

Strutting her naked, voluptuous body across the room, Rosa slid between the covers and all but purred in invitation. Marco removed his shirt and joined her. He kissed her full mouth and squeezed her bare breast, yet the taste of her seemed stale, and her breast felt flaccid in his hand. He caressed her nipple, listened to her sharp gasp of pleasure, and willed himself to grow more excited.

Rosa, meanwhile, was becoming very aroused, writhing and moaning in his arms. "Ah, *corazón*, you are such a big, bold stallion. Your hands slither across me so wickedly." She shrieked and squirmed with lust. "Oh, how depraved you are, to touch me there . . ."

Marco pulled back, holding up his hands and scowling. "Touch you *where?*"

All at once, as she stared at Marco's hands, Rosa's eyes grew as huge as saucers. She flailed about frantically for a moment, threw back the covers, bolted up from the bed, and screamed her lungs out.

Marco also leapt up, stunned and confused. He observed Rosa shrieking and pointing, then stared downward and at last spotted the head of a gray snake peeking out from the covers.

"God in heaven, what is this?" he cried.

Gingerly he grabbed the gray snake by the back of its neck. Rosa continued to scream hysterically as he bore the squirming serpent to the French doors, opened them, and hurled the creature out into the garden. Then he paused, glowering, for he was certain he heard the sound of feminine laughter coming from the distant foliage.

"That little brat!" Rosa cried from behind him.

Marco slammed the doors shut and whirled to face his seething mistress. "Now what are you ranting about, woman?"

"That hellion Christina put a snake in your bed!"

Marco was incredulous. "You must be jesting. Why would she do that?"

Rosa flung her hands wide in exasperation. "*Idiota!* To drive me away, of course! She wants to share your bed and she knows I sport with you each night."

"That is insane," Marco snapped. "The serpent must have wandered in by accident."

"This was no accident!" Rosa screamed, trembling in her rage. "*Madre de Dios,* I could have been killed!"

Marco raked his fingers through his hair. "The snake was of a harmless variety—I think."

Rosa shook a fist at him. "Well, I will tell you who is not of a harmless variety, and that is the little bitch you let stay in your home!"

Marco was becoming angered, his jaw tightly clenched as he faced down the Spanish woman. "Rosa, Christina is not a bitch."

"But I am a whore, *verdad?* And she comes first with you!"

"That is not true!"

"It *is* true! For years I have begged you to get rid of that spoiled little chit, but you won't! Are you blind? The little witch is in love with you. And one of us has to go!"

"Rosa," Marco said in deadly quiet tones, "this is Christina's home. She may stay here for as long as she pleases."

"Then you have made your choice," Rosa spat back. "For as long as that little *puta* stays in this house, I swear I will never again share your bed."

"Goddammit, woman!" Marco exploded. "You will not dictate to me!"

"I will do exactly what I please!" Tossing her head proudly, Rosa stormed off toward the door.

But even as she reached for the knob, his hand grabbed hers. "Just a minute."

Her dark eyes flashed defiantly. "Don't you dare try to stop me!"

"Oh, I won't try to stop you," he drawled cynically. He eyed her nakedness slowly, insultingly, then held up a mound of red fabric. "But wouldn't you prefer to leave clothed rather than stark naked?"

She grabbed the garment and hissed, "Go to the devil—you pig!"

With her frock in hand, Rosa stormed from the room, naked as the day she was born. Marco cursed explosively and slammed his fist against the closed door.

Marco crossed the hallway and pounded on Christina's door. "Christina!" he thundered.

"Come in," answered a sweet voice.

Marco flung open the door and charged inside, only to stop in his tracks as he spotted the girl sprawled across the bed in a handkerchief-linen nightgown, her womanly curves, beautifully gleaming hair, and bright smile taunting him remorselessly. Pansy lounged next to her. *Dio del cielo*, the girl was a vision! All of a sudden, Marco felt as if a rock had lodged in his throat—and a boulder in his trousers.

"Is something amiss, Marco?" she asked innocently.

Trembling with combined anger and lust, he managed to maintain a safe distance from the seductive little siren. "You know damned well that something is amiss, you little brat! You put a snake in my bed!"

"Me?" she asked, eyes wide with innocent astonishment.

"Don't bother to deny it," he snapped. "I heard you laughing in the garden when I tossed the serpent into the bushes."

She flipped her mane of glorious hair and lifted her chin proudly. "I am sure I have no idea what you are talking about, Marco. Besides, why would I pull such a prank?"

He laughed ruefully. "Following your disgraceful

behavior earlier today, I would hazard a guess that you wanted to scare off Rosa so you could claim me for yourself."

"Would I do such a thing?"

"At the moment, I would not put a tryst with the devil past you."

She chuckled. "And did I successfully chase off Rosa?"

Marco was beginning to see red. "Aha! So you admit your treachery, you little witch! Try a stunt like that again and I promise you, you will not be able to sit down for a week."

She laughed. "You would never spank me."

"Don't tempt me."

She stared at him with a sudden determination and intensity that all but blinded him. "You know, you really are mine, Marco. Fight it if you will, but nothing will change."

Marco was speechless. He turned and strode from the room, slamming the door.

"Come on, Monique, darling. Come to bed with me."

"Oh, but I am too ashamed, Marco. You are not my first."

"Please, that does not matter to me."

"But it matters to me. I am so wicked—I shall surely burn in hell."

A fortnight later, Marco was trying—without much success—to seduce Monique, one of the half-dozen "loose" women who lived on the island. The petite blond Frenchwoman was a striking beauty with her huge brown eyes and bigger breasts, but she also loved to play the coy innocent, forever claiming that she had slept with only one man before, when it was well known all over the island that she was a slut of the first water who had sported with anything and everything in trousers.

The past two weeks had been intensely frustrating for Marco. With Rosa off in a perpetual huff, he had become compelled to woo other women in an attempt to sate his lusts. But Christina had continued to sabotage his lovelife. The night he had tried to seduce Giselle, some unknown person had let Pansy loose in his bedroom at precisely the wrong moment. Just as he had been prepared to free himself from his breeches, the cheetah—who fiercely disliked all of the island whores—had leapt onto the bed, landing on his back, driving Giselle to hysterics, and plunging his seduction scheme into chaos.

A week later, when he had tried to sport with Minerva, both of them had started choking on smoke. Some anonymous soul had shoved a potful of burning rags through the French doors.

Both times, Marco had angrily confronted Christina. Both times, she had avowed innocence, while smirking at him with glee.

Tonight, however, he was determined either to meet with success in bed or to brow-beat Christina until she confessed and repented. If only Monique would cease playing the simpering prig! He could not be sure how much time they would have before that little witch Christina attempted another stunt!

"It was Luigi who ruined me," Monique now sniffed. "He threw me down and ravished me on the jungle trail. He is the reason I must come to you a soiled dove. I wanted so to be pure when we first made love, Marco."

He resisted an impulse to roll his eyes at her absurd histrionics. But that would not get him between her thighs. "You will always be pure to me, darling," he soothed. "Let us make a fresh start tonight." He grabbed her arm and pulled her toward the bed. "*Now.*"

"Well, if you really think—"

Impatient with her machinations, he hauled her up

into his arms, quickly crossed the room, and deposited her on the bed. "Indeed I do."

Marco shrugged off his shirt and joined her there. He kissed her without enthusiasm and began raising her skirts. Again he found that a state of proper excitement eluded him. If only he could get a decent erection, he could spread her thighs quickly and ease his sexual frustration—

But even as he was trying to will his uncooperative member to arousal, she shoved him away, pouting again. "Marco, no, I cannot face you. I am so ashamed ..."

Her coy game angered him—and anger aroused him. "You cannot face me, my love?" he mocked. His smile was utterly ruthless. "Then avert your eyes and turn over, darling, so you may hide your *great shame* and I may show you the great joys of mating as the animals do."

Now, to his delight, he had the wench totally flustered. A vivid blush stained her cheeks, and her mouth fluttered agape. "Marco, you cannot mean—"

"But I do, my darling, for this is, indeed, the perfect solution," he sneered, rolling her over.

She squirmed, all the while panting with lust. "Oh, Marco! This is—so very wicked—"

"And you are thoroughly enjoying every scandalous second!"

Marco was reaching for his trousers when suddenly the water came—by the feel of it, an entire cold bucketful! In the space of a split second, he, Monique, and the bed were thoroughly drenched. For a moment, both were too stunned to react. Then Marco whirled to the sound of feminine giggles, and he caught a glimpse of a handkerchief-linen gown and Christina's tanned legs skipping out his door.

Sopping wet, Marco bolted to his feet. "Goddammit! That little brat!"

Monique popped up as well. "*Mon Dieu!* This is surely divine retribution."

"It is retribution, all right, but straight from the jaws of hell," he retorted.

Wild-eyed, Monique crossed herself, then dashed for the door. "I must go pray."

Marco cursed vividly.

Still shirtless, and dripping wet, he charged across the hallway to Christina's room, threw open the door, and burst in.

"You little vixen!" he yelled, shaking a fist at her.

She stared at him calmly, avidly. "Why, Marco, you are all wet."

"Thanks to you! You deserve a good, hard spanking, and this time, by damn, you are going to get it."

But even as he braced himself to tackle her and thoroughly blister her behind, she only smirked at him, the little termagant, as if to dare him to venture even one step closer to her! Then she stared pointedly at the front of his trousers, where the drenched cloth clung tightly, outlining his manhood in exquisite detail. To his mortification, the searing hunger of her gaze made him spring to life before her eyes, in an erection more agonized than any he had ever before felt in his life.

Mother of God! Why could he *never* become aroused at the proper moment?

Christina's triumphant gaze flicked back to his face, and in that moment, they both knew precisely what he wanted to give her. It wouldn't be a spanking—but it would be *very* hard and so good.

"*Dio mio,*" Marco muttered.

With all the finesse of a blind man, he turned and stumbled from the room.

SEVEN

"Pansy, what should I do about Christina?"

This was the question Marco posed to his cheetah the following morning as he and the large black cat paced the verdant courtyard behind the plantation house. Unfortunately, neither Pansy nor *il Dio* seemed to have any answers for Marco at the moment.

Christina had staked her claim on him and now refused to let go. Thanks to her shenanigans, no woman on the island would come near him, as they all now feared swift and sure retribution at the hands of the little terror. He was powerless to punish the girl, for her triumphant gaze last night had indeed mirrored the truth—his hands on her backside would never do more than hold her body tightly pinned against his hungry, thrusting loins, reprehensible possibility though it was. Even now, sexual frustration burned in him, and he was in such a mean temper, he hardly trusted himself around other people.

Yet what exasperated him the most was that all of his sexual energy was now focused on one woman—the same little witch who was cheerfully ruining his life! He actually shuddered as he recalled his near-violent rush to arousal last night when she had smirked at him from her bed—mere seconds after she had drenched him with cold water! It amazed him that he had responded with such vigor under circumstances that would have temporarily frozen all sexual feeling in any other man.

Why was it that only she could stir him so? Even if he could manage to coax another female into his bed, Marco was beginning to have serious doubts about his own performance. He was almost to the point of marrying the little brat just to assuage this gnawing sexual hunger, and yet his conscience would never allow this. Indeed, he had prayed over his dilemma last night, and had come away with the strong feeling in his heart that he could never make any woman a decent husband, not with his constant absences and freebooting ways—not as long as he continued with his mission to avenge the deaths of his parents. He and his men were leaving on another voyage two days hence, and what would he do about the girl? She had totally gone to seed. Could he trust her not to seduce one of the field workers while he was away?

Perhaps her nurse might exert some influence over her. Much as he detested speaking with the virago, Hesper, he was desperate enough to deal with that devil's mistress at the moment.

Marco hurried up the back stairs, entered the shadowy recesses of the house, and went in search of the nurse. He found the hunched-over little woman sitting in the dining room near the window, doing her mending. Wearing a brown muslin dress and a white house cap, she was squinting at her lap as she worked her needle through a frayed napkin.

Standing in the archway, he crossed his arms over his chest and assumed a strong, determined pose. "I would have a word with you, woman."

Hesper set down the napkin and regarded Marco with a pursed mouth and narrowed eyes. "Why, of course, your lordship," she sneered.

Marco's jaw tightened. "You must do something about the girl, Christina."

Hesper appeared amazed. "I beg your pardon?"

He coughed. "The girl is running wild, like a cat in heat."

"And you think I am the one to remedy this situation?"

"But of course," Marco said sternly. "You are her nurse, are you not?"

Whatever response Marco had expected, it was not the one he received. The wrinkle-faced woman threw back her head and laughed herself silly. As Marco watched with a dark scowl, Hesper cackled and guffawed until tears sprang to her eyes.

"What is so amusing, woman?" he demanded.

Still laughing, Hesper rose and went over to stand before him, rubbing her gnarled fingers together gleefully as she regarded him with a mixture of scorn and triumph. "I knew this day would come!"

"What are you talking about?"

She snorted in disdain. "Where were you, your bleedin' lordship, six years ago, when I begged you to let me exercise some discipline over the girl and you turned a deaf ear? You and your heathen buccaneers have let the chit run wild and have done everything in your power to undermine my authority. Now she has gone to seed, you say? Well, I say this is chickens coming home to roost, and glad I am to see this day!"

Marco was hardly amused by this diatribe. "That is

quite enough, woman! I shall not have you criticizing the way I run this island or my household. I am merely pointing out that the girl is of an age where she needs a woman's influence—"

"Hah!" the shrew retorted. "The girl is beyond redemption, thanks to you and your kind! For years I begged you to listen to me regarding the evil doings on this island—the drinking and the fornicating. Now look around you, my fine lord, at all the little bastards you and your men have fathered. A few more years and every last one of them will be as wild and iniquitous as that wayward girl. Did you really expect her to grow up any different from the whole dissolute lot of you?"

Stunned speechless, Marco could only stare at the woman. What could he say to defend himself? She had spoken the truth.

Marco continued to ponder what he should do. Hesper had certainly been of no help. In two days he must leave, and Lord only knew what outrageous thing Christina might do next. He shuddered at the possibility of returning home to the discovery that she had become pregnant by one of the peasants.

Perhaps he should try to reason with the girl directly. Granted, she had acted incorrigibly of late, but they had been good friends for so many years before. Perhaps somewhere within her rebellious soul there still dwelled a trace of the sober, winsome child who had regarded him with worshipful eyes, had asked him for guidance, and had once promised that she would lay down her life for him. Yes, he would speak with her and see if she would not come around.

When a search of the house revealed no trace of her, he went searching for her along the verdant trails of Isola del Mare. Pansy ambled along beside him. He knew he was getting closer to the girl when, abruptly, Pansy paused and lifted her ears. As Marco glanced around with a scowl, Cicero swooped down, screeching, from his perch in a nearby *châtaignier* tree, and made a nosedive for Pansy. At first, the cheetah tried to hold her ground, growling and batting at the parrot as he zoomed in—

The result was a horrible mêlée—hissing cat and screaming bird and a murderous flash of lethal claws, bared talons, and brilliant purple-and-green feathers.

Within seconds, Pansy turned and bolted, shrieking with fear as Cicero flapped after her with deadly intent.

"Pansy, you big baby!" Marco called after the cheetah in disgust. "Come back here, you coward!"

When the only reply was the shrill sounds of more squawking and screeching in the distance, Marco chuckled, the shenanigans of cat and bird lifting his spirits a bit. Actually, Pansy was not too much of a coward, he mused. The cheetah feared only two other beasts of prey—Cicero and Hesper, both of whom had terrorized poor Pansy almost all of her life. The cat had definitely lost out in the pecking order with both. Otherwise, the cheetah was fiercely protective of her master, and had even tried to attack members of Marco's crew when he and his men had engaged in playful wrestling matches.

Marco gave up waiting for Pansy and continued searching for Christina. He knew that if Cicero was guarding the area, the girl must be nearby. Indeed, he was soon drawn by the sound of her laughter to the very dappled lagoon where she had accosted him years earlier as he bathed. He spotted her out in the shallow pond near a tinkling waterfall, holding one of the island children, one-year-old Roberto. The baby's older brother, six-year-old Gregorio, was swinging on a massive root above the pond. With a howl of laughter and a loud splash, Gregorio landed not far from Christina. The children's mother, Sophia, sat on the bankside weaving a basket.

Marco sat down beside Sophia and smiled. *"Buon giorno,"* he said amiably.

"Buon giorno," she repeated with a shy smile.

At that moment the sound of laughter stopped; Marco turned to see both Christina and the baby staring at him solemnly, while Gregorio swam happily nearby. The sight of the beautiful, wet girl holding the small child unexpectedly jolted him. The scene was so innocently sensual. Christina's hair and face were dripping, and the baby's brown arms were locked tightly around her neck. Marco even felt a twinge of jealousy toward the small child who snuggled so close to the very heart he coveted.

A shudder of longing racked his body. *Dio mio,* he thought, what was happening to him—again? He had come here to set the girl in her place. He could not begin his stern lecture with an insane urge to tumble her in the bushes and ensure that it would be *his* baby she held in her arms next spring!

"Cara, may I have a word with you?" he called out with as much calm as he could muster.

She regarded him petulantly. "I promised Sophia that I would teach the baby to swim."

"It is all right, Christina," Sophia called quickly as she gathered up her weaving supplies. "Roberto and Gregorio need their nap."

Christina shrugged. Taking Gregorio's hand and holding the baby securely braced in her other arm, she climbed out of the pool, her wet white shift clinging sensuously to her lovely curves. Marco swallowed hard, his heart hammering wildly at the vision of womanhood approaching him. Roberto giggled as Christina handed the fat baby over to his mother;

Gregorio tugged on Christina's hand until the girl leaned over and kissed him.

Suddenly Marco hungered for a kiss, too.

Watching Sophia leave with the brown, half-naked boys, Marco again recalled Hesper's warning. Would Roberto, Gregorio, and the other small children on the island grow up to become debauchees—just as Christina was rapidly showing signs of becoming?

The little temptress now strolled over to sit down beside him, crossing her legs and regarding him soberly. Catching a lungful of her intoxicating scent, as well as an eyeful of her tautened nipples straining against the soaked cloth of her shift, Marco hastily removed his shirt and wordlessly handed it to her. She draped the garment around her shoulders, sniffed the collar, and then smiled at him, in a display that was brazenly carnal. Desire racked his senses anew.

"What is it you wish to talk to me about?" she asked, slowly drawing her gaze over his naked chest.

Marco could barely speak, let alone breathe. He already intensely regretted taking off his shirt and handing it to her—yet was that not better than the alternative of staring at all the delightful curves and valleys of her body through the near-transparent cloth of her shift?

Dio, he was far too close to this siren! He stood and began to pace. "*Cara*, we seem to have reached an impasse, you and I, and I was hoping we might make our peace."

Christina stared up at him earnestly. "I have no desire to be at war with you."

His hopes soared. Perhaps this would not be so difficult after all. Already they were making significant progress. "Then you are willing to cooperate, I take it?"

Her lovely gaze narrowed. "Cooperate in what way?"

With an effort, he kept his voice calm and level. "Christina, how can you even ask that, considering your behavior lately? You must stop being cruel to my women. You must deport yourself as a young lady should. Then you and I can be friends again."

She laughed. "But I have no desire to be your friend, Marco."

Unaccountably, he felt crushed, regarding her with wounded eyes. "Do you not like me anymore? Is that why we cannot be friends?"

She stood, staring him up and down boldly. "I no longer wish to be your friend, Marco, because I am going to become your wife."

Marco's patience snapped. "Damn it, Christina! Why all of a sudden are you behaving in this provocative manner? When are you going to stop this absurd talk of our marrying?"

"It is not absurd! You promised me!"

"Now what are you talking about?"

She pointed to the stream and spoke passionately. "You were in this very pond, six years ago, when you gave me your word that you would marry me when I grew up."

Marco's mouth dropped open. "You remember that? But you were just a child—"

"Does that relieve you of your obligation to honor your promise?" she demanded indignantly.

"Christina, you were only twelve," he reasoned. "You cannot have possibly known what you wanted then—"

"Yes, I did know! I wanted you! And I still want you now!"

"But why?"

"Why?" she repeated with a bitter laugh. "Are you an idiot? Because I love you!"

"What?" he cried, staring at her, thunderstruck.

As he watched her intently, tears filled her beautiful eyes and her lower lip began to quiver. Suddenly it was all Marco could do not to pull her into his arms.

She spoke in a tortured whisper that further assailed his conscience and his heart. "You think I did not already love you the day I asked you to marry me?"

"Christina, please," he entreated, groaning.

A tear spilled off her eyelash and rolled down her cheek. "I have loved you from the very moment you rescued me on Edisto Island."

He clenched his fists. "Christ, girl, you must not say these things."

"Why?"

His anguished gaze met hers. "Because I am a man of the sea. I am committed to destroying the Spanish who robbed me of my family. Until then, I cannot be a proper husband for any woman."

"I think you are making excuses. You could still marry me if you really wanted to."

But he could only shake his head resignedly. "That is not true, *cara*. You deserve better than this island and a husband whose loyalties are torn."

"How can you say that? This island is my home, and you are all I want."

Stepping closer, he brushed a tear from her cheek and smiled at her sadly. "If those are your feelings, then all I can say is that you do not know any better. You have not seen enough of this world to understand what is best for you. And I must somehow remedy this lack in your education."

Her eyes flashed with sudden alarm. "You would send me away?"

He sighed. "I think that the solution for your life does not lie here on Isola del Mare."

"Well, you are wrong, and you will send me away over my own dead body!" She yanked off his shirt and flung it at him. "And furthermore, you gave me your promise and you *will* marry me, Marco Glaviano!"

She stormed off, leaving Marco to die a dozen slow deaths as he smelled the heavenly scent of her on his shirt and stared at the delectable curves of her retreating backside.

EIGHT

CHICKENS COMING HOME TO ROOST.

Marco was reflecting on this dismal thought as he sat in bed the following morning sipping hot tea, with Pansy dozing beside him. Every step he took to set things right with Christina only took him further into an abyss of unwelcome complications. Was the shrew Hesper right that he had brought them to this appalling pass himself?

How glad he was that he would leave tomorrow. Perhaps out at sea in the endless tranquility, he might be able to think things through and come to his senses regarding the girl, to get his thoughts and feelings back on the proper course. He would speak with his God and ask for guidance. If he stayed, he feared that Christina's antics would impel him to drag her to his bed within a week—and such a move would spell disaster for them both.

Didn't she have any idea what she did to him when she looked at him with those gorgeous green eyes welling with tears and told him that she had loved him from the very night they had met? Didn't she realize how she could stir a man by telling him she had adored him for years? Didn't she know she was tearing his gut to ribbons? Hesper had been right that the girl had been at an impressionable age when he had rescued her. He should have listened and laid down the law from the beginning, instead of letting the wench run wild and spoiling her rotten.

This was the result. He groaned. The hell of it was, he wanted her as much as she wanted him—but not in a way that would ever do her any good.

While Marco ruminated about their relationship, Christina sat on a chair on the front porch. She wore a simple white, off-the-shoulder frock. She was trying unsuccessfully to yank a hairbrush through her long, wild, recalcitrant locks. Cicero watched her from his perch on the gallery railing, frequently calling out, "Bad girl!"—and only adding to her irritation.

Marco—the coward!—had failed to make an appearance so far this morning. He was no doubt hiding out following their argument yesterday. Tomorrow, he would sneak off on another of his voyages, doubtless hoping that she would forget all about her feelings for him while he was away—

Well, he was going to be in for a fine surprise when he returned, for she would never abandon her love for him. Nor would she release him from his promise to marry her.

She would also not soon forgive him for his rejection of her yesterday. She had laid her heart on the line, telling him of her feelings, and he had slashed her heart to shreds. She did not for a minute believe his trumped-up excuse that as a privateer, he would never make her a good husband—he simply did not want to give up his wenching. Why couldn't he see

that she was woman enough to satisfy him? Though
she was still a virgin, she was well aware of what
transpired between a man and a woman in bed, especially after so many years spent on this libidinous
island. She was prepared to love Marco with all the
passion in her young body and soul—even a dozen
times a day, if that was what it took to satisfy the
rogue. Why did he not find her attractive?

Scowling, she raised her hand mirror and studied
her face critically. She saw pleasing lines and angles,
smooth golden skin, bright eyes, a strong chin, and a
full mouth. She could find no real flaws in her visage, and she knew from the stares and compliments
of the other pirates that they found her pretty. Why
didn't Marco?

A twinge of doubt needled her as she thought of
how most of his mistresses were far more voluptuous
than she. Did he like his women on the plump side?
Did he find her breasts too small, her bottom not
rounded enough?

Well, perhaps if she ate like a pig while he was
gone, she might be able to add a few more ripe
curves to allure and please him. In the meantime, she
had to do something to get his attention before he
left—she would not make it convenient for him to go
off and forget about her while he was at sea.

Luigi now emerged from the forest trail and
climbed up the front steps to the house. Grinning at
Christina, he asked, "Is the boss up yet this morning?"

Christina smiled at the swarthy, bearded Italian
who she knew found her very attractive. He was
dressed in well-fitting trousers and a shirt that was
half unbuttoned. She might have found him appealing, except that she could not help but compare him
with Marco—and there every other man came up
short.

"I haven't seen Marco today. I assume he is still
lolling about in his bed."

Luigi scowled. "He asked me to come fetch him early so we could inspect the hull of *La Spada* before we launch her. There is much to do in preparation for tomorrow's voyage."

Christina again tried to yank the brush through her tangled locks, and cursed her frustration. "I am sure you are indeed very busy," she muttered. "Why don't you go to Marco's room and rouse him?"

Now Luigi was staring at her intently, watching her struggles with the brush. "Oh, I would not want to risk disturbing the boss." He cleared his throat. "Tell me, are you having difficulty with your hair this morning?"

"Hah!" she retorted, gesturing her exasperation. "My hair is perpetually thick as seaweed and full of tangles. Marco used to brush it, but now he refuses to help."

Luigi chuckled as he stepped closer. "How inconsiderate of the boss. May I offer my assistance? You know, I used to brush my little sister's hair back when Marco and I lived in Venice."

Christina stared up at the lean, dark-eyed pirate. As he had moved closer to her, she had noticed a certain husky note creeping into his voice, and his obsidian eyes had narrowed on her with a near-predatory gleam. In the back of her mind, she knew that to encourage this man could be dangerous, but she refused to listen to that small, nagging voice. Normally, too, she would have cringed at the thought of having any man but Marco touch her—even if just to brush her hair. Yet now her resentment toward the blond giant took precedence over all other concerns. Why should she continue to be loyal to him in her heart when he no doubt betrayed her nightly with every whore on the island? And he was bound to come outside at any moment now, she mused with vengeful pleasure. Let him see that other men did not treat her with his own cold disregard.

Let him see that other men found her desirable. Marco's rejection of her yesterday had cut her to the quick. Now let him know what it felt like to watch another man minister to her needs!

She handed Luigi the brush and smiled. "Thank you. You are most kind."

He chuckled, took the brush in hand, and began slowly drawing it through Christina's long, dense locks. "You are wrong about something, little one," he murmured raspily.

"And what is that?"

He ran his fingers through a long strand and whispered, "Your hair is not like seaweed. It is baby-fine, soft as satin, and shiny as silk."

Christina wished she could feel charmed by Luigi's compliments, but she did not. Instead, she felt a stab of dismay, wishing Marco would say such lovely things to her!

Luigi continued to brush her hair, humming the strains of an Italian folk song. As the moments passed, Christina had to concede that the pirate was quite skilled with the brush, slowly and patiently disentangling each snarl. Yet when she felt an occasional tug of pain, she also had to admit that he was not quite as proficient as Marco, however commendable the boatswain's diligence might be.

When at last he finished, he handed her back the brush with a grin. "Now, do I get a thank-you, mistress?"

She rose to face him and smiled. "Thank you very much, Luigi."

He feigned a wounded expression. "After all that work, don't I at least get a small kiss as my reward?" he teased.

Staring at the grinning pirate, Christina suddenly found herself liking the idea of attracting him as a beau to make Marco jealous. Besides, what harm could one small kiss do? She might even be able to hook Luigi like a nice, fat fish and string him along for a while—so that Marco could consider how it felt to lose her to another.

"Very well, I suppose one kiss won't hurt," she murmured. Setting the brush down on her chair, she stretched on tiptoe to plant a brief, chaste kiss on his lips—

Luigi's response was sudden and frightening. Heaving a mighty groan, he yanked her into his arms and slammed his mouth brutally on hers, trying to pry her lips apart with his bold, insistent tongue—

At his unexpected assault, Christina felt at first paralyzed by shock and then consumed by fear. She had never expected this savage response to an innocent kiss! Luigi was holding her so tight that she feared her lungs would burst, and he seemed determined to invade her mouth with his tongue. Feeling sickened and repulsed by his advance, she continued to keep her lips tightly pressed together and managed to insinuate her hands between their bodies, balling her fists and struggling unsuccessfully to shove him away.

Her resistance enraged him. He pulled back, shook her by the shoulders until her teeth rattled, and hissed, "Stop it, you little bitch! Do you think you can tempt a man and then play the coy innocent? I am sure you sport with the boss nightly, so this game comes a bit too late! Now open your mouth wide, slut, just as you will soon spread those creamy thighs for me—"

Christina was appalled, horrified by the filthy things he was saying to her. "No!" she cried, but she was too late. Luigi's mouth descended brutally on her parted lips and his tongue ravaged her mouth. Christina gagged at the revolting taste of him, a sickening mix of stale tobacco and sour food. She began to fight him with all the strength in her body—

Then, suddenly, she was flailing at thin air as the pirate was pulled violently from her.

She looked up to see Marco restraining Luigi by the collar. Never had she seen him so enraged. Veins stood out on his temples, and his eyes were brilliant with fury. His fist was clenched and drawn back, seemingly ready to smash the other man's jaw.

"What in hell do you think you're doing?" he demanded of the boatswain.

While Luigi cowered before his livid boss, his tongue remained bold. "That girl is a tease! She invited me to kiss her—"

"I did not!" Christina cut in furiously.

"And then she tried to play the innocent!" Luigi accused.

"That is not true!" Christina cried.

"Get out of my sight!" Marco hissed to Luigi. "I will deal with you later!"

He flung the man away, and Luigi tumbled down the front steps, uttering several loud grunts of pain and sending Cicero flying off his perch with a protesting squeal. Despite a rough landing, the pirate staggered to his feet and limped off toward the jungle, hurling Christina and Marco a venomous glance over his shoulder.

Christina gulped as Marco advanced on her with murder in his eyes. "Now, you tell me what in hell is going on here!"

It took all of Christina's inner strength not to cower in his daunting presence. His voice was sharp as the crack of a whip. Watching his powerful chest fall and rise, glimpsing the anger tightening every muscle of his huge body, Christina began to fear for her own safety. Never had she seen him like this!

"Damn it, girl, I said explain yourself!" he roared.

Christina could not help herself; she wrung her hands and her voice came shrilly. "I only asked Luigi to brush my hair, because you will not help me anymore! Then he insisted on a kiss in payment, so I thought, why not? You do not care if I kiss another!"

She cringed as Marco violently kicked over the chair she had been sitting on. "Don't you dare tell me what I do or do not care about! Furthermore, have you *never* considered the consequences of tempting a grown man in this manner?"

"I tempted you and you only rejected me!" she railed. "Why should I not seek another beau now?"

Her words so exacerbated Marco's fury that he could not trust himself to speak. Instead, he clamped his steely fingers over her wrist, pulled her resisting body into the house and down the hallway to the tiny room that served as his office.

He yanked her inside, slammed the door, and pinned her shoulders against the door with his strong hands.

"You," he thundered, "will stop behaving like a strumpet and comport yourself as a young lady should!"

"I will not!" she blazed back.

Marco was on the verge of strangling her. "You will obey me or have your bottom soundly spanked—which is what the willful child you are deserves!"

"I am not a child, I am a woman!" she screamed at him, her fear taking a backseat to her outrage. "And I will not obey you! I shall do exactly what I please, just as I have always done ever since I came to this island. You think you can act like a big, mean bully, Marco Glaviano, but it will not work with me! It is too late for you to start ordering me around! And if you will not marry me, I shall take one of your men as my husband."

Marco muttered a blistering curse that actually left Christina blushing. His hands gripped her face with near-punishing force; his eyes blazed down into hers. "Get something through that thick, stubborn head of

yours! You will never take one of my men as your
husband! No man on this island is worthy of you!"

Even in the face of his superior strength and fulmi-
nating fury, she remained defiant. "Yes, there is such
a man—if he would only stop screaming at me and
honor his promise!"

"Goddammit, woman!" Reeling with frustrated
rage, Marco released her and backed away.

"If you will not honor your promise," she continued passionately, "then I will find another who is
man enough to live up to his word."

He shook a finger at her and laughed in cynical
disbelief. "You are such a naive child! You have no
idea what you are doing! You think you will find a
husband, but instead, you will find yourself flat on
your back, with your legs spread—and pregnant
within a fortnight."

"That is fine with me!" she flung at him recklessly.
"I want a baby anyway! And I can handle any man
on this island!"

"Oh, can you?" All at once, Marco was feeling utterly ruthless. "Let us see, then."

Intent on teaching her a lesson she would never
forget, Marco grabbed her roughly, shoved her back
against the door, ground his body into hers, and
kissed her thoroughly and insultingly. Even as his
tongue plunged and ravished her mouth, his hand
took one of her breasts. Banishing every tender emotion from his heart, he reeled with power and lust.
He told himself he had to do this to her. He must
conquer her, humble her, bring her to her knees—and
to her senses.

And yet, within seconds after his lips claimed hers,
he was left wondering just who was being mastered
here. While his own lips plundered and ravaged, her
mouth surrendered so sweetly to his drowning kiss.
While his brutal strength crushed her, her body trembled against him so eagerly. He felt the nipple of her

breast spring to life, tautening against his palm, and
his fingers uncoiled, now caressing rather than punishing. Her mouth felt softer than satin on his, her
lips warmer than the sun when it struck his face. Her
hands were stroking his spine, turning his blood to
liquid fire. He fought to ward off the devastating
flood tide of desire and tenderness that threatened to
hurl them both deep into the smoldering red vortex
of passion—

He wrenched his mouth from hers and spoke brutally. "A grown man will kiss you until your mouth
is bruised. He will squeeze your breasts until you cry
out. He will spread your legs and drive into you until you beg for mercy . . ."

If Marco had hoped to scare some good sense into
Christina, he could not have been in for a greater
shock when she sobbed and panted, "Oh, yes. Please,
love me, Marco."

Stunned, he backed away and stared down into
her bewildered, passion-dazed eyes. God in heaven,
what was he doing? This girl was dangerous! Another minute of this little game, and he would be the
one snared, humbled, and conquered. He would
bury himself to the hilt inside her—and then she
would never let him go until she dragged him to the
altar!

He began to pace the tiny room like a great, frustrated lion, while she watched him warily. At last he
turned to her and snapped, "I cannot handle this
right now."

She raised her chin. "What are you saying?"

He raked his fingers through his hair. "I will make
a bargain with you. Are you willing to listen?"

She shrugged. "I am listening."

"If you will comport yourself like a lady while I
am gone, we will settle this matter between us when
I return."

She eyed him suspiciously. "Settle it once and for all?"

"*Sì.*" Seeing her smile, he quickly held up a hand. "Mind you, I am not promising I shall marry you. Only that we will resolve things."

She bit her lip and considered that for a moment. He resisted an insane urge to grab her and chew that luscious lip in her stead.

"Well?" he prodded tensely.

"I suppose that is fair," she conceded.

"Do I have your word you will behave yourself while I am gone?"

"Very well," she said grudgingly.

He fought a smile at her petulant look, taking her chin in his fingers and tilting her face upward. "No chasing after the peasants in the fields?" he asked sternly.

"All right," she muttered.

"*Buono,*" he said, relieved.

He was turning to leave when she queried, "Marco?"

"Yes?"

She hesitated, now chewing on her finger and drawing his senses across a new rack of sensual torment.

"What is it, *cara?*" The scolding tone he tried to effect came out strained and husky instead.

She dropped her hand and stared at him with her heart in her eyes. "Will you kiss me good-bye, Marco?"

Long after, he would wonder how much a simple question could wreak such emotional havoc. Why did she have to stand there looking so ravishingly beautiful, so innocently seductive? Never had she looked more adorable to him than she did now, with her tight nipples straining against her dress, with her wide eyes and wet lips just begging him to kiss her! The uncertainty and vulnerability of her visage further twisted his heart. His chest hurt and his eyes stung with tears. If only she knew that he was a hairsbreadth away from crushing her in his arms again, kissing her senseless—and never letting her go!

Instead, he stared at the floor and helplessly clenched, then unclenched, his fists. "I can't, *cara.*"

He heard her disappointed sigh. "Then will you comport yourself like a gentleman while you are gone?"

He glanced up at her sharply. "What do you mean?"

She met his gaze boldly. "If I cannot be with another man, then you cannot be with another woman."

He could only stare at her, mutter a noncommittal grunt, and beat a hasty retreat.

Still immersed in turmoil, Marco fled the house and hurried down the path toward the beach to check on *La Spada.* Pansy sprang out of the bushes and fell into step beside him.

"Where were you when I needed you?" Marco asked the cheetah ruefully.

Pansy whined.

Luigi was waiting for them near the beach, and jumped up from the chunk of driftwood he had been sitting on.

"Boss, I do hope you understand about the girl—"

Marco glared at him and spoke in a charged, cold tone. "After we leave on our voyage, we will dump you off at Spanish Town like the loathsome sewage you are. You will be given a month's wages. Never return to this island again."

Marco turned and started off with Pansy.

Luigi's expression was incredulous and enraged as he charged after his captain. "You would ban me from your crew simply because I kissed a brassy wench? You would take the word of that girl over me? I tell you, she is a little slut—"

Marco hurled an oath, there was a mighty cracking sound, and before Luigi could blink, he was lying flat on his back and rubbing a jaw that felt broken by the force of Marco's fist.

Yet Luigi's ordeal had hardly ended. A split second later, a hundred pounds of enraged black cheetah landed, screeching, on his chest. As the terrified boatswain watched, wild-eyed, the cat's sharp, vicious teeth descended toward his throat—

"Pansy!" Marco yelled.

In the nick of time, the great cat hesitated, turning to hiss resentfully at her master. Then she hopped off Luigi and ambled back to Marco's side, eyeing him contritely and licking his hand.

Luigi was staring at Marco incredulously. "You want the wench for yourself!" he accused.

Marco's reply was lethally calm. "Touch the girl again, you bloody bastard, and I'll kill you."

He strode off toward *La Spada* with Pansy following, leaving Luigi to glower at his boss's retreating figure with a thirst for revenge burning in his heart.

NINE

WILL YOU KISS ME GOOD-BYE, MARCO?

On a balmy evening three days later as he stood at his post on *La Spada*, Marco was still pondering Christina's devastating parting question. Next to him, Giuseppe was manning the wheel as the brigantine plowed through the waves ten leagues southeast of Havana. Marco and his men were on the lookout for Spanish treasure galleons, which customarily took on booty in South America, then followed the sea lanes to Havana, meeting other Spanish treasure ships and forming flotillas before sailing back to Spain. Although so far their voyage had brought no plunder, Marco was hoping to snag a stray north-bound galleon loaded with Peruvian or New Granadan gold before the ship reached the safety of the Havana harbor.

Such had been his charge for six years now, during England's long war with Spain. As a privateer commissioned under letters of marque bearing the seal of

George II, Marco was allowed to keep better than half of his plunder; the balance would be turned over to his British liaison at Charles Town. But *La Spada* would prowl these waters for many weeks first, until her hold was near bursting with silver and gold bullion.

Normally, Marco relished his time at sea—the creaking of the ship's timbers, the rolling motion of the vessel, the snapping of the sails, the crisp wind and salty spray in his face. But on this voyage he had felt troubled ever since they had left Isola del Mare.

Traditionally, the entire population of the island came out to bid the pirates Godspeed. This time had been no exception, with numerous women and children lining the docks to wave, cheer, and throw out flowers to bless the departing vessel. Yet, standing in his customary place on the quarterdeck, Marco had eyes for only one—the beautiful young woman in white who merely stared at him so solemnly from the wharf, with Pansy on a leash beside her. Usually, Christina would have waved, laughed, and blown him kisses, and he would have responded in kind. Instead, when she had regarded him with such deep-eyed sadness, he had felt as if he had left his heart behind when he sailed out of port. Endlessly he wondered why they had come to this impasse in which they could no longer be friends.

Marco truly missed the comfortable camaraderie and affection that had been between them previously. For years he had never hesitated to wrap an arm around Christina's shoulders, to greet her with a great hug and a friendly kiss. He had soothed her and wiped her tears when she had skinned an elbow or twisted her ankle. He had listened to her patiently when she complained about Hesper or because he was gone too much. He had read her stories and allowed her to best him at cards. He had even dragged her in out of the rain, throwing the stubborn girl over his shoulder when she refused to return to the house during a nor'easter ...

Now those idyllic days seemed gone forever. Now everything had become so strained. He missed playing with her—for now the nature of the game itself had changed.

Why did he have to want her so, and she him? He was convinced that this mutual desire would bring them both nothing but trouble. Yesterday in the quiet, he had again prayed over their dilemma, and the answers had confirmed what he already knew in his heart.

The man he was today could never marry Christina. The man he was today would not give up his quest to avenge the deaths of his parents. Like the crusaders of old, Marco saw himself on a holy quest for justice and righteousness, and he was determined to do his part to decimate the Spanish corruption that had brought about the murder of his father. Taking a wife would not merely frustrate his goals; he could not serve two mistresses—the sea that drew him to battle, and the siren who drew him to her arms. He would never make a proper husband and father unless he laid down his sword forever.

Already, his strained relationship with Christina was affecting his position with his men. Two days ago, he had caught more than a few resentful glances when they had dumped Luigi off at the harbor in Spanish Town. The scuttlebutt had already gotten around Marco's crew that the boatswain had been banished for kissing Christina, and this information had not been well received. Of course, it was accepted by any man of the sea that a sailor could be lashed for dereliction of duty or summarily hanged for mutiny—but to punish a man for kissing a wench was unheard of, especially if the female involved was unattached, as Christina was presumed to be. Even Marco had been given pause by the look of rabid ha-

tred in Luigi's eyes when he had put the man off
with no more than the clothes on his back and a
month's wages.

His problem remained—what would he do about
the girl? He had thought of no solution other than to
see if he could not find her a suitable school while he
was in Charles Town. He had even considered the
possibility of trying to locate the girl's former guardian, Charles Rutgers, although he still instinctively
distrusted the man after he had placed Christina in
such peril on Edisto Island in the first place. Marco
knew that his nemesis, Carlos, had returned to plunder the island on several occasions, his raids reducing the village to a shambles. Over the years, Marco
had survived more than a few dangerous skirmishes
with the infamous Spanish pirate himself, and never
again would he allow Christina to be subjected to
such peril. Whatever place he found for her must be
both civilized and safe.

Lord, he would miss her so when she left, he
thought poignantly, remembering the splendor of
their kiss, the haze of desire and tenderness that had
consumed him. But the sad truth was, he would do
her no good if she stayed.

"Ahoy! A ship!" called a voice from the crow's
nest.

Marco raised his spyglass and scanned the horizon
until he spotted a three-masted Spanish galleon in
the distance, her billowing tiers of sails outlined in
the red-gold splendor of sunset. He emitted a hoot of
triumph! Their luck could not have been better! The
treasure ship was making unescorted for Havana,
and as low as she sat in the water, she was surely
loaded down with South American treasure.

Marco was well aware that galleons could be fierce
fighters when cornered, and were customarily heavily armed to guard their precious cargoes. He called
out an order to take in the topsails and approach

their quarry slowly. Claudio relayed his command to the seamen, who busied themselves hauling halyards or climbing the ratlines. Marco hoped that, if they approached unhurriedly, in a nonthreatening manner, by the time they raised their own British Navy flag, it would be too late for the doomed vessel to flee.

Unfortunately, the other ship soon caught on to Marco's game of slow pursuit; as he watched through the spyglass and muttered a frustrated curse, the galleon's decks swarmed with hands lashing cannon to the gunports, while other seamen clambered aloft to unfurl additional sail.

"Captain, she's bearing down for Havana four points to the wind and manning battle stations!" his navigator called out from the binnacle.

Yet Marco was not disheartened. "Let her run, then." To Claudio, he shouted, "Unfurl full sail and bear down to larboard. She cannot hope to beat a shallow draft vessel, not as low as she's sitting."

Marco's crew responded with energy and precision, sailors crawling out on the yards to untie canvas. True to Marco's prediction, with La Spada's full square sails catching the wind, she soon began to gain on the Spanish ship. When Marco yelled, "All hands to battle stations!" the entire crew sprang into action—gunners manning the dozen cannon on the gun deck, while powder monkeys loaded the rounds; sailors readying the boarding pikes and nets; Patrizio standing ready to act as surgeon; the new boatswain, Ugo, whistling commands to the sailors up in the rigging as the drummer boy tapped out a battle cadence.

Marco wondered if the galleon would give up without a fight. Traditionally, merchant ships did surrender, though an occasional determined captain would do battle with privateers and a horrible mêlée would ensue, with red-hot grape, chain shot, and grenades screeching through the air to blow apart men, masts, and hulls. Galleons often bore huge, razor-sharp blades on their yards that made grappling onto them and boarding a perilous business at best.

As they were now within firing range, Marco called out, "Raise the pennant and fire a round across her bow!"

Claudio relayed the orders, and in only seconds, *La Spada*'s port cannon blazed out a shot that sailed over the bow of the galleon and landed in the ocean with a huge boom and a mighty splash.

Seconds later, to Marco's dismay, the guns of the galleon cracked back, a trio of cannonballs landing just shy of *La Spada*'s port side. The brigantine's gunners re-aimed their own cannon and responded in kind, pelting out four more blistering rounds, and at last one of the shots met with success, hitting the other vessel high to starboard. As Marco observed the drama intently, the galleon heaved a mighty groan, and her foremast came toppling down across her gundeck, sending the gunners dashing about in confusion. Marco gave orders to cease fire, hoping that, with the galleon's starboard cannon disabled, her captain would quickly give up the fight.

On the brigantine, all waited tensely to see how the other vessel's captain would react. Then a shrill of victory went up from Marco's crew as the galleon struck her colors in the traditional gesture of surrender. Marco silently commended the wisdom of the Spanish captain for avoiding a cruel fate for himself and his men, had he chosen to continue to do battle. Of course, sometimes surrendering could be equally dangerous for a conquered enemy; however, unlike some pirates and privateers who slaughtered a surrendered foe with unrelenting barbarism, Marco and his men always behaved fairly and humanely toward their captives. Whenever possible, Marco preferred accomplishing his goals without violence. Thus, they would

raid the galleon's hold and hoist its plunder, relieve
the crew of their money, jewelry, and arms, and then
cut the other vessel loose to make for Havana.

As his men grappled onto the galleon and prepared to board, he wondered idly if the ship's hold
would sport a large emerald or a gold Indian mask to
please Christina. After each of his voyages, Marco
customarily brought her home a priceless bit of plunder to soothe her sulks and bribe her forgiveness following his long absences, and she customarily
rewarded him with a kiss—

Will you kiss me good-bye, Marco?

He groaned. If only Christina would give up the
fight as easily as the Spanish ship, he mused. Unfortunately, he feared that the kind of surrender she had
in mind would only spell his own defeat.

TEN

Two weeks later, in a sordid section of Charles Town not far from the harbor, Luigi Monza staggered out of the Pig and Whistle Tavern. His battered bicorne hat hung at a sloppy angle, his clothing was tattered, and his face was grimy and heavily bearded. His rolling gait attested to the fact that he had drunk much more than a sailor's customary portion of grog at the notorious punch house.

Late on this warm spring afternoon, the stench of garbage was heavy in the air, especially as the scavenger clattered past in the street with his red cart overflowing with slops and refuse. On the shell walkways, sailors out looking for sport intermingled with vendors hawking their goods, businessmen, constables, fancy ladies, black and Indian slaves.

Luigi had loitered about Charles Town for two days now, ever since the Spanish merchant ship that had given him passage from Spanish Town had dropped him off at the Charles Town harbor on the

Cooper River. His voyage with the Spanish had been
far from pleasant. The pigs had confiscated all but a
few shillings of his wages in supposed compensation
for his passage—and then the dogs had pressed him
into service manning the pumps on their galleon.
When he had protested, the bastards had tied him to
the mast and laughed cruelly as they repeatedly
lashed his bare flesh with a cat-o'-nine-tails. His back
still bore the same oozing red welts. Now, after two
days spent drinking and sporting in the harbor town,
he was destitute and near desperate. Indeed, he had
just lost his last few farthings betting on a cockfight.

He knew the sensible thing to do would be to sign
on to another ship. Yet Luigi was determined to remain in Charles Town until Marco Glaviano sailed
into the harbor on *La Spada*. Daily he haunted the
wharves, watching for any sign of the privateer's
brigantine. He knew that, sooner or later, Marco
would fill his coffers with Spanish treasure and sail
into port to unload the Crown's share of his booty.

And Luigi would at last be in a position to seek his
revenge. For he was familiar with Marco's habits. He
knew Glaviano liked to drink and whore while in
Charles Town—and one of these nights soon, Luigi
would be waiting for him in the shadows outside
some seamy grog shop or bordello.

Luigi blamed Marco for every ill that had befallen
him during the past weeks. After all, his troubles had
begun when the privateer had unjustly banished him
from Isola del Mare for kissing that slut Christina.
No doubt Glaviano sought his ease nightly between
the wench's thighs, making his condemnation of one
of his men—for no more than a brief taste of the
girl—all the more reprehensible. He had given the little tease only what she deserved for tempting him—
and Glaviano would now pay dearly for robbing him
of his dignity and disgracing him before the other
men.

Yet how would he survive until *La Spada* appeared in the harbor? Passing the storefront of a goldsmith, he paused and glanced through the front window. As he watched the smiling smith show several ornate pocket watches to a bewigged, elegantly dressed gentleman, a reckless idea occurred to him. He knew that stealing was dangerous, and could mean the workhouse or the public stocks here in the English colonies—but what choice did he have at the moment? Again he blamed Marco Glaviano for bringing him to this terrible pass whereby he was driven to the life of a street thief in order to keep body and soul alive.

He waited at the corner of the shop, his body obscured as he surreptitiously watched the gentleman purchase an expensive gold watch. He observed him stuff the watch and his fat purse back into the breast pocket of his stylish velvet coat. The portly man then shook hands with the shopkeeper and approached the door. Luigi stepped deeply into the shadows of an adjacent doorway as the smith's bell jangled and the gentleman emerged.

Luigi followed the man as he strode to the corner and turned into Meeting Street. While fewer people were on the streets now, Luigi knew they were moving toward a finer area of town, with respectable homes and prosperous churches. Anxiety skittered along his spine and his heart lurched sickeningly as he realized that he must soon make his move.

As his quarry passed along the shadowy gallery of a dry goods store that had already closed its doors for the day, Luigi sprang into action, leaping on the man from behind, tackling him, and hurling him to the ground. His victim heaved a huge grunt of pain, but before the stunned man could even catch his breath, Luigi had relieved him of both his purse and his new gold watch, and had sprinted off.

Half a block away, he could hear his victim's

hoarse, outraged cry: "Thief! Thief!" Panic threatened to engulf Luigi as people on the walkway turned to stare at him. Women gasped and pulled small children out of his path, while he raced on, not daring to look back.

And then—cursed luck!—just as he was making for the corner, two uniformed watchmen rounded it and emerged solidly in his path. Just out of their reach, Luigi skidded to a stop. The watchmen also paused to eye him suspiciously. Then, hearing the hoarse cry of "Thief! Stop him!" coming from the prone man down the street, the watchmen sprang into action. They brandished their nightsticks and charged hell-bent for Luigi, even as he spun on his heel and raced off again.

Lady Luck had not been with Luigi for many weeks, and today was no exception, as the watchmen caught up with him in front of St. Peter's Church. While one of them seized the thief by the collar, his partner viciously beat Luigi with his nightstick, bashing him across the face, arms, and shoulders, causing the captured man to scream in pain and beg for mercy. Once the watchmen seemed convinced that they had subdued the thief, they dragged the battered and bleeding man back to face his accuser. Luigi gagged on the blood trickling down his throat and feared his nose had been broken.

The gentleman Luigi had robbed was now on his feet and surrounded by a small entourage of concerned citizens. With wig askew and features livid, the old man glared at the thief.

One of the guardsmen handed the retrieved watch and purse back to the victim. "Is this the scoundrel who robbed you, Magistrate Rutgers?"

"Aye," the man said, his voice trembling with fury. "Take the miscreant to the guardhouse for the night, and then I shall deal with him in my court, first thing on the morrow."

"Aye, my lord," the other guardsman said.

As the two watchmen hauled Luigi off, he felt sick with shock and fear at what he had just done. Mary, Joseph, and Jesus! He had just robbed a magistrate of the Court of General Sessions!

The next morning, Luigi sat clamped in irons with the other felons in the makeshift courtroom of the Charles Town Court of General Sessions. He had spent a miserable night in the cramped, dank, mosquito-infested guardhouse nearby.

Now, at the bench, Magistrate Charles Rutgers was meting out a series of judgments to the unfortunate lawbreakers brought before him, and as each severe sentence was pronounced, Luigi felt more horrified. Already he had observed a sailor sentenced to a public whipping for stealing a bottle of rum, and now the guards were dragging away a shrieking, hysterical prostitute who had just been sentenced to the gallows after she, while intoxicated, had accidentally scalded and killed her infant daughter. Listening to the woman's piteous pleas for her life as the unfeeling guards towed her away, Luigi had no doubt that the punishment awaiting him would be equally harsh.

All too soon the clerk barked out his name, and he shuddered in fear as the sadistically grinning guards yanked him up and dragged him, irons and all, before the bewigged and black-robed magistrate. As he spotted the ugly bruise on Rutgers's forehead and the glint of bloodlust in his cold gray eyes, Luigi knew he was doomed.

Rutgers peered through his monocle to eye with contempt the criminal cowering before him. "Ah, Master Luigi Monza. Shall we see to it that you regret the day you accosted a magistrate of this court?"

Luigi was so intimidated, so sick with fear, that he

was reduced to helpless babbling. "Yes, your worship—I mean, no, your worship."

Rutgers's face was like stone as he nodded to the bailiff. "Read the charges."

The man complied, droning out the official language charging Luigi with thievery and bodily assault on a magistrate of His Majesty's court. Luigi listened and felt his life slipping through his fingers.

Afterward, Rutgers said coldly, "You, sir, are charged with crimes most grave. How do you plead?"

Luigi's voice became shrill and piteous. "Guilty, your grace, and I humbly beg your pardon and throw myself on your mercy."

Rutgers snorted. "And where was your mercy yesterday, man? I say an evil dog like you must be taught a lesson."

By now, Luigi could only pray for death. "Yes, your grace," he muttered with his head bowed.

"I hereby sentence you to the public pillory for a period of ten days." Rutgers rapped his gavel and nodded to the head guard. "Nail his hands and ears to the stocks, and at the end of his time, cut off his right hand."

"Aye—with pleasure, your lordship," the guard replied.

Luigi was appalled and petrified. "Please, your grace!" he pleaded.

Rutgers again pounded his gavel. "Get this reprobate out of my sight. Next case."

But as the men dragged him off, Luigi dug in his heels. "Please, your grace, have mercy! I—I can redeem myself! I can divulge the whereabouts of an evil pirate!"

Rutgers looked up with interest, motioning to the guards to wait. Charles Rutgers was well aware that no officer of the Crown could ignore an offer of information about a freebooter. Charles Town had a long history of nasty encounters with such notorious pirates as Edward Teach and Stede Bonnet. While piracy had been on the wane for almost two decades, buccaneers who threatened the peace and the shipping lanes were still ruthlessly hunted down and dealt with brutally.

"What pirate is it you speak of?" he demanded of Luigi.

Luigi gulped. "If I can furnish information leading to the capture of this villain, may I keep my hand, your grace?"

Rutgers uttered a sound of impatience. "I make no promises to curs such as yourself! But I will listen."

Hastily, Luigi confessed, "The freebooter is named Marco Glaviano, and he raids shipping all along this coast. He lives on an island in the Caribbean—"

Rutgers's snort of contempt cut Luigi short. "Do not give me this balderdash, thief! I know of this man. Glaviano is a privateer sailing under letters of marque from the Crown. He is of good repute and under no bounty." To the guards, he added impatiently, "Take the scoundrel away."

But as the guards yanked him off, Luigi screamed, "Glaviano kidnapped an English child, I tell you! He still has her with him in the Caribbean!"

"Halt a moment!" Rutgers called, scowling.

The guards brought Luigi back to the bench.

"Tell me of this girl," Rutgers commanded, his expression one of intense interest.

"The girl is English, and she was only twelve years of age when Glaviano kidnapped her on Edisto Island."

Rutgers had turned white. "Her name, man!"

"Christina." Frowning, Luigi added, "Christina Abbott."

Rutgers's voice became a tense whisper. "And are you telling me that this young woman is still alive and living in the Caribbean?"

"Aye, your worship. Glaviano has the girl on his island."

"Is she safe?" When Luigi hesitated, he barked, "Tell the truth, man!"

Luigi avoided the magistrate's eye. "That depends on what you mean by safe."

"Damnation, man! Is her life in danger?"

"No, your grace."

Rutgers nodded decisively. "Then you will draw up a map for my men showing them the location of this island. That is all."

As the guards again dragged Luigi away, he screamed, "Your grace! I beg you!"

Rutgers sighed and muttered, "See that the cur spends his days in the pillory. Afterward . . . the thief may keep his hand."

After he had concluded his docket for the morning, Charles Rutgers remained in his deserted courtroom, his mind consumed with turmoil. So it appeared that his ward, Christina Abbott, was alive after all. He had assumed that the Spanish privateers had killed her during their raid on Edisto Island six years past, but now it appeared that his presumption was false. He was not at all certain he was pleased by this annoying complication, though he supposed he was still obligated to the girl. Six months prior to Christina's father's final, fateful voyage, Richard Abbott had asked Rutgers to draw up his will and had persuaded him to agree to serve as Christina's legal guardian, should the necessity ever arise. Rutgers's promise, however reluctantly given, remained both a sacred duty and a binding legal obligation after both Abbott and the girl's stepmother had drowned.

Now, if what this thief had told him was true, the girl had been living with freebooters in the Caribbean for over six years, and she was no doubt thoroughly corrupted and despoiled by them. It was even possible that she would resist a return to civilization.

He sighed. He supposed he was now duty-bound to write to the girl's stepuncle in England, the kindly but meddlesome vicar, George Hollingsworth, who had never given up hope that Christina might still be alive. Hollingsworth had even journeyed to the colonies soon after the child had disappeared, in the hope of finding her. Before returning to England empty-handed, the man had appointed a solicitor to act on his behalf and continue the search. Rutgers still heard from the solicitor, or from Hollingsworth, on occasion.

If Hollingsworth did choose to journey to the colonies once again, the two of them would doubtless need to charter a ship and sail for the Caribbean to retrieve his ward. Eventually, too, he would have to choose a husband for the girl—assuming she could be salvaged in some sort of marriageable shape—and relinquish the fortune that had been kept in trust as her future dowry for six long years. In truth, he would miss his generous recompense for acting as trustee of the estate, and he had looked forward to receiving compensation for at least another year before the girl could be declared legally dead and her inheritance settled on the next heir in line.

Of course, he could simply forget that he had ever received this information from Luigi Monza. But logic argued that if the girl were truly alive, she would sooner or later surface to claim her legal due.

All in all, this was a most bothersome business, he decided.

ELEVEN

Two and a half months later, Marco Glaviano sat sipping a tankard of rum in a smoky corner of a seamy tavern ignominiously known as the Rat's Nest, in the Charles Town harbor district not far from the Cooper River. In his buccaneer attire—dark trousers, flowing white shirt with leather vest, and gold earring—he fit right in with the other freebooters and sailors crowding the rowdy establishment. Tonight, the noisy revelers were immersed in activities ranging from games of shuffleboard, dice, and cards, to the raucous cockfight going on in the pit in the next room, to the seduction of the serving wenches, which was being carried out both on the tavern floor itself and in the cribs overhead. On a small dais in a distant corner, a Cockney lass was trying her best to belt out an off-key rendition of "Drink to Me Only With Thine Eyes," her voice and the sawing of the fiddler accompanying her almost drowned out by the din. As if to do justice to the establishment's name, a trio

of fat rats scurried beneath the tables gathering
crumbs and morsels of meat, the rodents largely unnoticed by the inebriated clientele.

Marco felt filled with restless tension tonight, and
his intent gaze combed the disreputable expanse,
searching for a comely wench for him to bed. He and
his men had been at sea for almost three months
prowling for galleons; this was their third trip into
Charles Town to off-load booty, but their first actual
shore leave. The voyage, while lucrative, had been
unusually protracted; at one point, they had spent almost two weeks becalmed off the Florida coast,
quickly running out of water and provisions. Ultimately, they had been impelled to lower the long-
boats and make a daring midnight raid on
Spanish-held St. Augustine in order to replenish their
supplies. Their foray had been successful, since they
had managed to scale the city walls and steal the
needed supplies without alerting the sentries at
Castillo de San Marcos. Other than the weeks they
had spent trapped in the summer doldrums, fortune
had sailed with *La Spada* as she completed her entire
voyage unchallenged and unmolested. Marco had
not even once sighted his nemesis, Carlos, even
though the Spanish privateer normally seemed to
possess an uncanny ability to predict and harass
Marco's movements.

While the voyage had been successful, its extended
length, coupled with the fact that Christina had
driven off all of Marco's women before he had sailed
from Isola del Mare, had left him a man in dire need
of a willing female. *Dio*, he had not lain with a
woman in over three months now! As a man of
strong urges who was accustomed to taking his ease
with a wench whenever the fancy struck him, he was
now literally seething with sexual frustration. Thus,
after he had met with his British liaison this last time
and had turned over the Crown's share of his booty,

he had given his men forty-eight hours of leave here in Charles Town.

He felt a stab of guilt as he remembered the promise he had exacted from Christina before he had left Isola del Mare. She had agreed to behave herself during his absence, and then had requested the same level of abstinence from him. Well, he had not actually promised the girl anything, had he? he asked himself irritably. Besides, decent women were expected to be chaste—men were not. That was simply the way of the world.

But his world had changed ever since the minx had laid claim to him. And his plans for sport left him battling a nagging conscience.

Marco chuckled as he watched a seasoned, bearded sailor with an eye patch and a peg leg hoist a plump whore into his arms and make for the stairs, his wooden limb thumping loudly across the floor. At the foot of the rickety steps, the squirming wench managed to convince the sailor to set her down; Marco observed her scolding the old salt for almost breaking both their necks—whereupon the sea dog kissed the wench loudly and smacked her behind. Marco shook his head and grinned as the two staggered up the staircase arm in arm.

A premonition of impending danger streaked along Marco's nerve endings as he caught a flicker of motion from the corner of his eye. He turned to see his enemy, Carlos, enter the tavern with several of his men. The tall, bearded Spaniard wore dark breeches and a black jacket crisscrossed by bandoliers bearing numerous knives and pistols. A tricorn hat dangled at a rakish angle atop his unruly black hair.

Marco automatically tensed, his hand moving to the pistol at his waist. He would like nothing better than to spring up now and shoot the Spanish jackal or gut him with his cutlass. He was tired of the Spaniard dogging his path for so many years. But his hands were bound at the moment. According to the unwritten law of the freebooters, disputes between warring pirates were settled at sea, never in port. In port, even the most bitter enemies ofttimes drank from the same pitchers, laughed over games of dice together, and walked the streets unmolested. Over the years, Marco had been compelled to share a few tankards of rum with Carlos, though he had never liked the bastard.

Truth to tell, the Spaniard was being quite a nervy scoundrel at the moment, strutting about in Charles Town, brazenly seeking his sport, with an English bounty hanging over his head. But turning Carlos over to the authorities would net Marco no satisfaction; he wanted the pleasure of defeating the miscreant in person.

Spotting Marco, the swarthy pirate grinned and made a mock salute. As Marco returned the greeting with equal derision, Carlos spoke briefly with his lieutenants, then strode across the room to stand before Marco's table.

"Señor Glaviano, *buenas noches*," Carlos drawled, bowing elaborately.

"*Buona sera*," Marco replied.

"May I join you?" Carlos inquired.

"By all means, please yourself," came Marco's less-than-enthusiastic response.

Chuckling, Carlos took a chair, tossed his hat down on the scarred table, and motioned to a serving wench. As the pretty young woman came up, Carlos gave his order. "A pitcher of molasses beer for myself and my friend." Winking at the girl, he added, "I am hoping the molasses may sweeten my *compadre*'s disposition."

The girl—quite a comely wench with her dark hair and eyes, and pink cheeks—smiled sympathetically at Marco, and he smiled back. As she headed off, he stared at the retreating swell of her buttocks, and Carlos grinned as he took note of Marco's scrutiny.

"What brings you to port, *amigo?*" Carlos asked casually.

Offhandedly Marco replied, "The usual pursuit of pleasure."

"Then you would not be turning over treasures stolen from the Spanish Crown to the British authorities here?"

Marco chuckled. "England and Spain are at war. Any goods confiscated from your merchant fleet constitute legitimate spoils of battle."

"A most convenient excuse for piracy," Carlos drawled.

Marco snorted with contempt. "And this from the very blackguard who has plagued British merchant ships from Savannah to Charles Town, and now has the nerve to walk these streets inviting arrest—and the hangman's noose."

Carlos was far from intimidated. *"Touché.* Rumor has it that we just missed each other off the coast of St. Augustine a fortnight past."

Marco raised a brow in feigned shock. "Listening to rumors can be dangerous."

"Be assured that the next time you are on the high seas, *amigo,* our rendezvous will be kept."

Marco raised his tankard in a mock toast. "I shall anticipate the day with great relish."

The serving wench returned bearing a pewter pitcher and two tankards. She smiled shyly as she set a filled tankard of beer before Marco. He looked her over again. With her big bosom and rounded bottom, she seemed a fair enough candidate for the night's sport—

Then memories of his bargain with Christina rose again to needle him, and he realized with frustration that this would never work. Damn! Why couldn't he get the maddening minx out of his mind?

"Will there be anything else, sir?" the girl asked Carlos.

The Spaniard winked at Marco. "In due course, woman. For now, my belly aches. Bring me some food—fish and bread and rum pudding. As for my friend, I'm sure he will let you know where his appetites lie."

She turned eagerly to Marco. "Will you, sir?"

Not about to lose face in front of Carlos, he grinned. "Soon enough, wench."

She giggled. "Aye, sir," she said in a sultry purr as she looked over the handsome blond giant. "I shall look forward to hearing of your pleasure."

As she started off, Carlos howled with ribald laughter. "You want the wench," he taunted Marco.

Marco shrugged and continued the pretense. "If you have no objection?"

"The night is young," Carlos replied. "I prefer to fill my own gut before I plug a squirming wench's belly with my manroot."

Marco chuckled. "I shall try to leave you a scrap of the woman to nibble on."

A jovial Carlos lit his pipe. "Speaking of wenches, how is the girl, Christina?"

A stab of alarm streaked along Marco's spine. It caused him no end of vexation that Carlos had evidently witnessed his rescue of Christina Abbott that long-ago night on Edisto Island. Carlos had inquired about the girl several times over the years, and had even managed to wrest her name out of one of Marco's lieutenants while they had been in port a few years back. Marco had severely whipped and discharged the sailor who had been so easy with his tongue while tippling with Carlos and his men at the Bowling Green House. Still, Carlos's interest in the girl concerned Marco greatly. He always answered the Spaniard's queries about Christina casually, lest he let his foe know how much the girl really meant to him. As far as he knew, Carlos had never discovered the location of his base in the Caribbean, which gave him at least some measure of peace regarding the girl's safety. He could not doubt the Spanish mongrel might kidnap Christina and ravish her just to spite his enemy.

"*Amigo?*" Carlos prodded with a smile.

Marco took a gulp of beer and muttered, "I'm afraid she took the ague and passed away last winter."

Carlos's dark gaze narrowed. "Ah, such a pity. She would have made a fine piece to warm a buccaneer's bed. Perhaps yours, *amigo?*"

Rage welled in Marco. His fingers clenched on his tankard and the line of his jaw hardened. In the nick of time, he managed to restrain himself from charging up and smashing his fist through Carlos's face. Such an explosion would do little to ensure Christina's safety, he reminded himself grimly.

To Carlos, he forced himself to shrug and say, "Actually, she became a rather homely and whining creature as she matured. Her death caused me no great grief."

Carlos did not comment, but regarded Marco with an abstracted frown.

The wench ambled back, placing a plate heaped with food before Carlos. Eager to escape the Spaniard's loathsome presence, Marco pulled the woman into his lap, amid her shrieks of surprise and glee.

"Are you going to bed her here, *amigo?*" Carlos asked.

Marco nudged the giggling woman to her feet. "Let's go," he told her.

"Save a piece of her for me, *amigo,*" Carlos added as he tore off a chunk of bread.

"The barest morsel," Marco jeered. He and the woman crossed to the stairs in the wake of Carlos's bawdy hoots.

Marco led the wench up the narrow steps to a

dark, dusty corridor. The sounds of torrid moans drifted out from behind several closed doors.

"Which room is yours?" he asked.

She grinned and took his large hand, leading him into a tiny, stale-smelling cubicle furnished with little more than a cluttered, sagging dresser and a filthy, unkempt bed. An oil lamp on the dresser provided the only scant light.

The wench licked her lips as she looked Marco up and down. "My, but you are a big 'un, m'lord."

"Don't get all excited, love," he drawled back. "You shall be compensated for a night's sport—but I shall not be bedding you."

Her expression was crestfallen. "Then why—"

"Frankly, I was tiring of the Spaniard's company downstairs."

She moved closer and regarded him with wounded eyes. "Don't you find sweet Mary desirable?"

"You are lovely," Marco responded diplomatically, "but I have made a promise to another."

"We'll never tell," the whore teased.

"But she will know, damn her eyes," Marco muttered ruefully. "Unfortunately, so will I."

"She must be some lady."

"That she is."

Marco noticed a pack of cards and some dice on the dresser. He walked over and picked up the deck. "Can I interest you in another game?"

Mary wagged a finger at him. "You want your friend to think we have coupled."

"Sì," Marco replied. "And he is not my friend."

Marco and the whore proceeded to have a rollicking time playing several games of hazard and cards. Even though the pursuits were innocent, visions of Christina kept intruding on Marco's thoughts, and his desire for her continued to burn. He found himself fantasizing about small, uptilted breasts that

would fit perfectly in his large hands; about tiny,
tight nipples he hungered to suckle; about a nicely
trimmed bottom he longed to knead with his fingers;
about long, slim legs he hungered to feel wrapped
around his waist—or, better yet, draped over his
shoulders. At one point, he sucked in his breath
sharply as Christina's beautiful face swam before
him—the luscious, pouting mouth and huge, beautiful green eyes silently reproaching him for even considering sport with another woman.

Later, Marco left the tavern and strode down the
darkened, squalid streets past carousing sailors and
night watchmen. His sense of sexual frustration
seemed a constant with him these days, with no cure
in sight. For he knew now that only one woman held
the power to arouse him. And she was the very minx
forbidden to him, even as he was about to explode
with unassuaged lust!

If only he could bed Christina and get her out of
his blood—but that was not a choice open to him.
Certainly, Marco was no saint, and could not claim
that he had never before seduced an eighteen-year-
old. But the children of the island had always
seemed different to him—innocent, untouched, un-
corrupted, even sacred. Now this—this budding siren
laying claim to his body and spirit, even when they
were apart! What should he do? Send her away? Engage a schoolmaster? Bring back a priest to imbue
her with religion? Ah, such a dilemma ...

Marco continued to pace through the streets, heading back toward the boardinghouse where he had let
a room, and unaware that a shadowy figure was
stalking him. Carlos the pirate hovered ten paces behind Marco, following the blond Venetian through
the alleyways of the harbor district.

Carlos smiled to himself in grim satisfaction. Tonight, Glaviano had claimed to him that the English
girl, Christina Abbott, was dead. But Carlos sus-

pected otherwise. He had a strong intuition that Marco had lied, and he was determined to ferret out the truth.

For he had been paid—paid very well—to locate the girl Glaviano had carried off six years ago. And once he found Christina Abbott . . . The very thought of his instructions sent a sadistic thrill coursing through him.

TWELVE

The following afternoon, the casual observer glimpsing the handsome, stylishly dressed gentleman strolling down Church Street in Charles Town would never have recognized the man as the privateer Marco Glaviano. He very much appeared the dashing man about town in his royal blue silk coat with side pleats, a satin waistcoat topped by a lace jabot, stylish breeches, hose, leather shoes with brass buckles, and a black felt cavalier hat with a flowing white plume. Carrying an elegant walking stick with a gilt tip, he strode past shops and verandaed houses, smiling and tipping his hat at the many graciously attired ladies who eyed him with such open appreciation as they headed home followed by menservants bearing the bounty of their shopping expeditions.

The late August afternoon was muggy and overcast. In anticipation of the coming storm, shopkeepers were bringing in their produce and wares, vendors scurrying for shelter with their carts. In the distance, Marco could see the stately ships bobbing about in the bay as they made for the crowded, bustling wharves of the harbor.

Marco had much on his mind. Realizing that his badly craved sexual gratification would be denied him during the current port leave, he had decided to throw himself into the pursuit of finding a solution for Christina's situation—and getting the little termagant out of his hair once and for all. He had told himself that surely, if he could only find a place for the girl, get her removed from Isola del Mare, then after she was gone, his life—most particularly, his *love* life—could at last return to normal.

His first inclination had been to find a church or school willing to take her under its wing, but so far his inquiries had proved fruitless. Charles Town was in many ways still a fledgling Crown colony; while there were half a dozen churches in the city, there was only one school, the Free School sponsored by St. Philip's Church, and Marco had already discovered that the ramshackle structure housed little more than a charitable institution for orphans and the poor. The headmaster had also expressed grave misgivings about taking on an eighteen-year-old.

Dio, he had allowed the girl to run wild for too long!

His one ray of hope had come when he had spoken with the parson of the Baptist meetinghouse. The rector had suggested that Marco contact a Madam Snyder who ran a boarding school for young ladies on Bay Street. He was bound for there now, and if this inquiry also failed, he was left with only the option of contacting Christina's legal guardian, Charles Rutgers. That was a prospect Marco had resisted for over six years—not only because he felt that Rutgers had failed Christina as a guardian, but also because, if Rutgers should learn the truth regarding

Christina's disappearance and Marco's role in it, he feared that the magistrate would almost certainly misunderstand his motives in rescuing her and might well have him arrested for kidnapping instead.

He was scowling over his dilemma as he rounded a corner and bumped against an older, robust gentleman wearing a bagwig and an elegant Continental suit.

"*Scusi*, signore," Marco muttered, standing aside so that the man, who was accompanied by a wife and several grown children, could pass.

Suddenly, the gentleman grabbed Marco's sleeve and cried, "Marco Glaviano! By the saints, is it you, boy?"

Marco scowled perplexedly at the man who had addressed him, then grinned as he recognized a neighbor of his family's back in Venice. He pumped the man's hand, exclaiming heartily, "Don Giovanni Renaldi! What a pleasant surprise!"

"Indeed, my boy! And the pleasure is all ours!"

"How wonderful to see you here in Charles Town!" Marco glanced toward the wife and children. "And have you brought your entire family with you to America?"

"I have." Don Giovanni gestured proudly toward the lady, a pretty, round-cheeked matron who wore a high-necked taffeta gown with hoops and a large straw hat. "You remember my wife, Donna Flora?"

Marco took the hand of the smiling, dark-eyed lady and gallantly kissed her glove. "Signora, I am most honored to see you again."

"As I am, Marco," Donna Flora replied with a bright smile. "My, but you have truly become a man since we last saw you."

At the sound of feminine titters, Don Giovanni motioned toward three plump, smiling young ladies who were staring at Marco with unabashed admiration. "And, my friend, may I reintroduce my three beautiful daughters—Seraphina, Calista, and Jovita?"

Marco glanced at the trio. Despite their fashionable frocks and ribboned bonnets, all resembled their large-nosed father and seemed to be even more homely than he remembered. "Ladies, I am most honored—as well as enchanted by your loveliness." He kissed the hand of each daughter in turn, prompting a plethora of blushes and giggles.

Don Giovanni now turned to a tall, thin, sober-looking young man whose visage was partially obscured by a tricorn hat and a curling, shoulder-length wig. "And here is my beloved son, Vittorio."

"Vittorio," Marco repeated, shaking the boy's hand. "I believe the last time I saw you, you were still wearing sailor suits."

"I am a man now, as anyone can see," Vittorio replied self-importantly, thrusting his head high and straightening his silk cuffs.

"But of course." Marco glanced at Don Giovanni. "What brings you to the colonies, my friend?"

"I should ask the same question of you, my boy."

Marco was struggling for an appropriate reply when, all at once, a thunderclap boomed out, followed by a spattering of hard, fat raindrops. As the women gasped in dismay and opened their parasols, Don Giovanni said urgently to Marco, "By the saints, we cannot complete this reunion on the walkway. Come sup with us, my boy, and we shall all become reacquainted."

"I am honored," Marco replied.

The group hurried inside a nearby eatery and settled at a large table near the front windows. Amid the sounds of the downpour outside, Don Giovanni ordered seafood soup, grilled shrimp with rice, wine, and bread for all.

"What in heaven's name are you doing in Charles

Town, my boy?" Don Giovanni asked as he took a hearty gulp of wine.

"I must insist that you speak first, my friend," Marco replied smoothly. "I had never thought I would see you here in the colonies. I do hope your venerable family has not fallen on hard times back in Venice."

Though his expression was regretful, Don Giovanni shook his head. "We have managed to hang on to our holdings, both the glass factory on Murano and our vineyard in the country—no thanks, of course, to the barbaric Spaniards and other foreigners who have victimized our great republic for centuries. Actually, we have come to America for a most propitious occasion." He grinned at the homeliest of his daughters. "Our dear Seraphina is betrothed to the son of my old friend Lorenzo Palermo, who some time ago settled with his family in nearby Beaufort. We have all come to South Carolina for the wedding."

"Ah, congratulations," Marco murmured, smiling warmly at the blushing young woman.

"And we are so delighted to see that you have settled here as well, Marco," Seraphina replied with a flutter of thin eyelashes.

"Indeed—now you must tell us what has brought you to the colonies," Don Giovanni added.

Marco's expression grew wistful as he began quietly. "You surely know that there was not much left for me in our homeland after I lost my dear parents."

Don Giovanni sighed and murmured sympathetically, "Ah, yes, my dear boy. It was such a tragedy to see your father, our most distinguished ambassador and a man with the noblest of motives, turned over to the Inquisition by the Spanish jackals. As for your mother . . . *Il Dio* knows that poor Elena was never the same following Betrando's death."

Marco nodded morosely. "*Sì*, it killed me to watch

Mama waste away like that ..." Sighing heavily, he finished with, "I suppose I felt I must get away from all the bad memories."

"I understand," Don Giovanni concurred. "But what made you choose Charles Town, my boy? Have you some enterprise here?"

At the inevitable query, Marco hesitated. During the past few minutes, he had decided it would be best not to tell these visitors from Venice about his privateering activities. While the Renaldi family had never been truly close friends of his own, he much preferred that his old neighbors think that he was involved in more dignified and honorable pursuits.

"Actually, I do not live in Charles Town," he explained. "I am now the owner of a sugar plantation in the Caribbean, and I am here to meet with my factor and buy needed provisions for my estate."

"Ah," Don Giovanni murmured approvingly. "I always knew you were a young man who would accomplish much in this world." Nodding toward his daughters, he added, "You would not be in need of a wife, would you, my son? We've two more of these lovelies to wed off, you know."

This comment prompted gales of laughter from the plain daughters, and left Marco forcing a wan smile.

"Giovanni!" Donna Flora scolded. "You must not embarrass poor Marco!"

Don Giovanni waved off his wife. "The boy is old enough to know his own mind—and the desires of his own heart."

"But perhaps not quite old enough to settle down as yet," Marco finished deftly. He tossed a quick grin at the girls. "As much as the beauty of these young ladies inspires me."

At the lavish compliment, the daughters murmured a collective "Aaaaah!" of ecstasy, while Don Giovanni tapped Marco's sleeve and taunted, "Perhaps, my boy, you are yet planting a few wild oats amongst your cane plants?"

"Giovanni, really!" Donna Flora scolded. "Remember that your daughters are present."

Don Giovanni was chuckling. "I understand my old friend Don Lorenzo has several unwed sons, so we may fare better in Beaufort." He nodded toward Vittorio. "Then when we return to Venice, we need only to find a proper bride for my son, so that he may continue the family name and enterprises following my passage."

As Don Giovanni uttered those words, a light seemed to spring to life in Marco's brain. He turned to Vittorio. "Do you desire to marry soon, my friend?"

Vittorio replied stiffly, "Such is my father's desire. As a grown man of twenty, I shall of course do his bidding, much as I would have preferred to become a priest and consecrate my life to *il Redentore*."

Don Giovanni waved off his son. "The boy is our only male child and my sole heir. He would be a fool to forgo our wealth and commit himself to a life of poverty."

"Indeed," Marco murmured, his mind humming as he stared at Vittorio. All at once, he felt he was looking straight at the solution to all his problems. Casually, he said, "As a matter of fact, I personally know of a most eligible and beautiful young lady."

All six Renaldis looked at Marco with intense interest.

"Who is this young woman?" Don Giovanni asked.

Marco thought fiercely for a moment, then replied, "My niece, Christina."

"Your niece?" Don Giovanni exclaimed. "However did you acquire a niece, my boy?"

Marco was inventing his story even as he spoke. "You do remember my dear sister, Bianca?"

"Ah, yes," Donna Flora murmured with an expression of intense sympathy. "Was she not the sweet young woman your parents sent to convent school in Florence?"

"You have a fine memory," Marco said.

"And if it serves correctly, did she not die there, *Dio* rest her poor soul?" Donna Flora continued.

"*Sì*, tragically, we did lose her, but not before she married and bore a child."

"She married? And had a child?" Donna Flora gasped. She frowned in bafflement. "Why do I not remember these things?"

Marco shrugged. "It was long ago, Donna Flora. Bianca married an English chap by the name of—er—Abbott. At any rate, the baby was a girl, Christina. Unfortunately, Bianca died in childbirth, and then a few years later, Christina's father, a soldier of fortune, was killed helping the Neapolitan army battle the forces of Don Carlos when the Spanish once again attacked and subjugated Naples."

All six of the Renaldis gasped in horror and crossed themselves.

"Oh, the poor child!" Jovita said. "To lose both parents at such a tender age. And for such tragic reasons."

"*Sì*," Marco concurred. "About that time, my beloved mother passed away, and thus, before I left for the colonies, I retrieved my young niece and her English nurse from Florence and brought both of them here to live with me."

"How old is the girl now?" Don Giovanni asked, thoughtfully stroking his jaw.

"She is eighteen. She is also"—just in time, Marco managed to quell a guilty smile—"quite beautiful, very devout, and most obedient."

Approving sighs flitted over the table, and even the stern-faced Vittorio appeared intrigued.

"Actually," Marco went on, "Christina is at the point in life where I need to choose a proper husband for her." He slanted a meaningful glance toward Don Giovanni. "And, of course, I intend to provide the very substantial dowry myself."

"Naturally," Don Giovanni murmured, his dark eyes gleaming with intense interest.

"The only difficulty is, our island existence is so very isolated," Marco lamented. "I would feel so much better if my niece could live somewhere more civilized, with proper society, culture"—he paused, glancing meaningfully at Vittorio "—and churches, of course. Christina is very pious, you see." As Vittorio made a sound of appreciation, Marco brought his fabrication to an end. "Truth to tell, my fondest dream is to see my beloved niece back in Venice, married to a man of distinguished family and high moral fiber."

"I am certain you must want the best for her," Don Giovanni remarked sagely.

"If I may ask, how long are all of you to remain in the colonies?" Marco inquired offhandedly.

"For some months," Don Giovanni answered. "The wedding is scheduled in Beaufort, but not for several more weeks, so that the proper prenuptial festivities can be held. After we see our Seraphina happily wed, we thought we might tour a bit of the country before we return home." He smiled at his wife. "Donna Flora longs to shop in your city of New York and see your art exhibits in Boston."

"But you cannot return home without our having a more extended visit," Marco protested. "As a matter of fact, I would like to invite all of you to come to my island as my guests."

As the Renaldis murmured appreciative comments, Don Giovanni replied, "Your offer is most generous, and we would love to see your plantation, my boy. When would you like us to come?"

"As it happens, I must sail for home on the morrow," Marco told him, "but I would be delighted to send my brigantine back to Beaufort in a few weeks to fetch you. You see, I would like all of you"—his gaze again settled on Vittorio "—to meet my beautiful young niece."

"We would be most honored," Don Giovanni quickly answered.

"The honor is all mine," Marco murmured.

As the women chatted excitedly among themselves, Marco leaned over toward Don Giovanni, cupping a hand around his mouth. "In the meantime, my friend, would you be free to breakfast with me on the morrow? I must set sail for the Caribbean at noon, when the tide rolls out, but first I have a business proposition to discuss with you—a proposal I think would be much to your interest and our mutual benefit."

Don Giovanni smiled sagaciously and shook Marco's hand. "I shall look forward to our discussion with great relish, my boy."

THIRTEEN

MARCO GLAVIANO STOOD NEAR THE STERN OF *LA SPADA* with spyglass raised, scanning the blue waters of the Caribbean for his first glimpse of Isola del Mare. The early September day was bright, cloudless, and hot, the mood of the sailors exuberant as they manned the pumps and worked the rigging, all the while singing a sea chantey and eagerly scrutinizing the horizon for that first heartwarming glimpse of home.

Marco well understood his men's good humor. Their voyage had been most lucrative, and many of his crewmen had already spent their portion in Charles Town buying gifts for sweethearts and children. Most of his men could look forward to a hero's welcome—wives and children to hug their necks, and tonight, a willing woman in their beds to make their reunions complete.

While this should have been a happy occasion for Marco as well, he, by contrast, could look forward only to a continuing battle between himself and

141

Christina, a conflict more deadly and volatile than that between the English and Spanish—

Especially when he told her his news. He lowered his spyglass and groaned. Before he had left Charles Town, he had met with Don Giovanni Renaldi and arranged for Vittorio and Christina to wed. Any lingering doubts Don Giovanni had harbored had vanished when Marco mentioned the sizable dowry he intended to transfer to Christina's husband—a king's ransom by any standards. Don Giovanni was nothing if not an immensely practical man; indeed, Marco suspected that Don Giovanni had continued to flourish in Venice through courting the favor of the various foreigners who had so exploited his country. Though concerns regarding Don Giovanni's loyalties did trouble Marco, he was also well aware that the Renaldi son, Vittorio, was a high-minded, upstanding young man, and that Christina would have a much better life with him in Venice. At least the political climate in his homeland was stable; Venice, unlike so many of her sister city-states, had managed to maintain a tenuous independence.

Thus, in one month's time, he would send *La Spada* back up the American coast to Beaufort to fetch the Renaldis. That gave him only five weeks to make Isola del Mare appear to be a prosperous sugar plantation. His biggest challenge, of course, would be reforming Christina and impelling her to behave like a lady; when he told her of his intentions—not the least of which was that she pose as his niece—she would kick and scream every inch of the way. Yet he retained a strong conviction that he was doing the right thing for the girl.

"Land ho!" came a voice from high in the rigging, and Marco again raised his spyglass, staring at the beautiful, verdant expanse of Isola del Mare—the coral reefs, the rocks and tide pools, the gleaming white beaches, the palm trees waving in the breeze.

Despite all his misgivings, his heart leapt with joy at this first sighting of home in so many weeks—and at the thought of seeing Christina again. Though it bedeviled him to admit it, he had really missed the little brat. She had never been out of his thoughts.

As *La Spada* moved closer to port, Marco busied himself giving orders to strike the sails and maneuver the craft into harbor. Glancing ahead, he saw that women and children had already begun to gather on the wharves and were waving and cheering at the approaching ship. Automatically, he scanned the pier for the one he sought—and his heart sank a bit when he did not spot her.

Yet he soon became distracted by his duties as the crew maneuvered the vessel into port, dropped the hefty anchor, and moored *La Spada* to the wharf. Immediately, women and children began to overrun the vessel—the sounds of sails being lashed and rigging stowed mingling with cries of joy, the chortles of children greeting their fathers, and the smacking sounds of sweethearts kissing.

Marco felt strangely bereft, left out of the hearty homecoming, until he saw her standing alone on the wharf, with Pansy on a leash beside her. His heart seemed to tumble into his belly. *Dio del cielo*, how he had deceived himself, trying to convince himself that he did not want her. She looked so solemn, so exotically beautiful standing there in her flowing white dress with a trailing of island flowers in her hair.

Marco could not help himself. He ran for the gangplank and quickly strode down it to join her. A few feet away from her, he paused warily, not certain how to react as both of them regarded each other with so much longing—and so much mistrust.

"Hello, *cara*," he said at last.

"Hello, Marco."

Pansy, sharing none of their caution, abruptly

whined and tugged Christina forward. Smiling, Marco reached down to pet the cheetah, who was purring and affectionately nuzzling against her master's thigh.

Marco glanced back up at Christina, and when he spoke, he could not restrain a tremor of emotion in his voice. "You look very beautiful, *cara*."

"You look wonderful, too," she replied almost shyly. "And very brown."

He chuckled, stepped closer, and awkwardly kissed her smooth brow. The slightest taste, the merest scent of her, inflamed him, and he stepped back quickly, as if burned. Both of them stood there awkwardly as people began streaming down the gangplank.

"Walk with me back to the house," Marco told her stiffly. "And we will talk."

With Christina leading Pansy, they fell into step with the others, who were laughing and singing as they started toward their various homes.

"You were gone so long," she murmured.

"We were becalmed off Florida. I hope you didn't worry overly."

She did not answer directly. "Was your voyage successful?" she asked.

"Yes, very," he replied with an irony she could not hope to comprehend. Alas, when she found out how very successful his voyage had been, he added to himself ruefully, there would be the very devil to pay before she was convinced to cooperate.

As they walked along the dappled forest trail, Marco continued to admire the young woman striding beside him. *Dio*, not touching her was purest agony—it was all he could do not to pull her into his arms and greet her properly. If anything, she had become even more beautiful while he was away. Her hair was as bright and shiny as gold, her skin warm and softly tanned. Examining her curves slowly and thoroughly, he felt a worried frown drift in. Was she, perhaps, just a little more slender than before? While her body appeared as svelte and alluring as ever, he selfishly took heart at the thought that she might have missed him so much that her appetite had been affected. This possibility was followed by the equally irresistible, wicked thought of fattening her up, of feeding her grapes and olives, cheese and wine—in his bed.

For she was a feast that his starving senses refused to ignore. He eyed appreciatively the shape of her lovely hands and long fingers, and the contours of her bare feet as she moved along the soft forest floor. The fact that she was barefoot—by no means an unusual occurrence—seemed rivetingly sensual to him today, especially with the exotic black cat walking beside her.

By the saints, how could he take this wild, beautiful, untamed creature and impel her to wear the boned corsets and hoops, the torturous shoes, and all the other accoutrements of proper womanhood? Marco had spent hours at a Charles Town couturier buying Christina these needed items, as well as many lengths of fashionable fabric to provide her a new wardrobe. Now he feared his plans to whip her into a proper lady could be doomed. She seemed to belong not in some stuffy drawing room, but here among the iridescent ferns, the exotic flowers, the ripe tangle of life. To change her would be tantamount to plucking a luscious wild orchid and crushing it within his hand. The daunting truth was, he adored this enchanting creature just the way she was. Indeed, the thought of her one day padding down the forest trail in her bare feet, flowers in her hair, Pansy by her side, and his baby in her belly, was enough to set him reeling.

With a massive effort, Marco pulled himself to his senses. Could he not see how wrong his lustful thoughts were, how limited her future would be with him? His determination to harass the Spanish had not changed. This girl was pure quality, a prize beyond all riches, and she deserved so much better than to share a pirate's bed. Hadn't he prayed over this dilemma for weeks now? Hadn't he always come to the same heart-wrenching, inevitable conclusion? Could he set them both on a path that might well end in heartache for her?

Christina, walking beside Marco, was also studying him with great admiration and longing. Oh, she had missed him so desperately while he was gone! He now appeared to her more glorious than ever—his hair longer, thicker, more shiny and sun-bleached, his skin deeply bronzed. He wore his leather vest without a shirt, and she could not resist staring at his tight stomach muscles and the magnificent sinews of his broad chest, his powerful shoulders and arms. He had not even touched her when they had met on the wharf, other than the brief moment when his lips had so tormentingly brushed her brow. How she longed to be crushed into his strong arms, nestled against his beating heart. When he had left, there had been so much unsaid between them—the knowledge of their rift had caused her untold anguish while he had been away. Would he now settle things between them at last, as he had promised? Or would the war of words and torn feelings continue? Since he had arrived, he seemed to stare at her hungrily one minute, then frown and retreat into himself the next. So far she did not like the way things were shaping up between them.

By the time they reached the plantation house, the others had turned off for their homes. They climbed the steps with Pansy, and as he opened the front door for her, Marco murmured, "We shall talk in the salon."

They continued into the large room together. Marco lounged near the door, while Christina moved toward the center and removed Pansy's leash. The cheetah went to crouch down near the fireplace.

Lacing her hands together tightly, Christina said forthrightly, "You told me you would settle things with me when you returned. Are you ready to do so now?"

He whistled. "My, you are so businesslike, *cara*. Haven't you forgotten something?"

It took Christina a moment to realize that Marco was teasing her. Then she remembered their time-worn ritual, the little vignette they enacted each time he returned from a voyage. She found it rather sweet of him to insist on the comfort of tradition.

She smiled at him coyly and uttered her expected line of dialogue. "Do I get a present?"

"Indeed you do." He grinned and crossed over to her, taking a glittering necklace from his pocket and dangling it before her.

"Oh, Marco! It is exquisite!" At once, Christina was all winsome child again, staring in wonder at the dazzling, square-cut emerald dangling from a fabulous serpentine chain.

"As green as your lovely eyes," he murmured.

"Where did you get it?"

"Off a Spanish galleon."

"Did you kill someone for it?" she asked eagerly.

Marco roared with laughter and could not resist reaching out to tug one of her curls. "Brat! What a terrible thing to say! No, I did not kill anyone for it."

She appeared disappointed. "Was there at least a battle?"

He feigned a scowl. "Only a token protest of cannon, followed by an immediate surrender."

She smiled at him then, quite brazenly, and he could have kicked himself for his unintended double entendre. He quickly clasped the chain around her neck, and as his fingers brushed her baby-soft skin, good sense seemed to desert him. She was so beautiful, so tormentingly near. His heart hammered like a wildly beating drum in the explosive silence. They both knew what he always said to her next, and how very foolish it would be for him to say it now—

He said it anyway, with a husky note in his voice as he leaned toward her and gazed into her wide, gorgeous eyes. "Do I get a kiss?"

For a moment, they continued to gaze at each other, sexual longing seeming to electrify the very air between them. He watched avidly as Christina's lips parted slightly, heard her catch a sharp little breath. He was on the verge of grabbing her and kissing her senseless when she delighted and intrigued him by turning curiously shy. Avoiding his eye, she stretched on tiptoe to quickly peck his cheek—

The chaste kiss ignited Marco's desires as the most passionate embrace never could. That was when he again smelled the flowers—smelled her—and his longing for her burst in him, along with the bittersweet knowledge of how very much he had missed her—

He had only himself to blame for what happened next. He hauled Christina into his arms and voraciously claimed her soft, sweet lips. He sucked in her warm breath, tasted her deeply, languished in the feel of her slender body against his. When she began to kiss him back, nipping his lips gently and teasing his tongue with her own, lust engulfed him with a force that left him reeling. All restraint fled, and he devoured her mouth like a starving man, crushing her luscious body against his with a vehemence that threatened to crack her ribs. He realized fleetingly that the stark force of his desire would surely frighten even the most seasoned courtesan, yet Christina was all eager acceptance, all surrender . . .

At last his lips moved to her delicious cheek and he whispered intensely, "*Cara*, I have missed you! So very much!"

"And I've missed you! Oh, Marco, tell me at last that you are mine!"

The words hit his aroused body and inflamed senses like ice water. Belatedly, he managed to remind himself that Christina was adept at dousing the flames of his ardor with buckets of water. He thrust her away, muttering, "*Dio!* What am I doing?"

He began to pace, wearing a ferocious scowl and muttering to himself in Italian.

Across from him, Christina appeared both hurt and bemused. "I thought you said you would settle things with me when you returned!"

He turned to her, thrusting his fingers distraughtly through his hair. "Not like this."

"Then how?" she cried.

He drew a heavy breath. "*Cara*, sit down."

"No!" she flared.

"Do it!"

Glaring at him, she went to sit primly on the edge of the settee.

Marco settled his large frame into a wing chair across from her. Staring at the rebellious, gorgeous creature, he thought, *Dio* help me! He must not let her see his fear. He must be stern and implacable. Otherwise, he would be doomed.

He leaned toward her, laced his long fingers together, and spoke firmly. "Christina, while I was away, I did manage to find a solution for you. Though you may resist it at first, I think that eventually you will realize that I have acted in your best interests."

Already her mouth was trembling, even as her eyes blazed at him. "You are planning to send me away!"

"Not immediately," he hedged.

"What does that mean?"

Marco decided he might as well bite the bullet. "Actually, I have arranged for you to marry."

"What?" She sprang up, her expression incredulous.

"Sit down."

"No! Tell me what you mean by that demented statement!"

"Sit down and I will tell you!"

She flounced back down, crossed her arms over her chest, and glared at him.

He cleared his throat. "While I was in Charles Town, I ran across some old friends, the Renaldis, from Venice."

"So?"

"The Renaldis are a fine and prosperous family. They have a son named Vittorio who is twenty years old, and he is in need of a wife. Thus, I have arranged for you to marry Vittorio and go to live with him in Venice."

She popped up again, her expression eloquent with rage and defiance. "What? You have arranged for me to marry some foreigner—and to live in an alien land—without even asking me?"

Now he was standing, too, trying very hard to control his surging voice and temper. "Christina, you will be much better off in Venice."

"You may as well send me to hell! It's halfway around the world! I'll never see you again!"

"We have to think of what is best for you."

"You think it is best that I am totally miserable?"

"You haven't even met this young man," he argued. "He and his family will be coming here in a few weeks—"

"They are coming here?" she repeated in stunned disbelief. "And you did not even ask me my feelings?"

"I am sure that you and this young man will get on well, if you will only give him a chance. He can give you a good life in Venice—a life based on family, society, church, culture—"

"I do not want these things! I want you."

"Christina," he said, his fists so tightly clenched that the veins stood out. "this attraction between us is wrong—"

"That does not stop you from kissing me until my eyes feel as if they're popping out! How can you kiss me like you just did and then give me to him!"

He heaved a giant breath. "I made a mistake."

"You have made several," she uttered haughtily. "And the biggest is in thinking you can marry me off to some foreigner against my wishes."

"Christina, you will obey me in this," Marco said, his anger rising. "Furthermore, it is critical that we make a good impression on the Renaldis when they come to visit."

Now Christina was growing suspicious. "If, as you say, this is such an exalted family, then why would they be arranging a marriage for their son through a pirate? And just how did you explain me to them?"

Oh, the little minx did not miss a beat, Marco thought in despair. Avoiding her eye, he muttered, "Actually, they do not know that I am a privateer. Since this is a venerated family and appearances are critical to them, I have told them that I am a proper sugar planter, and that you"—he gritted his teeth— "are my niece."

"Your niece?" Christina was horrified, gesturing wildly and half screaming at him. "You go around kissing me all the time, and now you plan to pose as my uncle? That is depraved!"

"Christina, we will not be kissing anymore. You must understand—I have to get you married off, or . . ." He stared at her with conflicted longing, and groaned.

"Why are you so afraid of loving me?" she demanded.

He crossed the room and grabbed her by the arms. His eyes were brilliant with emotion. "Do you have any idea what it is truly like to be a pirate's woman? To be without him for months on end? To wonder each time he leaves if it will be the last time you will ever see him alive? To risk being left pregnant, alone and vulnerable, with no one to provide for you? I cannot put you through that, Christina! You may have the body of a woman, but you still have the innocent heart of a child, and loving me would destroy you."

"I am a woman and I am not afraid!"

"What if we married?" he demanded. "What if I were killed? Who would you love then? Who would you hold?"

Tears welled in her eyes, and the exquisite torment on her face slashed at Marco like a saber as she whispered, "I would love you in my heart for the rest of my life—and if God should smile on us, I would hold your baby."

Frustration and anguish burst in Marco. He uttered a string of vivid curses in Italian, picked up a Ming vase, and hurled it across the room. The vase crashed against the fireplace, the explosion just missing Pansy and sending the cheetah into a shrieking tailspin.

Reeling at his own violent outburst, Marco whirled to glimpse Christina's dazed, stricken face. Oh, God, what had he done? Confused her. Frightened her terribly.

He reached for her, too late, as she fled the room.

He turned to comfort the still screeching cheetah. "Pansy—"

Pansy hissed venomously at Marco and hurried out after Christina.

Marco collapsed into a chair and buried his face in his trembling hands. He could not go after Christina. If he did, she would be his wife within the week.

FOURTEEN

MARCO FARED A LITTLE BETTER WITH HIS MEN THAN HE had with Christina. The next morning, it was a rowdy crew—all fifty of them—who gathered in front of the house at his command. Since normally time spent on the island belonged to each man to do with as he pleased, the pirates displayed their resentment at being summoned in this peremptory fashion by indulging in free-wheeling shenanigans.

When Marco emerged on the porch with Giuseppe and Pansy, it was to observe his crewmen gathered loosely in a circle, hooting, clapping their hands, and stomping their feet, while portly Patrizio careened around drunkenly, dancing a jig, and Ugo sawed out an off-key accompaniment on his fiddle. Taking in the chaos, Marco groaned. He grimly studied his men—so many of them swarthy and bearded, wearing turbans, earrings, and other jewelry. *Dio,* they looked as disreputable as a band of thieves! Was the feat he had in mind truly impossible?

First, he must gain the attention of these derelicts! *"Silenzio!"* he called out loudly.

There was little response—other than a few mutinous glares and a surly comment or two.

"Eh, Captain, why are you spoiling our frolic?" called an indignant voice.

"Sì, me and my woman were trying to put a loaf in her oven when you botched our cooking," drawled another, prompting gales of ribald laughter.

Exasperated, Marco motioned to his towering quartermaster, Claudio. The large, bearded man stepped forward and fired his musket into the air.

At last the din abated and the fiddling stopped. Patrizio tottered around indecisively, then crashed into the wall of men, almost toppling several seamen. With some additional grumbling, the pirates turned their resentful attention to their leader.

Marco glared at the group. "That is better. Now you had best listen to me, you bilge rats, before I drown the lot of you!"

"Why have you summoned us here, boss?" called an irate voice.

"If you will all shut up, I will tell you."

More grumbled complaints ensued, followed by grudging silence.

"Thank you," Marco muttered sarcastically. "I have assembled you here to tell you that there will have to be some changes on Isola del Mare."

At this, the men exchanged perplexed glances and murmured to one another.

Marco held up a hand. "In a few weeks' time, we shall have some distinguished visitors here on the island—some friends of my family back in Venice."

Now there was only reverent, absorbed silence and appreciative glances; many among Marco's crewmen hailed from the homeland, and thus, this was an announcement of great interest.

"Our guests will be Don Giovanni Renaldi, his

wife, Flora, and three of their children—two daughters and a son. These guests are to be treated with the utmost respect by all of you—is this understood?"

There were numerous respectful nods and murmurs of assent.

"But why are these people coming here?" Ugo asked.

"I am getting to that," Marco said. "The truth of the matter is, I have arranged for the English girl, Christina, to wed the Renaldi son, Vittorio. I have told the Renaldis that I am the girl's uncle."

Now there were comments of amazement, and snickers among the ranks. "Do the Venetians know the wench has lived among pirates for six years—including her lusty *uncle?*" called Patrizio, prompting new gusts of merriment.

"Silence!" Marco shouted. "No, they are not aware of our privateering activities, and that is the main reason I have gathered all of you here today. We must never let on to the Renaldis that we are freebooters. While they are here, we must all pose as proper sugar planters."

Now the men could only shake their heads and stare at one another in bewilderment.

"Why must we go through with this ruse?" Francesco demanded. "For that matter, why do you wish to get rid of Christina—so much so that you would pretend to be her uncle?"

"Yes, we enjoy having the English wench here," added another, and laughter again erupted.

"That is just my point!" Marco exclaimed. "The girl deserves better than her life on the island. Furthermore, you are all going to cooperate and see that my guests are given the right impression!"

Irritable comments and mutinous expressions now flitted through the ranks.

"Listen to me!" Marco snapped. "During the next four weeks, we must all do everything in our power to make this island both habitable and respectable. Every cottage must be cleaned and repaired, the beaches and wharves cleared of any debris. Furthermore, all loose women"—he placed much emphasis on the word *loose*"—are to be herded up, given a small sack of gold apiece, loaded onto *La Spada*—and then I shall assign a skeleton crew to dump the wenches in Havana."

Chaos broke out among the ranks. "You are taking away our wenches?" one seething voice demanded.

"You would rob a man's very bed?" called out another.

Marco had to shout to be heard over the din. "You misunderstand me! I am only talking about the island whores who have no mates and children."

"And what if a man fancies one of the beauties as his mate?" shouted an indignant voice.

"Then install her in your cottage—and the sooner the better."

Turning to Giuseppe, Marco snapped his fingers, and his helmsman stepped forward and handed him a small wooden chest. Marco set the container on the gallery railing and flipped it open, the pirates looking on in curious silence. The interior—as everyone could plainly see—was filled with gold rings, some bejeweled and others plain.

Marco held up a couple of the glittering bands. "My friends, these are rings that Giuseppe and I painstakingly gathered from the treasure room. They will certainly suffice well as wedding bands. If you wish to keep your wenches with you, you must all pose as proper married couples." Amid new mutterings of protest, he added, "And mind you, only one *wife* per man. Indeed, I hereby decree that any woman caught without a ring on her finger by day's end will be carted up and sent with the others to Havana."

"What about the English girl?" a testy voice demanded. "Will dear 'Uncle' be putting a ring on her finger by day's end?"

As bawdy merriment broke out among the ranks, Marco could feel hot color rising in his face. "You forget that all of this is being done to secure the girl a proper husband," he replied coldly. "Once that is done, we no longer need worry about the trappings of propriety here on Isola del Mare." He held up the chest. "The choice is yours, my friends. Pretend your women are your wives—or be prepared to give them up."

The pirates stormed the steps to get the rings.

While Marco was persuading his men to go along with his charade, Christina was deep in the forest, with Cicero flitting about nearby.

During Marco's recent absence, she had painstakingly carved an image of his face on a mangrove tree. Now she was throwing daggers at her wood etching. She had gathered seven from the room where the weapons were stored back at the house—and now knives protruded from Marco's ears, eyes, mouth, and nose.

"I hate you!" she screamed as she hurled her last knife deep into his forehead. "I hate you so much!"

Yet even as she said the vehement words, she fought tears. The problem was she didn't hate him— she didn't hate him at all.

She collapsed onto her haunches and tried to swallow the painful lump of emotion in her throat. While Marco had been gone, she had missed him desperately, had worried over him endlessly, and her love for him had only deepened. She had prayed every night that when he returned, he would at last profess his love for her, and make her his bride. At times she had been so anxious for his return that she had not eaten or slept. She had been forced to abandon her plan to gain weight to please him, and she had watched herself grow skinnier and more distraught with each day that passed.

Yesterday, she had been overjoyed to see him. Being held in his strong arms and kissed by him so passionately had been purest ecstasy. Then he had cruelly forsaken her, thrusting a knife deep into her heart when he had told her he had given her hand to another—a foreigner!—without even consulting her! He had betrayed her love and her trust. He was sending her away forever—the heartless cad!

She looked around her achingly, watching Cicero soar about, feasting her eyes on the smoky sprays of light that filtered down through the lush canopy of green, inhaling the unique, intoxicating scent of woods and dew, earth and nectar.

This island was in her blood—*he* was in her very soul. How did he dare do this to her—forcing her to leave him, and this place she loved so much! There was only one solution. She would never cooperate. She would die first!

Marco's meeting with the household staff was less successful.

Hesper almost split her sides laughing after Marco made his speech in the dining room. "Those idiots you call your crewmen are going to pose as sugar planters?" she scoffed. "And you are going to pose as Christina's uncle?"

"You will cooperate, woman," Marco thundered, "or I will wring your scrawny neck!"

Meanwhile, the cook began her own tirade. The Greek woman charged forward with hands balled on her hips and eyes blazing. "Five more mouths to feed! You are treating me as slave labor! I demand that you double my wages!"

"*Another* increase!" Marco retorted incredulously. "Woman, you will obey me, or I will throw your ungrateful carcass off the island!"

Eunice almost collapsed from the force of her mirth. "You would starve, you fool!"

Marco threw up his hands. Suddenly, he had a splitting headache. "Very well!" he snapped at the cook. "You will get your increase. Now get the hell out of my sight, all of you!"

The others fled, but Hesper lingered, eyeing Marco quizzically.

"What is it, woman?" he demanded.

"You know you will never succeed in this ruse, my lord."

Marco ground his teeth. "Do you want the girl in a better situation or not?"

"Indeed I do. For the first time since you abducted us and brought us here, you have done something on behalf of the girl that makes sense."

"Then why are you complaining?" Marco half shouted.

Hesper laughed shrilly. "Have you seen the way Christina dresses, much less acts? Do you honestly think you can pass off that hoyden as a lady?"

"I brought back from Charles Town all the trappings of a proper wardrobe for her."

Hesper waved him off. " 'Twill be like dressing up that Pansy of yours in laces, a bonnet, and a wig, and bringing her to tea."

Marco groaned. "I intend to work on—er—the girl's ungovernable behavior."

"It is not just the girl who will bring you to ruin," Hesper continued vehemently. "My lord, have you even considered the disgraceful way your men dress and act? If they are sugar planters, I am the Archbishop of Canterbury. Furthermore, where is the church on this island? Where is the school?"

Marco's headache was not improving. "This is so much more complicated than I had feared," he muttered, rubbing his forehead.

Hesper stood. "I shall help you, my lord. I shall

gather some of the womenfolk together and see that proper costumes are made for all."

Marco regarded the crafty old woman through narrowed eyes. "And what do you want in return?"

"To accompany the girl when she leaves."

"Very well," Marco said wearily. "But what about the church and the school?"

Hesper laughed. "That is your problem, my lord."

Ten minutes later, after being summoned by Marco, Giuseppe and Patrizio appeared in his office doorway. As usual, the hefty Patrizio was drunk, slobbering and leering at Marco; he remained upright only because the smaller man, Giuseppe, somehow managed to support his staggering weight.

"Giuseppe," Marco began tersely, "you will gather a corps of men and build a chapel and a school on this island."

The helmsman stared at his captain, wild-eyed. "But, boss, I know nothing about carpentry—"

"You will do it! At once! Patrizio will help you."

Giuseppe glanced askance at the insensible man. "Yes, boss."

"Then, when our guests arrive, you, Giuseppe, will pose as the island priest—and Patrizio will pretend to be the schoolmaster."

Giuseppe was so stunned that he released Patrizio. While he stared at Marco openmouthed, Patrizio fell flat on his face on the floor, belched loudly, and then began to snore.

FIFTEEN

Sundown brought a really low-class scene. Every member of *La Spada*'s crew had to be summoned to help gather up the remaining "loose" women on the island. The woods rang with screams as the wenches raced hysterically down the jungle paths, trying to outrun the determined pirates stalking them. At times the women retaliated, hiding in the foliage and tripping the pirates with branches, or hurling coconuts at them as they passed. Soon, the sounds of male cursing and groaning mingled with the female shrieks.

Success came slowly but surely. Marco stood on the wharf where *La Spada* was tied, supervising the operation with Pansy by his side. With the pink-gold rays of sundown outlining his tall form and his long golden hair whipping about his face, he towered there with arms akimbo, a fierce scowl gripping his handsome features as he watched two of his crewmen approach with the first captive. The woman was

161

bound, gagged, and lashed to a yardarm that the two men balanced over their shoulders. As they passed Marco, the female's dark eyes glared murder at him.

"Wait a minute," Marco commanded his men. "Is it necessary to truss up this wench and carry her on board like a pig on a spit?"

In answer, the first crewman glowered at his captain and extended his forearm, which was covered with angry gouges and vicious bites.

Marco coughed. "I see that it is necessary. Sorry," he muttered to the enraged female, standing aside so that the two crewmen could pass with their venomous quarry.

The next woman was pulled down the wharf on a leash which two of Marco's crewmen had tied to her bound wrists. As the exasperated pirates tugged the obstinate female toward the boat, the wench dug in her heels and spewed out a harangue of blistering expletives that left even Marco's ears burning and impelled poor Pansy to turn tail and run, scampering up a nearby tree. Marco hastily jumped back when the wench tried to land a kick to his shin and called him every vile name he had ever heard of—plus a few more he never had.

Next came Marco's quartermaster, bearded, muscular Claudio, who bore a kicking, screaming Rosa over his shoulder. Marco watched his former mistress approach in a wild flurry of flying legs and flapping petticoats—and then, as Claudio passed, Rosa caught sight of *him*.

"Marco Glaviano, you pig! You bastard! How dare you cast me and the others from the island!" she screamed, waving a fist.

"Claudio, a moment," Marco called wearily, striding after them.

Claudio turned and set down the seething woman. Rosa confronted Marco with bosom heaving and hands balled at her waist.

"Well, Marco Glaviano! Explain this cruelty—if you can!"

"Rosa, I simply felt that you and the others would be better off in Havana—"

"So you cast us from our homes? You wrench us away from everything we hold dear?"

Marco's temper was rising. "All you hold dear, Rosa, is the price you will exact for your next bedding. And you have been paid handsomely for your troubles, have you not?"

Uttering a graphic profanity, Rosa dug in her pockets, removing the sack of gold doubloons she had been given as recompense for her eviction and hurling the bag at Marco. He winced as the sack of heavy coin hit him squarely in the belly.

"That's what I think of your money, you coward!" she spat.

"My God, woman, are you trying to maim me?" he asked hoarsely.

"And do you think you can buy my cooperation with your pieces of gold?" she retorted with contempt. "It is that girl, isn't it? That slut, Christina! You just cannot wait to get beneath her pristine skirts, can you?"

At this scathing insult, Marco was so affronted that he actually drew his hand into a fist. He watched Rosa cower.

"Take her away!" he yelled to Claudio.

With a grunt, the trusty seaman again heaved the kicking, screaming wench over his shoulder.

"I'll make you sorry!" Rosa shrieked, waving a fist at Marco as she was carried off. "I'll make you rue the day you were born, Marco Glaviano! And I shall make you pay if it is the last thing I do!"

Marco turned from the raving female with a groan. Women! Why did they all have to make his life so difficult?

* * *

La Spada returned from Havana several days later. The crew brought back with them the many additional supplies Marco had requested—everything from lumber, nails, and paint, to countless bolts of fabric for new clothing and draperies, to the fine wines and cheeses Marco would use to entertain his guests from Venice.

In the days and weeks that followed, Isola del Mare became a busy, industrious place. The beaches were cleared of their debris, flotsam, and discarded rigging. Crews were assigned to hack away at the greenery encroaching on the many jungle trails. All buildings on the island were cleaned and repaired, and many were given a fresh coat of whitewash. Giuseppe and his corps of "carpenters" were hastily throwing together the two huts that would suffice as the island church and the school, while their women sat nearby, giggling and thatching panels for the roofs.

Marco's house became a bustling command center. The dining room and grand salon were soon covered wall to wall with fabrics; the island women chatted merrily as they sewed everything from a cassock for Giuseppe to new play clothes for their children, new linens and draperies for the main house. Marco made his daily rounds to inspect everyone's progress, and he was beginning to feel that his ruse would actually work—

Except for one area, in which all his efforts remained an unqualified disaster. Christina still categorically refused to cooperate with his scheme. They had daily, violent arguments regarding her obstinacy. She steadfastly insisted that she would never leave this island, she would never pretend to be his niece, and she would *never* marry the man he had chosen.

Marco was nearing his wit's end, only to have his patience completely snap one balmy September morning. He was striding down a jungle path when he spotted his own image carved on a mangrove tree. Actually, the etching was a fine likeness of his face, except for the fact that seven daggers protruded from his eyes, ears, nose, mouth, and forehead! He had no doubt regarding who had left him this malevolent little souvenir! *Madre del Dio!* The girl had turned into a demon straight from hell! By damn, something must be done about her!

He stormed back to the house, intent on finding her. He strode around slamming doors and bellowing, thoroughly unnerving the women who were busy sewing in the grand salon and dining room.

He finally found the little shrew on the back veranda. She was sitting on the porch floor, humming a song and petting Pansy, while Cicero complained loudly from his perch in a nearby gum tree. Marco felt his defenses weakening. How seductively innocent the girl looked in her perpetual, virginal white. He wanted to throttle her—almost as much as he wanted to haul her up into his arms and devour her alive.

"So there you are," he snapped.

She glanced up at him rebelliously. "Hello, Marco. If you have come to try again to force me to cooperate, you can forget it!"

"I saw the memento you left me in the jungle," he drawled sarcastically.

She laughed, stood, and faced him. "I was wondering when you would discover my little keepsake. Were you pleased by my talent? I thought it an excellent likeness of your face."

"Oh, *sì* it is—although I am not sure I can bear the kindness of your motives."

She merely shrugged. "You deserve it for the way you have treated me."

"Christina," he began, shaking a finger at her.

"It is true," she cried. "You are cruel, and all you can think of is getting rid of me. You will likely have your men haul me away, just as you did with the whores."

He flung his hands wide in exasperation. "I had them sent away for your benefit!"

"Yes—so you can carry out your absurd charade and get rid of me," she reminded him with resentment.

He heaved a great sigh. "Christina, I have decided that I have tolerated your defiance long enough. Therefore, I have come to inform you that if you do not begin cooperating with me at once, there will be consequences." He pinned her with a stern glance and added meaningfully, "*Severe* consequences."

"Such as?" she challenged, undaunted.

"I'll chain you up in your room," he threatened.

"I'll go on a hunger strike!" she blazed back.

"I'll send you to a convent!"

"I'll corrupt the nuns—and then I'll run off with a gypsy!"

He took an aggressive step closer, his voice rising. "I'll lash you to *La Spada*'s mast and beat the stubbornness out of your hide with a cat-o'-nine-tails!"

She was totally unrepentant, her bright green eyes just daring him to try it. "I won't make a very appealing bride, will I, with my back shredded to ribbons?"

"Goddammit, woman!" he exploded. "What will it take to make you cooperate?"

She didn't bat an eyelash. "You—as my husband."

"That is impossible! You are behaving like a child."

"I was a child when you promised me!" she accused bitterly. "What could be crueler than breaking a vow made to a twelve-year-old?"

"I tell you, you want something the two of us can never have! You know I cannot marry as long as I must roam the seas and do battle with the Spanish."

"And I tell you I shall have you—and no one else! Furthermore, I am tired of your excuses. Such 'noble' motives have never stopped you from taking other women to your bed."

Marco was so frustrated, he began to pace with fists tightly clenched. He had to make her cooperate—no matter what it took.

At last he turned to her and said in cold, cruel tones, "Christina, I have tried to be patient with you, knowing you are still a child at heart. But obviously, the time for coddling is past. The truth is, you are making a fool of yourself with me. So listen well, you wayward brat—I do not love you and I do not wish to marry you."

Her expression began to waver. "You are lying."

"I am not."

Her chin came up. "You need me."

"I need no one."

"That is not true!" she flared. "I know you want me!"

He forced himself to eye her slowly and insultingly. "*Sì*, I would enjoy bedding you, *cara*. But there is a big difference between *wanting*, and wanting to marry."

At last he got to her—with a vengeance. As he watched in agony, her lower lip trembled and tears filled her eyes. How he managed not to pull her close then, to beg her forgiveness and kiss her until all her tears melted, was totally beyond him.

She faced him with a pride and defiance that only made him want her all the more—and hate himself utterly. "Very well, then. I will marry this—this foreigner! And I hope you rot in hell, Marco Glaviano."

Before he could reach for her, she fled into the house. Marco slammed his fist violently into a pillar, then shouted in pain.

Christina had a broken heart. She lay on the bed in her room, sobbing disconsolately, feeling shattered by the heartless things Marco had just said to her.

He had told her he did not need her, did not even want her other than in a purely physical sense. She remembered that night so long ago when he had told her of how he found peace and contentment within himself. Was he truly an island unto himself, as in the poet's words? Did he need any woman, or did he view them all—herself included—as no more than convenient outlets to assuage his lusts?

Well, she would not let him off the hook so easily. He *did* need her, whether he was ready to admit it or not.

And he had promised her as an innocent child that he would marry her when she grew up, and she was not about to let him forsake his vow. Did he think she was a creature without pride, without feelings? He was about to find out how strong, determined— and vindictive—she could truly be. She would get her revenge on Marco Glaviano. She would make him want her, need her, and love her—to the point of madness. She would use his scheme to turn the tables on him, and especially to *make him sorry*.

And then she would make him her husband.

Marco had two broken fingers.

"How on earth did you manage this, boss?" Giuseppe asked as he sat with Marco in his office and carefully bound the injured digits.

"Don't ask," came Marco's terse reply.

Giuseppe wisely fell silent and continued his ministrations.

Marco sat brooding and feeling very sorry for himself. Actually, he felt more miserable over the things he had just said to Christina than he did regarding his own mangled hand. He wondered where everything had gone wrong. How he missed the golden days when he and his men used to spoil Christina and take joy in watching her grow up. Why had they come to this terrible pass where he must now hurt her? Oh, *Dio*, the look on her face when he had said those cruel things!

Still, he remained convinced that his actions were absolutely necessary and for her own good. He would never make any woman a decent husband. He would never be willing to give up his freebooting ways. He only wished Christina could understand how noble his motives truly were. As for the not-so-noble problem he was having, in that his manhood seemed willing to salute only one woman—surely this was just a temporary inconvenience that would fade once she was gone—

"Goddammit, man!" Marco was wrenched violently from his tortured thoughts as Giuseppe tightened the bindings on his fingers.

"Sorry, boss," Giuseppe muttered.

"You are not nearly as sorry as I am," Marco muttered back.

Later that day, Marco and Christina passed each other in the hallway. She saw his two broken fingers, and quickly glanced at his face—in a brief, unguarded moment that slammed them both like a fist in the gut.

He saw her broken heart, and it hurt him more than the physical and emotional anguish already tearing him apart.

SIXTEEN

IN A SMOKY TAVERN NEAR THE HAVANA HARBOR, ROSA DE Leon was behaving scandalously. She sat atop a scarred pianoforte, her features florid, her skirts hiked disgracefully up to her thighs. She was waving a tankard of grog and leading the crowd of seedy harbor rats in a bawdy song, to the off-key accompaniment of the pianoforte.

Just as an inebriated sailor staggered over and began pawing Rosa's bare thighs, the door to the establishment swung open and Carlos the pirate strode in with three of his lieutenants. At once, his dark gaze became riveted on his former mistress.

He smiled to himself cynically. He could not believe his good fortune. He and Rosa had been lovers for some time before a spat had impelled him to dump her off in New Providence over six years ago. Afterward, he had heard, to his chagrin, that she had taken up with his enemy, Marco Glaviano. Now Marco must have tired of the Spanish slut, for it seemed she had been cast adrift again—this time, in his waters. His senses quickened at the thought of the lusty roll she would provide him tonight. But most of all, his innate greed and thirst for revenge were heightened by the possibility that this woman could—and would—lead him to Marco Glaviano and to the English girl whose capture would net him such a handsome bounty.

Now the drunken sailor was leaning over to bury his face between Rosa's thighs, to the lusty cheers of the other men, and the brassy wench made no protest. Carlos was tempted to thrash her soundly. His rage piqued, he quickly strode across the room, pulled the nervy bastard off Rosa, and slammed his fist into the smaller man's jaw. Seconds later, the unfortunate man was staring up at Carlos dazedly from the filthy floor of the tavern.

Carlos shook a fist at the whoreson and bellowed, "Keep your filthy hands off my woman!" His threat brought more hoots and lewd comments from the other customers, as well as a convulsive nod from the defeated sailor.

Carlos turned to Rosa to find her staring at him, agog.

"Carlos!" she managed in a shocked whisper.

"Yes, it is I, Carlos!" he snapped. "And you, woman, had better learn to behave yourself!"

Yanking down her skirts and setting aside her grog, he heaved the plump woman over his shoulder, slapped her firmly on the behind, and strode off with her to the enthusiastic huzzahs and catcalls of the other men.

He bore her to one of the banquettes at the side of the room. The small cubicles had been set behind half-doors to afford privacy to amorous customers who wanted to fondle their wenches while still benefiting from the bawdy atmosphere.

And Carlos was feeling very amorous—as well·as

bawdy—at the moment. Closing the half-doors behind them, he sat down, and as Rosa slid into his lap, he leaned over to kiss her soundly.

"*Querida*, it has been very long," he murmured.

"Far too long, my big stallion," she purred wickedly as she reached down between their bodies to stroke him.

He sucked in his breath between gritted teeth. *Caramba!* She had not lost her touch! "You have missed me?"

"Oh, yes, Carlos!"

"But you have been well occupied, servicing my enemy," he complained.

"What was I to do after you abandoned me on New Providence?" She pouted. "Marco saved me from being raped by the barbarians occupying the island."

He chuckled. "Given your prurient appetites, my pet, I find it difficult to believe that you truly wished to be saved from such a treat."

"But I did—and I damned your eyes for deserting me!"

His expression turned quizzical. "Ah, yes, the silly spat that separated us. What was it about?"

"Who remembers?"

He cuddled her close and pawed her breast. "Then it was a trifle, indeed. The point is, we are together now."

She stroked him wantonly and panted, "Ah, yes, that is the point."

He laughed ribaldly, ran his large hands over her breasts and belly, then murmured, "Why are you here, *querida*? You must tell me what happened between you and Glaviano."

"That bastard!" she retorted. "I do not wish to speak of the coward."

"Then I must assume that he has courted your ill favor?"

She laughed bitterly. "You assume correctly."

He stuck his tongue in her ear and thrust it about boldly, delighting in her earthy moans. "What if I should offer to help you seek your revenge?"

She pulled away, staring up at him as realization dawned. "Now I see what you are about! You want me to betray Marco!"

"Are you saying Glaviano is not deserving of betrayal?" he demanded angrily. Shaking her slightly, he went on aggressively. "Are you still in love with the bastard? Because if you are, I'll strip you bare and beat your bottom with a salted whip!"

But she merely touched his mouth with her finger and chuckled sensually. "Ah, Carlos, you are so very passionate."

His dark eyes twinkled with merriment. "And you, wench, are shameless."

Rosa was on the verge of telling him that this was what Marco always called her, but she caught herself in the nick of time and merely smiled at him luridly.

He groaned. "Ah, wench, what shall I do with you?"

She was caressing him again, so skillfully, and writhing against him in unabashed invitation. "As I seem to recall, you needed no instruction previously."

He laughed heartily, but soon a grim frown drifted in. "Tell me about you and Glaviano."

"And what do I get in return?" she demanded petulantly.

His response shocked even Rosa. Chuckling devilishly, Carlos hiked up her skirts, unbuttoned his trousers, and quickly impaled her womanhood with his rigid member. She gasped in ecstasy and brazenly wiggled closer. To the casual passerby, she was still sitting in his lap; but to Rosa, heaven had never loomed closer.

"Oh, *mi corazón*, you are such a wicked stud," she purred, rocking against him greedily.

"Now tell me what happened with you and Glaviano," he urged.

"You wish to speak of such things at a time like this?"

"*Sì*. What better time, my love, then when your—er—defenses are down." His hands at her waist restrained her lusty movements and his voice was suddenly laced with steel. "Now speak, woman—or forgo your satisfaction."

She moaned her frustration. "Very well! The pig threw me off his island—along with several other women."

"He did?" Carlos nibbled at her neck as he thrust slowly inside her. "But why, *querida?*"

"Some nonsense about marrying off the English girl," Rosa said, panting. "Did you know he rescued that spoiled brat six years ago?"

"*Sì*, I knew." Suddenly, Carlos was all attention, his manhood once again motionless inside her. "Go on."

"Carlos, at a time like this—"

"Go on!"

Hoarsely, urgently, she confessed, "He claims that he has found a husband for her—the son of a prominent Venetian family. The entire group of foreigners is supposed to be visiting the island in a few weeks. Now Marco argues that he must turn respectable in order to properly impress his guests—and to secure the girl's marriage. This is why he claims he cast me and the others from the island like so much trash."

"Ah, poor darling," Carlos murmured, rocking her on his phallus again.

She shuddered violently.

"You know, the last time I saw Glaviano, he told me that the English girl was dead," Carlos said.

"Hah!" Rosa cried. "I am not surprised that he

lied. He is behaving like a fool over her. What he really wants is to get beneath the little brat's skirts."

Finding that to be an immensely pleasurable thought himself, Carlos began to pump forcefully inside Rosa, making her cry out wantonly.

"And what of the English girl? How does she like the prospect of being married off?" he inquired.

"She is fit to be tied, that one," Rosa replied with relish. "She has hungered to ride Marco's mast for ages now."

"Has she?" Carlos's ardor was rapidly increasing at the thought of bedding yet another woman who lusted after his enemy.

"*Sì.*" Rosa's reply was punctuated by a tortured gasp. "The jealous little bitch even put a snake in my bed to get rid of me—and then Marco took her side."

"How ungallant of him."

"*Sì.*"

"Tell me how to get to Marco's island," he commanded.

"Oh, Carlos, you ask too much of me." She heaved the words amid frenzied groans of delight. "If Marco ever found out that I betrayed him in that manner, he would slit my throat."

"And if you don't tell me, I'll wring your miserable neck." He punctuated his threat with quick, hard jabs, locking his strong forearms at her waist to heighten her torment and forbid escape.

"Very well!" she half screamed, her fingernails tearing gouges in his forearms as the savage coupling drove her to madness. "I'll tell you . . ."

The instructions were almost lost in the wail of animal pleasure that was abruptly torn from them both.

While Rosa and Carlos were mindlessly fornicating in Havana, Charles Rutgers was receiving Christina's stepuncle, the Reverend George Hollingsworth, in the drawing room of his house on Bay Street in Charles Town.

"Good afternoon, Reverend Hollingsworth," Rutgers said, crossing the room to greet the black-clothed vicar. "It has been some time since we have seen you here in the colonies."

"Indeed it has—and good afternoon to you, Magistrate Rutgers." Hollingsworth, a tall, thin man in his mid-thirties, with pale brown hair and even paler eyes, shook the hand Rutgers extended. "I very much appreciate your contacting me regarding my stepniece's whereabouts."

Rutgers shrugged. "As the girl's guardian, I felt it was my duty to do so." He motioned toward the silk brocade settee. "By all means, Reverend, take a seat."

"Thank you." Hollingsworth strode to the settee, while Rutgers resumed his place at the wing chair near the fire.

"I trust you have recovered from your malaise?" Rutgers asked.

The vicar nodded morosely. "I would have called on you weeks ago, except for the dysentery that has plagued me ever since we sailed from London."

Rutgers glanced at his guest sharply. "You have recuperated sufficiently to travel now?"

"I have." Hollingsworth leaned toward Rutgers, lacing his long, slender fingers together. "Your letter said that Christina has been living in the Caribbean with these privateers for six years now. I presume that nothing has since changed?"

"Nay—at least, not as far as I know."

Hollingsworth frowned. "Do we have any way of knowing whether or not this Marco Glaviano has adequately provided for my stepniece's safety and well-being?"

Rutgers took a moment to dip snuff from an elaborate hand-painted tin. "The man is a privateer for the Crown, but of course I cannot attest to his character—or lack thereof. As you are aware, his kind are essentially a lawless breed. In fact, I suspect that Glaviano is currently in favor with the Crown only because the war has legitimized his piracy."

Hollingsworth's thin lips twitched in distaste as he watched the magistrate snort his snuff. "What of this Luigi Monza who told you of Christina's whereabouts in the first place? Was he able to provide any additional details about Glaviano or this Isola del Mare you mentioned?"

"Unfortunately, no," came the emotionless reply. "Although, as I indicated in my correspondence, the felon did provide us with a map to Glaviano's island."

"Would it be possible for me to question this Monza?"

Rutgers shook his head and laughed cynically. "The miscreant died of lockjaw while in the public pillory—mayhap because his ears and hands had been nailed to the stocks."

Hollingsworth shuddered. "May God rest his soul. Then I presume there is naught for the two of us to do but to sail for this Caribbean island to retrieve my stepniece?"

Rutgers sighed heavily. "Aye. As the girl's guardian, I am obligated to accompany you."

Hollingsworth scowled at the magistrate's obvious lack of enthusiasm for their undertaking. "I have already made some inquiries about chartering a schooner and engaging a crew."

Rutgers nodded as he turned to expectorate loudly into the nearby spittoon. "I shall sail with you, then, to secure my ward's return to civilization." He stood, regarding his guest with an impatient frown. "You will, of course, notify me when you are prepared to leave Charles Town?"

Hollingsworth also rose. "I shall."

"Then I shall await your word. May I see you out?"

As the two men headed for the door, Hollingsworth murmured, "By the way ... I presume Christina's inheritance is still in order?"

Rutgers's cold gray eyes gleamed with suspicion as he flicked his gaze to his guest. "Just what are you implying, man?"

Carefully, Hollingsworth replied, "I feel that it would be—regrettable—for the girl to return to society only to discover that she had not been properly provided for. Indeed, I would be most dismayed if you have not—er—adequately handled my stepniece's affairs."

Rutgers's color had darkened to an unbecoming scarlet, and his chest puffed up with indignation. "Are you making an accusation, man?"

"Not at all," Hollingsworth replied smoothly. "Merely an observation."

"The girl's affairs are in order!" Rutgers snapped, and promptly escorted the vicar to the door.

SEVENTEEN

THE RENALDIS ARRIVED AT ISOLA DEL MARE ON A BALMY morning in late October.

As if subconsciously aware that today would finally be the day he would greet his distinguished visitors from Venice, Marco awakened well before dawn. He hopped out of bed, splashed water on his face, and tugged a comb through his hair. He then made a lather and began awkwardly shaving his face. While his broken fingers had healed, the digits tended to be stiff when he first awakened.

He laid out his most elegant clothing, as he had on every recent morning. The lookouts posted at the redoubts in the harbor had been given orders to inform him at the first sighting of a sail. Nonetheless, should *La Spada* suddenly run in on the tide, he could not risk being caught wearing his traditional vest without a shirt, or even greeting his venerable guests shirtless.

His toilette completed, he donned a ruffled linen

179

shirt, dark breeches, white hose, and flat leather shoes with large brass buckles. He added a brocaded beige waistcoat, a tailored gold silk coat with turned-back, brass-buttoned cuffs, and a black cravat. Disdaining the powdered wigs so popular for gentlemen both in Europe and in the colonies, he wore his hair down and loose, and crowned his outfit with his black cavalier hat with its white plume.

Grabbing his gilt-tipped walking stick, he left the house to make his daily inspection of the preparations. The islanders had made remarkable progress cleaning up Isola del Mare over the past weeks. As he strode down the jungle trail, taking deep breaths of the air so redolent with nectar, dew, and greenery, he felt pleased that he did not encounter the usual loose chickens and pigs—not to mention half-naked children. The island animals had been confined to corrals and pens, the children to their yards.

The trail took him past the cane fields, where the tasseled stalks waved high in the breeze. The furrows were being weeded by a number of his crewmen, most of whom were now clean-shaven and wore conservative broadcloth jackets, trousers, and sugar-loaf hats.

Yet Marco was dismayed to note that a couple of his men had not yet fallen into line. Spotting two unkempt pirates weeding a furrow together, he paused and called out, "Francesco, what in the name of heaven are you doing out here without a shirt? And, Ugo, go shave off that beard—and get rid of the earring!"

The two men straightened up to glower at Marco. "Do we have to, boss?" Francesco replied irritably as he brushed his gritty hands on his trousers. "It is bad enough that you have us out here weeding the fields like bloody peasants!"

"*Sì*, Captain, the mosquitoes are eating us up alive!" protested Ugo.

"Do it, and quit complaining!" Marco ordered, and
the two grumbling men trudged off.

Wearing an expression of grim satisfaction, he continued on his rounds. He noted that the nearby cottages were refurbished, their chinking repaired, their
roofs freshly thatched, their yards cleared of debris.
The pirates' women sat in the swept yards, sewing or
weaving baskets or scaling fish, their plump bodies
now attired in modest, high-necked gowns with
tightly laced bodices. Marco felt intensely relieved
that the females had relinquished their usual loose
shifts worn without undergarments, although he had
to stop to caution a couple of the wenches who had
brazenly hiked their skirts up over their knees, or
were wearing their bodices open or unlaced. He endured their blistering complaints about the restrictive
clothing and charmed them all with ready smiles. As
he left the area, he observed that even the small children playing in the yards were decked out in traditional jackets, hats, and trousers for the boys, and in
demure dresses over lacy petticoats for the girls.

Marco took in everything with an approving eye.
Hesper and her confederates had done well outfitting
the pirates and their families. The island was actually
beginning to resemble a respectable community
rather than a den of iniquity. Now if only his disreputable cronies would pass muster with the Renaldis,
without committing too many blunders!

He continued his inspection, passing the northernmost cove, where he spotted half a dozen of his men
fishing in the breakers with their nets. He admired
the clean white expanse of sand, now cleared of flotsam and discarded rigging, as well as the neat row of
buckets filled with fat mackerel and rainbow run-
ners. He waved to his crewmen before moving on.

Striding past a smoky lagoon, he came upon his
helmsman, Giuseppe, who was now decked out in a
black, belted cassock and leather sandals. Giuseppe's

hair had been cropped closely around his face, his
beard was neatly trimmed, and he wore a bejeweled
gold cross on a heavy chain around his neck. He was
mumbling to himself in Latin, and was so deeply immersed in the opened missal he carried that he did
not even notice Marco as he swept past.

Marco chuckled to himself and turned off down
the narrow trail that led to the just-completed schoolhouse. He wanted to check on Patrizio's progress before he returned to the house.

The thatched hut appeared neat and beckoning,
but as Marco stepped inside, what he saw hardly
pleased him. To be sure, the low benches and small
tables were perfectly arranged, and cluttered with the
papers, primers, and slates that bespoke recent learning activity. Unfortunately, though, there were no
students in sight. Although the schoolmaster was at
his desk at the front of the room, beneath the taste-
fully displayed charts and maps, he was passed out
at his post, snoring blissfully with his head on his
desk and his hand curled around a cask of rum that
Marco was positive had just been drained dry!

He uttered a sound of disgust. Obviously, with
their schoolmaster dead to the world, the children
had all run off to play. Now what could he do? No
one among his crewmen was as learned as Patrizio.
He was still the best candidate to pose as schoolmaster—yet how would Marco keep the man sober
during the Renaldis' visit?

"Patrizio!" Marco barked, beating his cane on the
dried mud floor.

The drunken man lifted his head, blinked at Marco
dazedly, and slurred out, "Aye, Captain?" Then his
head slammed back down on the desk, like a dead
weight falling, and he began to snore even louder.

"Never mind!" Marco half shouted to the insensible man. "I will send a woman with hot coffee!"

He hurried to the nearest cottage and asked the

woman to fetch Patrizio a pot of coffee, and to see to it that he drank several cupfuls. Marco then pulled several of his men off the nearby beach, ordering them to herd up the island children and propel them back to the school. He was heading back to the house when he heard the low, mellifluous notes of conch horns. A moment later, one of the guards, Vincente, hurried toward him along the path.

"Boss! *La Spada*'s sail has been sighted just west of Barnacle Reef! She should be gliding into the harbor within a half hour!"

"Thank you. You may go back to your post, Vincente," Marco said briskly.

As the young man sprinted off, Marco hurried on to the house. He would have to fetch Christina and take her with him to the docks to greet the Renaldis. He sighed. He had seen little of the girl since their disastrous argument several weeks ago. She spent most of her time either sulking in her room or hiding out deep in the island along the salt flats or lagoons. Although Hesper had assured him that a proper wardrobe had been prepared for the girl, every time he had caught sight of her lately, she had still, defiantly, been wearing one of her loose shifts—a skimpy garment he well knew the Renaldis would find scandalous. Her cooperation this morning was critical; she must look, act, and dress like a lady, even if he was compelled to force her into the proper garments himself. If she should revolt again, he really would have no choice but to thrash her into submission, as much as he hated the prospect of taking her to the wharf with her mien sullen and her face still streaked with tears.

He hurried into the house and rushed down the corridor to pound on her door. "Christina! Christina, our guests are arriving, and you must come with me to the docks at once to greet them."

To his utter astonishment, she emerged from the room, attired as he had never before seen her.

"Good morning *Uncle* Marco," she greeted him sarcastically as she twirled her lacy parasol.

Marco could only gape at the ravishing creature who stood before him. Christina was dressed in a gown of green silk that was every bit as bright and vibrant as her gorgeous, spiteful eyes. The frock was low-cut and tight-waisted, revealing the creamy flesh of her upper chest and the tantalizing cleft in her bosom. He could see the barest trace of the whalebone stays that thrust her ripe breasts so enticingly high. The hooped skirt swept wide, allowing an alluring glimpse of slim ankles veiled in silk stockings and shapely feet encased in satin brocade slippers with silk bows and Italian heels. She wore the emerald necklace he had recently given her, along with gold bangle earrings. Her hair had been painstakingly arranged in tight sausage curls that dangled well past her lovely bare shoulders, and she wore a wide-brimmed straw hat bedecked with small silk flowers. Her face was strikingly beautiful, her color exquisite, even without rouge, and her chin was thrust high. All in all, she resembled a magnificent ice princess.

Marco could not contain the slight tremor that racked his voice. "You look lovely, *cara*," he murmured.

"Lovely enough to barter away?" she sneered.

"I wish you would not see it in that light."

"But this really is a business transaction, is it not? I have been thinking much about this arranged marriage. What could persuade this exalted Venetian family to come to this castaway island in the Caribbean to secure their son a bride—if not a very substantial dowry?"

"Of course there is a dowry," Marco snapped at

her. "You will not find a respectable marriage that is arranged without one."

Her lovely mouth tightened. "So you wish to get rid of me so badly that you're willing to pay these people to take me off your hands?"

"I could not possibly be acting in your best interest, could I?" he demanded in exasperation.

"How much did you have to pay them to get me a husband?" she countered.

"That is none of your affair. And furthermore, *niece*, we are due at the docks."

Marco grabbed Christina's arm and pulled her resisting body from the house. As they started down the path toward the pier, he spotted Giuseppe coming toward them, still immersed in his missal and now mumbling the Latin Credo.

"Giuseppe!" Marco called. "*La Spada*'s sail has been spotted. Come with us to the wharf to greet our visitors!"

A few yards away from them, Giuseppe stopped in his tracks to stare at them in horror. "The guests are here already? But this is terrible, boss! I am not prepared!"

Marco dismissed his protest. "Oh, just mutter some Latin over them and you will be fine. Let me assure you that you are in much better shape than our illustrious schoolmaster, Patrizio."

Tucking his missal under his arm and crossing himself, Giuseppe rushed over to join them. "I have a feeling this is going to be a disaster," he lamented. "Poverty and celibacy have never been my long suits, boss."

"Indeed," Marco drawled irritably. "Consider your appointed role as divine retribution for all your lusty behavior over the years."

The three strode quickly down the path and emerged onto the pier just as *La Spada* glided into view, the crew busily maneuvering the craft and ty-

ing down sails. Spotting the Renaldi family together
at the rail at midships—their ranks minus the now
married Seraphina—Marco waved, and all five cheerfully waved back. Christina, meanwhile, stood sullenly by his side. Soon, the gangplank was lowered
and Marco towed Christina over to wait for their
guests at its base. Giuseppe trailed behind them.

"Marco, my friend!" Don Giovanni bellowed as he
escorted his wife onto the pier.

Favoring his stiff fingers, Marco gingerly shook his
friend's hand, then quickly kissed the cheek of
Donna Flora. "Welcome to Isola del Mare, my dear
friends. I trust that all of you are well, and that fair
winds sped your journey?"

"But of course," Don Giovanni replied. He glanced
shrewdly at Christina. "And who is this ravishing
young beauty?"

"May I present my niece, Christina Abbott?"
Marco replied solemnly.

Now five sets of dark eyes were riveted on
Christina, and as a plethora of greetings and hand-
shakes were exchanged, she in turn quickly sized up
the Renaldis. Don Giovanni and Donna Flora were
both prosperous-looking as well as extravagantly
dressed, but something about their effusive manner
put her off. The two daughters, Calista and Jovita,
were elegantly attired, and though both were homely,
they seemed very nice. Indeed, Christina felt touched
when Calista warmly hugged her, while Jovita told
her that they would be proud to have her as their
new sister.

That left the Renaldi son, her ostensible fiancé, toward whom Marco now tugged her. "Christina, I
would like you to meet a very fine young gentleman,
Vittorio Renaldi."

Christina carefully regarded the lad, who was
handsome, if sharp-featured and slender, and very
solemn-looking. He was dressed in a blue silk coat, a

satin waistcoat, breeches, and hose. His pompous-looking powdered wig curled to his shoulders, and was topped by a black tricorn hat.

"How do you do?" she murmured.

"Signorina." As he bowed before her, she automatically curtsied in return. He took the hand she extended, kissing her gloved fingers. "I am enchanted to make your acquaintance."

"I am pleased to meet you as well," she replied, flashing him a dazzling smile that she hoped Marco would take note of.

Don Giovanni stepped forward to pound his son's back. "By the saints, you must be enchanted, my boy!" He winked at Christina, then turned to his host. "Marco, you neglected to mention that your niece is such a prize. My son will be the envy of all Venice when he bears home his bride. Why, she is utterly *magnifica!*"

Marco's quick glance at Christina was strangely intent. "That she is."

Meanwhile, Christina could no longer bear being the center of so much attention. "Uncle Marco is around me all the time," she sweetly informed the others. "Let me assure you that he is the last person to notice my looks."

Now the focus was shifted back to Marco. He coughed and tugged Giuseppe forward by the sleeve of his cossack. "Our priest, Father Giuseppe, is here to greet all of you and bless your arrival."

Tossing Marco a mystified glance, Giuseppe quickly stepped into the midst of the newcomers and shook each person's hand, alternately murmuring, "Bless you, my son," and "Bless you, my daughter," between extravagant bouts of crossing himself.

As the Renaldis exchanged bemused glances at the priest's odd behavior, Marco suggested, "Shall we all go on to the house, then? I am sure you would like to freshen up, and luncheon will be served shortly."

Don Giovanni clapped Marco across the back. "*Sì*, my boy. We are eager to get better acquainted with your estate."

Catching Marco staring at her again, Christina turned to Vittorio and preened. "Will you escort me to the house?"

He gulped, then at once bowed and offered his arm. "Of course, signorina. I am deeply honored."

She placed her fingers on his sleeve and smiled at him brilliantly. She could have sworn she could hear Marco's teeth grinding.

The procession started off, first Marco and Don Giovanni escorting Donna Flora, then Christina and Vittorio, then the two Renaldi daughters with Giuseppe, and finally, half a dozen crewmen bearing the many trunks of their guests.

As the party descended the wharf, Don Giovanni glanced askance at the nearby redoubts manned by Marco's men. He regarded his host with a raised brow. "Cannon, my friend?"

"One cannot be too careful in these parts of the Caribbean," Marco replied. "There are savage Indians on the nearby islands, and pirates have been spotted in these waters as well."

"Ah, pirates. The scourge of the seven seas."

Behind them, Christina rolled her eyes.

Soon, Marco led the others into the freshly white-washed, immaculate house. As the group milled around in the central hallway while an amazingly civil Hesper gathered hats, walking sticks, gloves, and parasols, Pansy abruptly bounded in from the dining room to join them. The cheetah whined as she ambled up to Marco.

Spotting the fierce-looking black cat, Donna Flora and her daughters gasped and shrank back, while Don Giovanni eyed Pansy in fear. "Marco, what is this wild animal doing in your home?"

"Please do not worry," Marco hastily reassured

them, petting the cat, who stood by his side, panting, with her mouth open. "Pansy is harmless."

"Harmless?" Don Giovanni repeated skeptically, staring at the cheetah's huge, sharp teeth.

"She is just a big, overgrown baby," Marco insisted with a grin.

Hesper harrumphed loudly and strolled off.

Meanwhile, Pansy began to prowl among the guests, carefully sniffing each person. "Are you certain the beast is harmless?" Donna Flora asked shrilly as Pansy chewed on the lace of her cuff.

Marco snapped his fingers, and the cat quickly returned to his side. "I assure you, Donna Flora, that Pansy is as tame as the lovely flowers on your hat. You see, I raised her from a small cub after I—er—rescued her from a cage at a tavern in Havana."

"Whatever was the cat doing there?" Don Giovanni asked.

Marco shrugged. "I assume she was captured by Spanish slavers in Africa. At any rate, she does help protect our household." He cleared his throat. "May I show you all to your rooms?"

The Renaldis hastily accepted Marco's offer. Pansy tagged along, seemingly oblivious of the tension she was causing. All of the newcomers gave the cheetah a wide berth as Marco escorted them to the suite of three rooms that had been scrubbed from top to bottom, with snowy linens, fresh fruit, and flowers laid out.

Christina was able to retire to her room until luncheon. As she sat at her dressing table freshening up, Hesper slipped inside the room.

"I saw your young man," she said.

Christina turned to regard the wrinkled old woman, who looked almost comical decked out, as a respectable housekeeper, in a black bombazine dress, lacy apron, and white house cap. "And what do you think of him?"

"He seems very handsome and upstanding. He will make you a fine husband."

"I suppose so," Christina murmured without enthusiasm.

Hesper stepped closer, frowning. "Are you still fighting this match? The marriage will get both of us away from this stinking island, you know."

Christina tightly clenched her jaw. "There is nothing I want more than that," she agreed vehemently.

"Good girl." Patting Christina's shoulder, Hesper slipped from the room.

Yet Christina frowned as she rearranged an errant curl. She had to admit that, as a fiancé, Vittorio was indeed far from a disaster.

The problem was, he was not Marco.

At luncheon time, everyone gathered in the dining room. Marco sat at the head of the table, with Don Giovanni opposite him at the other end. Donna Flora and her daughters sat across from Christina, who was seated between Vittorio and Giuseppe.

As Eunice and the three peasant girls assisting her brought in the first course of hot bread and conch stew, Marco and Don Giovanni chatted about Seraphina's wedding in Beaufort and the Renaldis' voyage to Isola del Mare. Christina noted one of the serving wenches, Antonia, smiling shyly at Vittorio as she offered him a slice of hot bread, and him nodding back and murmuring his thanks. Her spirits lifted slightly at the thought that at least she was betrothed to a man whom other young women found attractive.

As the cook and her company left the room, Marco looked at Giuseppe. "Would you kindly offer thanks, Father Giuseppe?"

At the request, Giuseppe turned a miserable color of red, then pulled out his missal, fumbling through the pages with an expression of bewilderment. At last he lurched to his feet, and as the others hastily bowed their heads, he muttered, "Father, forgive us, for we have sinned." Making a hasty stab at crossing himself, he sat back down.

Marco groaned, and Christina covered her giggles with her napkin. Don Giovanni tossed his host a confused glance, while the other Renaldis murmured to one another in perplexity.

"You must forgive *Father* Giuseppe," Marco drawled at last. "He has been in the Caribbean far too long. The sun has affected his brain."

Don Giovanni laughed nervously and swilled his wine. "Ah, yes." Raising his glass, he saluted Giuseppe. "You poor man."

Christina glanced at her reticent fiancé. "I would wager that Vittorio could return proper thanks for us."

At this, the young man at last sprang to life, his dark eyes gleaming with a fanatical joy and a broad smile sculpting his thin lips. "It would be my honor and privilege." He glanced at Marco. "As long as our host is willing."

"Of course," Marco replied.

Vittorio stood up and launched into a lengthy prayer in Latin. Christina was stunned—but soon very bored.

When at last he sat down, she smiled at him gratefully—to torment Marco—while inwardly groaning at the thought of being married to a religious zealot.

After luncheon, while the women napped and Vittorio immersed himself in a theology book in the library, Marco showed Don Giovanni about the estate. They walked along the verdant trails amid hazy shafts of light, Marco pointing out the various flora and fauna. He mused darkly that at least the excursion helped ward off his black, jealous thoughts regarding the way Christina had already taken to the

Renaldi son, the coy smiles and little touches she used to charm the boy. *Dio*, it had been ages since she had smiled at him that way!

Of course, Marco's conscience reminded him that this was exactly the result he had wanted—for Christina to respond positively to the young man he had chosen as her husband. And yet, on a strictly emotional level, he found himself thinking dark, possessive thoughts about her—his physical nature at war with his higher intellect.

He took Don Giovanni by the schoolhouse, hoping that by now Patrizio had sobered up. But as the two men stepped inside, it was only to see the tables once again vacant of students and Patrizio once again passed out and snoring across the desk. At least there was no cask of rum present this time, Marco noted grimly, although the smell of soured liquor was heavy in the room.

He turned to his guest, who was eyeing the scene with a bemused frown. "Ah—I forgot that it is nap time for the children," he muttered.

"And for the schoolmaster as well?" Don Giovanni countered, inclining his head toward the snoring, drooling man.

"Yes—well, intensive learning can be so prostrating." With these words, Marco hastily led his guest from the building.

He took Don Giovanni past the fields, where both admired the robust cane plants waving in the island breeze. They continued on to a small stone building.

"This is our sugar mill," Marco explained. "In a couple more months, we shall cut the cane. The juice will be pressed from the stalks in the mill, and then the liquid boiled down outside over open fires." He pointed to a row of huge cast-iron pots. "Later, *La Spada* will bear our hogsheads of sugar crystals off to Charles Town to be sold through our factor."

Don Giovanni nodded approvingly as he gazed

about at the fields and prosperous cottages. "You have made a good life for yourself here, my boy, as well as a fine home for your niece." His smile turned thoughtful and he murmured behind his hand, "How do you think it goes with the young couple, eh?"

With great effort, Marco managed not to frown. "They seem to be getting on."

Don Giovanni elbowed him. "I would say they are highly compatible, no?"

"Perhaps so," Marco conceded.

Don Giovanni was still chuckling as they strode off again, and Marco reluctantly forced a smile.

"Will you miss the girl when she is with us in Venice?" Don Giovanni asked.

"*Sì*," Marco replied with much more vehemence than he had intended.

"Why don't you return with us to our homeland? Then you can see your niece whenever you wish."

And within a fortnight, I would have her committing adultery, Marco replied to himself ruefully. To his friend, he uttered solemnly, "I cannot return to Venice—not with the city's greatness so diminished by the Spanish and other foreigners."

"Has it occurred to you, my boy, that you cannot help your mother country by being here in the New World?"

It was on the tip of Marco's tongue to tell Don Giovanni that he was helping his countrymen by raiding Spanish shipping and thus aiding the English in their war against Spain, but he caught himself in the nick of time. Privateering was considered by most an ignoble provision, only a step away from outright piracy. Don Giovanni would never understand such a questionable activity.

He turned to his guest and said simply, "I have found my life here."

Gazing at the tropical splendor, Don Giovanni nodded. "I understand."

The two men were continuing down the trail when they almost collided with one of Marco's men, who bore a shrieking, giggling wench over his shoulder, her petticoats and legs flapping wildly. Marco groaned at the spectacle, while Don Giovanni appeared both taken aback and amused.

Meanwhile, the abashed pirate at once set the wench on her feet and smoothed down her skirts. Grinning lamely at the two other men, he explained, "Sorry, boss. The wench—that is, my wife—stepped into a bed of ants. Just trying to rescue her."

The woman, meanwhile, ruined everything by convulsing into giggles.

"Yes—well, be about your business, then," Marco told the man gruffly. As the two dashed off, wearing guilty smiles, he turned to Don Giovanni and shrugged. "Peasants. You know how it is. One tries to reform them, but . . ."

Don Giovanni wagged a finger at Marco. "I thought I spotted a few wild oats growing out in those cane fields, my boy."

Marco chuckled. "What can I say? We are in the tropics, after all."

Don Giovanni laughed heartily and wrapped an arm around the younger man's shoulders. "Now, my dear Marco, let us get back to that ravishing niece of yours, and my very fortunate son. Regarding the transfer of the dowry . . ."

EIGHTEEN

Toward sunset, everyone moved down to the beach. At one end, Marco had his men set up several folding Venetian chairs and a small gateleg table. He, Don Giovanni, and Claudio sat smoking, sipping wine, and playing cards, while Donna Flora lounged nearby, embroidering linen napkins for Seraphina and her new husband. Pansy lay crouched at Marco's feet, trying her best to feign invisibility in order to hide from the monster parrot Cicero, who was overseeing all from his perch high in a palm tree.

Down the beach, Christina and Vittorio walked together, followed by "Father" Giuseppe with a Renaldi daughter on either side of him. The scene was cool, brisk, dreamy, and beautiful. Beyond the promenaders, the sunset was glorious, a kaleidoscope of pink, gold, and orange rays slowly sinking into the sea. The pounding surf thudded in their ears as the mighty breakers flung huge cascades of spray into rock tide pools. Fingers of waves teased at their feet as the wind surged and whipped at their hair and clothing.

Jovita and Calista amused themselves by chatting with Giuseppe and throwing stale crusts of bread to the swooping, screaming gulls. Ahead of them, Christina and Vittorio spoke more solemnly.

"Tell me of your life in Venice," she urged him.

His expression turned wistful. "My family and I live in a grand villa on a prosperous vineyard out in the country. We also own a town house in Venice and a glass factory on an island near the city. We divide our time between our two homes."

"Your existence sounds quite varied and interesting."

He smiled. "It is. I think you will find our life in Venice to be most lively and diverse compared with your isolated existence here."

Christina was silent, feeling bemused. Vittorio's was a life of culture and civilization that she could only dream of—yet it was also meaningless to her. She could never tell him that she would be content to be stranded in the entire world alone with only one man—as long as that one man was Marco Glaviano.

"As I grew up, I was tutored by our priest, Father Giorgio," Vittorio continued. "I was provided a classical education—Greek, Latin, art, literature, and music—as well as my studies in catechism." Glancing at her hesitantly, he confided, "Naturally, I had hoped to devote my life to the church, but my father had other plans for me, that I continue our family-business dynasty."

"I see," Christina murmured. So she was dealing with a less-than-enthusiastic bridegroom, a man whose devotion would always be first to God and not to woman. While it might prove a little more difficult to lure Vittorio into her planned scheme, at least she need not worry unduly about hurting him when she later cast him adrift—after winning Marco over, of course.

"Does it bother you that you are destined to lead a secular life?" she asked.

Surprisingly, he flashed her a quick smile. "One can also serve God by becoming a good husband, father, and provider—just as my own father has done."

"That is true," Christina agreed, smiling back at him.

"And yourself, Christina," he went on. "What has it been like for you growing up here on this island?"

"Well, as you said, very secluded." Quickly, she added, "Although I had the influence of both a teacher and a priest, as well as Uncle Marco to set a familial example." Christina stunned herself by making her last statement with a straight face.

Vittorio was nodding solemnly. "Ah, yes. You were very fortunate to have such a fine uncle to take you in after you were orphaned at such an early age back in . . ." He paused to frown. "Was it Florence?"

"Er—yes," Christina stammered. She felt intensely uncomfortable with the subject matter, since Marco had told her little about the fictional background he had fabricated for her. "Of course, I was so very young when we came to the New World that I remember little beyond my life here on Isola del Mare."

Vittorio glanced over at the crashing waves. "I would think that it would be very enriching to grow up close to the sea, so near to the source of life itself. That is much our feeling in Venice as well."

She nodded, reflecting that perhaps this young man was not nearly as shallow as she had first assumed.

"Are you comfortable with the prospect of spending the rest of your life in a foreign country?" he asked tentatively.

"Oh, I am delighted," she assured him. "Uncle Marco has told me much about Venice, and I am eager to see it."

He appeared pleased by her response. "There are so many places I would like to take you to in the city—the opera at Teatro la Fenice, the Piazza San Marco, the Grand Canal, the magnificent bridges. As befitting the Worthy Ones, our family is often invited to the formal receptions and dinners at the Doges' Palace. There you will see splendor beyond your wildest imaginings—halls lined with gold, sculptures by Sansovino, as well as the holy paintings of Titian, Tintoretto, and Veronese. Ours is a most esteemed and cultured city."

"It does sound fascinating," Christina said.

"Then you will not be distraught at the prospect of leaving your home and your uncle?" he went on rather tensely. "I realize that this marriage was arranged without our ever meeting—"

She reached out to touch his arm. "Vittorio, I assure you that I am most content with the prospect of becoming your bride."

Appearing taken aback by her frankness, he blinked at her almost dazedly. "Yes, well—"

"And what are your feelings about the contract your father and my uncle arranged?" she pursued deftly.

He coughed, then said awkwardly, "Of course, I agree with my father. I think I shall be a most fortunate young man."

"Then it is settled," she said brightly.

With his brow furrowed and his mouth tight, he appeared less than completely convinced. "You must understand that if we do marry, our life will be largely based around family and the Church."

"Oh, but of course—I am most devout myself," Christina quickly agreed.

"That is what your uncle said," he murmured.

Christina had to struggle not to laugh. "Do not worry, Vittorio. As we become better acquainted over the next few days, you will quickly discover how utterly pious I am."

"*Buono*. Of course, my parents wish us to marry at St. Mark's in the Piazza."

She chewed on her bottom lip. "Oh—then they want us to wed in Venice?"

"*Sì*, that is my family's preference, since we must sail for home before long anyway. I had hoped we could return to Venice in time for the Yuletide festivals in December. We have already missed the *vendemmia*—the harvesting of the grapes."

"I see."

"Will you uncle be journeying back with us for the nuptials?"

"I doubt it," Christina replied, her voice edged with a trace of bitterness she could not quite contain.

They paused, and Vittorio leaned over to pick up a large, striking pink conch shell that blocked their path. Brushing off the sand, he solemnly handed it to Christina. "This bounty of our Creator is so *bellissima*. But not nearly as lovely as the lady I present it to."

"Why, Vittorio, I am charmed," she murmured. She fingered the shell and slanted him a happy look, while inwardly feeling delighted that she was winning the lad over that first, tiny bit.

At the end of the cove near the tide pools, the procession made a slow turn, and then the strollers proceeded back toward Marco and the others. Christina could hear the Renaldi daughters giggling as Giuseppe regaled them with the story of a troublesome goat that had once plundered his garden. As the group neared the card players at the other end of the beach, Christina deliberately slipped her free hand into Vittorio's. At first, her fiancé shot her a flustered look and his fingers trembled in hers; then he surprised her once again by clutching her hand tightly in his, and she had to marvel at the strength of his grip.

Down the beach, Marco could only stare at the obviously lovestruck young couple who now approached, smiling into each other's eyes and holding hands.

"Uncle Marco—look what Vittorio found for me!" Christina called out, proudly holding up the shell.

Marco continued to gawk.

"Marco, have you forgotten that it is your turn to deal?" Don Giovanni asked irritably.

By now Marco was so distracted that, as he tried to shuffle the deck, his less-than-agile fingers slipped and he sent a spiral of cards spinning into the air, a flurry at once caught by the capricious wind— impelling all three men to scurry about, mumbling curses and overturning chairs, as they tried to retrieve the scattered pack. Pansy, meanwhile, scampered off, thoroughly unnerved by the confusion.

Late that night, Marco sat on the windowsill in his room, sipping wine and staring out at the black, fathomless sky. Outside his window, the tropical foliage rustled in the breeze. The scent of honeysuckle wafted over him and he heard an owl hoot in the distance.

Pansy, snoring softly, lay behind him at the foot of the bed. But Marco could not sleep, for his mind still teemed with thoughts of Christina. All evening, the image of her holding hands with Vittorio and smiling at the lad had haunted him. Never had he anticipated what his own response would be when he saw her with the young man.

He had put into motion the plan to win her a better life, and now he had succeeded. She seemed very pleased with his choice of Vittorio, and ready to marry him and go live with him in Venice.

Dio! She would lie in Vittorio's bed, give her glorious body to him, bear his children! The lucky young dandy! As for himself . . . An unexpected anguish rent Marco through and through. Once she was gone, he would gaze out at the vast, star-dotted heavens and dream of her, imagine her in Vittorio's arms, while his own throat ached and his own arms were empty. Once she was gone, nothing would be the same.

He groaned and shut his eyes against the beauty that seemed so alien without her. Heaven help him. He had not realized how much the girl had come to mean to him, how hard it was going to be to give her up. Yet he was bound by his commitment to his mission, and his desire to launch Christina upon a brighter future.

In doing what was best for her, had he consigned himself to a living hell?

Across the hallway, Christina lay in bed, smiling in the darkness and feeling inordinately pleased with herself. Much of her suffering at Marco's hands had been vindicated today when she had paraded before him holding hands with Vittorio. The look of stark longing on his face had brought her the fiercest pleasure; watching him make a fool of himself fumbling the cards had amused her immensely.

He wanted her! She knew he did! And though he might not yet be ready to admit that he needed her—needed anyone—he would come around soon enough, and take her as his wife. Now she had only to torture and torment him a while longer by bedazzling Vittorio, and he would be doomed—he would be hers. Especially when she put her coup de grace into motion. What she planned for Vittorio might be wicked, but Marco had only himself to blame for forcing her hand and abandoning his promise to her. She might well have to risk losing her virginity to succeed—but she would win Marco over!

NINETEEN

Several days passed. Christina and Vittorio became better acquainted. Marco spent much time with Don Giovanni, the two old friends fishing, hunting, and playing cards together. Donna Flora and her daughters took long naps and spent many lazy hours at the beach, wearing huge hats and long dresses to protect their delicate skin from the sun's damaging rays. Giuseppe was frequently seen chatting with Jovita and Calista, or taking the two young ladies for strolls; the trio often served as chaperons when Christina and Vittorio walked around the island together.

While seeing Christina with Vittorio continued to torture Marco, he kept his emotions in check. His charade maintained its fragile illusion. There were awkward moments due to additional faux pas committed by the pirates—such as on Sunday, when Giuseppe's attempt to perform a Latin mass could only be termed a disaster; or on Monday, when

Marco and Don Giovanni stumbled over Ugo and Vincente having a spirited wresting match on the path to the beach; or on Tuesday, when the two men happened upon Francesco and his woman, both naked and cavorting wildly in a water barrel. But for the most part, the Renaldis continued to accept Marco's assertions that he and his confederates were sugar planters, and that Christina was his niece.

The ruse began to unravel one day at luncheon. Marco and his guests were busily discussing the wedding plans over white wine, fish soup, and sourdough rolls. The repast was again served by a taciturn Eunice and her assistants. Christina, sitting next to Vittorio, felt somewhat bemused when she noted her fiancé and the serving girl, Antonia, again exchanging shy smiles and furtive glances.

Don Giovanni was outlining the family's agenda and trying to persuade Marco to return with them to Venice for the nupitals. "We really need to begin our journey home within a fortnight," he explained. "I have neglected my business in Venice for far too long. As for the wedding ceremony, of course we could always have a small service here"—he paused to stare meaningfully at an obviously horrified Giuseppe—"but then all our friends and neighbors would miss out on the celebration. Besides should not the young couple marry in what will be their homeland? For centuries, many esteemed Venetians have married at St. Mark's in the Piazza. We will hold a big feast afterward, and every exalted family in the Golden Book will be in attendance, of course." He nodded decisively at Marco. "Thus, the most logical solution is for you to sail with us back to the homeland, *amico mio.*"

Marco was frowning and loosening his cravat. "I appreciate the offer, Don Giovanni, but I really cannot leave my duties here."

"What duties?" Don Giovanni scoffed. "The cutting and pressing of the cane? Have you not inferiors to see to such trivia? I would think that you have gone native quite long enough, my boy. Besides, you are actually going to allow your dear niece and sole relative to be married off with none of her family in attendance?"

Marco was appearing at a loss when Christina graciously intervened. "But, Don Giovanni, are not you, Vittorio, Donna Flora, and your lovely daughters all my true family now?" She flashed Marco a poisonous smile. "As much as I shall miss Uncle Marco, I shall hardly pine away if he remains here."

While Marco ground his jaw, Don Giovanni grinned at Christina. "But of course." He winked at Marco. "She is a jewel, this one."

"That she is," Marco muttered, his voice oddly charged.

Donna Flora was about to add a comment of her own when all at once everyone became distracted by the sound of loud, bawdy singing out in the hallway. Above the approaching din, Hesper's outraged voice could be heard, loudly exclaiming, "Get out of here, you drunken riffraff!"

"Marco, what is going on here?" a perplexed Don Giovanni demanded of his host as the commotion increased and there was a crashing sound out in the hallway.

Even as a bewildered Marco was struggling for a reply, half a dozen slatternly-looking women—led by Marco's former mistress, Rosa—staggered into the room, accompanied by half a dozen equally disheveled men. All twelve interlopers were shabbily dressed, sopping wet, littered with seaweed, and reeking of alcohol. The dozen were linked, arm in arm, in something of a chorus line, a couple of them waving empty kegs of rum as all belted out a very bawdy song. The group was followed by a glowering Hesper, whose beady eyes shot daggers at Marco.

At first, the mystified diners could only stare at the intruders. Marco was able to catch just a couple of lines of their obscene ditty—yet these were sufficient to curl his toes:

> Hike your skirts, wench, let us roll,
> Lash your sails to my love pole.

As the prurient lyric scorched everyone's ears, the Renaldis uttered a collective gasp of horror. Christina struggled to hide her giggles behind her hand. Marco groaned and raised a hand to his brow, while Giuseppe crossed himself and implored the heavens.

Meanwhile, the drunks were swaying to and fro as they launched into another ribald ballad, this time led by the Frenchwoman, Monique.

"Marco, who are these miscreants?" Don Giovanni demanded over the bedlam.

"I've never seen them before in my life," Marco shouted back.

But even as he uttered these words, Rosa de Leon broke ranks and staggered over toward Marco. Her heavy breasts jiggled in her low-cut, sopping-wet gown as she held her arms wide. "Marco, *mi corazón!* It has been far too long, my big, lusty stallion!"

And in front of the mortified Renaldis, Rosa grabbed Marco by the waistband of his breeches, yanked him to his feet, and greeted him with a lurid, sloppy kiss, all the while keeping her fingers indecently tucked at his waist.

A moment later, she released him, grinning saucily and licking her lips. He slid back into his chair, his expression stunned as he watched Donna Flora swoon into her soup, saw Don Giovanni spring up to help her, and observed Giuseppe trying to shield the eyes of the two stupefied and equally fascinated Renaldi daughters.

Christina, meanwhile, was staring murder at

Marco as a wide-eyed Antonia walked in with dessert. When one of the drunken men made a grab for the serving girl, she scurried away, lost her balance on the wet floor, then slid into the table and dumped her tureen of rice pudding all over the insensible Donna Flora. Vittorio sprang up to rescue the appalled Antonia and his mother.

Marco prayed that lightning would strike and put them all out of their misery.

Standing in the island schoolhouse ten minutes later, Marco still wished he were dead. What had happened in the dining room could only be termed a debacle—thanks to Rosa and her dissolute cronies. Donna Flora, still unconscious, her face gritty with fish soup and her fashionable coiffure ravaged by rice pudding, had been borne prostrate to her bed. Don Giovanni was now sitting with his stricken wife, while Giuseppe attempted to pray over the fallen matron. The other Renaldis had gone to their rooms shaking their heads.

As for Christina, Marco was certain the brat was now laughing herself silly over his failure. For, from the indignant look Don Giovanni had cast Marco's way as he carried his insensate wife from the room, Marco feared that all his well-laid plans to marry off his "niece" were now in a shambles.

At least he had managed to take charge of the interlopers. Since there was definitely no learning taking place on the island, Marco had ordered his men to herd all the drunks together and drive them to the schoolhouse. The dozen debauchees now lolled about before him at the various tables, singing another salacious chantey, while Patrizio snored blissfully in the background. Marco stood before the schoolmaster's desk, glowering at the degenerates; three of his lieutenants were posted nearby with muskets primed and cutlasses drawn.

From what Marco had managed to ascertain so far, Rosa, Monique, and the other women had convinced six Spanish fishermen from Havana to bring them back to Isola del Mare. Well, he would see to it that Rosa's scheme to return would result in failure—especially after she and the others had so humiliated him before his friends. He intended to be rid of all these unwelcome drunks as quickly as possible.

"*Silenzio!*" Marco commanded, and the rowdy chorus slowly died out, the drunks turning to regard him dazedly.

"Rosa, explain this intrusion!" he commanded.

She slanted him a sultry smile and rose. "*Mi corazón,* I missed you so—"

"Sit down!" he cut in furiously, dreading a repetition of her earlier kiss. As she sullenly complied, he went on aggressively. "You and the others were paid—paid well—to leave this island, and told never to return."

"That is true, but—"

"Now explain what the hell you are doing back here!"

"*Corazón,* don't be cruel," Rosa beseeched, pouting. "There was nothing for me and the other women to do off in Havana."

"Rosa is right," put in Monique, who coyly batted her lashes at Marco. "You were heartless to exile us, *mon ami.*"

"So we all decided to come back," Rosa continued, pausing to gesture toward the men, "and these Spanish fishermen offered to give us passage."

"Well, they can damn well give you passage back!" Marco retorted.

One of the drunken fishermen turned to Marco with a look of trepidation. "Oh, no, *capitán.* Our vessel, she is ruined."

At Marco's bewildered expression, Claudio stepped toward him and explained, "The man is speaking the truth, *capitano*. These drunken fools gutted their fishing sloop on Barnacle Reef. I'm betting the tide will pull her off and sink her tonight."

"Damnation!" Marco muttered. To Claudio, he ordered, "Then herd them all onto *La Spada* and dump them—oh, I don't know, at St. Kitts or Spanish Town."

At this directive, pandemonium broke out amongst the drunks. All of the men seemed to be talking in Spanish at once, and were seemingly horrified about Marco's suggestion.

"What is the problem now?" Marco demanded of Monique.

"You cannot send us to Spanish Town or St. Kitts," she replied. "The rest of the islands are quarantined with the plague."

"And you are lying," he snapped.

"No, *capitán*, it is true!" protested another of the Spaniards. "Even Road Harbor, she is closed. The British governor, he would not even allow us to stop to take on fresh water."

Marco groaned. To Claudio, he muttered behind his hand, "What are we to do now? There is no time to take them all back to Havana. I have promised Don Giovanni that *La Spada* will be available to take his family back to Beaufort."

Claudio shrugged. "We could always string the lot of them up from *La Spada*'s yardarm."

Unfortunately, the fishermen overheard Claudio's cynical suggestion. Amid exclamations of terror, all six collectively began to plead for their lives, three of them sinking to their knees and wailing supplications while two others brought out rosary beads and wept openly.

The emotional chaos became too much for Marco. There was nothing worse than a bunch of drunks getting religion. "Quiet!" he yelled.

The men at once complied, staring at Marco in awe

and fear. He was attempting to gather his thoughts when Patrizio emitted a particularly raucous snort. He turned to the unconscious man and bellowed, "Will you kindly shut up!"

Patrizio snorted even louder, then mercifully fell silent.

Marco scratched his head. "Where was I?"

The Spaniards exchanged confused glances, and several of the women giggled.

"*Capitán*," one of the captives interjected, "the others and me, we will sign on with you. Rosa, she tell us that if we just bring her and the other women here, you make us buccaneers like yourself." He thrust out his chest and grinned broadly.

Marco was fuming as he turned to his former mistress. "Rosa, for the love of heaven, what have you been telling these simpletons?"

She was literally purring as she looked him over. "You must forgive me, *mi amor*," she murmured huskily. "I am a woman in love, desperate to get back to you."

Marco threw up his hands and turned irritably to the Spaniard who had made the suggestion. "Get something through your dim-witted head. We are not buccaneers here! We are respectable sugar planters. Is that clear?"

"*Sì, capitán.*"

"Furthermore, even if I did need to sign on additional manpower, I could do without the questionable navigational skills of you and these other cretins."

At his harsh criticism, all six fishermen appeared so crushed that Marco almost retracted his words.

He turned in exasperation to Claudio. "I don't know what the hell to do with these imbeciles. I suppose for now, keep all twelve of them here under guard."

"*Sì, capitano.*"

He started for the door, only to have Rosa chase after him. "But, *mi corazón*—"

He whirled, bracing a hand on her shoulder to hold her at bay. "As for you, you conniving strumpet, stay the hell away from me! You have caused me quite enough grief for one day." Shoving her aside, he regarded the entire glassy-eyed crew one last time. "And that goes double for the rest of you. If you give my men any trouble, I'll have you keel-hauled, the lot of you!"

Amid new exclamations of dread, he stormed out of the building.

On the way back to the house, Marco spotted Don Giovanni heading toward him along the path. His old friend was grim-faced, and a feeling of impending doom gripped Marco at the sight of him.

"My boy, we must talk," Don Giovanni called ominously.

"Yes, we must. How is Donna Flora?"

"Conscious, but suffering from a most excruciating headache," came the cheerless reply.

"I'm sorry," Marco said as the two men fell into step together. "Indeed, my friend, I must abjectly apologize for the entire disaster in the dining room."

Don Giovanni shook his head. "I had thought that you had truly done something with your life, my boy. But after witnessing this scandalous exhibition in your very own home, now I cannot help but have doubts— grave doubts—not only about you, but about having my only son associated with your family."

As much as Marco could see his friend's point, he also fought a rising indignation at Don Giovanni's maligning Christina. "It is not fair that you blame my niece for my own failure," he pointed out in a tense, if controlled, voice.

Don Giovanni sighed. "That is true. Nonetheless, I must consider what is best for Vittorio's future back in Venice. After all, our family is among the Worthy Ones—"

"And my family is not?" Marco countered.

Don Giovanni slanted Marco a glance of mingled sympathy and admonition. "I can understand, as I have previously stated, your sowing a few wild oats, my boy. But a gentleman must always be discreet. Now you have brought disgrace to both our families through your association with these—reprobates—"

"I must explain that," Marco cut in quickly.

Don Giovanni's laugh was rueful. "By all means, please do."

For a moment, Marco felt at a loss. Then he carefully admitted, "The truth is, I did have a—liaison— with the woman, Rosa, in Havana. Over the years, I have been most discreet in taking my manly ease—so as not to set a bad example for my niece. I suppose the woman must have gotten the wrong impression from our brief tryst in Havana, for she persuaded half a dozen Spanish fishermen to bring her and the others here."

"And that is the entire story?" Don Giovanni asked skeptically.

"*Sì*, that is everything," Marco smoothly lied. "Furthermore, I have all the interlopers under guard now, and I give you my solemn word that they will not again harass you or your family while you remain on Isola del Mare."

Don Giovanni was scowling. "I am not sure, my boy. Donna Flora is ready for us to return to Venice even now."

"And you would disavow the marriage contract we have made for your son and my niece?" Marco asked, struggling not to betray his rising frustration.

Don Giovanni scratched his jaw and replied shrewdly. "It is a dilemma, my friend. Of course, the beautiful young lady will so *enrich* our esteemed family, but at this point, it may be difficult to assuage my wife's—er—severe misgivings."

Marco at once caught his friend's hidden meaning. Thoughtfully, he murmured, "You know, Don Giovanni, it occurs to me now that while we were discussing the dowry last week, I seem to have neglected to mention a few of the assets I shall be transferring to Christina's future husband."

"Indeed?" All at once, Don Giovanni's expression was one of intense curiosity.

"*Sì*. Perhaps we should talk more, you and I, and thereby come up with a fitting strategy to allay Donna Flora's reservations."

Don Giovanni grinned broadly and clapped Marco across the shoulders. "My boy, I am your captive audience."

Marco suppressed a cynical laugh. They both well knew who was being snared and bilked here—and it was definitely not Don Giovanni Renaldi.

TWENTY

Moments later, Marco headed back to the house in a very foul humor. He had left Don Giovanni at the beach, fishing with Claudio. The marriage plans would proceed, but only because he had consented to all but double Christina's dowry.

Not far from the house, Pansy, who had obviously been out prowling the jungle, fell into step beside her master. "I am a fool, am I not, Pansy?" Marco asked ruefully, pulling several cockleburs from the cat's thick black mane. "The indignities I have been forced to endure in order to get that little witch out of my hair! Never before have I offered to pay so much money on behalf of a female I will not even get to bed!"

Pansy panted and stared at her master with sympathetic golden eyes.

Marco was still scowling murderously as he and the cat ambled up the front steps and entered the house. He strode down the hallway with Pansy at his heels, intent on going to his room, having a few shots of strong whiskey, then napping off his ill humor.

Yet as Marco was turning a shadowy corner, all at once a slight, bearded man with dagger in hand leapt out at him, hissing a deprecation in Spanish and aiming his blade straight for Marco's heart!

Marco was so startled that he almost missed his opportunity to react. In the nick of time, he managed to grab the smaller man's wrist and deflect the blow. The knife clattered to the floor, yet his attacker's other fist came hammering down on Marco's recently healed fingers, provoking a cry of pain and rage from him as he was forced to release his assailant's forearm.

"Why are you doing this?" Marco demanded.

The quick, aggressive Spaniard only screamed a bloodcurdling curse and aimed a savage blow squarely at Marco's jaw—a jab the larger man just managed to duck.

At this, Marco's patience snapped. While his opponent was still spinning in mid-swing, Marco slammed his fist into the other man's gut, then punched him hard in the jaw.

With a groan, the Spaniard crumpled to the floor. As Marco stood breathing hard and staring at the unconscious man in perplexity, Pansy sprang on top of the assailant with a hiss of rage.

"Pansy, no!" he cried, stopping the cheetah just as her vicious teeth were about to clamp on the man's throat.

The cheetah growled, then dutifully leapt off her quarry. Marco sank down next to the fallen man. "Who are you and why are you trying to kill me?" he reiterated furiously.

But his assailant was dead to the world.

"Damn it!" Marco cursed, turning to Pansy. "We should have questioned the bastard before I knocked him out!"

Glancing toward the corner of the hallway, Marco felt a near panic encroaching on his already frayed nerves. *Dio,* he must get the man out of here before one of the Renaldis spotted him—and a fresh crisis ensued! The villain could awaken at any moment; he would need someone to guard him.

Marco dashed through the house and spotted Giuseppe scowling over a theology book in the library. "Giuseppe, come quickly! I need your help!" Marco called out in a tense whisper.

Giuseppe dutifully sprang up, and the two men rushed back to the hallway, where Pansy still stood guard over the unconscious man.

Giuseppe gasped and crossed himself. "Who is this, boss?"

"You tell me," Marco snapped. "The miscreant leapt out of the shadows and tried to assassinate me."

"Is he still alive?"

"*Sì.*"

"But how did he get in here?"

"Who knows? For now, you must help me take him to the sugar mill, and then you must assign a man to guard him. Perhaps when he recovers consciousness, we can question him."

"Sure, boss."

Marco leaned over and grabbed the man under his arms. "We must hurry now, and get this scoundrel out of here before one of our guests discovers him!"

"Yes, boss."

Giuseppe took the man's feet, and he and Marco quickly bore the assailant out the back door, through the garden, and into the woods. Pansy loped along beside them.

"Where do you suppose the assassin came from?" Giuseppe panted as they hurried along.

Marco stared at the man and shook his head. "He does not appear to be one of Rosa's Spanish fishermen—although perhaps he stowed away and came here on their vessel."

"Do you suppose Carlos sent him?"

Marco's frown was bleak. "That is precisely what I'm afraid of."

Giuseppe's eyes widened. "Then Carlos may have discovered the location of our hideout!"

"*Sì*. In fact, it is entirely possible that my enemy followed Rosa and those other bumbling idiots on their voyage from Havana. I must assign a crew to take *La Spada* around the nearby cays and coves, to make certain that Carlos's schooner is not lurking in the vicinity."

Giuseppe muttered a supplication to the heavens. "And what about security here on Isola del Mare?"

"First, you must order the lookouts to be doubled down at the harbor. Post guards around the house as well—but instruct them to be discreet. Tell them to pretend to play cards or to hide in the bushes. We can't risk alarming the Renaldis."

"*Sì*. And what are you going to do, *capitano*?"

Marco laughed humorlessly. "After we take our prisoner to the mill, I'm going to wring the neck of a certain Spanish slut."

"You had better start talking, and make it fast."

An hour later, Marco's mood had gone from foul to black. Just as he and Giuseppe had tied up the intruder at the mill, the Spaniard had regained consciousness. Marco had tried to question him, but the belligerent bastard had spoken no English, and thus the only response Marco had received was more blistering foreign expletives—and a spray of foul saliva spewed in his face.

Infuriated, Marco had left the mill. After grabbing a cat-o'-nine-tails from *La Spada*, he had yanked Rosa out of the schoolhouse, dragged her deep into the jungle, and cornered her against a mangrove tree.

Now he stood slapping the whip ominously against his thigh, while Pansy paced nearby, occasionally turning to hiss at the Spanish woman.

In the face of Marco's fomenting rage, a more sensitive woman—or a less foolhardy one—might have collapsed into sobs or pleas for her life by now. But so far Marco's attempts to intimidate Rosa had brought him only frustration. Despite several moments of intense interrogation, despite repeated threats of a savage thrashing, the maddening wench claimed to know nothing at all about the Spaniard who had just tried to kill him. Indeed, the Jezebel was smirking at him, leaning indolently against the tree even as he stood inches away from her with chest heaving and nostrils flared. Her impudent manner alone made him ache to break his own strict rule of never striking a woman and slap the haughty grin off her face.

"I said, tell me where the man came from!"

She shrugged. "*Quién sabe?* All this nonsense about assassins. I have no idea what you are talking about, or where the man may have come from."

Marco seized her arm. "He was Spanish—and you came here with six Spanish fishermen!"

Her gaze was brightly defiant. "So he was Spanish. So is the Cardinal of Spain. That does not mean he sailed here with us."

"Did you idiots even think to station a watch to make certain you were not followed from Havana?"

"Why should we?" she asked insolently.

Marco was so enraged by her impertinent reply that he actually drew back the whip. Yet she only faced him down with a defiant smile, as if to dare him to slice her to ribbons.

At last, with a formidable effort, he lowered the whip. "I take it, then, that you did not station a watch?"

"That is correct."

"Then you could quite easily have been followed from Havana to Isola del Mare?"

"Sì."

Marco's fingers clenched on the whip handle. "Get the hell out of my sight before I kill you."

She emitted a sultry laugh and looked him over greedily. "You could always punish me with your magnificent body."

"I could," he snarled. "But you would not survive it."

She arched against him. "**Are** you so sure, *corazón*?"

He shoved her toward the path. "Go peddle your wares elsewhere."

As Marco angrily propelled Rosa back to the schoolhouse, a self-satisfied smile curved her lips, and the sound of her throaty laughter filled the air.

TWENTY-ONE

Over the next few days, the courtship between Christina and Vittorio proceeded, if on somewhat shakier ground at first. The two again strolled the area near the house and talked, with "Father" Giuseppe and the two Renaldi daughters following them to ensure an air of propriety. Donna Flora recovered from her vapors and often sat knitting or embroidering on the front gallery. Don Giovanni spent more time with Marco, though the esteemed Venetian frowned a good deal of the time. Marco suspected that his old friend's stern visage was affected mainly for show, so as not to let on that he was entirely satisfied with the current financial arrangements. Indeed, during unguarded moments, Marco often caught a gleam of keen pleasure in Don Giovanni's eye—and he knew that his compatriot was mentally tallying up the vast fortune that would soon be transferred from Marco's control to the Renaldi family coffers.

The fact that he was being so thoroughly fleeced by his old friend was hardly foremost on Marco's mind. For one thing, he was still going quietly insane watching Christina and Vittorio together. Every time he observed them laughing on the jungle path, or holding hands in the courtyard, or talking quietly as they walked on the beach, he died a little inside. If only the girl did not appear so damned happy—the very image of the blushing, blissful bride as she clung to her future bridegroom's arm and hung on his every word. Part of Marco perversely hungered for Christina to be as miserable at the thought of leaving him as he was at the prospect of losing her. But no, she appeared to be captivated by Vittorio, and spent practically every waking moment with him!

Marco had other pressing troubles on his mind as well—for would-be assassins continued to pop up on Isola del Mare. The second one appeared the morning after he had captured the first. Marco was opening his armoire to select his clothing for the day when a small, dark man leapt out at him with dagger raised and voice hissing blasphemies in rapid Spanish. While caught off guard, Marco had wrestled with the man, the two hurling curses and swinging at each other, overturning the furniture and smashing vases. Finally, Marco had tripped the bastard to the floor and pinned the knife to his throat. He had demanded to know who his assailant was and what he was doing here, but the scoundrel's only reply was, "No hablo inglés." In disgust, Marco had taken the interloper off to be guarded at the mill. It had unnerved him that one of these devils had managed to get so far inside the house.

Later that same day, his men had to kill a third intruder whom they caught trying to slither into the house through Christina's window. Alarmed that the girl might have been hurt, Marco again doubled the watch, and ordered a guard posted at Christina's window twenty-four hours a day.

Then, the next morning, another near calamity occurred when Marco was walking down the hallway with Don Giovanni. As he led his friend around a corner, he was appalled to see two of his men ahead of them, grunting as they carried away the unconscious, battered body of yet a fourth would-be assassin. Marco was forced to spin around and all but collide with Don Giovanni, hastily leading his confused guest off in the opposite direction before he could spot the intruder.

Marco was deeply concerned by this sudden proliferation of assailants. He had assigned Francesco, who spoke both Italian and Spanish, to interrogate the captives, but so far they had not been forthcoming with information. Ugo had suggested staving or beating them until they spoke, but Marco refused to sink to such a level, not after his own father had endured the horrors of *la Inquisizione*. Marco did know that none of the prisoners came from the ranks of the Spanish fishermen—all of those dimwits remained under guard at the schoolhouse, although the women had been set free to roam the island, with a stern warning that they would be throttled if they came within fifty yards of the house or bothered any of the guests.

Regarding just who had sent the villains, Marco suspected that his old nemesis, Carlos, was behind the plot to do him and his confederates harm. He had a strong feeling that Rosa was involved, too. After all, she was Carlos's former mistress. Plus, she had just returned from Havana, which was definitely Carlos's playground. At the very least, Carlos had likely followed Rosa and the bumbling fishermen when they had left Havana, and had thus learned the location of Marco's hideout.

The fact that his mortal enemy had quite possibly

discovered the whereabouts of his base camp made
Marco feel very vulnerable. Isola del Mare possessed
only one decent harbor, but it would be impossible
for his men to guard the entire perimeter of the island. All Carlos had to do was to glide his schooner
in close to the island's blind side, dispatch his assassins in a longboat, and then hide his own craft in a
cove or lagoon of any of the nearby Leeward Islands.
Marco had sent out *La Spada* with a skeleton crew to
reconnoiter the area, but the brief voyage had uncovered no trace of Carlos's vessel.

Still, Marco suspected that his adversary was indeed lurking nearby, and was likely moving around
to elude capture. Ordinarily his response would have
been to load everyone onto *La Spada* under stealth of
night and quickly make for a new headquarters in
the Caribbean. But an evacuation was impossible as
long as the Renaldis remained here. What possible
explanation could he give his already suspicious
friends? That they must all flee because he was being
stalked by his mortal enemy, a Spanish pirate—who
sought to kill him because he himself was a privateer
for the English?

He could only hope that he and his men could
continue to apprehend the villains before someone in
the house got hurt. The Renaldis were planning to
leave with Christina in a few more days. If only he
could maintain a facade of normalcy until then!

On the day after the fourth intruder had been
caught, Don Giovanni fell ill. Donna Flora sent Marco
a message at breakfast that she would spend the day
sitting with her ailing husband, who had contracted
a bilious fever. Marco mused cynically that his old
friend was much more likely hung over, since he,
Don Giovanni, and Claudio had stayed up half the
night drinking and playing cards. He was hardly
feeling in the prime of health himself, but as a youn-

ger man, he tended to snap back more quickly from such sprees.

He began the day by checking on the various guards he had posted around the island. As he headed toward the northernmost beach, he came across four of his men burying two assailants near a salt marsh.

"Not again!" he muttered, glancing from the sweaty, filthy men digging the graves to the corpses that had been shrouded in strips of discarded sails.

"We caught them sneaking onto *La Spada* at dawn, *capitano*," Ugo told him as he heaved sand with his shovel.

"Did you have to kill them?" Marco asked.

"*Sì*. The bloodthirsty bastards charged us with their cutlasses drawn," explained Ugo. "They cut Vincente's arm badly—Patrizio is sewing him up now."

"*Dio*, what a disaster." Marco thrust his fingers through his hair. "Were you able to question them at all?"

Another of the crewmen shrugged. "One of them muttered, *'No hablo inglés,'* right before he died."

Marco groaned. "This is a nightmare! Pretty soon my guests will be stumbling over these graves."

"We will try to space them out properly," a third crewman replied irritably as he swatted at a mosquito.

"Yes, yes, I'm sure you are doing your best," Marco said. "Carry on, then."

He strode back to the house, wondering what in hell he was going to do about these troublesome scoundrels who seemed to be popping up in more profusion than the cane plants.

He decided he would go to his room and have a drink.

Christina sat with Vittorio in the courtyard behind the house. The two were huddled together on one of the stone benches as hummingbirds and parakeets flitted about and the fountain played its soft music in the background.

Cicero was perched on Christina's arm. She was scratching the parrot's head, while he affectionately chewed on her finger and squawked, "Bad girl!"

Christina chuckled. Was she a bad girl? She did feel perversely pleased that she had managed a few moments alone with Vittorio; she knew that Giuseppe and the girls would join them shortly, as soon as they finished breakfast.

So far her time alone with her fiancé had proved anything but exciting. He had spent the past ten minutes lecturing her on his proposed religious training of their future children. While outwardly Christina professed to be fascinated with the subject, flashing him frequent smiles and eager nods, inwardly she was dying of boredom. Even his appearance cloyed on her nerves, she decided—his perpetual formal velvet coat, frilly shirt, pompous hat, and powdered wig. She hungered to be around Marco, with his raw male appeal—Marco with his shirt hanging open, his hair whipping about his handsome face. And with Rosa, Monique, and the other loose women now back from Havana, she felt she had not a moment to lose in implementing her scheme to win him over. Every time she remembered Rosa luridly kissing him in the dining room, jealousy burned in her anew. A few times since then, she had spotted the wench lurking near the house and eyeing Marco covetously; with great restraint, she had managed not to tear after her and claw her eyes out.

She took heart from the great progress she had made with Vittorio over the past week. The young man was as stiff as a starched shirt and a hopeless prig besides, but by baldly playing up to his interests, she knew she had snared him in her web. He looked at her with much greater interest now, and he held her hand more frequently—although, to her dismay, he had yet to kiss her.

Christina was hardly disappointed because she *wanted* Vittorio to kiss her. On the contrary, she simply realized that she would never be able to attain her goal with Marco unless she first made Vittorio desire her. She had even asked him once, outright, to kiss her, but he had been mortified, insisting that such intimacy was totally inappropriate until they were wed. And much to her chagrin, he still seemed fascinated by the serving girl Antonia, and stared at the wench whenever she was around. Christina felt frustrated by this evidence of how tenuous her hold on her fiancé might truly be. At least, when she observed Vittorio ogling Antonia, she felt a little less guilty for making him a pawn in her own relentless game.

Now she nodded as Vittorio made some inane comment about the credentials of the priest who would one day instruct their children. She was about to murmur a platitude when all at once her attention was diverted by two separate flurries of movement. She saw Antonia emerge from the kitchen with two cups on a silver tray, and, nearby, she observed the curtain at Marco's window moving just slightly.

Vittorio, too, became distracted. He fell silent, staring avidly at Antonia as she approached with the tray. Christina inwardly cursed, her fingers tensing as she stroked the parrot. Suddenly, she wanted to throttle her obviously fickle fiancé.

The dark, lovely serving girl curtsied before Vittorio. "Sir, I thought that you and the lady might enjoy some tea."

Vittorio stood and solemnly took both cups, setting one down on the bench beside Christina. He smiled shyly at Antonia. "Thank you, signorina. You are most kind."

Smiling back and curtsying once more, the girl

turned and slowly moved off, amid a seductive sway of her hips which hardly passed unnoticed on Vittorio's part.

Watching her fiancé gulp as he gazed after the girl, Christina fumed. Cicero, sensing his mistress's agitation, squawked stridently and flew off. Christina stood to confront Vittorio.

"What is going on between you and that serving girl?"

He paled, turning to her in alarm. "What do you mean?"

"Are you in love with her?" she demanded.

"You are asking if I am in love with the maid? Certainly not!"

"Then why do you keep staring at her?"

A thoughtful smile pulled at his thin lips. "You mean you have not noticed?"

"Noticed *what?*"

Reverently, he murmured, "Why, Antonia is the very image of Raphael's Madonna."

Christina was appalled. "You mean you are lusting after the Holy Virgin? You have decided you want her instead of me?"

"Of course not!" he heatedly denied, his expression horrified. "I would not dream of dishonoring my parents' wishes."

"And that is the only reason you are marrying me, is it not?" she continued petulantly. "If not for the contract your father made, you would much prefer to wed that serving girl!"

"No, Christina! That is not true! Just because I admire the visage of a woman who resembles the Virgin Mother does not mean I am not devoted to you."

Christina glared at him, while again catching a flicker of movement at Marco's window. She realized that now was the perfect moment to press her advantage. Stamping her foot, she accused bitterly, "You do want her! I just know you do! You are only toying with my affections, and you will surely break my heart!"

Vittorio's countenance betrayed his growing exasperation. "Christina, you are becoming irrational. That is simply not the case."

Christina surprised herself by the ease with which she burst into tears. "It is!" she wailed. "You cannot abide me! You cannot even bear to kiss me!"

At this juncture, Vittorio had no choice but to do what any red-blooded male—even the most straitlaced—would have done under the circumstances. He pulled his disconsolate fiancée into his arms and kissed her.

Christina found Vittorio's kiss sloppy, unskilled, and far too chaste. Nevertheless, she was in heaven, her heart soaring with the knowledge that Marco was now observing her in another man's arms . . .

Marco was in hell.

He stood at his window, unaware that he was slowly shredding the curtains to bits as he watched Christina and Vittorio kissing so passionately out in the garden. *Dio*, to see her mouth on another's, when he so hungered to feel those lips on his own again!

When he had spotted them outside his window, he had rationalized his obsession to watch them, telling himself that he was thinking only of Christina's safety, that more assailants could be lurking in the bushes. Obviously, no peril hovered—save to his own, now decimated peace of mind! He had made himself no better than the demented old fellows who peeked in other people's windows and watched them make love.

Nonetheless, he could not take his eyes off the ardently embraced couple. Would they never stop kissing? he wondered, battling an insane urge to charge out there and pry the two lovers apart. Why did

Christina have to appear as if she were enjoying it so much?

Dio, he loved the little brat! He knew that now—even as the devastating realization shook him to the core of his being, making him more of a wreck than the ravaged curtains.

He felt so torn. He knew that marrying her off to Vittorio was the right thing to do. His conscience, his prayers, repeatedly confirmed this. Yet he still wanted Christina so! His arms ached to hold her.

And he was giving her to a pompous young whelp who could never love her as thoroughly or as well as he could.

At sunset, he was striding down the beach in a very foul temper.

At sunset, she sought him out.

Marco was startled when he saw Christina fall into step beside him. For the first time in days, she wore one of her simple white dresses, and her hair was down and free, tangling in the wind. Barefoot, with her shapely brown feet skipping through the sand, she appeared primal, virginal, and totally desirable.

"Christina," he greeted her gruffly. "To what do I owe the pleasure?"

"I wished to speak with you," she replied smoothly.

He glanced around in mock bewilderment. "What, without your lapdog fiancé in attendance?"

She shrugged, but mischief danced in her eyes. "Why, Uncle Marco. What do you have against Vittorio?"

"Nothing," he snapped. "He truly is a prince of a fellow, is he not?"

"He is the man you chose for me," she pointed out smugly.

"So he is."

"As a matter of fact, that is why I have sought you

out, *Uncle* Marco." She stretched her arms dreamily, then admitted, "I wanted to tell you that you were right."

This surprising admission stopped him in his tracks, and he glowered at her. "Right about what?"

"That I should choose a husband and leave this island. Really, I had never even realized how lonely I was until the Renaldis came here. Now I feel as if Don Giovanni and Donna Flora are my new parents and Jovita and Calista are my sisters." Eagerly, she continued. "As for Vittorio, he is such a fine, moral young man, and the idea of living in Venice with him does sound so wonderful—"

"Splendid, then," Marco cut in sarcastically, pivoting hard and striding off again.

She hopped into step beside him. "And knowing him has also made me realize that what I felt for you was only childish adulation."

He glanced at her sharply, blinking rapidly. "A very heartwarming admission. So everything is resolved, then. Why don't you get the hell back to the house?"

She appeared bewildered. "Uncle Marco, why are you so angry with me?"

He sighed, thrusting his fingers through his hair as he considered her question. What could he tell her? *I'm angry because I want you in my lap, dancing like a lovely sail upon my mast?* It was not her fault that he had set this chain of events into motion, and that it had succeeded. Hell, as far as she was concerned, she was only abiding by his wishes.

He forced a thin smile and reached out to brush a strand of hair from her brow. "I'm sorry. Actually, I think I have become preoccupied with the assassins."

Her eyes went wide. "Assassins?"

He nodded grimly, then confided in a low voice, "Please do not alarm the Renaldis, but armed cutthroats have been appearing here ever since Rosa and her confederates returned. So far my men and I have had to capture or dispatch six of the villains."

"Six? That is terrible."

"*Sì.*" He regarded her with sudden anxiety. "One of them was even trying to get into your room."

She shrugged. "If another should attempt to harm me, I shall kill the scoundrel. Giuseppe taught me well."

Marco could not contain a chuckle. She was forever the brave, defiant lioness, and this knowledge made his newfound love for her all the more painful. "I am sure he did." Clearing his throat, he forged on. "At any rate, I have doubled all the watches, since I do not wish our guests to meet with foul play—or even to alarm them unnecessarily."

"Do not worry. My lips are sealed."

Her lips . . . They had come to the end of the beach, and as both of them paused, he stared irresistibly at her luscious, inviting mouth and reached out to touch her cheek. A shock wave of tenderness bolted through him. *Dio*, she was so soft! Soft as a baby, yet all woman . . .

"You will be careful now, won't you?" he asked huskily.

She smiled. "I will. You are kind to show such concern."

"I have always been concerned about you, *cara.*"

Pride gleamed in her eyes. "Have you? That does not stop you from sending me away."

"Perhaps because I know what will happen to you if you remain here with me," he murmured ironically.

Her gaze flashed to his. "A pity I shall never know."

They continued to stare at each other, desire seeming to smolder in the very air between them. "You will have a good life in Venice, *cara*," he said at last. "Much better than here. That is all that matters."

"And what of you?" she challenged. "What will your life be like without me? Will you miss me?"

"I miss our being friends already."

"Just friends?" she asked poignantly.

Her words were a deliberate invitation, and Marco was anything but immune to it. With a groan, he clamped an arm around Christina's waist and hauled her slender body close, lowering his lips to hers. He drank in her woman scent, felt her sweet, hot breath on his lips, saw the rush of expectation to her bright eyes just before he claimed her mouth passionately.

Oh, how good she tasted, how long it had been since he had held her thus! Love and desire soared within him. She might belong to Vittorio now, but he would show her one last time what a real kiss was! He stroked her lips expertly with his tongue, teasing and retreating. He gloried in her low moan as she opened to him, and his heart felt near bursting as she curled her arms around his neck to make her surrender complete. He slipped his tongue inside her mouth, tasting her sweetness at his leisure, retreating, then plunging, ravishing. She kissed him back, running her own tongue over his lips and teeth, taunting him until he responded with barely repressed violence, crushing her against him and plundering her mouth. His hands ached to cup her hips, her breasts, until he realized that if he did so, he would not stop until she was pinned beneath him on the sand, her maidenhead breached by his driving heat.

When he abruptly pulled away, both were breathing convulsively. It was on the tip of Christina's tongue to demand to know why Marco had kissed her—but then she saw how unnaturally bright his eyes were, and she could only stare at him in anguish, her own heart twisting with longing.

"*Arrivederci, cara*," he whispered, turning and slowly striding away from her.

Watching his beautiful, towering body move down

the beach, Christina was trembling, her heart aching and tears spilling from her eyes. He had given up on her—he had given her to Vittorio!

Well, she would not! She would never give up until he was hers! Tomorrow, she would continue her campaign with Vittorio, and she would not stop until she had the lad precisely where she wanted him. If only she could attain that one goal, then Marco would not have a chance.

TWENTY-TWO

THE NEXT MORNING, AS CHRISTINA AND VITTORIO walked the beach together with Giuseppe and Vittorio's two sisters trailing behind them, Christina followed up on her plan to snare her fiancé deeper in her web. She once again complained bitterly, insisting that Vittorio did not really want to marry her and that he was actually enamored of Antonia.

Vittorio tied to reassure his petulant fiancée, claiming that he was devoted to her and to the marriage contract his father had made. He squeezed her hand and stared earnestly into her eye as he argued that he really did want her for his bride.

Behind the small group, down the beach, stood a tense, scowling, bleary-eyed Marco. He had spent a sleepless night agonizing over Christina, and now he felt doubly tortured as he watched the two young lovers converse so intently and gaze into each other's eyes.

After spending another excruciating moment

233

watching them, Marco had had enough. He muttered
a curse, turned on his heel, and strode off. Although
he had promised to spend the morning boar hunting
with Don Giovanni, he decided he would again ask
Claudio to serve as substitute host. As for himself, he
preferred to take *La Spada* out on a brief run to reconnoiter the neighboring islands for any sign of Carlos.
Indeed, it would be a privilege to get away from
Isola del Mare for a few hours!

Christina, some fifty yards away, had spotted
Marco standing down the beach, staring at them so
intently, then turning and striding off. Inwardly she
gloated over another small victory, while outwardly
she continued to feign a pout to Vittorio.

"Christina, are you listening to me?" he asked, exasperated.

She turned to him quickly. "But of course I am."

"Then why won't you answer my question?"

"What question?"

He heaved a frustrated sigh. "I said, what will it
take to convince you that I really do want to marry
you?"

Frowning at his query, she glanced over her shoulder to make certain Giuseppe and the girls were out
of earshot. All three appeared fascinated by a courting male frigate bird who was strutting around with
red pouch fully expanded, trying his best to impress
a hen crouched in the mangrove bushes.

Restraining a smile at the sight, Christina turned
back to Vittorio and whispered, "Come to my room
tonight."

"What?" he cried, thunderstruck. "Have you taken
leave of your senses? That would be scandalous, totally improper—"

"And if you are, as you say, devoted to me, then
you will risk it," she cut in vehemently.

"But why?" he demanded, clearly bewildered.

"Because I cannot know for certain if you truly do want me as your wife until you kiss me again."

He flung his hands wide. "Christina! If your uncle knew I was even contemplating such a treason, he would kill me."

"I must have another kiss before I can be sure," she insisted stubbornly.

"But why must you have it in your room?"

"It is the only place where we can be assured of privacy. We were extremely lucky, yesterday morning, to catch even a few moments alone in the garden before Father Giuseppe and your sisters joined us. I doubt we shall be so fortunate again."

Vittorio's gaze implored the heavens. "If I do this crazy thing and rendezvous with you, will you promise, no more arguments about marrying me? No more doubts about this serving wench?"

She affected a look of passionate sincerity. "There is no love without risk, Vittorio. If you are willing to gamble all to see me tonight, then I shall never again question your devotion, or the fact that we truly are meant for each other."

He nodded grimly. "Where is your room, then? And when do you wish me to meet you there?"

Christina almost could not contain her glee as she gave him her carefully prepared instructions.

At dusk, Marco was awakened by a sharp rap at his door.

He sat up in bed and groaned. Pansy, who had been dozing at the foot of his bed, shook her head, perked up her ears, and stared at him.

Marco recalled coming back to his room following his unsuccessful run on *La Spada* to search for Carlos. He had tumbled himself into bed, and now it was dark again. *Dio*, he had slept through supper!

The knock sounded again. "Who is it?"

"Giuseppe."

"Come in!"

Giuseppe, in his cossack, slipped inside. "I am sorry to disturb you, boss—"

"What is it?"

"It is the cook. She went on a tirade during dinner tonight, and now she refuses to prepare the lamb for tomorrow's Festa del Cristo."

"Ah, hell," Marco muttered, sitting up at the side of his bed and running his fingers through his mussed hair. "What brought on this revolt?"

"I am afraid Donna Flora criticized Eunice during the evening meal, asking her to take away the oyster stew and insisting that the last batch had made Don Giovanni ill."

Marco mouthed a vivid curse. "What next? Every female on this island is driving me insane!"

Giuseppe grinned crookedly. "Women are known to do that, boss."

"I cannot believe the cook is being so stubborn, with all I pay her! You go tell that spoiled harridan that she had better get back to her stove, or else—"

But Giuseppe was backing away, shaking his head as he pressed the flat of his hand to his heart. "Boss, I cannot tell that one anything. She refuses to speak with anyone but you."

"Madre del Dio!" He reached for his pants and boots. "I shall go speak with the witch myself, then!"

When Marco left the house minutes later, he looked most unkempt. Given his foul humor, he had not even bothered to comb his disheveled hair or to button the shirt that hung from his powerful shoulders. A ferocious scowl sculpted his handsome visage, and a shadow of whiskers along his jaw lent him an even more fearsome look.

He stormed inside the small stone kitchen, a short distance away from the main house. To his immense irritation, Eunice took no note of him as she sat on a stool reading what appeared to be a book of poetry.

The kitchen itself was in a shambles, with dirty pots and dishes stacked everywhere, the leg of lamb lying raw on the chopping block, and no pots simmering on the cluttered stove.

"What is this, woman?" he demanded. "Why are you not attending to your duties for tomorrow's feast?"

The plump, black-haired woman set aside her book and stood to confront him with a sneer. "So His Highness has finally deigned to come visit the scullery where we menials slave away."

"Why do you refuse to cook for my guests? With as much as I am paying you—"

"No one can pay me enough to be insulted as I have been!" she cut in. "In front of everyone—my serving girls and all your guests—that Italian she-devil accused me of poisoning her husband!"

Marco gritted his teeth. "That was most unfortunate. You see, the truth is, Don Giovanni was too much in his cups the night before last. In our culture, it is considered the height of bad taste for a man to get drunk, so I am certain that he lied to his wife to cover his own faux pas, and instead told her that the food had made him sick."

"That does not give the battle-ax the right to blame me!"

"You are right, of course," Marco said, trying his best to feign sympathy, while inwardly wishing the troublesome woman would simply shut up and go back to her cooking.

"No one appreciates me!" she accused in trembling tones.

Fearing that she was about to burst into tears, he decided to try charm. He flashed her a lusty grin. "I appreciate you, woman."

But her eyes flashed ominously and she held up a hand in warning. "Oh, no, you don't! I will have you know that I am a middle-aged widow with grown children, and I know all about the tricks of evil lechers such as yourself."

He could not restrain a chuckle. "Eunice, if you will simply be patient for a few more days, my guests will be gone—"

"No! No!" she protested in a fit of pride, setting her arms across her bosom. "I refuse to prepare one more morsel for those ingrates. As far as I am concerned, they can all starve."

"I shall give you another increase," he offered desperately.

"You could bring me my own treasure galleon, and even that would not persuade me!"

"What will it take to make you see reason?"

She glowered at him. "You do not really care about me or my problems. All you care about his having food on your table."

Marco rolled his eyes.

"Furthermore, you have no idea at all what is really involved with cooking!"

"Eunice, please! What is it you want?"

She balled her hands on her hips and stared him down. "If you and your guests want a meal on your table tomorrow, then you can start helping me."

"Me?" Marco was so stunned, he almost toppled over.

"Yes, you."

Near frantic, he pleaded, "I will go fetch another of the women to help you—"

"No! No!" she interrupted defiantly. "I will cook for tomorrow's feast only if you *personally* assist me."

He remained astounded. "Surely you jest."

She pointed to the sideboard and said imperiously, "You may begin by scrubbing those filthy pots, and then you can beat conch for the soup." As a vengeful gleam lit her dark eyes, she predicted, "You, my fine lord, are going to learn more about cooking this night than you ever wanted to know."

Marco could only stare at the woman, utterly flabbergasted, while she glared back with absolute determination.

"Well?" she prodded.

Marco threw up his hands. "Women! You will never rest, any of you, until I am in Bedlam!"

With a defeated curse, he trudged off to pick up one of the filthy pots.

Outside the kitchen window, Christina was eavesdropping, and giggling so uproariously behind her hands that she feared her sides would burst.

Her plan was falling into place perfectly!

First, before dinner, she had mentioned to Donna Flora that she was certain that it was Eunice's soup that had made Don Giovanni sick two nights past, and that others had fallen ill previously after sampling the cook's dishes. She had known that Donna Flora would then insult the cook at dinner, and that Eunice, being the proud woman she was, would rebel.

Now she realized that her scheme could not have produced better results. Marco would be busy in the kitchen for some time, appeasing Eunice—and giving *her* ample opportunity to put the rest of her plan into motion!

An hour later, Christina stood in Marco's room, wearing only a diaphanous pale blue gown and a wrapper. Her hair gleamed in the soft light, and her thick curls were interlaced with fragrant orchids.

A few minutes earlier, she had sneaked back to the kitchen window one last time. Feeling confident from the sounds she had heard that Eunice and Marco were finally finishing up, she had hurried back to the house and slipped a note under Vittorio's door as the two of them had arranged earlier. Then she had rushed to Marco's room with her gown and negligee,

hurriedly undressed, and put them on. Letting Pansy
out through the French doors, she had scurried
around tidying up the room, making the bed and
stuffing Marco's discarded clothing into the armoire
so Vittorio would not be aware of her ruse until it
was too late.

He should be joining her at any moment now, and
the prospect filled her with a thrill of combined fear
and exhilaration. As far as she knew, Vittorio was
still blissfully unaware that she had given him instructions to the *wrong* room! Oh, she could not wait
to see the look on Marco's face when he discovered
the two of them together. If the sight of her seducing
another man in his bed did not shake Marco out of
his resistance, then nothing would!

Oh, she was bad, depraved to her very soul to pull
such a dirty trick on both men. Yet, perversely, she
anticipated the coming drama with great relish. She
was a woman in love, and as far as she was concerned, ruthlessness was entirely in order.

Her excitement soared as she heard the soft rap at
the door. "Who is it?" she called in a whisper.

"Vittorio," came the equally low, tense reply.

"Come in."

He entered, and for a moment the two of them
could only stare at each other. Vittorio looked so different to Christina. Gone was his wig; now, for the
first time, she glimpsed his short, thick black hair,
and noticed how dark his eyes were. He wore a
white shirt and black trousers. Seeing him at last
without all his velvets and ruffles and folderols made
her realize what a truly handsome young man he
was—

Although, of course, he could never compete with
Marco, not in any way!

He in turn was staring at her intently, devouring
her curves, which the gown and negligee did little to
hide.

Hoarsely, he said, "Christina, I did not expect you to be—"

"Dressed to receive my future husband?" she cut in boldly. "Does it shame you to see me thus?"

"N-no, of course not," he managed, drawing himself up with pride. "Our Creator did not make us in His image to feel shame."

"I agree."

He stepped toward her, smiling slightly, and then she noticed that he was holding out an object in his hand.

"For you," he murmured.

Christina moved toward him eagerly and took the beautiful hand-painted porcelain cachepot. She removed the lid and gasped as she viewed the lovely loose pearls. "Why, Vittorio, they are exquisite."

"I bought them for you in Charles Town, and intended to have them strung before I presented them to you on our wedding day."

"How sweet. And I am proud to have them just the way they are. We can always get them strung later."

Replacing the lid on the cachepot, she moved away from him toward the bed, under the guise of putting her gift down on the night table. After doing so, she turned to him and said in a sultry purr, "Now, come here so that I may thank you properly."

He gulped, then started obediently toward her. When he took her in his arms, she wantonly arched her curves against him. He groaned and clutched her close, and his kiss, though inexpert, was urgent, just as she knew it would be.

It was a very dazed Vittorio who pulled back a moment later to stare at her. "Christina, we must take care here. We could easily lose control—"

"But I want us to lose control," she urged passionately. Kissing his jaw, she murmured, "Make me yours, Vittorio! Let there be no turning back between us!"

He appeared both horrified and fascinated. "But, Christina, we must not! There could be a child—"

"Oh, yes, that I would love, my darling," she whispered hoarsely. "If you give me your child, your beautiful, dark-eyed baby, then I can be certain that you are devoted to me." Insinuating her fingers inside his shirt and stroking his chest brazenly, she murmured, "After all, are we not soon to become husband and wife? Would it be such a sin for us to consummate our love tonight?"

With his nostrils flared and his chest heaving, Vittorio could only stare at the seductive enchantress. Then Christina sealed his fate when she stretched on tiptoe and kissed him. He crushed her against him and ardently kissed her back.

Within seconds, she was able to pull him onto the bed with her. In the moments that followed, Christina's mental state hovered between glee and panic. She felt an intense, vengeful pleasure at the thought of Marco's response when he caught her with Vittorio. But she had not counted on the fact that her fiancé was both young and virile. From the way Vittorio was now thrashing around on the bed with her—from the feel of his demanding lips on hers and the shock of his hardness pressing against her—he was rapidly become very aroused. Thus, dread hovered at the edge of her mind at the thought that this normally restrained young man might well dispense with her virginity before Marco even appeared. She was willing to risk these moments in bed with Vittorio in order to make Marco jealous and to crumble the barriers between them, but she could never condone giving her virginity to any man but Marco!

Fright threatened to consume her as Vittorio ground his mouth into hers and began boldly hiking

up her gown. She grabbed his strong fingers and
struggled to restrain him while thinking wildly,
Marco, where are you?

As he left the kitchen and returned to the house,
Marco was in a mood to make a human sacrifice—
and it would not be himself. He was exhausted, his
wrists aching from beating conch with a mallet, his
hands wrinkled from scalding dishwater, his ears
burning after listening to Eunice's diatribes and
cooking instructions for so many hours.

The lamb had been left to stew throughout the night.
Just as the cook had promised, Marco had learned
more about cooking this night than he *ever* wanted to
know. Indeed, never would he divulge to anyone everything that had transpired in that steamy kitchen,
and all he had suffered. It was too humiliating.

Back inside the house, he strode down the hallway
and threw open the door to his room. He stopped in
his tracks—

At first, he was certain that his eyes must be de-
ceiving him! But no, it was true—

Vittorio was in *his* bed, on top of Christina, his
hand brazenly touching her bare upper thigh as he
thrust his loins against her.

For a moment, Marco could only stand there, staring at the two of them and trembling violently. Rage
blinded him and fury threatened to choke off his
breathing.

At last anger goaded him into action. He stormed
across the room and yanked the young man off
Christina by the collar of his shirt. As Vittorio stood
tottering, gaping at Marco in horror, Marco demanded, "What in hell do you think you're doing?
Fornicating with my—my *niece* in my own room, my
own bed?"

Vittorio shook his head in disbelief. "This is your
room, sir?"

"Damned right it is!"

"But Christina never told me—"

"Christina evidently was *not* in a position to be talking!"

"B-but, sir, I had no idea—I mean, I never intended—"

Marco flung him away. "Spare me the revolting details of your intentions and get the hell out of my sight before I kill you!"

"Yes, sir."

Vittorio stumbled wildly for the door and dashed out, slamming it behind him.

Marco turned on Christina, glaring at her, magnificent in his wrath. "As for you, you conniving little—"

But she only smirked at him as she reached for the cachepot on the night table. Removing its lid, she calmly showed him the pearls. "Look what Vittorio gave me, Marco. Are they not splendid?"

Marco snapped, grabbing the cachepot and flinging it against the wall. An explosive crash was followed by the sound of pearls spinning off in every direction.

At last he saw the fear in Christina's eyes and he smiled. Vindictive pleasure and searing lust stormed his senses.

And then he was on her.

TWENTY-THREE

"Is this what you want?" Marco demanded, his eyes blazing into Christina's. "To play the whore, to give yourself to a man without benefit of marriage?"

With these harsh words, he savagely kissed her, his lips hot and bruising, his face rough with whiskers, abrading her soft skin. He held her in a bone-crushing grip, and a less intrepid woman would have been terrified at the rage vibrating through his huge, powerful body.

But, pressed beneath him in his bed, with the scent and taste of him inflaming her, Christina hardly cared what Marco said to her. She did not care if he hurt her, insulted her. All she knew was that at last he was *hers!* Joy soared in her heart that she had finally broken his restraint.

In the meantime, his hands were roving everywhere on her, his lips devouring her as he raised her gown and wrapper and boldly kneaded her bare breasts. The stimulation was unspeakably erotic to

245

her, making her break out in shivers, making her
ache to join herself with him. She managed to insinuate her hands between their bodies. She clawed at
his shirt, ripping off buttons, then caressing his
warm, muscled flesh. She heard him groan with pleasure.

Marco felt tenderness pulling at him, threatening
to tow him under. He fought off the enervating tide
of feeling and instead stoked the fires of rage, jealousy, and wounded pride that still threatened to consume him. She had insulted him as no woman ever
could, seducing another man in his bed. She had behaved like a strumpet, and he was going to see that
she regretted it. She might think she was beyond
shame, but she would soon learn otherwise. He
would shock and punish her this night for her brazen, hurtful behavior. He was just the man to do it.

He hiked her gown to her neck, and his mouth
boldly took her bare breast. He felt her shudder, and
glancing upward, he smiled at the look of sudden
uncertainty on her flushed face. Lust seared him as
he stroked her tautened nipple with his tongue and
whispered hoarsely, "Did you enjoy it when he did
this to you? Did it pleasure you to know that I would
get to watch . . ."

As much as Marco's hot mouth and skilled tongue
were driving her crazy, Christina managed to protest,
"Marco, Vittorio and I—we didn't—"

He pulled back and glared at her magnificently,
and was pleased to see fear widening her eyes.
"Don't make it worse by lying. I saw precisely what
the two of you were doing! Any woman who se-
duces one man in another's bed deserves precisely
what she gets!"

He demonstrated with a punishing kiss, his tongue
ravaging her mouth. Her smothered, fearful cry only
increased his rage and passion as his hand moved
between her thighs. He felt her wet readiness, and

madness threatened to choke off his breathing as he realized that her response could well be for another. That thought sent his hand determinedly to his breeches to free his teeming erection. He glared into her panic-filled eyes and pressed aggressively.

Her cry of pain stopped him as he met the resistance of her virginal barrier. At once he took her face in his hands and stared down at her questioningly. "*Cara?*"

Feeling the huge, hard tip of him impaling her, Christina reeled with a pain that was far from just physical. Tears spilled from her eyes. "I lied. I do love you!"

"Oh, *cara.*" Abruptly, all the anger in Marco died. Pressing his lips to her wet cheek, he felt like an utter bastard. Still, he managed to scold, "You have some explaining to do, young lady. Why did you try to seduce Vittorio in my bed?"

He drew back to hear her reply, watched her lower lip tremble, her eyes fill with new tears.

"Why, Christina?"

"To make you jealous, so you would love me," she whispered convulsively. "So you would do just what you are doing now."

He shut his eyes and groaned as guilt continued to assail him. "Oh, *cara.* I am not loving you. I am only trying to punish you."

Abruptly, he withdrew from her, and despite his previous ruthlessness, she cried, "No!"

He sat up at the edge of the bed, his body rigid with tension and sexual frustration, his heart aching with torment and regret.

She knelt behind him, kissing his strong shoulder, and he clenched his teeth in anguish at the feel of her wet mouth on his flesh, her soft, naked thigh pressing against his bare back.

"Marco . . ."

His voice was very rough. "I think you had better go, Christina."

She reached around him, taking his swollen maleness in her fingers. "Please do not make me leave. I want you."

He shuddered violently.

"I'm sorry. Please love me now."

While Marco's emotions remained torn, his manhood had already hardened to a shaft of agonized steel in her tormenting fingers. Yet it was ultimately her apology, the abject tears in her voice, that slayed him. After what he had just done to her, she was apologizing to *him*?

A raw cry escaped him. His arm whipped around and caught Christina's slim waist. He pulled her into his lap and buried his face in her fragrant hair. And then his lips seized hers in a devastatingly tender kiss.

Feeling his hot mouth on hers, his tongue driving deep and bold, Christina was in heaven. She kissed him back with all the love welling in her heart.

Pausing only to pull off his boots, Marco tumbled her back on the bed. Some distant voice warned him that he must stop, that this was madness, yet he was powerless over the need consuming him. Never had he so hungered to possess a woman. He was near bursting for her, on fire. Even as he eased up her gown, she eagerly pulled it off. He knelt between her spread thighs, running his large hands, his fervid gaze, over her gorgeous body—her exquisite face, her lovely hair falling bright and free over her aroused breasts, her flat belly, and her long, supple legs. His burning gaze lingered for a long moment between her thighs as he caressed the mound of silky hair, then dipped his finger lower to touch the portal he would soon lovingly breach. He heard her soft gasps of arousal and glanced upward to see her staring at him adoringly, her eyes dilated and her lips parted. The expression of utter trust and love on her face was almost more than he could bear. He lay on top of her, kissing her mouth, her lovely smooth throat, then moving lower, taking her nipple with his teeth.

"I've wanted to do this for so long, *cara*," he whispered urgently. "It feels like forever."

"I've wanted you to do it forever, darling," she whispered back.

The word *darling* excited Marco as no aphrodisiac ever could. He sucked the tip of her breast into his mouth and flicked his tongue over her taut nipple.

Christina squirmed in delight, drawing her fingers through Marco's thick, shiny hair and arching her breast eagerly into his mouth. He felt so wonderful on top of her, with the warm flesh of his massive chest crushing her belly and his mouth firmly latched onto her aching nipple. She wanted him so badly, it was difficult to breathe. She felt his hand slipping between her thighs again, his finger sliding inside to prepare her, while his rough thumb moved higher, finding and stroking the tiny bud that sprang to life so eagerly at his touch. The stimulation was so acute that Christina gasped wildly, writhing to get away. Yet Marco held her firmly, his mouth smothering hers again as his skilled hand continued to torment and tease, arousing her to a fever pitch, until she actually hurt from wanting him and was left begging him to take her, moaning his name.

He heard her woman's plea. He quickly shucked off his breeches, then his hair-roughened thighs spread hers wide as his rigid shaft eagerly sought out her small crevice. He paused to give her a moment to relax, planting soft kisses all over her face and then lingering at the side of her sweet mouth.

"Kiss me now, *cara*," he whispered. "Kiss me hard."

She fastened her lips on his and sucked his tongue

deep inside her mouth. The brazen invitation was too
much for Marco to bear. Heaving a mighty groan, he
dug his fingers into her hips, lifting her as he shattered the fragile barrier. He felt her teeth sink into his
lip, heard the soft sob in her throat, but she did not
pull away.

The hot, wet tightness of her sent his desires spinning out of control. She was irresistible, so warm and
sweet and eager, and he devoured her like a starving
man would, burrowing deeper into her velvety, snug
sheath, until he thought he might die at the pleasure
of joining himself with her.

Christina felt the burning flash of pain as Marco
drove into her, followed by the incredible pressure of
him filling her until she was taut and throbbing, then
filling her even more. She clung to him in a frenzy of
unbearable pleasure. Her heart was beating madly, her
breathing was sharp and out of control, and she was
bursting with him. She caught a glimpse of his beautiful face, the features so tightly gripped by passion, and
never had her love for him burned so brightly in her
heart. Never had she felt anything as glorious as this
intimacy, this melding, this joining of two hearts and
bodies and souls. Nibbling at his jaw, she reached
down, sinking her fingernails into his hard, smooth
buttocks, then cried out when he responded with solid,
rocking thrusts and rapacious kisses.

Marco plunged into her repeatedly, powerfully, in-
undating them both in passion's heat, propelling
them both past all barriers or restraint. When he felt
Christina's fingers relax against his buttocks, felt her
hips arch upward to take him, he lost control, pounding into her with the riveting strokes of his climax
until her soft sobs sent him tumbling over the edge
with her, and spiraling to rest against her womb.

She slept, and after withdrawing from her gently,
Marco pulled on his breeches and went to sit on the

windowsill. He stared at her, naked and so glorious on his bed. He watched her flip over onto her stomach, until she lay with her hair spread wide across the pillow, her beautiful body bathed in moonlight. With considerable restraint, he managed not to go over to her and nibble at the delicious curve of her hip.

Lord, what had he done? He had fallen right into the little temptress's trap, fallen straight into the arms of heaven . . .

He groaned. Never before had being with a woman jolted him so. How would he ever give her up?

As if his thoughts had somehow reached her, she stirred, smiling at him sleepily from across the room. He patted the windowsill beside him and grinned back. He watched her reach for her wrapper and don it. Her movements were gingerly as she got out of bed, and tenderness swept him at the thought that her body now bore the mark of his lovemaking.

She crossed the room in the diaphanous wrapper, looking as innocent and delectable as a Botticelli nymph.

He reached for her, pulling her down into his lap and kissing her ardently.

"You are sore, *cara?*"

"Oh, yes," she replied ruefully.

They lay there for a long moment with her body positioned over his, the moonlight pouring down upon them. Beyond the window, the breeze stirred the tropical foliage, wafting the sweet night air over them.

Marco pressed his lips to her temple and reached down to massage her lower belly. "Does that help?"

"I am not sure it helps," she replied breathlessly. "It makes me want you again."

He chuckled and continued his slow caress. Yet his voice held a slight tremor as he murmured, "I cannot believe the lengths to which you went to get my attention tonight. So that entire, passionate scene with Vittorio was done simply to make me jealous?"

"Yes." She smirked at him. "And I succeeded, didn't I?"

"You did. And you are a very bad girl, *cara*."

She turned her rapt face up to his. "Am I?"

"Except when you are good," he teased, and kissed her again.

They snuggled together for a moment, then he sighed. "Oh, *cara, cara*. What a muddle you have gotten us into."

She laced her fingers through his and spoke tremulously. "Have I? Is it such a terrible muddle?"

"Horrible." He nuzzled his lips against her brow. "But let us not think of that tonight."

She twisted around to stare up at him.

Catching her earnest, vulnerable expression, he tugged on one of her curls. "What is it?"

Her eyes had turned strangely bright. "It is just that—you are so beautiful."

Tenderness sculpted his features. "So are you, of course."

Straddling his body with her knees, she looked him over intently. "But you are incredible. The way the moonlight hits your hair. And your face—your wonderful eyes, your strong nose, your magnificent mouth." She paused to kiss that handsome mouth, then murmured against his lips, "I have never seen a man's visage so perfect."

"*Cara*," he scolded, "you are about to get yourself in deep, deep trouble."

Yet she was heedless, drawing her gaze down his body as she boldly caressed him. "Your chest and shoulders are so muscled, so powerful. I love even those faint scars you received in battle." She kissed the old injuries to demonstrate, and he groaned.

He tangled his fingers in her thick mane of hair,

but only half tried to restrain her. "You, my lady, are about to be impaled in my lap," he teased.

That comment brought a smile to her lush mouth as she stroked his thighs through his trousers. "Your legs are so splendid. I loved the rough feel of them as they drew mine apart—"

Marco was no saint. He grabbed Christina around the waist and drew her upward so she could feel precisely what she was doing to him. "My legs are not all that is powerful."

"I know," she whispered raptly, drawing a moan from him as she playfully slid off his lap. Again straddling his thighs, she unbuttoned his breeches. "Here you are beautiful, too—"

"*Cara.*"

"Even if you are huge."

"Huge?" His eyes danced with laughter.

She smirked at him. "I thought you were going to rip me in two, but I forgive you."

"Do you?"

She stared down at him unabashedly, causing him to become even harder before her very eyes. "Do all men swell up like this when they are aroused?"

He laughed heartily and touched the tip of her nose with his finger. "Nice girls do not ask questions like that."

"I should wager nice girls do not end up in your bed."

"You are the first."

"Am I?" she asked dreamily.

And then she leaned over and kissed him there.

A mighty groan rumbled from him, and the next thing Christina knew, she was in his arms and he was carrying her back to the bed.

"*Cara,* I fear you are not going to forgive what happens next."

By now Marco was in so much pain that he did little more than fling her onto her back on the bed and position himself between her spread thighs. Yet she was so eager, stroking him as she wrapped her long, slim legs around his waist. He plunged into her, watched her toss her head from side to side, heard her cry out softly as she absorbed his full length.

He fell upon her, kissing her greedily.

"Marco?" she murmured.

"Yes?" he murmured back distractedly as he thrust into her.

"I don't think I mind—"

"Mind what?"

"That you are huge. In fact, I think I shall get used to it."

That comment sent him spiraling into her, harder, deeper, faster, until he shuddered in ecstasy.

TWENTY-FOUR

"**A**RE YOU GOING TO MARRY ME NOW?"

It was barely dawn the following morning, and Marco was at his mirror shaving when Christina abruptly asked her question from his bed. As the words impacted him, he nicked himself and cursed vividly. Wiping off the shaving soap, he turned to stare at her and desire stormed him anew as he viewed the seductive temptress in his bed. She was naked, her mane of wheat-colored hair wild and disheveled, the sheet draped about her midsection. With the rosy light from the French doors pouring over her delectable shoulders and upturned breasts, she was the most enthralling sight he had ever seen—the most desirable woman he had ever had in his bed. Regret seared him that he still could not give this glorious creature what she most wanted and needed.

"Well, are you going to marry me?" she prodded impatiently.

255

To himself, Marco replied, *I am going to marry you off before I succumb to you again, and quite possibly get you pregnant.* To her, he said sadly, "*Cara,* I just do not see what has changed."

From the bed, Christina glared at him. Marco stood across from her, looking devastatingly handsome in his dark trousers and, especially, with no shirt. Yet she could not believe what he had just said to her! After all that had transpired between them last night, how could he cast her aside this way?

Her chin came up proudly. "Last night did not change anything for you?"

He took a step toward her. "Christina, I am still making war with the Spanish. And I still cannot give you what you need."

"You did last night."

She watched a muscle twitch in his jaw, and his voice vibrated strangely. "I feel you would be better off in Venice."

"Then take me there."

Marco stared at her, so proud and tempting. Never had he wanted so much to grab her and kiss her, to drive himself into her until she cried out with pleasure. Instead, he clenched his fists and said miserably, "I can't."

She flounced off the bed, dragging the sheet with her. "You mean you won't."

"If you prefer, then I won't," he said tightly.

"You aren't willing to give up your other women, are you?" she accused bitterly.

"Christina, it is not a matter of other women. You know damn well how I feel about our marrying as long as I remain a privateer. I just want what is best for you—"

"Was it best for me that you took my innocence last night? And now that you have ruined me, you are merely going to abandon me to Vittorio?"

Anger sparkled in his eyes. "So now I ruined you last night? I thought we made love."

"If we had made love, you would stand by me. Instead, it is clear that you only wanted to take advantage of me last night."

"I took advantage of you?" he repeated incredulously. "You are the one who was brazenly seducing another man in my bed, and now I have taken advantage of you?"

She moved angrily toward him. "How do you think Vittorio will feel about having a bride who is soiled goods?"

"Soiled goods?" He laughed ruefully. "I doubt that pup is worldly enough to know the difference."

She slapped him.

He grabbed her hand and glared at her. "You had better leave before I respond in kind, or before the others discover we have spent the night together."

"Heaven forbid!"

Hastily wrapping herself in the sheet and grabbing her clothing, Christina stormed from his room, slamming the door, and Marco cursed in helpless frustration.

That day, the atmosphere remained strained between Marco and Christina as they again visited with the Renaldis. The guests seemed to note the resentful glances that "uncle" and "niece" frequently exchanged. Vittorio in particular acted jumpy following last night's debacle, spilling his tea at breakfast and tripping over his own feet when he left the room. The unfortunate lad tried whenever possible to avoid Marco's eye and even his presence.

Early that afternoon, as Vittorio and Christina strolled along the beach in the crisp air and early fall sunshine, he raised the subject of the disaster. Glancing behind them to make certain that "Father" Giuseppe and the girls were out of earshot, he asked tensely, "Christina, why did you deceive me last night and give me directions to your uncle's room instead of to your own?"

Christina frowned in sudden uncertainty. Vittorio had raised a very natural and inevitable question, but one that, given her own worries, she was ill-prepared to answer.

She shrugged. "I suppose I did it as a joke."

"A joke?" He appeared incredulous.

"I was angry at Uncle Marco and I wanted to teach him a lesson."

"Some lesson—at my expense! It is a miracle that your uncle did not kill me."

"I am sorry," she admitted distractedly. "I suppose I did not really think things through."

"I cannot believe you did such a thing as—as simply a prank!" Vittorio was shaking his head in disbelief. "Does your uncle still want us to marry?"

Christina glanced at him sharply. "I should think that Uncle Marco would be very angry with you if you backed out of our arrangement now."

"What if my parents should discover what happened?" he went on in a low, urgent tone.

"There is no one to tell them—unless you do." When his response was to grind his jaw in silence, she continued impatiently. "Very well, Vittorio. Speak your mind."

He gestured in frustration. "It is just that, after last night, I cannot help but have doubts about you, Christina. I had thought you were a most serious and devout young woman. But now this . . ."

Christina was losing her patience. "Very well, I shall admit it! I acted impetuously, even recklessly, and I do apologize. It will never happen again. There—are you satisfied?"

He sighed resignedly. "I suppose you are right and that our only recourse now is to marry as planned."

"I agree," Christina said bitterly. "Indeed, I cannot wait to leave this island."

At dinner, more furtive, angry glances were exchanged between Marco and Christina, but somehow everyone managed to survive the meal.

Later that night, as Christina stood in her room in her nightgown, brushing her hair while she prepared for bed, she struggled to fight off tears as she considered Marco's cruel behavior. How could he love her so passionately last night and then cast her away? Well, she would not give up—she simply would not. She would somehow make him love her again—she would tear down his barriers if it killed her.

With her resolve firmly in place, she was putting down her brush when suddenly, she was grabbed from behind! While startled, she also found herself frantically hoping that it was Marco who had seized her, that he had come to her again. But a hasty glance into the mirror revealed the terrifying reality that she was caught in the grip of a slight, bearded man with a knife in his hand. A sliver of fear impaled her as she realized that this was surely another of the cutthroats Marco had mentioned. And he was thrusting his dagger straight toward her throat!

Christina grabbed her attacker's wrist and struggled to deflect the dagger while shouting desperately, "Marco! Help me! Please!"

Meanwhile, her assailant was screaming deprecations in rapid Spanish and shoving the knife, with increased pressure, toward her neck. Gasping for breath as she fought with the strong, wiry man, Christina realized she could easily knock him off-balance, flip him over her hip, and shove the knife into his belly. Yet she held out, hoping that Marco might still rescue her, willing to risk her very life to bring them together again. She continued to cry out his name while praying that he would come before this animal killed her.

At last, the door to her room crashed open and Marco loomed there. She caught a brief, electrifying glimpse of his face—white with fear and rage—and a split second later, the Spaniard was yanked off her. Christina backed away as the two men fought over the knife. Marco finally wrenched the knife away from the smaller man, punched him in the jaw, and then, as the assailant staggered toward him, Marco banged him over the head with the handle of the knife. The villain crumpled to the floor.

As Marco caught his breath, Pansy sprinted into the room, charged over to the unconscious man, and hissed viciously.

Christina gasped and stared at Marco.

He was breathing hard and gazing at her with deep concern. "*Cara*, are you all right?"

She nodded, stepping forward to soothe the spitting cheetah.

He strode over to the window. "Where is that imbecile who is supposed to be guarding your room?" He paused and bellowed, "Ugo!"

One of Marco's men popped up unsteadily from the grass. He squinted at Marco confusedly, rubbed a head bulging with a goose egg, and grimaced. "I'm sorry, boss. Someone sneaked up behind me."

"The same cutthroat who almost just killed Christina!" Marco shouted back. He strode to the middle of the room, muttering, "What in the name of heaven is going on here? I cannot make it through a single day without battling at least half a dozen assassins!" Gently, nudging Pansy out of the way, he picked up the unconscious man and bore him back to the window. Shoving the man through the opening into Ugo's arms, he ordered, "Here—take him to be guarded at the mill with the others."

"Yes, boss." Grunting, Ugo staggered off.

Marco pulled the curtains closed and turned back to Christina. His expression was eloquent with worry. "Are you certain you are all right?"

Her lower lip quivered. "Why do you care? You hate me!"

He started toward her, his expression miserably torn. "No, *cara*, that is not true. I just want you to have a better life."

"If you did, you would marry me," she asserted.

Next to her, he paused, his eyes bright with anguish. "Christina, you are still shaking. Are you certain he did not hurt you?"

"He almost slit my throat!"

He touched her arm. "You are frightened, aren't you, darling?"

She willed the helpless tears to come. "Yes!"

The rest happened so quickly, it set them both reeling. Suddenly, she was in his arms and his lips were crushing hers. "*Cara mia*," he whispered tormentedly into her mouth. "To think that you could have been killed, my sweet darling . . ."

He swept her up into his arms and bore her quickly to the bed. Her head spun with the dispatch with which he hiked her gown to her neck. Then his hot, wet mouth took her breast, and he thrust himself into her so hard and deep that she could not bear the pleasure. His strong hands dug into her hips, lifting her into his exquisite plunder, holding her inexorably to his utter possession.

With a cry of rapture, Christina gripped his rough face with her hands, drawing him upward to take her hungry, trembling kiss. Her fingers ripped open his shirt, bringing his hard, warm chest crushing down on her aroused breasts. His thumb settled between her thighs, relentlessly stroking her as he drove her toward her climax. Christina's rapture was so intense, she could not seem to breathe. Her hips moved with his, intensifying the friction and pressure for them both, reducing them to helpless moans. She tangled her fingers in his wild mane of hair and held his face to hers, uttering small, sharp sobs as he pushed them both into the vortex of hot, shattering pleasure . . .

After he poured his seed deep inside her, Marco could only stare down at her, feeling stunned and humbled by what had just transpired. Christina's face had been abraded by his whiskers, her lips were bruised by his kisses, and she was staring up at him with such love. He had not intended for this to happen, but, *Dio*, what ecstasy she had given him again! Tenderness welled in his heart and brought his loins surging to life once more. He knew that to take her again this night would be a mistake—

A mistake he was surely about to make.

Indeed, he was leaning over to claim her lips when he paused, bemused, at the sound of purring. He felt something wet and cold on his back. He twisted around to see Pansy with her head propped on the edge of the bed, staring up at him with her huge golden eyes.

He chuckled. "Pansy, what do you think you are doing?"

The cheetah purred.

Christina giggled. "She was so quiet that we forgot about her. I guess she is happy to see us together."

"Hah!" he cried. He shook a finger at the cheetah. "Pansy, you are a voyeur."

Pansy purred all the louder.

Still laughing, Marco turned his attention back to Christina. He stroked her flushed cheek and stared at her tenderly. Why was it he could not leave her alone? What was this strange powerlessness he felt around her? He must love her—nothing else could hurt this much and yet feel so wonderful. He wished the night could last forever—and take away with it all the barriers that prevented them from having a future together.

"Come with me to the beach, *cara*," he whispered.

"To the beach?" Her eyes widened; then an impish grin settled in. "Won't it be dangerous?"

"Pansy will protect us," he assured her solemnly.

"What if someone sees us?"

He winked at her. "Let's risk it."

She glowed with happiness.

They dressed quickly, Christina donning a loose shift, Marco throwing on his breeches and a shirt now bereft of buttons. He grabbed his cutlass, and then, with Pansy sprinting ahead, they hurried down to the beach, holding hands and laughing like two children as they raced barefoot along the moonlit trail.

Wanting a secluded spot to make love to her, Marco led her to a rock tide pool. With Pansy standing guard on a cliff above them, they sat together at the edge of the pool, dangling their feet in the bubbly water as the spray drenched them and the cool breeze caressed their bodies. The silvery ocean beyond them was glorious, the palms and tropical foliage behind them rustling softly.

Marco leaned over to kiss her, then chuckled, touching the tip of her nose. "I think you have been a very bad girl again, *cara*."

"Me?" she replied irately. "Who just threw me down on my own bed and ravished me?"

He shook a finger at her. "Who played the helpless victim tonight? You forget that I have seen you training with my men, *cara*. You are utterly ruthless. Indeed, you could have easily disarmed and killed that villain yourself."

"Then why did I not?"

"So I would charge in to rescue you, of course."

"And why did you intervene?"

"Because at the time, I thought your life was in

danger. Now I must wonder if I am not the one who was truly in peril."

"Ah, yes—I put you through such unspeakable agonies just now," she teased, wrinkling her nose at him.

"And I should probably strip off your shirt and give you a thorough spanking," he taunted back.

She smirked at him. "Every time you threaten to spank me, Marco, you really want to do something else to me."

All at once his gaze turned smoky, and he tenderly stroked her lips with his finger. "I always want to do that with you, *cara.*"

She took his large, strong hand and kissed it. "Always?" she whispered achingly, holding his palm against her damp cheek.

She looked so adorable, Marco almost could not bear it. He caught her closer with a groan. "Let us not think of 'always' tonight. Let us just enjoy each other—and this moment."

"But, Marco, sooner or later, we must—"

Her protest was smothered by a drowning kiss.

"Strip off your shift," he uttered hoarsely. "I want to see all of you."

"Take off your shirt—and your pants," she challenged.

"Wench!" he teased.

"Lecher!" she taunted.

They both undressed, never taking their eyes off each other. Afterward, when both sat there gloriously naked, Marco feasted his gaze on her. Outlined by the moonlight, with the wind and the spray teasing at her glorious hair and supple skin, she appeared like a wild, primal goddess, his to claim and tame. He railed his fingertips enticingly over her high, proud breasts, her flat belly, her silky mound, and smiled at her sharp gasps of pleasure. He nibbled at the gooseflesh on her wet arms. Reaching behind her, he ran his hands boldly over her soft back and rounded buttocks. His hands slid to her waist and he pulled her onto his lap. Her silken sigh ignited a storm of desire in him as he cupped her breasts, sank his mouth onto her shoulder, and murmured urgently, "Why is it you so fire my blood? I could devour you alive again, this very moment!"

Christina gasped ecstatically, loving the feel of his hands and lips on her, his warm, muscled chest against her back, his swollen shaft pressing so brazenly against her bottom. She tilted her face to give him a fevered kiss, and he crushed her against him.

Abruptly, she slid out of his embrace, kneeling next to him to feast her eyes on him in the moonlight. With his naked body and fierce features sculpted in silver, he appeared as beautiful and barbaric as an ancient warrior come to claim her. She kneaded the strong muscles of his shoulders, delighting in his satisfied groans. Her fingertips trailed over his massive chest and tight belly, brushing against his swollen shaft. She watched his nostrils flare as he tried to haul her close again. But again she eluded his grasp, moving behind him to kiss his magnificent back as she ran her fingertips over his muscled buttocks.

His hand closed over hers convulsively. "I want to feel your fingernails there when I drive into you."

"You will," she promised.

She was grabbed forcefully, pulled onto his lap, and kissed until she was certain their mouths and tongues and teeth had fused. All the time, his hand was between her thighs, his fingers preparing her with rough urgency. Her desperate whimpers only increased his ardor. He leaned over and slowly, so slowly, drew the tip of her breast into his mouth. He sucked hard, and she thought she would die of pleasure. Her sudden, wild squirming proved useless. She heard his husky chuckle as he held her tightly and continued to torment her thoroughly. At last he moved to pull her down into the cool waters with him.

Yet she resisted, slipping out of his embrace. He grabbed her and brought her astride him at the edge of the pool, his features ferocious as his manhood stood poised to plunder her.

"Christina," he warned fiercely, "tease me at your peril."

"No," she pleaded breathlessly. "Not yet."

"Why?"

She nuzzled his neck, his chest, and rubbed her breasts against him. "I long to please you first, to drive you crazy. Tell me how I may please you."

His groan was tortured. "Your mouth is like hot velvet," he murmured intensely. "I long to feel it on me."

"Where?"

With a provocative movement and a smile, he showed her.

Christina slipped off his body and into the chest-deep tide pool. She gasped ecstatically as her naked flesh was enveloped by the bubbly coolness. The effervescent water felt exquisite against her hot flesh and aroused breasts as she insinuated herself between Marco's spread thighs. She began kissing him, starting at his knees and then moving slowly, inexorably higher. His strong hands reached down to hold her breasts.

At her tender, intimate kisses, Marco found himself trembling violently, as if a fever had taken him. When that hot, sweet mouth latched onto his manhood, he thought he would climax then and there, so burning was the pleasure, so intense the spasms of ecstasy. She alternately teased him with her tongue and drew him into her wet warmth. He tangled his fingers in her hair and gritted his teeth in agonized arousal.

Somehow, through the haze of desire, he managed to pull away before he spent himself. He slipped into the pool, lifted her onto him, and impaled her as a powerful wave breached the wall of the pool, crashing over them. *Dio*, the water was so cold, and she was hot, so very hot. While she trembled against him, she took him fully, holding nothing back, her legs wrapped tightly about his waist as cries of pleasure burst from her. As his fingers dug into her bottom, he felt her fingernails, as promised, sinking into him. He went wild, thrusting into her again and again.

Cradled in his arms and feeling him to the hilt inside her, Christina sobbed her joy. She thought of how strong he was as he held her there. The currents pulling at their bodies did not even sway him on his feet and could not compare with the power of his deep, jolting strokes. Whatever happened tomorrow, he was hers tonight, truly hers, and she would cherish this moment in her heart forever.

When the explosion came, their mouths joined in a soul-rending kiss.

TWENTY-FIVE

"Can your men take us back to Beaufort on the morrow, Marco?" Don Giovanni asked.

Late the following morning, Marco, Christina, and the Renaldis sat together in the salon. The girls and Giuseppe had gone off to paint with oils at the beach. Marco had been staring at Christina, who sat with Vittorio on the settee. He had been reliving last night's glorious passion and wondering how in the world he would now give her up. Indeed, he had been musing that he was not at all sure he *could* give her up—her best interests be damned!—when his friend abruptly spoke. He was so startled by Don Giovanni's query that he almost dropped his teacup. Setting the cup and saucer safely aside, he glanced again at Christina, who stared back at him with bright defiance. Then he turned his attention to Don Giovanni.

"Must you and your family leave so soon?" he asked somberly.

"*Sì*, my friend, we have delayed our journey home for far too long," Don Giovanni replied.

"And we've a wedding to plan," Donna Flora added happily as she clicked her knitting needles.

Marco glanced at Christina again, and their gazes locked for another meaningful moment. He was tempted to blurt out, *The hell you have a wedding to plan! Christina is staying here—as my wife!*

Instead, he muttered distractedly to Donna Flora, "So you do."

"For the last time, won't you reconsider and come back to Venice with us?" Don Giovanni implored. He gestured toward Christina. "Surely the young lady would be much more comfortable marrying with her uncle present."

"I have explained before . . ." Staring starkly at Christina, he finished tightly, "It is impossible."

Meanwhile, Christina turned to Don Giovanni and related with cheery sarcasm, "Uncle Marco only wants what is best for me."

Don Giovanni was scowling, trying to digest this odd comment, when all at once everyone was distracted by the sound of voices out in the hallway. As they watched in confusion, a group of five entered the room—an agitated Hesper escorting two strange men, followed by Claudio and Ugo. One of the newcomers was elderly and bewigged, elegantly dressed, while the other was much younger, tall and thin, dressed in austere black with a flat, round hat.

"Signore Glaviano, we have guests," Hesper announced with barely repressed sarcasm.

As an obviously baffled Marco jumped to his feet, Christina and the Renaldis continued to regard the newcomers with perplexity. Christina found that the older gentleman appeared vaguely familiar. She watched him stride over to Marco.

"You are Marco Glaviano?" he asked.

"Yes," a scowling Marco replied. "And who are

you, sir, and why have you invaded my home in this manner?"

The man drew himself up with dignity. "I am Charles Rutgers, Magistrate of the Court of General Sessions in Charles Town." He glanced sharply at Christina. "I am also Christina Abbott's legal guardian. I presume this is the girl here?"

At these aggressive remarks, Marco paled and he stared at his inquisitor coldly.

Meanwhile, a thunderstruck Don Giovanni surged to his feet. "Marco, what nonsense is this man babbling about?"

While Marco regarded Don Giovanni in uncertainty, Rutgers pressed angrily. "Well, Signore Glaviano? Is this girl my ward, Christina Abbott, or not?"

Marco nodded. "She is."

As the Renaldis exchanged astounded glances, the second man hurried toward Christina. Startled, she stood to face him warily, and he embraced her. "Christina, my dear, to think that after all this time, I have found you and we get to meet at last!"

Christina wiggled away from the mystifying stranger. "Who *are* these men?" she demanded of Marco in a frantic undertone.

Before he could reply, Rutgers stepped toward her and smiled benignly. "Christina, dear, I realize we have met only on a few occasions, but surely you must remember me. I am your guardian, Charles Rutgers. Remember, I took charge of your affairs after your dear stepmother and father were lost at sea?" He motioned toward the black-clothed man. "And this is your stepuncle, the Reverend George Hollingsworth of England. The good reverend has been frantically worried about your whereabouts ever since you disappeared from Edisto Island six years ago."

"I see—I think." Christina bit her lip and stared at

the vicar, who, despite a prominent wart on his left cheek, was a pleasant-enough-looking man with thin features and pale brown eyes. "You are my stepuncle?"

"I am."

She went over to him and extended her hand. "How do you do?"

He squeezed her hand, beamed at her, and replied feelingly, "I am doing splendidly, my dear, now that we have at last met! After I heard the tragic news of my sister's death, only ill health prevented me from spending every minute of the past six years trying to find you."

Meanwhile, Don Giovanni was throwing up his hands in exasperation. "Marco, what on earth is going on here? Do you mean to tell us that Christina is not your niece?"

"His niece?" Charles Rutgers turned to Don Giovanni with a look of amazement on his face. "His niece, indeed! Why, I've never heard such balderdash." He pointed an accusing finger at Marco. "This man, Marco Glaviano, is anything but Christina's uncle. He is in fact a brazen opportunist who kidnapped the girl from Edisto Island six years ago."

"He kidnapped her?" Don Giovanni gasped, reaching out to steady his wife, who was pale and tottering on her feet.

"Indeed," Rutgers continued with contempt. "I would have brought along an armed escort of the British Navy to arrest the blackguard, except that I happen to be aware, through my friendship with Commodore Jenkins, that Glaviano is a privateer in our service."

While Marco groaned in helpless frustration, Don Giovanni turned to him. "A privateer? Do you mean to tell me, Marco, that you are little better than a pirate who abducted this girl?"

Christina rushed to Marco's defense, confronting

Don Giovanni with her hands balled on her hips. "Marco did not kidnap me! He rescued me from the Spanish pirates who would have raped me!"

Such stunned silence fell in the wake of this disclosure that at first, Don Giovanni appeared to take no note of the fact that Donna Flora had crumpled to the floor in a swoon.

When he and Vittorio at last noticed the fallen matron and rushed to her aid amid panicked utterings in Italian, Hesper came forward to face Rutgers. "The girl is speaking the truth, your lordship. Surely you must have been aware that Spanish raiders attacked the island on the night Christina disappeared. Had it not been for Marco Glaviano, the cutthroats would have carried off the girl and done God only knows what with her."

Rutgers fell silent, scowling.

Christina pressed their advantage. "So you see, Mr. Rutgers, far from kidnapping me, Marco Glaviano saved my life that night. Instead of maligning him, you might ask yourself why you left me and Hesper in such peril on the island." She glanced at Marco, and took heart when he smiled at her. "Marco told me it was most imprudent of you to leave us there."

Again Rutgers seemed at a loss for words, watching Vittorio and Don Giovanni help the staggering but revived Donna Flora back to the settee.

Hollingsworth intervened with a kindly smile. "May I suggest that we all cease making these bitter accusations and take joy in the fact that we have at last found our Christina?" He touched her arm solicitously. "My dear, are you all right? That is, I hope no one . . ."

As his voice trailed off meaningfully, Christina raised her chin proudly. "Marco has always shielded me from all harm."

"Aye, he has," Hesper affirmed to Rutgers. "Signore Glaviano has even arranged for the girl to marry with this fine lad here—"she paused to gesture at Vittorio—"and the signore is providing the dowry himself."

"I suppose that is commendable," Rutgers admitted grudgingly. He glanced at a white-faced Vittorio. "Is this true, young man?"

Vittorio opened his mouth, glanced around in utter befuddlement, then clamped his thin lips shut.

"It is," Don Giovanni answered in his son's stead. He glared at Marco. "Leastwise, that was the case until I discovered just now that my old friend has deceived me, that he entered into this contract under fraudulent circumstances—"

"Don Giovanni," Marco began helplessly.

"You lied to me, my boy!" Don Giovanni accused, shifting his furious gaze to Christina. "This girl is not your niece—she is merely some waif you picked up on a sea island—"

"Now wait just a minute!" Charles Rutgers cut in indignantly. "I will not hear Christina Abbott so maligned! The girl is the daughter of a merchant, Richard Abbott, who was wealthy and respected in Charles Town. After she lost her parents, Christina became an heiress. I should know, as I am the trustee of her legacy."

Don Giovanni stared at Rutgers in utter fascination. "The girl is an heiress?" The words were barely audible.

"She is. The Abbott fortune lies in trust in Charles Town for Christina's future husband."

At once a huge smile split Don Giovanni's face. He turned to Marco and held out his arms. "Marco, my friend! Forgive my impetuosity! Obviously, this is all just a minor misunderstanding that we can easily clear up between us." He turned to Hesper and ordered impatiently, "Bring wine and glasses to your master's study, woman. The other gentleman and I have much to discuss."

* * *

Several hours later, Marco sought out Christina. He found her sitting on the front steps of the house with her chin propped in her hands, staring ahead moodily.

He offered his hand. "Go for a walk with me, Christina?"

"What?" she replied irritably. "And add even more grist for scandal to this memorable day? I doubt the others could survive it."

A muscle jumped in his cheek. "Please come with me? I must have a word with you."

With an exasperated sigh, she took his hand and let him help her to her feet.

They headed down the dappled trail toward the harbor, not touching, each locked up in private, tumultuous thoughts.

"Where are the others?" she asked.

"Our guests are all resting now," he replied ruefully. "I suspect the disaster this morning has exhausted them all."

She laughed cynically. "That was truly some scene—my guardian and stepuncle charging in and ruining your charade, not to mention accusing you of kidnapping me."

"I know," he replied grimly. "But I think the misunderstanding has been smoothed over. Both Rutgers and Hollingsworth appear to be reasonable men who have so far accepted my motives in rescuing you. And they do want to get to know you better."

"I am touched. How did the two of them learn of my whereabouts, anyway?"

He kicked a coconut out of their path. "You remember Luigi?"

"Yes."

"It seems he committed some thievery and landed in Rutgers's court in Charles Town. Hoping to improve his own prospects, he told your guardian all

about your supposed abduction and our whereabouts. Rutgers then wrote to your stepuncle in England. Hollingsworth sailed for Charles Town, where
he subsequently chartered a schooner to bring himself and Rutgers here to Isola del Mare. So here they
are."

She was shaking her head. "What else happened in
your office? The five of you were in there for hours."

He avoided her eye and muttered, "It was a
lengthy discussion, all of us trying to decide what
would be best for you."

"You would not dream of consulting me, would
you?" she flared bitterly.

He ignored that, continuing matter-of-factly. "The
result is that both Charles Rutgers and Reverend
Hollingsworth seem very impressed by the Renaldis,
and by my choice of Vittorio as your husband. We
have all decided that it would be best to proceed
with the wedding as planned. Indeed, Don Giovanni
insisted that the contract be honored."

"Of course he did! Now that he knows I am an
heiress."

Marco's smile was ironic. "My old friend is a most
practical man."

"Try 'mercenary.' "

He chuckled, then regarded her curiously. "Did
you know?"

"Know what?"

"That you are such a wealthy woman."

She shrugged. "Not really. I have a vague memory
of living with my father and stepmother in a fine
house in Charles Town. Then, after I lost them, Magistrate Rutgers sent me with Hesper to live on the island. Our cottage there was modest, and I suppose I
was never truly aware that my parents were so rich."

"How do you feel about being an heiress?"

"Oh, I do not know," she responded offhandedly,
straightening the lace on her cuffs. "I am not sure it

makes that much difference—other than making Don Giovanni a very happy man."

He chuckled. "At any rate, everything is settled."

She paused. "So you are just giving me away, Marco?"

He groaned and gestured his frustration. "Don't you know that I have agonized over this? This morning, I all but blurted out . . ."

"What?" she demanded in a charged voice.

He shrugged fatalistically. "It does not matter. It is clear to me now that you belong in a different, more civilized world, that you should not waste your life on this primitive island."

"Heaven forbid that I disagree!" Recklessly, she continued. "Perhaps now that I am an heiress, I do not need any of you. Perhaps I shall just go back to Charles Town—or somewhere else—and to hell with you, Vittorio, and everyone else."

He spoke with growing impatience. "Christina, you forget that you are a woman, and as such, you have no real rights. If you refuse to marry Vittorio and still leave this island, you will be returned to Charles Rutgers's guardianship. Eventually he will choose a husband for you. Is that what you want?"

"You could let me stay!" she blazed. "You could fight for me!"

His hands seized her shoulders. "Christina, look at it from my perspective. I am a sea rover, not a proper husband for you—especially not now that you are an heiress. Besides, we are walking a very fine line here in convincing the others that you are . . . still chaste. If I told your guardian that I desire to wed you, he would no doubt order me slapped into irons and borne back to Charles Town, there to swing at Hangman's Point."

"Heaven forbid that you stick out your neck for me!" she cried with anger and hurt. "You know I would do anything for you."

He pinned her with an earnest glance. "If I thought it would be best for you, I would take on them all."

Losing patience, she shoved him away from her. "Save me from your high-mindedness, Marco Glaviano! I discovered last night what you *truly* want—and it is definitely not a wife! Why don't you admit that you can't be content with just one woman?"

She would have fled, but he grabbed her hand. "Christina, can we not, for once, cease hurling angry words at each other?"

She was silent for a moment, staring at the ground, her lower lip trembling. "Why?"

"Because I must know something." He raised her chin with his fingers and stared into her tumultuous eyes. "Why did you defend me today?"

While she tossed her chin free of his grasp, his solemn gaze ultimately needled her conscience and compelled honesty. Drawing a deep breath, she admitted, "Because it was not right for them to accuse you of all those horrible things. You were always good to me, Marco, and no one has ever molested me or Hesper here—just as you promised us."

He nodded. "I tried, *cara.*"

"Not hard enough," she was compelled to add.

"Perhaps not," he acknowledged tightly.

She smiled at him sadly, and for a moment each shared a feeling of grief over the friendship and rapport now lost to them both.

"You always let me have everything I wanted," she went on in trembling tones.

"You were very easy to spoil," he said huskily.

"The only problem is . . ." She stared at him achingly, her heart pounding in her ears. "Now I want you."

"I know, darling."

They stood there gazing at each other with stark longing, their bodies mere inches apart. Then

Christina could not bear the torment any longer—she thrust herself into his arms.

He clutched her close and kissed her hair, inhaling the heavenly scent of her.

"Come to my room tonight?" she whispered in a small voice.

His voice was tortured. "I'm sorry, *cara*. I cannot."

She slipped out of his embrace and fled, before he could see her blinding tears.

TWENTY-SIX

"I AM THE VICAR OF A SMALL VILLAGE IN SOUTHAMPTON," George Hollingsworth said. "It is truly one of the loveliest shires in England—gentle hills, beautiful rivers, and thick forests."

The following afternoon, Christina sat with her stepuncle in the garden behind the house. He had suggested that they take some time to become better acquainted, and Christina had already discovered that she truly liked the soft-spoken clergyman.

"It does sound so beautiful," she replied eagerly. "Was that where you were raised? Was my stepmother born there as well?"

"Indeed."

Her eyes darkened with sadness. "I was only eleven when I lost her. I remember her as being very kind."

His expression grew equally wistful. "Virginia was a gentle creature, a lady in every way."

"Tell me more of how you remembered her—back in England," Christina encouraged.

"Certainly, dear. Everyone loved Virginia. She was devout, but she also took much joy in living. She dressed beautifully, she was a wonderful dancer, and she did exquisite needlework."

Tears clouded Christina's vision. "She was really more a mother to me than my own. Ever since the shipwreck, I do so want to remember my stepmother and my father—but sometimes over the years, I find their images fading."

He patted her hand. "That is only natural, my dear. You were still a child when the tragedy occurred."

She bit her lip. "And my father—did you know him well?"

"Oh, yes." Bitterness hardened George's thin lips. "Richard Abbott was a powerful, determined man. He came from a family of titled aristocracy—he himself was the Earl of Somerset. When his first wife— your mother—died, he was left a widower with an infant. He met my sister at a village fair, and he set his cap on her at once. Doubtless, Virginia could not resist the romance of the tragic widower with a small, motherless daughter. She fell in love with both of you, making it easy for your father to sweep her off her feet."

"You sound rather disapproving of him."

He smiled. "I'm sorry, my dear. But you see, from the outset I was opposed to Richard's wild scheme to take you and Virginia off to the uncivilized American colonies. She loved him, of course, and by then she had become devoted to you as well. To Richard's credit, I must confess that he became a very successful merchant in Charles Town. Still, I cannot help but wonder if, had all of you remained in England, mayhap the terrible tragedy at sea would never have occurred."

Christina nodded morosely. "I can certainly see your point. As a matter of fact, I would love to see England. Of course, I was born there—but I remember nothing."

"You could always come back with me," he offered generously.

"Could I?"

"I realize that your guardian has agreed to your marriage with this Venetian lad, but if you are not truly amenable to the match, I would be happy to intervene on your behalf."

Christina's eyes gleamed with new hope. "Would you?"

He nodded. "Although I am no actual blood relation of yours, I do feel a deep bond toward you because of Virginia. Perhaps your guardian might thus be persuaded to turn over control of your affairs to me."

"Oh, that would be wonderful." Abruptly, a troubled expression pulled at Christina's mouth. "Do you think you might be able to persuade Magistrate Rutgers to let me stay here?"

"Here?" Hollingsworth appeared flabbergasted. "Why ever would you want to stay here, my child? To live on this uncivilized island among these disreputable privateers? Given the fact that you have been at their mercy for six years, it is truly a wonder that none of them have ever—"

"Marco would never allow that!" she cut in passionately. "He has always protected me and has demanded that everyone else here treat me with respect!"

Hollingsworth's gaze narrowed. "You seem quite fond of this pirate."

"He is a privateer!" she corrected. "And why wouldn't I be fond of him? He saved my life and gave me everything I could ever want."

Hollingsworth snorted in contempt. "The man may

have helped you, and I must admit that he has arranged for you a fitting marriage. However, I have grave doubts about his being the best influence for a young lady of your—er—impressionable age."

"What do you mean by that?" Christina asked tensely.

He sighed. "Why, only this morning as I journeyed to your chapel to have a few moments of quiet prayer, I spotted your Signore Glaviano on the path, having an intent discussion with—er—a very slatternly-looking female."

Christina felt the color draining from her face. "Was she dark?"

He shook his head. "On the contrary, she was quite fair—a blond woman, as I recall." He coughed. "And I must say that she seemed to be having a difficult time—er—keeping her hands off your Signore Glaviano."

Christina inwardly seethed at this revelation. After rejecting her again yesterday, was Marco already up to his old tricks with other women?

"So you see, my dear," Hollingsworth continued smoothly, "you must relinquish your insane desire to remain in this unacceptable environment. Your choice is either to marry this Venetian boy or to return with me to England, where I will be happy to serve as your protector and arrange a proper marriage for you."

Christina's eyes flashed mutinously. Men! she thought. They all wanted to take charge of her, to run her life, to tell her what to do! Marco Glaviano, most of all!

During the next day and a half, Christina drifted in an endless purgatory as the males around her continued to blissfully plan the rest of her life. She, Hollingsworth, Rutgers, and the Renaldis were all to leave for Charles Town on Monday, taking the schooner Hollingsworth had chartered. In Charles Town, legal papers would be drawn and signed and her guardian would transfer control of her affairs and her fortune to Don Giovanni. She would then set sail with the Renaldis for Venice.

Of course, she realized that she could always take her stepuncle up on his offer to intervene on her behalf, but that would only put her at the mercy of another man, largely a stranger, who would then take charge of her life and choose her a husband. At least with Vittorio and the Renaldis, she knew in advance what she would be getting into, and that was perhaps preferable to the prospect of braving uncharted waters.

Christina felt so betrayed, and she blamed Marco for her woes. Surely he could not love her, then turn her over to these others so easily! Indeed, if what her stepuncle had told her was true, Marco might even now be sporting again with Monique or Rosa. This possibility tortured her. Knowing how vulnerable she was right now, how could he even consider such hurtful behavior? Could he not wait the few days until she was gone before he selfishly sought his own ease? Whenever she was around him, she flashed him hot, accusing, embittered glances; when she saw the answering pain and guilt in his eyes, she took perverse joy. Let him suffer for his sins, and most deservedly so! He still did not care enough to fight for her—or to give up his womanizing!

Christina's rage came to a head on the third evening after her stepuncle and guardian had arrived. She was strolling down the hallway toward her room when she practically collided with Rosa, who was brazenly emerging from Marco's room! The woman wore a low-cut peasant blouse and a garish printed skirt; she reeked of cheap perfume.

Christina glared at her. "What were you doing in Marco's room?"

Rosa crooned a sultry laugh. "Why, I was waiting for him. We have a rendezvous set up for later tonight."

Although the Spanish woman's claim assailed her with new doubts—especially following her stepuncle's claims—Christina faced her enemy with pride and disdain. "You are lying! You have not been in Marco's room for months now. I would have known if he was still bedding you!"

Rosa's dark eyes blazed with contempt. "So you think you would have known, you little meddler? You are such a stupid, naive child! The truth is, Marco and I have been forced to be more discreet ever since you started acting like such a jealous little bitch." Stepping closer, the woman continued with malicious relish. "Instead of meeting in his room, Marco and I now couple at the beach, or deep in the jungle. Why, when he went on his last foraging raid, he even had me rendezvous with him at St. Kitts. He laughed with me over the way we had fooled you, and he called you a spoiled brat."

Her lower lip trembling, Christina retorted, "Marco would never do that—or say that about me!"

"Wouldn't he?" Rosa challenged. Spitefully, she taunted, "You are *una idiota*. There are other women, too. Marco is an insatiable lover. Sometimes he wears me out so badly that I allow him to take his ease with Minerva or Monique. I do not care as long as I remain his favorite."

By now Christina was so stunned and infuriated, she could only glare at the other woman, her chest heaving.

"Now I am carrying Marco's child," Rosa went on with vengeful triumph, "and I am most proud to do so. Did you really think you were woman enough to please him?" She looked the girl over with scorn, and made a clucking sound. "He becomes so easily bored with inexperienced schoolgirls. He calls you a scrawny chicken. Did you know that, you little *puta?*"

"You are a lying whore!" Christina flared.

She yanked back her hand to slap the other woman, but Rosa grabbed her wrist, successfully blocking the blow. For a moment, the two women glared at each other with raw, burning hatred.

Then Christina jerked her hand free and hissed, "Marco is mine! Come near him again, and I will kill you!"

She shoved past the other woman, whose cruel laughter followed her all the way down the corridor.

When Marco returned to his room late that night, it was to find Christina waiting for him, pacing and in a rage. She was wearing a thin white muslin dress—enticingly maidenly—and her wild hair trailed behind her as she stormed about. Pansy, equally agitated, was prowling the room at the girl's heels, whining abjectly and looking forlorn.

"What are you doing here?" Marco asked tensely.

Christina charged across the room and slapped him, hard. "You pig!"

"Now what have I done?" he demanded, rubbing his stinging cheek.

"You got Rosa pregnant!"

"I did *what?*"

"Don't bother to deny it, you miscreant! She told me the truth tonight, right outside your bedroom door. All this time you have been sneaking off and sporting with her! And with Minerva and Monique, too!"

"Minerva and Monique? What lunacy is this?" he cried.

"George Hollingsworth told me he saw you on the path early yesterday with Monique!"

His face went blank, then he snapped his fingers

and said quickly, "Oh, that. Monique asked my advice regarding Ugo's recent advances toward her—"

"So you offered her a few *advances* of your own?"

Marco's patience was wearing thin. "Christina, I did no such thing!"

"Should we expect *her* to make an appearance tonight as well?" she ranted. "Surely you would enjoy such a ménage—as *insatiable* as you are!"

"Christina, be reasonable!"

Yet she was heedless, still storming about. "I should have known you would take up with whores again. How could you do that while you were kissing me? How could you make love to Rosa at the beach, after what we did there?" Catching a convulsive breath that was half a sob, she glared at him and whispered, "How *could* you?"

"Christina," Marco said, struggling to keep his voice level, "there is nothing between me and Monique. As for Rosa, she has lied to you. I have not lain with her in over half a year, ever since you . . . laid claim to me. She could not possibly be carrying my child, since her belly is flat even now."

Uttering a blistering curse, she came up to him and shoved him hard. "Oh? So you are that familiar with the state of her belly, are you?"

He groaned. "Besides, there are ways that a man can prevent conception—"

"Such as?" she demanded.

He sighed. "A man can don a protective sheath, or withdraw before his seed is spilled."

"You never use these sheaths or withdrawals with me!" she accused.

He stared at her burningly. "Never with you, *cara*."

For a moment, she looked ready to relent, or burst out sobbing. Then she threw up her hands and ranted. "Well, I do not believe you! I would die for you, and all you can think about is fornicating with these others! You have lied to me, betrayed me . . ."

She paused to catch a convulsive breath, and the cheetah whined loudly. "Furthermore, you have upset Pansy!"

With an expression of amazement, Marco watched Christina as she continued to rave and pace. He realized that never had she looked so glorious, the very image of the enraged lioness as she railed at him in every possible way. Instead of becoming justifiably irate, he found that her jealousy aroused him unspeakably. He felt himself burning to wipe the pout off her lips, to melt her anger with his hard heat. He realized that it had been so long since he had been able to spoil and charm her—

Seduce her. That wildly erotic possibility sent him reeling.

Fool that he was, he would do so now. *Dio*, he was only a man, after all, and the girl could tempt a saint! He clucked to Pansy, crossed the room, and let the cheetah out the French doors. Christina appeared too agitated even to notice.

"And you don't like my body!" she finished angrily.

"What?" He turned to her and laughed.

Crossing her arms over her chest, she appeared on the verge of tears again. "Rosa said you called me a scrawny chicken."

"She said that? Darling, I would never—"

"Don't bother to deny it! And don't dare call me darling!" She shook a finger at him. "I know you like your women fat and voluptuous. I tried to get fat while you were away. But every time I ate too much, I would only retch."

Marco could not believe his ears. She was magnificent, trying to become fat for him! Suddenly, he knew just how he could help her achieve her goal, and the realization made his breeches feel several sizes too small.

"If you were carrying my child, you would become fat," he teased huskily.

"Would you find me desirable then?"

"I would find you irresistible—as I do now."

"Not irresistible enough to fight for."

Enough! he thought, staring at the gorgeous, defiant angel. Ah, he was so bad for her! But ultimately, she had only herself to blame for being so damned desirable. She was asking for a thorough bedding, and she was going to get it.

"Are you so sure?" he teased. "Come here, *cara*."

"No!"

Marco was accustomed to willing women, and her resistance only poured more fuel on the flames of his ardor. In two quick strides he came to her, pulling her mutinous body into his arms.

"We must correct a misconception here, you and I," he murmured, touching the tip of her adorable, stubborn nose. "Darling, I do love your body."

"You do not."

"Are you going to force me to demonstrate?"

"Yes!"

Marco laughed his delight. She was tempting him, defiantly and recklessly, and getting herself in deep, deep trouble. He grinned and reached down, quickly unfastening her bodice, popping buttons in his haste. He chuckled at her cry of shock and surprise as he leaned over and took an aroused nipple in his mouth.

"I love your breasts," he murmured intensely, wetting and stroking her. "They're perfect to fill my hands—or my mouth."

She moaned and thrust her breast more deeply into his mouth, tangling her fingers in his hair. "Do you?" she whispered with a tentativeness that twisted his heart.

"Oh, yes, darling."

He sank to his knees, continuing to pull down her

clothing, tearing it in frustration, and then his hot mouth was pressed against her bare, quivering stomach. "I love your flat belly . . ." His hands reached behind her, cupping her hips. "Your charming little bottom." His hands slipped beneath her skirts to caress lower. "Your incredibly long, soft legs." He reached around to her front again, insinuating his hand between her thighs and then burrowing a finger inside her, until she gasped and dug her fingers into his shoulders.

He glanced up at her face and love welled in him as he drank in her expression of intense longing. Her lips were slightly parted, her eyes brimming with tears. Intensely, he whispered, "I especially love you where you are so tiny, so tight, and yet you take all of me eagerly, so deeply."

"Oh, Marco!"

"No one loves me like you do, *cara*—no one."

With a shattered cry, she slipped to her knees beside him, kissing him with desperate need. "When will this purgatory end?" she whispered achingly against his mouth. "I cannot bear it anymore . . ."

"I know, darling."

Half shocking him with her brazenness, she braced the flat of her hands against his shoulders and pushed hard, tumbling him onto his back and straddling him. As he watched her, wide-eyed and equally captivated, her nimble fingers made short work of the buttons on his breeches. Then she sank herself onto him with a greediness that had him responding with a deep, rapacious thrust. She gasped and stopped dead as their bodies were locked tighter than ever before.

Marco chuckled at the sight of her, brazenly straddling him with her bodice down, her skirts bunched between her thighs and all of him buried inside her. She was panting, breathless, undone—exactly the way he liked her. And yet she had about her the air of a starving hoyden who had sunk her teeth into a huge treat and was now trying to swallow it whole.

He reached up, drawing his finger over her wet lips. "Bite off more than you can chew, *cara?*" he teased.

Waiting for her response, he grew fascinated by the expression in her eyes—at first wild and uncertain, then hot, passionate, determined.

Her knees clenched against his sides. And then she took him.

Oh, *Dio,* yes, she was taking him, riding him, rolling her hips, grinding into him, killing him so sweetly that he was dying of the pleasure. His fist pounded the floor and he moaned helplessly. He stared up at her, watching her bite her lip in tortured passion while her eyes were clenched tightly shut in ecstasy. The rise and fall of her proud breasts was so beautiful to him, and with her clothing undone, her hips quivering as she absorbed the shock waves of their deep coupling, she appeared utterly, wantonly ravished. His large hands reached up to take her breasts, and he gently tugged her toward him, taking her lips in a fevered kiss. When her eyes opened and he glimpsed the mindless passion, the bright tears there, he knew just what she had meant when she had told him she could not bear it. *Dio,* neither could he!

She was right, he thought. This was madness. Almost nightly, he poured his seed inside her, as if perversely obsessed with getting her pregnant so he need no longer worry about saving her from himself. If she carried his child, *never* would he let her go—

Never would he let her go anyway! The realization was so powerful, so jolting, that it seared Marco's heart and soul and sent his passions spiraling uncontrollably. His arms clenched around her waist, holding her to his convulsive thrusts. The love he felt brought tears to his eyes as he listened to her raw cries and pressed home greedily, spilling his seed inside her once more—

He crushed her to his heart as their lips met in a tender kiss. And in that moment, she became *his*.

TWENTY-SEVEN

*S*HE WAS HIS, A PIRATE'S WOMAN.

This remained Marco's tender thought an hour later as Christina lay asleep beneath him in his bed, with his manhood still wedged inside her. After they had made wild, passionate love on the floor, he had carried her to bed, stripped her naked, and they had claimed each other again insatiably until both were too sore to move.

He stared down at her exquisite face, at the lush mouth and lovely cheeks pink and puffy from his kisses and his whiskers, at the long lashes that quivered slightly as she slept. He brushed a strand of hair from her smooth brow, and had to smile with pride at the girl's determination. What spirit! Never had she given up until he was hers.

Then a frown drifted in. How would she fare being his wife, having his babies, worrying about him while he was away? After all, a fortune lay in wait for her in Charles Town. Would she not one day want to claim her legacy and put down respectable roots somewhere else? If she did, could he change for her? Could he give up the sea and his mission of harassing his Spanish enemies?

And what of the others—Rutgers, Hollingsworth, not to mention the Renaldis? There would be the devil to pay when he defied the lot of them and announced his own decision to wed her. His friendship with Don Giovanni would be ruined irrevocably, and this possibility filled him with sadness. Yet he loved this brave, proud girl so much now that he would withstand them all. He would even defeat her if need be—and this possibility also filled him with regret. When she discovered that marriage to him was hardly the heaven on earth that she had anticipated, she might well balk. Then she would discover what true ruthlessness was. For he would offer her no choices—never would he let her go.

Indeed, the very thought made him throb to life inside her once again. He watched her bite her lip and utter a small cry that held the heavy breathlessness of desire. Even in her sleep she wanted him, and the knowledge made him harden to agonized readiness. He suddenly ached to thrust himself into her— slowly, deeply, endlessly—all night long.

Dio, he could not do this to her again; they would both be rendered incapacitated! Yet even as his conscience scolded him, his lips tenderly sought her breast, and he sucked her incredibly warm, sweet nipple into his mouth. Still sleeping, she tossed her head from side to side, dug her fingernails into his bare shoulders, and arched her hips into him. That brazen wiggle had him pulling back and easing in deeper, until her eyes flew open on a gasp.

"See what you do to me, *cara?*" he teased, taking her soft hand and kissing each lovely, tapered finger. "Now I must love you until we both are raw."

The possibility seemed to please her, judging from

her greedy, unabashed smile and the way she coiled
her arms and legs tightly around him. Then both of
them froze at the sound of a sharp rap at the door.

"Oh, Marco, *mon amour!*" called a lyrical, French-
accented voice. "I can face you now, my love, and I
am here for our rendezvous."

At the baffling arrival of Monique outside his door,
Marco scowled in perplexity, then looked down in
panic to see Christina glaring at him with hatred.

"So it *is* true!" she gasped. "You have been wenching again—with both Rosa and Monique—just as
Rosa told me!"

"No, darling, it is not true!" he cried. "I have no
idea why Monique is—"

"Get off me, you bastard!" she hissed.

"*Cara*, please, listen to me! I haven't—I didn't—"

"Get off me!"

Uttering a miserable groan, Marco withdrew from
her flesh, even as Monique again crooned out, "Oh,
Marco!"

Furious, he leapt out of bed and grabbed his
breeches. "*Madre del Dio!* What is this—a damned parade? What in hell is that woman doing here?" he
asked himself in exasperation.

Meanwhile, Christina was savaging him with angry, accusing glances as she yanked on her own
clothing. "What is Monique doing here? Why, she
is simply here for your little lovers' tryst, just as
the two of you no-good liars arranged yesterday
morning!"

Marco rushed to her side. "Darling, you must
believe me! Monique and I never arranged a rendezvous. She must have gone mad. Just let me get rid of
her—"

Shrugging on her torn dress, Christina shoved him
away. "You go to the devil!"

"But, Christina, I didn't do anything!"

Meanwhile, Monique called out, "Marco, darling, please hurry! I am so hot for you, *mon amour!*"

"Goddammit!" he roared as he buttoned his breeches.

Christina was laughing in contempt as she attempted to fasten her bodice. "So you didn't do anything? Don't let me keep you, Marco! After all, your slut is waiting. Or should I say your *sluts?*"

She stormed off toward the French doors, and he followed her, staring in horror at her ruined clothing. "Christina, you cannot leave the house like this. Your dress is torn and you are in a disgraceful state!"

"Thanks to you!" she hurled over her shoulder, flinging open the door, exiting, and slamming it shut just inches from his nose.

Marco cursed explosively, not knowing which way to turn as he watched Christina flee into the garden and again heard Monique crooning his name out in the hallway. Rage contorted his face. *Why* was the Frenchwoman doing this to him? He would go catch Christina, but first, he would strangle Monique for making him look like a liar and a cheat in front of Christina!

He stormed across the room and flung open the door. Monique stood there grinning at him.

"What the hell are you doing here?" he demanded.

She feigned a hurt expression. "Why, Marco, *mon amour*, have you forgotten the note you sent me?"

"What note?"

"The note in which you asked me to meet you here tonight."

"Dammit, woman, I sent you no note!"

"Then who . . . ?"

For a moment, both appeared baffled; then Marco snapped his fingers. "Ah, hell," he groaned. "I suspect that Rosa is behind all this. She has been trying to create trouble between me and Christina, and confronted the girl outside my bedroom tonight."

"You mean that you are bedding Christina now?" Monique asked, wide-eyed.

At once Marco's expression grew murderous and he shook a finger at the Frenchwoman. "Say a word about it to anyone, and I swear I will kill you!"

Her countenance grew pouty. "I do not mind you bedding her—but I do regret our never having made love." She slinked up close to him and batted her eyelashes.

He shoved her away. "Monique, get this through your head. I have no interest whatsoever in bedding you! Now get the hell out of my sight before I make you rue the day you were born!"

Sighing as she gave Marco's body a last, covetous stare, Monique sullenly turned and left.

Marco retreated inside his room, slammed the door, and cursed. Damn that Rosa! He would have a good talk with the wench, and would likely wring her neck. He would not allow her to further sabotage his relationship with Christina—

Oh, God, Christina! She had fled into the garden alone, half clothed, and there might still be cutthroats lurking about! If anything happened to her, he would *kill* Rosa!

Marco quickly grabbed his bandolier and cutlass, and raced out of his room into the garden ...

Christina had arrived on the beach. She sat with her forearms crossed over raised knees, her head resting on her arms. She was sobbing her heart out, unable to believe that Marco had made such a fool of her. Perhaps he had been right all along when he had claimed that he would never make her a decent husband. She had been a naive child to so trustingly believe he would give up other women for her.

She bet he and Monique were having a good laugh over her even now, scorning her as an idiot for the way she had thrown herself at him ...

"Well, what have we here?"

At the sound of this frightening, alien voice, Christina gasped and jerked around to see four turbaned, bearded Spanish pirates circling her. A scar across the cheek of one, an eye patch on another, and a peg leg on a third gave evidence that these men were seasoned, ruthless fighters. As she watched in dizzying horror, they stalked her, staring at her with bald lust and depraved smiles. Fear made her nauseous, and she quickly crossed her arms over her gaping bodice.

"Look at the wench!" one of them said derisively, pointing at her with a gnarled finger. "Her clothing is shredded, and she has no doubt been riding her master's mast tonight."

As ribald laughter rippled over the lot of them, another added lustily, "Which will only ease the way for us."

"*Sì*, we are inviting you to go on a little ride with us, señorita," jeered the one with the peg leg.

As the four closed in on her, Christina felt her heart pound frantically. She watched the villains with the eyes of a cornered animal. She knew she was a strong fighter, but she was also no fool. Here she was clearly outnumbered, and her only hope for escaping certain rape and death would be to outrun these bastards.

Like a bolt of coiled energy, she was up, racing for her life down the beach. She took only a few steps before a huge black fishing net was hurled over her. Helplessly ensnared, she crashed to the ground with a bone-jarring thud. Feeling the grit of sand on her cheeks and in her mouth, she screamed oaths and fought frantically, uselessly, for her freedom, while in the background, the pirates only laughed cruelly.

Unable to find Christina in the woods, Marco was racing for the path to the beach when all at once four

Spaniards leapt out of the bushes to confront him and block his path. The men were small and wiry, facing him with daggers and cutlasses drawn.

Mother of God! Assassins again! And Christina was out here alone, unguarded! Marco yanked out his cutlass and assumed an aggressive stance, with feet braced apart and knees bent.

"Get out of my path, you bloody bastards!" he yelled.

The four converged on him with weapons flying, shouting profanities in Spanish. Marco swung his cutlass with the skill of a master and the rage of a demon. The air rang with the sounds of steel striking steel—the hard thrusts, the banging blows, the shrieking parries. Lunging forcefully, Marco drew blood—and screams—from three of his assailants, slashing one across the arm, slicing an earlobe of another, and felling a third with a thrust to the heart. He made a valiant fight, but ultimately, he could not deflect every blow from the three still standing, aggressive swordsmen. Even as he blocked a thrust, he glimpsed a second sword swinging at him and tried to feint. He felt the cutlass slice across his belly; he felt an iron belaying pin bang against the side of his head. Then his legs gave out beneath him and he crumpled to the ground.

Reeling with pain, Marco watched the three men close in for the kill, and he knew he was done for. Then his spirits heartened as he heard a familiar, lethal scream, and Pansy charged into the fray.

Turning slightly, Marco saw the magnificent black cat leap out of the night and sail over him. The cheetah was a coiled bolt of fury, charging his assailants with a shriek of bloodlust, razor-sharp teeth flashing and bright eyes spewing vengeance.

Marco heard the men's screams of surprise and agony as Pansy's teeth evidently hit their mark. There was a sudden wild frenzy all around him. He was

kicked and trampled in the mêlée, and he groaned in
helpless torment. He wanted to go to the aid of the
trusted cat, but he was too weak to move.

The pirates were yelling curses, lashing out wildly.
But ultimately, Pansy, too, could not defeat the three
remaining swordsmen. Marco heard the cat's sharp
yelp of pain; then she collapsed on top of him. Poor
Pansy . . . was she still alive? Yes, he could hear
moanlike sounds, could feel her muscles tensing as
she crouched protectively over him.

Meanwhile, the assailants were stalking about,
grunting in pain and heaving labored breaths.

"Where did that demon cat come from?" he heard
one demand of another.

"*Quién sabe?*" answered another. "I think I knocked
the beast cold with my belaying pin. Now I shall finish the job—"

Yet as the man stepped closer, Pansy emitted such
a menacing, feral snarl that even Marco's teeth went
on edge.

He heard one of the men whistle, heard footsteps
as all the pirates seemed to be retreating.

"Let us rejoin the others before the monster charges
us again," he heard one of them mutter. "Besides,
Glaviano is done in."

Feeling his own world going black, Marco believed
him . . .

Still helplessly entangled in the net and blinded by
the darkness, Christina felt herself being flung into
the wet, brackish bottom of a longboat. Disgusting,
slimy water oozed over her face and body, especially
as several men climbed inside and the boat rocked
precariously. She cried out as she was kicked and
bruised by the uncaring men as they took their
places. At last the tiny vessel achieved stability.
Christina could hear the slap of the oars in the water

and could feel the small vessel's rise and fall as the oarsmen plowed it through the waves.

The men were talking low in Spanish, and from the many voices mingling at once, Christina guessed their ranks had swelled from four to seven or eight. She had no doubt that she was now in the custody of Marco's mortal enemy, Carlos. Dread made her nauseous as she imagined the horrible fate awaiting her once she reached the pirate's ship. Her fight with Marco seemed almost silly now, especially as she realized that in all likelihood she would never again see him, or know his sweet loving.

Yet surely he would discover she was missing and come after her. Or would he be too busy bedding Monique or Rosa to care? That thought made rage well in her anew. If he did not care enough to at least try to rescue her, she vowed she would go to her grave hating his very guts.

Her thoughts scattered as the longboat slammed into the side of a larger vessel and she rolled about on the bottom of the boat, hitting her head painfully against its sides. The longboat rocked precariously, and a wave splashed over her as the men began disembarking. She heard a shout of "Lower the boom!" Then one of the men gathered up the net and pinned a huge hook through the bunched top of it. An instant later she was heaved, horrified, into the air, her body banging against the sides of a ship as she was hoisted over its rails and high above its decks. Then she was slowly lowered toward the deck, and looked down in sickening fear at fifty or more Spanish pirates who awaited her, leering rapaciously, screaming out hoots and catcalls, their evil faces awash in the oily yellow glow of lanterns.

Oh, Marco! Christina thought desperately. *Please come! I shall forgive you for anything—everything!*

Christina knew her bodice was gaping open, her skirts tangled around her waist, her legs scandalously bared to the scrutiny of the crew of miscreants. Oh, God, how would she survive being raped by all of them? She would never live through the night!

Indeed, as she was lowered to within their grasp, the whole smelly lot of them converged on her, laughing lustily as they boldly grabbed and pawed her. Within seconds, every inch of her body felt violated, bruised, poked, or prodded by their rough, filthy hands.

"Enough!" roared a loud voice.

The pirates drew back slightly, grumbling loudly to one another. Christina twisted around to look up at a bearded, black-haired giant, who stood staring at her and grinning. With his ruthless smile and the gleam of raw lust in his eyes, he was somehow more frightening than any of the others.

"The wench is mine!" he announced.

Marco awakened in a haze of excruciating pain. The side of his head was throbbing horribly. He felt weaker and dizzier than before—and Pansy was licking his face with her rough tongue.

"Pansy, are you all right?" he uttered feebly.

With a trembling hand, Marco reached up and touched the cheetah's head, hearing her yelp of pain as his finger brushed a huge, wet goose egg.

"Battered the two of us, did they?" he murmured. "Poor Pansy . . . You saved my life."

Indeed, Marco thought, had not the noble cat instinctively thrown herself across his body during the fray, he would now most certainly be dead.

Dead. *Dio*, what about Christina? Where was she?

Marco tried to struggle to his feet, only to cry out in agony and collapse on the path, retching and gasping for breath. Pansy remained there next to him, nudging his arm with her face and whining softly.

Marco willed himself to rise again, but his legs—

heavy, enervated, almost paralyzed—did not respond. His cheek lay against the path, and the grit of sand stung his eyes. Around him, the night was dark and cool, throbbing with night sounds, and the air—ironically—smelled sweet with island nectar. The labored pumping of his heart alarmed him, and reaching toward his waist, he felt a sickening wetness. *Dio*, how much blood had he lost? He could not afford to die now! Those bastards likely had Christina, and he must save her!

As if she had read her master's thoughts, Pansy again whined at Marco and took the leather strap of his bandolier between her teeth. The cheetah dug in her paws and began to pull hard, backing away and trying to drag her massive master with her. Somehow, with Pansy's continued nudging, Marco managed to half drag himself, half crawl down the path. Each time he slipped out of consciousness, Pansy wailed or licked his face until he awakened.

Vaguely, Marco was aware that Giuseppe's cottage lay between him and the house. If only he and Pansy could get that far ... As he made his tortuous progress, he felt several furry night creatures scurry past him and the cat. Despite the distractions, Pansy did not stray from her purpose, and Marco prayed that a poisonous snake would not strike out from the bushes and kill one of them. He practically jumped out of his skin when an owl hooted directly over their heads, and Pansy, the seasoned night prowler, hissed in retaliation.

At last, Marco spotted Giuseppe's cottage ahead of him, awash in moonlight. Grunting in intense torment, he pulled himself up the steps, crawled over to the door, and banged his fist loudly against the middle of the panel.

When no immediate answer came, he grabbed the doorknob and yanked himself upward, groaning at the unendurable pain the movement brought.

Abruptly the door opened in a wavering shaft of light. Marco stumbled inside and crashed to the floor. Pansy bolted in after him, whining at Giuseppe frantically.

"My God, boss, what has happened to you?"

Giuseppe stood over Marco in his nightshirt, holding a lantern and staring down in horror at his captain's bruised temple and blood-soaked trousers.

"Assassins," Marco muttered.

"I will get help!"

But Marco grabbed his friend's ankle. "No, not for me," he whispered convulsively. "Christina . . . went into the jungle alone . . . Bastards—may have gotten her. You must . . . save her."

With this frantic plea, Marco succumbed to the relentless blackness once more.

TWENTY-EIGHT

WHEN THE PIRATE CAPTAIN ANNOUNCED THAT THE CAPtive woman was his, chaos erupted on the decks of his schooner. Fifty of his men seemed to shout protests at once as they continued to swarm around Christina and eye the kidnapped wench with rapacious lust. Only the few crewmen who were busy hoisting sails or manning the helm refrained from joining in the tumult on the main deck.

Christina, meanwhile, stared in contempt at the man who had just claimed her. Though she had never met him before, she had no doubt that this dark, husky giant with black eyes and a cruel smile was the nefarious Carlos. Everything about him was repugnant to her, from his heavy beard to his blunt, crooked nose and tobacco-stained teeth.

The crewmen continued to yell their objections and even wave their weapons. Yet their leader's voice was more powerful; his bellowed *"Silencio!"* at once brought the complaints down to a grumbling lull.

The pirates glanced at one another in uncertainty, their eyes hot, dark, and resentful.

"But, *capitán*," one of the men who had abducted Christina protested in a near whine, "Juan, Manuel, Jose, and I, we capture the wench. She is our plunder."

"You kidnapped her at my orders!" Carlos roared back, shaking a fist at the man. His lascivious gaze swung back to Christina. "Take the wench below, strip her, and tie her to my bunk." He reached out, pawing her leg—and only chuckled when Christina spat at him and glared at him with hatred. "But first, wash her down but good. She is filthy." Wiping his hand on his own grimy breeches, he nodded to the others and added generously, "All of you may watch."

As a bawdy roar went up from the ranks, Christina could only listen in sickened fear and frustrated rage. But she had to grudgingly admit to herself that Carlos was a shrewd man. In handing his crew a morsel of herself, in giving them permission to see her stripped, washed, and no doubt thoroughly humiliated here on deck, he had forestalled a possible mutiny and bloodbath. But the fact that she was to be raped by one instead of by fifty was little comfort to her now. Indeed, she preferred death to lying beneath any man but Marco.

The hook was removed and, still net-bound, she was borne toward the mainmast by several howling Spaniards. She was dumped out of the net roughly. Landing on her knees on the splintery deck, she faced down the bastards like a wild creature, with eyes burning and teeth bared.

"Look how proud the wench is!" one said contemptuously.

"She won't be so proud once this night is over!" another put in.

Then at least a dozen of them converged on her. Christina fought, kicked, screamed, and attempted to bite the devils as they clawed at her body and clothing. Once she was stripped to her chemise, their leader again intervened, evidently fearing that his men would lose control and spoil his own sport.

"Enough!" Carlos yelled. "Wash the bitch!"

Again she was flung to the deck, and this time bucket after bucket of ice-cold seawater was dumped over her, making her gag and retch, rendering her chemise all but transparent as the men whistled, leered, and yelled insults.

"*Por favor, capitán*, let us have a go at her!" one implored.

"Julio! Roberto! Miguel! Take her below!" their leader barked back.

As the pirates looked around indecisively, Christina seized her one chance. She was up like a shot, bolting for the side, preferring a watery grave to what was to come.

Half a dozen steely hands grabbed her at once, digging cruelly into her flesh, bruising her. She screamed insults and fought viciously, but it was useless. Within seconds, her wrists, ankles, and midsection were all bound by links of greedy fingers.

"So the señorita is feisty," Carlos called, leering at her. "Perhaps I shall take my quirt to her backside later. For now, tie her to my bunk as ordered. We'll see how proud she is, naked and a slave in my bed."

While the crew laughed uproariously, Christina was borne down a companionway to the area belowdecks. The nauseating smells of mold, rotting food, human excrement, and bilge water assailed her.

She was carried into a small, poorly lit cabin. She groaned in pain as her hip slammed against the sharp edge of a desk. After being handled so roughly on deck, her entire body felt battered.

She was flung down on a smelly bunk with yellowed sheets, and stared up mutinously at the four men who had carried her below. She knew better than to attempt an escape now; such a reckless move would likely only provoke the men into raping her. Even if she could make it back up the companion-way, she would still have to confront over two score of the villains up on the main deck.

The men were eyeing her warily and consulting among themselves. The vile smell of them made her nauseous.

"Do you suppose we could have a taste of the wench?" one asked while stroking his stubbled jaw. "She does look a hot piece."

"She is not worth being skewered on Carlos's cutlass," another pointed out.

"*Sì*, the *capitán* has a terrible temper," added the third. "He might keelhaul the lot of us."

"Then we had best obey *el capitán*'s orders," decided the fourth. "Surely when he tires of the wench, he will give the rest of us our ease with her."

Amid bawdy chuckles, they set to work to strip Christina of her chemise. She again fought wildly, spitting, kicking, and screaming. While she was clearly no match for four men, vengeful pleasure did consume her when she managed to viciously bite one of the jackals. Yet he backhanded her so brutally that her jaw felt near smashed and her teeth rattled in her head.

"The wench is a she-devil!" the wounded man cried, rubbing his bleeding forearm. "We will never get her stripped."

"Ah, leave her be," suggested another in disgust. "The captain can finish stripping her—and he will see to it that the bitch regrets thwarting his orders."

"Gag her like the madwoman she is!" said another.

The men cruelly tied her wrists to the head of the bunk and her ankles to its feet. Her mouth was bound with a repulsive, coarse woolen rag.

"There! Not so proud now, are you, slut?" the one she had bitten asked with malicious pleasure.

The four turned to leave her there, gagged and helpless in the cold cabin. Still sopping wet, Christina was already trembling violently.

Then a surprising thing happened. One of the men—the one who had pointed out to the others that Carlos, if defied, might keelhaul the lot of them—slipped back inside the cabin. Christina watched in terror as he approached, certain he had returned to rape her. He was a small man and appeared rather young. Unlike the others, he was smooth-shaven, and she even reflected illogically that he had rather kind eyes. So she would be raped by a bastard with mellow brown eyes! What an irony!

Next to the bed, he stunned her by picking up a moth-eaten woolen blanket from the floor and tossing it over her, covering her near nakedness. He stared at her with an odd expression of compassion.

Christina gave him a look of helpless gratitude as he turned and slipped from the cabin . . .

Back on deck, Carlos and his lieutenant, Juan, were discussing the successful raid on Isola del Mare. "What of Glaviano?" Carlos asked.

Juan grinned broadly, displaying broken, filthy teeth. "We did in the bastard."

Carlos pounded him on the back. "Good work, *amigo!*"

"You will be eager to tell the girl of her lover's death—no?"

Carlos shook his head, and his dark eyes gleamed shrewdly. "No. Let the wench think instead that her lover does not care enough to rescue her."

Juan laughed heartily. "You are a cruel man, *capitán*—but a very wise one."

Carlos grinned. "I am a man determined to get between the wench's thighs."

* * *

" 'Twas a very bad wound," Hesper said. "I did my best to sew him up. 'Twill be touch and go, I'm telling you. The cat, however, will live."

Back on Isola del Mare, Charles Rutgers, Don Giovanni, George Hollingsworth, Claudio, and Giuseppe were all gathered in Marco's room around his bed, looking down at the deathly pale man who lay unconscious before them. Next to Marco lay the ever-faithful Pansy, who now appeared rather ludicrous staring up at the others with her doleful golden eyes and her head wrapped in a huge white bandage.

"Do you think Signore Glaviano will survive?" Don Giovanni asked Hesper anxiously.

She shrugged. "That drunken fool he calls a surgeon would have killed him. Like I said, I tried my best, your grace. But the lad has lost much blood. Mayhap he will live, if the fever or infection don't do him in. 'Tis in the Almighty's hands now."

"If only there were something we could do," George Hollingsworth fretted. "Signore Glaviano may well know just what happened to Christina."

"What happened to the girl is Glaviano's Spanish enemies carried her off!" Hesper put in heatedly, confronting the lot of them. "And what are you fine gents going to do about it?"

The others, save for Claudio, appeared perplexed. "What can we do?" Charles Rutgers asked. "By the time we sail for Charles Town to get a Royal Navy escort, God only knows where the girl may be or what these Spanish pirates may have done to her."

"Do not concern yourself," said Claudio proudly to the others. "I am gathering a crew this night and we are setting sail to rescue Christina." He nodded decisively toward Marco. "It is what the captain would want."

Don Giovanni gratefully shook Claudio's hand. "Good for you, my friend. *Buona fortuna e buon*

viaggio. My son will, of course, be distraught until his
fiancée is returned."

"Aye, he'll be distraught at losing the girl's pot of
gold!" Hesper put in cynically. To Claudio, she
wagged a finger and added, "You find the girl, now,
or you will have Hesper to reckon with."

"You know I will try my best, woman," Claudio replied gravely.

"Aye, I know. Godspeed."

As Claudio left the room, Don Giovanni turned
impatiently to Giuseppe. "Well, what are you waiting
for, Father? Say a prayer for my friend's recovery—
before you are required to perform extreme unction!"

When Giuseppe merely gulped and appeared at a
loss, George Hollingsworth offered generously, "I
should be happy to say a prayer for Signore
Glaviano."

Don Giovanni waved him off. "An Anglican prayer
is useless."

While George stepped back, looking much re-
proved, Giuseppe crossed himself unsteadily, then
gripped his cross and began to mumble in broken
Latin. Don Giovanni slipped to his knees beside the
bed. After exchanging bemused glances, Rutgers and
Hollingsworth followed suit.

TWENTY-NINE

"Good morning, *querida.*"

A week later, Carlos grinned down at Christina, who lay helplessly bound and gagged in his bunk, her eyes spewing raw hatred at him. He sighed. This business with the wench was growing tiresome. He had strict orders to kill her—indeed, he had been paid very well to do so—and yet he preferred to bed her first. Perhaps he had been a fool to think that he could convince her to come to him willingly. He liked such mental games of enticement, domination, and subjugation. And his fierce male pride argued that if Marco Glaviano could seduce this girl, then so could he.

Daily he had tried to poison the wench's mind against Marco, to convince her that Glaviano had abandoned her. Yet all his efforts so far had proved for naught. God only knew what went on in that stubborn head of hers, but she treated him with unflinching defiance and loathing. In fact, the wench

311

was downright dangerous. The first time one of his
men had untied her bonds so she could see to her
needs, she had knocked the poor bastard senseless
and had escaped to the main deck with the man's
cutlass. If several of his crew had not possessed the
presence of mind to throw a net over the spitfire, she
would likely have gotten away. Now she was led to
her washings, and to the crew's head, like a dog,
with a leash around her neck and her hands mana-
cled behind her. Despite these humiliations, the girl's
spirit never flagged. Even when she was thrown to
her knees on deck for her bath, even as she crouched
there, near naked and shivering violently as his men
threw buckets of cold water on her and jeered cruelly, she never displayed fear. Instead, rabid rage and
contempt forever gleamed in those bright green eyes.
If only he could unleash that feisty spirit in a more
carnal manner; if only he could bed this hot piece
without raping her. The very idea sent lust shooting
through his loins.

He crossed the room to her and tore back the
moth-eaten blanket, ogling her brazenly. Her filthy
chemise hung in tatters on her body, and her skin
was covered with numerous small bruises. Still,
never had she looked more desirable, especially as
her chest heaved, her nostrils flared, and her eyes
blazed malice at him.

Taking perverse satisfaction in her helpless wrath,
he sat down beside her, drawing a rough finger over
her upper, bared chest. She struggled violently, uselessly, against her restraints, and he chuckled.

"Feisty today, aren't we?" he asked with deceptive
mildness. "You know, Christina, I am beginning to
wonder why I put up with this willful behavior. A
night spent on your back with fifty of my men to attend you would surely divest you of this defiance."

Her eyes grew huge, but still she revealed no fear.

"Are you putting on this show for the sake of

Marco?" he asked. "If so, you are a fool, *querida*. Did
I tell you of our last exploits together in Charles
Town? Marco sported with a comely wench in my
very presence. Indeed, he had the woman screaming
in passion right there in his lap. Afterward, he
laughed over how you had fallen in love with him.
Did you know he thinks of you as a silly, annoying
child? He said he might bed you just for the sport of
it. But you are a fool if you think any woman will
ever win Marco Glaviano's heart. His first mistress
will always be the sea."

He paused to gauge her response. Her eyes were
eloquent with rage. Cruel satisfaction surged in him.
Perhaps he was touching a nerve, making progress.

"Tell me this, *querida*," he went on. "If Marco truly
is devoted to you, why does he not come to rescue
you now? Perhaps he is too busy bedding the Spanish wench, Rosa, no? Or perhaps another of his
whores? You know, he mentioned to me that he was
having to sneak around to bed his women, since you
had become such a jealous nuisance."

Now the girl's eyes took on a wild, haunted quality, and Carlos felt a sadistic thrill. If only he could
convince her that Marco was toying with her affections, persuade her to hate this man, then maybe he
would still have a chance. He wanted to taste her before he killed her. Not that he relished the prospect of
driving his knife into her slender breast—but, after
all, business was business, and he had been paid well
to dispatch her. Perhaps he would leave that unpleasant task to his men, turn her over to them once he
had tired of her. She would never live through a
night of the horrors they would subject her to up on
deck.

He leaned over, loosened her gag, and removed it.
"Well, what have you to say about your lover, querida?"

She spat at him, spewing saliva all over his face.

"Puta!" he roared.

Despite his rage, Christina's chin snapped up, her eyes defied Carlos to his soul, and she smiled a smile of malignant triumph.

"Slut!" he screamed, shaking a fist at her. "I should have you tied naked to my mast and thrashed until you are dead!"

Her defiance still did not waver.

Hurling a string of Spanish oaths, Carlos shoved the coarse cloth between Christina's teeth and tied it brutally tight at the back of her head. He left the cabin in disgust. He was tiring of this game.

After Carlos left, a tear slid down Christina's cheek. Her throat and chest ached with sorrow and helplessness. ¯

Over the past week, her life had been a living hell. Daily she was subjected to endless humiliations—being tied to the bunk with nothing to keep her company but her hunger and terror; being led about like a dog; being washed, half naked, on deck while the men ogled her and jeered insults. Sometimes, much of a day would pass before she was brought food or drink. Miguel, the sailor who had showed her kindness on the night she was abducted, tried his best to secure her provisions, but the scant rations the pirates alloted her—maggoty gruel and foul water—qualified more as insults than as sustenance.

Being with Carlos was the worst of all. The man was a pig, dressing, eating, belching, farting, and even relieving himself in her presence. He was also brazenly trying to seduce her, and she expected that any day his patience would end. Only yesterday he had drawn a chair up to her bunk, and as she watched in helpless horror, he had pulled out his huge, ugly member and fondled himself in her presence. Each time she had looked away, he had forced her head around, making her watch, sickened, as he spewed his seed all over his hand.

And the things he said about Marco! She had always known that Carlos and Marco were enemies, but only now did she realize that they had also been *compadres* for years while in port. At first, she had dismissed Carlos's wild stories of their exploits together, but then she had understood, to her intense dismay, that Carlos simply knew too much about Marco to be making up everything. He knew of Rosa and of Marco's other mistresses, as well as details of Marco's activities over the years. When Carlos told her of how Marco had bedded so many women in Charles Town, even on his last voyage, she found it more and more difficult not to believe him. And his claim that Marco and Rosa were still lovers matched Rosa's story in every detail. It seemed impossible that both Rosa and Carlos could be lying. How could they fabricate identical accounts when they had had no contact with each other? All this made Christina realize that Rosa surely was carrying Marco's child— that he was likely sporting with her and with others, even as her own life hung by a thread. The realization only deepened her despair, hurt, and sense of betrayal. The anguish of knowing Marco had deceived and forsaken her was often more than she could bear.

What daunted her the most was the question Carlos asked her daily: *If Marco truly cares for you, then why has he not rescued you?* The answer seemed so obvious, so heartbreaking, that Christina often cared not whether she lived or died.

"Where *the hell* is Christina?"

The Renaldis, Giuseppe, Hollingsworth, and Rutgers all gasped in unison as a gaunt, white-faced Marco stumbled into the dining room wearing only a dressing gown.

Don Giovanni bolted to his feet. Tossing Marco a look of concern and embarrassment, he quickly turned to his wife. "Take my daughters out of this room."

Nodding vehemently, Donna Flora sprang up, grabbing Jovita and Calista and towing the two wide-eyed girls from the room.

Meanwhile, Don Giovanni was hurrying over to grab Marco, who was ashen-faced, obviously in severe pain, and wobbling on his feet. "My friend, you should not be out of bed!" he scolded. "You lost so much blood, and you have been delirious for days!"

"Where is Christina?" Marco repeated impatiently.

"I realize that you have been calling out for her. But she—that is, the girl—"

"Dammit, man, tell me the truth!"

The force of uttering this furious command left Marco staggering and clenching his teeth in agony. Don Giovanni also swayed as he tried to prop up his friend's massive body.

George Hollingsworth hurried over to help. "Here, my son, let us get you back to bed—"

"Take me to my chair or I shall kill both of you!"

The two men exchanged helpless glances, then began dragging the ailing man toward his chair. The brief journey across the room caused Marco excruciating pain, and once he was deposited in his chair, he caught several sharp, tortured breaths while reality swam in and out before his eyes. He buried his face in his hands, shook his head, and groaned.

At last the dizziness passed. He glanced up to find Charles Rutgers seated to his left. "Tell me where Christina is," he demanded.

The older man nodded morosely. "I fear that my ward has been abducted by Spanish pirates— probably the same brutes who wounded you."

"God in heaven! That's just what I was afraid of!" Marco surged to his feet, only to collapse in pain.

"You must not strain yourself in this manner and possibly hasten your own death," Hollingsworth admonished frantically. "We are relieved to see that your fever has at last broken, but you have also been at death's door for over a week now. Any exertion at this point would spell disaster."

"But—Christina . . ." Marco's voice was a tormented whisper.

"Listen to me, my boy," Don Giovanni put in. "Claudio and a crew of your men sailed off to rescue Christina the very night she was abducted and you were so gravely wounded. I am sure your able crewmen have found the girl by now and are fetching her safely home."

Yet Marco was shaking his head violently. "No . . . I must go after her myself. I am much more familiar with Carlos's haunts than they are."

"Who exactly is this Carlos?" Rutgers queried.

"He is a privateer for our Spanish foes, and has been my mortal enemy for many years. And I must sail after him at once."

"But, my boy, you no longer have a ship," Don Giovanni pointed out.

Marco stared contemptuously at Christina's guardian and stepuncle. "I shall take the schooner these two chartered out of Charles Town. Lord only knows why they are not using it to track Carlos and rescue Christina."

Hollingsworth and Rutgers looked at each other askance.

As Marco's pain faded, he regarded the two men with a suspicious frown. Turning to Don Giovanni, he murmured, "You know, it does make a man wonder."

"Wonder what?" his friend replied.

"We have recently learned that Christina is an heiress. And all these mysterious cutthroats started popping up about the same time her guardian and stepuncle became aware of her whereabouts. Now the girl has been abducted." He glanced challengingly from Rutgers to Hollingsworth. "Any comment, gentlemen? Is it possible that either of you might benefit from the girl's disappearance—or her death?"

Hollinsgworth appeared outraged. "You cannot actually mean to suggest that one of us might have been a party to my stepniece's abduction!"

"Were you?" Marco demanded in a lethal tone.

"Of course not!"

"What you are inferring is most contemptible!" protested a red-faced Rutgers. He threw down his napkin in disgust. "Signore Glaviano, you cannot blame us because your own reckless privateering activities have put your life and that of my ward in peril. If you are looking to assign fault, blame yourself and this Carlos you spoke of."

Marco glared at Rutgers. "Why do I get the feeling that the current crisis goes way beyond my Spanish enemies?"

That question was met with cold, tense silence.

Marco's patience was exhausted. "I shall sail at once to retrieve Christina," he announced decisively. He heaved himself to his feet with a labored grunt, took two steps, and doubled over from the pain.

Don Giovanni rushed up to rescue Marco, motioning to George Hollingsworth to help him. "Let us get the boy back to bed, pour brandy down him, and pray that he will sleep. Otherwise, he will kill himself before this day is out."

THIRTY

Ten days later, Christina's plight had not improved.
She was still in the wretched, stinking cabin, with
Carlos tormenting her daily. She remained bound
and gagged on the filthy bunk, with bedbugs biting
her and sometimes even rats scurrying across the
blankets.

The only bright spot in her deplorable existence
was Miguel, the sailor who still showed her occasional kindnesses. She had even been able to glean
some information from him. One morning, when he
had actually brought her a fresh banana and a
mango, she had questioned him and he had admitted
that they had just taken on fresh supplies and produce in Havana.

And over the past few days, when the ship's cannon had boomed out nightly and screams had rent
the air, Miguel had come belowdecks to offer her a
few words of comfort, informing her that she was in
no danger, that they were now off the coast of the

American colonies and were attacking British merchantmen. Yet even though the sailor had sought to reassure her, Christina had lain in terror during the nightly battles, smelling the acrid scent of smoke and listening to the bloodcurdling cries of men being tortured and killed, and to the piteous wails of Englishwomen. The cruel laughter of the Spanish pirates revolted her the most. At times, she could have sworn she could even smell the sweet stench of blood down here belowdecks. She had been certain she was hallucinating, until one night she felt something wet and sticky trickle down her arm and she realized to her horror that human blood was actually dripping down on her from the broken skylight above! She had screamed and screamed, but no one had heard—or cared.

Night after night the torment continued. One evening Christina lay cowering on her bunk, listening to the shriek of shells as yet another battle ensued. Who were the pirates attacking now? Another merchantman? A British warship? Did she dare hope that Marco had at last found her?

The earsplitting volleys continued for a few more moments, until a mighty crash jolted Christina violently. She assumed they had come alongside another vessel and the Spanish pirates were grappling on.

Then the screams came—of men, women, even children. Christina sobbed and trembled in fear for the poor victims. Doubtless the bastards were sacking another British merchantman. Oh, God, how she wished her hands were not bound and she could shield her ears against those harrowing cries! How she wished she had a weapon and could dispatch a few of the Spanish pigs!

All at once her door crashed open, and Carlos charged in with a bloody cutlass in his hand, followed by two of his lieutenants. There was a thin slash across Carlos's cheek and his body was streaked with red.

To his lieutenants, he snarled, "Bring the haughty little bitch up on deck and tie her to the foremast. I want her to see how we deal with uppity English wenches."

Despite Christina's protests, Carlos's two henchmen cut her loose and dragged her from the cabin, pulling her resisting body up the companionway.

A nightmare awaited her on the main deck. As the two lieutenants lashed her to the foremast, Christina looked around wildly. Across from the pirates' ship, a British merchantman was brightly ablaze and listing badly, its crewmen jumping into the water to a certain death as sharks circled around.

The sight on deck of the pirate ship was even worse. Several corpses of British sailors lay strewn about; the few officers and male passengers who were still alive were being flogged or tortured by Carlos's men. Most harrowing of all, a group of women and children had been tied to the mainmast across from Christina; all were wailing in abject horror as they watched the men and officers being thrashed and cudgeled.

Christina would have collapsed had she not been tied to the foremast. She prayed for death to release her from this hell.

Then Carlos once again loomed before her, with half a dozen of his compatriots surrounding him. "Tell the crew they are free to kill the men and rape the women now," he ordered, staring Christina straight in the eye. "And let the bitch watch."

"No," she pleaded weakly. "Please don't."

Carlos stepped up to her and stroked her quivering chin. "Not so proud now, eh?" he asked with a sadistic grin, while his cronies laughed.

"Please, just don't hurt anyone else," Christina implored. "I'll do anything you say."

"Anything?" he repeated meaningfully.

She stared at him with raw hatred. "Anything."

Snapping his fingers, Carlos turned to a lieutenant. "Tell the men to stop the slaughter."

"But, Captain—"

"Do it now! Then bring that chest of lady's clothing we retrieved last week down to my cabin, and fetch the wench a bath." He stared at Christina with contempt. "She smells, and I want her scrubbed before I bed her."

"Aye, Captain," the lieutenant replied grudgingly.

Two of the lieutenants dragged Christina below-decks, while several others hurried off to stop the bloodletting. One lagged behind to speak with Carlos.

"*Capitán*," he warned in low, tense tones, "you must allow the men their sport or they will mutiny."

Carlos dismissed his words with a wave of his hand. "Do not worry. I only staged this demonstration to bring the little wench to heel. Just keep the men restrained long enough for me to bed her. Afterward, you may all have her, as well as the other women. You may kill their husbands and the rest of the British officers. Then we shall throw the sorry lot of them to the sharks."

The lieutenant grinned from ear to ear. "*Sì, capitán!*"

On the same night, Marco stood on the quarter-deck of *La Spada*, desperately scanning the waters ahead for any sign of Carlos's schooner.

He thought of all that had transpired over the past ten days. After he had awakened from his fever to the horrifying discovery that Christina had indeed been abducted, the others had done everything in their power to restrain him from sailing at once to rescue her. Then that very evening, Claudio and most of his men had slipped into port on *La Spada*, all of

them in dour humor after having found no trace of
Christina during their eight-day voyage.

Marco had prepared to set sail with Claudio and
the other crewmen the following dawn. Before leaving, he had aggressively questioned Charles Rutgers
and George Hollingsworth regarding whether either
man had had a hand in Christina's kidnapping. Both
had steadfastly avowed their innocence, and finally,
Marco had been compelled to give up his interrogation and leave. However, he had left Giuseppe in
charge, instructing him to remain on guard for any
suspicious behavior on the part of either man. He
still suspected that a conspiracy might be at work
here, and that Hollingsworth or Rutgers could well
be after Christina's inheritance.

As for the Renaldis, they had vowed to remain at
Isola del Mare until Christina was safely returned.
Marco still had not informed Don Giovanni that he
intended to marry Christina, but he would once he
arrived back with her.

For, during this long, desperate voyage, nothing
had become clearer to him than his love for Christina
and the hopelessness of his life without her. How
foolish his pride, his hesitation, and all their prior arguments now seemed, especially when juxtaposed
against the reality that he could lose her! Daily he
battled the sickening fear for her life that could so
easily drive him to madness or desperation. Nightly
he prayed to God to give him direction, to help him
point *La Spada*'s bow toward the woman he loved.
He had solemnly vowed that if only he could find
her, he would profess his love for her, marry her, and
make her the queen of his heart for the rest of his life.

Evidently, *il Dio* had been listening, for of late, they
had uncovered clues concerning Carlos's whereabouts. During a brief stopover in Havana, they had
questioned some barmaids, and had learned that
Carlos had been in port there a week ago. And only

three days past, they had encountered a British warship. Marco had conversed briefly with the captain, who had informed him that Carlos had plundered and sunk two British merchantmen off the South Carolina coast. Marco had set sail for the area at once.

"*Capitano*, do you see it?"

Distracted from his thoughts, Marco turned to Claudio, who stood by his side at the helm. "See what?"

Claudio pointed to the horizon, and at last Marco spotted the red glow in the distance. "By God, it is a ship ablaze!" he cried, raising his spyglass and leveling it on the scene.

"It could well be Carlos sacking another British vessel," Claudio said.

Marco nodded. "Set a course due north at once!"

Claudio relayed the order, and *La Spada* tacked into the wind, making steadily for the distant blaze.

At last they were close enough for Marco to make out details through his spyglass. Exultation soared in him as he recognized Carlos's schooner; beyond it, he saw a British merchantman aflame and listing badly to port.

He scanned his spyglass back to the deck of the pirate ship, observing the hands busily tying up prisoners, heaving corpses over the sides, and washing blood from the decks. A group of women and children were tied to the mainmast, but he did not spot Christina amongst them. Carlos was nowhere in sight either, and so far none of the pirate crewmen seemed to note their approach.

Christina! he thought with a terrible ache in his chest. *Dio*, let her be alive and unharmed!

Closer to their quarry, Marco ordered the sails struck so that they could glide in, hopefully still unnoticed by the Spaniards. Their luck held until they were almost within boarding distance. At last the

Spanish pirates spotted *La Spada* looming out at them in the night, and they swarmed around in confusion, trying to pull back the cannon from the gunwales and load the guns. But their efforts proved too little, too late. *La Spada* slammed into the side of the Spanish vessel, and Marco's men were ready with boarding pikes and grappling hooks. Within seconds, they overran the decks of Carlos's vessel, screaming bloodthirsty cries as the hand-to-hand battle began.

Marco joined them, grabbing a line and vaulting across to the other vessel. He landed on his feet, drew out his cutlass, and went to work, swinging and hacking at his hated Spanish enemies. Within a minute, he had dispatched three pirates, lopping a hand off one, a nose off another. The air became thick with the sounds of screams and the smell of blood. Around Marco, his men were meeting with equal success, as the Spaniards fell with shrieks of agony. In less than two minutes, it was all over—the rest of the Spanish pirates had given up and were begging for quarter.

Marco grabbed one of them and pinned him to the deck with his cutlass against the man's belly. "Where is the girl?"

"What girl?" the man asked hysterically.

"The English girl, Christina. Speak, you bastard, or die!"

"She is belowdecks!" the man screamed. "The captain is bedding her."

"So, *querida*, are you ready for me?"

Wearing a high-necked red satin dress, Christina lay on Carlos's bed and watched the repulsive pirate advance on her. At least she had had the satisfaction of a thorough bath and a shampoo a few minutes ago, even if afterward she had been forced to endure the humiliation of dressing up in the garish clothing

Carlos had laid out for her. Now the bastard had returned to claim his prize.

She looked him over. How did he dare accuse her
of smelling when he was disgustingly filthy, his face
blackened by soot and dirt and his body still streaked
with blood. His shirt was open, revealing his black-
furred chest, and he wore a small dagger in a sheath
at his waist. She stared at the bulge in his trousers
and forced herself to lick her lips and recite the lines
she had already rehearsed.

"I have watched you play with your big member
for days now," she murmured in a sultry purr, batting her lashes at him. "I long to feel it inside me this
night."

She watched the pirate gulp, saw his eyes go
crazed with animal lust, and then he lunged for her.
It was the very opportunity she had been waiting for,
praying for—for him to drop his guard, just once!
Christina knew she was weak from her ordeal, but
she was also deadly determined. Using all her training, she dodged Carlos's bulk, flipped him over her
onto his back on the bunk, and grabbed his dagger
with her nimble fingers.

Before Carlos even knew what had hit him, the girl
was on top of him, slitting open his trousers from
waist to crotch and then shoving his razor-sharp dagger between his legs!

While she had not yet sliced him, Carlos was too terrified, too petrified, even to move. "What in God's
name are you doing?" he gasped in a tortured whisper.

"Move an inch and I'll cut your balls off, you
bloody bastard!" she said with steely quiet.

Carlos's fear-crazed eyes met her bright, near-rabid
gaze. "Please, you must not—I would sooner die—"

"Not so proud now, are we?" Christina mimicked
with a cruel sneer. "How does it feel to be held helpless and humiliated?"

"Please—you must not—"

"You sat here for days playing with your disgusting member right in front of me!" she continued with rage and disgust. "Did you truly think I would not get my revenge? Did you think you were impressing me?" She glanced downward and laughed. "Why, you poor little thing is so puny compared to Marco's that I may just cut it off to put you out of your misery." She smiled. "I am certain none of your women would even notice the difference!"

Carlos was speechless, his nostrils flaring as he gulped in frantic breaths.

Then, suddenly, the entire vessel was slammed violently and Carlos flinched as Christina nicked him.

"Mother of God, are we being boarded now?" he cried, hearing the sounds of a battle going on above them.

Moments later, with cutlass in hand, Marco kicked open the door of Carlos's room and crashed inside, terrified of what he would see, sick with fear that he would be too late—

What he saw astounded him. Carlos lay flat on his back on his bunk, his eyes wide with abject horror. Christina, wearing a red satin frock, was crouched over him with a dagger at his groin.

Carlos spotted Marco, and at once began pleading shrilly. "Marco, my friend! Please, you must save me! This termagant is trying to castrate me!"

As Carlos spoke, Christina's gaze swung around to Marco, focusing on him intently, but her dagger did not move. For a moment Marco stared back at the two, the girl with naked rage and bloodlust fomenting in her eyes, the man shrinking beneath her in terror.

The entire tableau unfolding before Marco was such an anticlimax that he simply could not contain himself. He began to laugh, to laugh so hard that he became light-headed. Here he had worried himself sick about Christina when the ruthless, splendid creature was obviously perfectly capable of castrating even his own mortal enemy! *Dio*, she was *magnifica*. Indeed, it was Carlos, not she, who was in need of saving!

When at last he was able to control himself and steady himself on his feet, he gazed at the other two, who had not moved an inch—

Neither appeared amused.

Another chuckle escaped him, and then he heard Carlos plead, "*Please*, Marco!"

Marco scratched his jaw. "Well, I am not so certain just what I should do here." He stared tenderly at Christina. "Do you want to castrate him, *cara*?"

She nodded vehemently.

Marco turned to the horrified Carlos and shrugged. "You heard what the lady said."

Carlos crossed himself and began to murmur supplications to the heavens.

Marco stepped closer, and his eyes were perfectly serious as he gazed at Christina. "Are you all right?"

She nodded again.

He drew a pained breath, then stroked her pale cheek and asked gently, "Did he rape you? Tell the truth, now."

"Marco, can you not see for yourself?" Carlos cried desperately.

Ignoring that, Marco was still staring questioningly at Christina. "Did he?"

She shook her head.

His hand reached down to restrain her fingers. "Then don't, *cara*."

For a moment, he observed her inner struggle, watched her blink rapidly and chew her bottom lip. Then, muttering a blasphemy that scorched even Marco's ears, she removed the knife from Carlos's crotch and hurled it into the headboard just inches above his nose.

As the girl at last moved off him, Carlos went spinning off the bunk, crashed to his knees on the floor, and began retching violently.

Christina fell, sobbing, into Marco's arms.

THIRTY-ONE

THE NEXT FEW MOMENTS PASSED IN A FLURRY OF ACTIVITY, cutting Marco and Christina's reunion woefully short.

No sooner had she fallen into his arms than Claudio charged into the cabin with a dozen pressing questions. What was to be done about the English officers and passengers? About Carlos and his crew?

Thrust back into a role of leadership, Marco was forced to abandon Christina at a time when he knew she was emotionally very fragile, very vulnerable. He returned to the decks of Carlos's schooner and began issuing orders. The remaining dead were wrapped in canvas, weighted down, and dropped overboard. Christina and the English refugees—the surviving officers and passengers of the sunken merchantman *Odyssey*—were transferred to *La Spada*. Marco promised the English citizens that he would give them safe passage to Charles Town.

Marco then had his men herd Carlos and his remaining crewmen on deck of the Spaniard's schooner. Staring at the twoscore of captives, Marco pondered their fate. With the exception of Carlos, who regarded him with pride and contempt, the Spanish pirates were obviously fearful for their lives; several were weeping or praying openly, and all clearly expected no quarter.

Indeed, Marco's first inclination had been to slaughter the lot of them for what they had done to Christina. But now, looking out at this sea of frightened, vulnerable humanity, he realized he could not do that. After all, Christina had been returned to him, unmolested. And he could not live with himself or with his God if he massacred helpless men. A man, even an enemy, did not deserve to die this way; a man deserved a fighting chance.

An even more central realization jolted him. He could not give Christina the love and commitment she needed unless he first gave up his quest for revenge. Indeed, how meaningless his vendetta now seemed, compared with all he had nearly lost.

However, one matter he could—and would—settle.

He motioned to Carlos to step forward. As the Spanish pirate strode up to face him with courage and defiance, Marco murmured, "I am willing to release you and your crew, *amico mio*. However, there are conditions."

Carlos appeared fascinated. *"Sì?"*

"First, you must give me your word that you will never again assault anyone on Isola del Mare."

"Done, *amigo*."

"And you must tell me who hired you to kill Christina."

Carlos hesitated for only a moment, and then he spoke . . .

Convincing Christina that he had made the right decision regarding the Spanish pirates was another

matter altogether. Marco was stunned by the depth
of her outrage over his action.

Half an hour later, the two stood on the deck of *La
Spada*, arguing bitterly as they watched Carlos's
schooner disappear into the night. The English refugees had been settled in the crew's quarters belowdecks, and *La Spada* was now making for Charles
Town.

"How could you just let Carlos go?" Christina demanded. "He and his men tortured and killed the
British sailors. They tied me and the wives and children to the masts and made us watch!"

In the scant light of the moon, Marco stared at
Christina. She still wore the high-necked red satin
dress; her damp hair was whipping in the cold, brisk
breeze. While she looked clean and kempt, he considered how thin and drawn she appeared, with the
pale circles under her eyes and the hollows beneath
her cheekbones. She had the countenance of an angry, wounded child, and he wanted nothing more
than to pull her into his arms and comfort her. But he
knew that such a step would only enrage her further
right now.

"What would you have me do, Christina?" he
asked patiently. "Keelhaul the lot of them?"

"Yes!" she replied vindictively. "It would give me
the greatest pleasure to watch them all suffer and die
deaths as agonizing as those they forced on the British seamen! At the very least, you could have taken
them all to Charles Town to be tried—"

"And hung," he finished cynically. "You must try
to understand, Christina. There is a code among pirates. I do not simply slaughter helpless crews after I
have captured them. Moreover, any trial in Charles
Town would only be a joke, with no doubt at all as
to the outcome."

She flung her hands wide in exasperation. "So you
just let them go? Do you actually believe that under

similar circumstances that barbarian Carlos would show you the same mercy?"

"I would hope he would. Even if he would not, that does not give me license to reduce myself to his level. The fact is, Carlos is a legitimate privateer sailing under letters of marque from the throne of Spain. It is his charge to harass British shipping—"

"Is it his charge to treat me so cruelly? How can you let him go after he abused me the way he did?"

He reached out to stroke her cheek, his expression troubled. "He did not rape you, *cara.*"

She shrank from his touch, shaking her head in pained disbelief. "You really do have the heart of a pirate, don't you, Marco Glaviano? Is that all you care about? Whether or not your prize has been sullied?"

"Do you actually think I regard you as a prize?" he countered, his patience wearing thin.

"Yes!" Her voice held a frantic edge. "All you care about is whether or not he got beneath my chemise. Don't you understand that there are other kinds of violation? The way they humiliated me, laughed at me—"

He grasped her shoulders and stared at her earnestly. "Christina, you are becoming hysterical. I realize that you have been through an ordeal. You need time to recover, then you will see that I am right—"

She shoved him away. "You are right? You who were too busy bedding Rosa or Monique to even come after me for weeks on end?"

Now his patience snapped. "That is a lie!" he retorted, shaking a finger at her.

"I don't know why you bothered to come, anyway," she went on spitefully. "All you have ever cared about is being rid of me!"

"Christina!"

"Why don't you just discard me in Charles Town with the others? I shall claim my fortune, and good riddance to you, the Renaldis, and my guardian! God knows I have no need for a man whose loyalty goes no farther than his breeches!"

Marco's voice was rising. "So you actually think that I didn't come after you because I was too busy wenching?"

Hot tears flooded her eyes. "Yes! I know you have betrayed me repeatedly! You are the worst kind of scoundrel! And I have no desire to be part of your harem, Marco Glaviano—that is, until you tire of me and dump me on Vittorio!"

Marco had reached his wit's end. "Damned ungrateful little chit!" he swore. "I do wonder why I bothered to save your spoiled little hide!"

"See—you admit it!"

"Get belowdecks!" he roared. "Before I throttle you!"

She shot him a look of blazing malice, then whirled and tore off for the companionway.

Marco remained at the railing, seething with confusion, anger, and wounded pride. He realized that Christina had suffered grievously over the past weeks, but that did not excuse her unjust accusations. How could she treat him so cruelly? He had gone to perdition and back for her, sailing off to find her when he could barely stand on his own two feet. He had worried himself sick over her, agonizing endlessly about her fate up until the very moment he had rescued her. Then he had been prepared to profess his love and to give up everything for her—his pride, his women, even the sea itself. Now this! How it rankled him that she had accused him of wenching—wenching, even as he lay on his own deathbed! *Wenching*—when he had not been able to bed another woman for over six months, ever since the blackhearted little witch had laid claim to him. He had gone through bloody hell for her—and his reward had been to be attacked by her viciously.

She owed him an apology—in spades. He would bear her home now. In time, after she had suffered enough, he would even marry her. In the meantime, he might even bed her again—

Correction, he said to himself in a sudden burst of passion. He would *definitely* bed her again.

But he would never let her see how deeply she had wounded him. He would withhold his heart from her until she came to *him* and set things right between them.

After donning the nightgown she had brought back with her from the schooner, Christina lay sobbing in her bunk in the small cabin across from Marco's. She felt so hurt and confused. Of course, she had been ecstatic when she had first watched him charge into Carlos's cabin to rescue her. Her heart had soared when she had feasted her eyes on his magnificent face after what had seemed an eternity apart from him. The moment when she had fallen into his arms, felt his trembling lips on her forehead, and breathed in his comforting essence had been heaven, her joy near blinding.

Then he had enraged her by releasing Carlos and the other pirates, even though she had known in her heart that he was right, that slaughtering the Spanish in the barbaric manner she had demanded would have been despicable. Still, she was desperate to receive some sign from Marco that he really did love her, that he valued her above all others, that he had missed her as much as she had missed him. So far, she had received none.

And doubts about Rosa and the others continued to plague her. Why had he waited so long to come after her, unless he was indeed too busy bedding the Spanish whore—just as Carlos had claimed?

She groaned and thrashed about as her conscience needled her. Had she really given him a chance to ex-

plain when she had attacked him so angrily on deck?
Even if he had not sailed off immediately to rescue
her, at least he had come. How could she excuse all
the vicious things she had said to him? To be brutally
honest with herself, she could not really blame him
for being enraged, for it was unlike her to be so
cruel—

Abruptly, Christina jumped and clutched her covers as her door crashed open and Marco loomed in
the doorway. He was shirtless, his massive body and
long blond hair outlined in stark relief by the light
spilling in from the companionway. Her wide-eyed
gaze became riveted on him. Never had he appeared
more frightening, more powerful—all vengeful pirate. His muscles were tense, his hands balled in fists
at his sides. He was enraged, and justifiably so.

He would kill her now.

He came over to her. "You are right, *cara*," he muttered, tearing back the sheet. "A pirate has a right to
his plunder. You are mine until we return to port."

And he hauled her up into his arms. Her heart
thudded wildly as he bore her across the corridor.
One glance at his grim face, the harsh features set off
by the wavering light, made her dizzy.

Just inside his cabin, he kicked the door shut and
paused to claim her lips in a ravenous kiss. At the
merest taste of him, all the emotion welling in
Christina burst. With a half sob, she gave herself to
him, kissing him back passionately and coiling her
arms around his corded neck.

She felt him heave a mighty shudder, and then his
anger, too, turned to tenderness and feverish desire.
He crossed the cabin quickly, depositing her on his
bunk and covering her face with kisses.

"*Cara, cara*," he murmured achingly.

"I missed you so," she whispered convulsively as
he covered her with his wonderful, hot body.

"Me, too, darling," he whispered.

"I was so scared ..."

"Me, too. *Dio*, I was frantic."

Feeling starved for him, Christina moved her hands over the smooth muscles of his chest, then began unbuttoning his breeches. She heard him grunt as if in pain as her hand curled over his warm, splendid erection. He was so hard, he felt as if he would burst in her fingers, and she yearned to feel his rigid length deep inside her.

"*Cara mia*," he murmured, nipping at her mouth as his impatient hands boldly hiked her gown over her waist, "let us give up our anger this night. Our reunion has been delayed far too long."

"I know."

His hands caressed her thighs and buttocks. His mouth took hers in a drowning kiss, his tongue plunging deep, possessing her utterly. His manhood thrust against her tightly coiled fingers and she heard him groan again, as if he were indeed in some physical discomfort. Before she could reflect on the oddity of this, he gently disengaged her fingers, kissing her palm with great tenderness as his strong thighs spread hers. He drove powerfully, embedding himself to the hilt inside her—

The intimacy was shattering, hot and heavenly, and Christina cried out. His lips captured hers again passionately, smothering her cries and calming her. She coiled her legs tightly around his waist and accepted him greedily. Yet after a moment, Marco was again uttering those odd sounds of pain. He gently withdrew, sat up against the headboard, and pulled her astride him. She gasped as his hands clutched her waist and pressed her deep into his lap.

He raised his knees to heighten the sweet torment. Reaching beneath her gown to caress her breasts, he eased her back. "Relax, *cara*. Arch your beautiful back and let me savor you."

She did, only to shutter and gyrate in a frenzy of

need as he rocked her slowly, exquisitely, driving her to an ecstasy she could not bear, wrenching a wild sob of climax from her. Her cries of pleasure broke his restraint as well. Thrusting powerfully, he swiftly took his own release, groaning and pulling her tightly to him.

Afterward, he stroked her silky hair, his expression bemused as he felt her tears on his cheek. When he asked in a tortured voice if he had hurt her, she cried, "No, no," and covered his face with kisses.

She could not bring herself to tell him that she wept because never had their lovemaking been more beautiful, never had they been more physically intimate, and yet she hungered for the same emotional intimacy as well.

A long moment later, Marco got up and lit the lamp. He turned to smile at her, and was about to suggest they share a glass of wine when he saw the rope burns on her neck. Glancing lower, he saw the bruises on her beautiful thighs, her knees.

He glanced at her face quickly, questioningly. She suddenly became embarrassed, and began scrambling to pull down her gown.

He grabbed her hands, restraining her. "Get up," he commanded, "and take off that gown."

Christina stared in confusion at the white-faced stranger standing over her. Was Marco now angry because she was bruised and emaciated? Did he seek to humiliate her, to make her reveal her battered, half-starved body?

"No," she pleaded weakly.

He whispered a blistering oath, and she was pulled to her feet. "Take off that gown!"

His voice brooked no challenge, and Christina had no choice but to comply. Trembling, she took off her gown, flung it to the floor, and stared at him in defiance, a hairsbreadth away from bursting into tears again.

He stared at her incredulously. "My God, you are
so thin! When you wore the red dress, I could not really tell. Did they starve you, *cara?* And your neck—
what in the name of heaven did they—"

"What did they do?" Rage and anguish burst in
Christina, and her eyes were brilliant with bitter, un-
shed tears. "They fed me maggoty gruel! They led
me around like a dog on a leash! They threw me to
my knees on the deck and washed me down, half naked, while all of those filthy bastards jeered insults!"

His voice was barely audible. "Christina, did
they—did anyone—"

"Did they rape me? No, they did not! There, are
you satisfied?"

"Satisfied" far from described Marco's mental
state. Frenzied rage toward Carlos and agonizing
pain over the torment Christina had endured threatened to choke off his breathing. His chest hurt with
the force of the emotions welling up in him.

"Turn around, *cara,*" he somehow managed to
whisper.

She complied, and Marco could have murdered
Carlos a thousand times over when he glimpsed her
equally bruised backside. He leaned over and, with a
violently shaking hand, retrieved her nightgown.
Then he went to his desk and picked up a jar of
salve. He walked back to her, reached around her,
and put the jar in her hand.

He could barely speak. "Here, *cara,* this is an oint-
ment. It should help . . ."

He could say no more. Marco left the cabin and
hurried across the corridor to her cabin. He slammed
his fist into the bulkhead, then stifled a cry of pain.
He wanted to run screaming across the entire, vast
world. To her, away from her, he did not know.

She had been right, he realized. He should have
keelhauled the lot of those Spanish bastards and let
her watch!

Belatedly, he realized that he still held her night-gown. He raised it to his face, smelled her, and then he wept.

Christina applied the salve and, unable to find her nightgown, crawled back into Marco's bunk, turning her face to the bulkhead. Doubtless he found her so physically revolting now that he had gone off to sleep elsewhere. Nonetheless, she had left the lamp burning, just in case he should return.

She was dozing off when she felt him slip in beside her and curl an arm around her waist. "You are quite naked, *cara*," he teased.

She reached behind her, unceremoniously gripping his turgid organ, and then she harrumphed. "So are you. Not to mention disgracefully randy."

He chuckled. "I am a marauding pirate. What is your excuse?"

"You took my nightgown," she replied petulantly.

Marco pressed his mouth to her soft cheek. He could not tell her that he had left her nightgown, still damp with his tears, in the other cabin. Instead, he murmured huskily, "You will not need it tonight." He nibbled at her jaw for a moment, then added rather sternly, "Did you apply the salve as I told you to?"

"To my front," she replied. "I cannot reach my back."

"We will remedy that, then." He twisted around and found the jar on the chair next to the bed. He pressed her onto her stomach, and wrenching emotion welled up in his heart as he tenderly applied the salve to the welts on her neck, her too-thin shoulders, and the rest of her backside. A tear burned his eye when he heard her sigh contentedly. When he finished, he set the jar aside, then pulled her back against him, spoon-style. He reached around her and began absently to caress her between her thighs. She

moved wantonly against his rough thumb and dug
her fingernails into his forearm. He was glad she
could not see his face then.

When at last he screwed up the courage to speak,
his voice vibrated oddly. "You are a very brave girl,
cara. I . . . I am sorry for all you have had to endure."

The sound of his heart beating seemed to explode
in the silence as he waited for her reply. Though she
said nothing, he felt her shudder against him.

Tell me you're sorry, too, Christina, his heart begged.
*Say you were wrong to mistrust me so cruelly. Say it so
that we can be one in body and soul from this moment on.*

Still she said nothing, and anguish rose in him at
the chasm that still gaped between them. But when
she squirmed wantonly against him, it was more
than he could bear. He slid down beneath her hips,
then thrust vigorously upward, embedding his
sword in the snug sheath of her womanhood. She
gasped in startled delight and arched back against
him again, deliberately heightening his torment and
her own pleasure.

Marco hovered between agony and ecstasy.
"Sweet, darling girl," he murmured, reaching around
her to cup and knead her breasts. He wanted to pro-
long her rapture, to torture her all night long if he
could, but her next brazen wiggle submerged him in
madness. His arms clenched around her slender
body; his lips fluttered at her ear, whispering love
words in Italian. When she began to twist and writhe
with the force of her own climax, he held her to him
fast. In a storm of deep, lusty strokes, he spent himself inside her; and, thus joined, they slept until
dawn.

THIRTY-TWO

At dawn, *La Spada* began to pitch and roll. Christina awakened as she felt Marco gently withdraw from her flesh. A moment later, she twisted around to get a glorious view of his magnificent backside as he reached over to retrieve his breeches.

"What is wrong?"

"There's a storm blowing up," he muttered, turning to her. "I must get up on deck, make sure the ship is gale-rigged and everything is battened down."

Yet Christina might not have heard him. Her gaze was suddenly riveted on the angry red scar just beneath his navel. "My God—what happened to you?"

His eyes went cold, and he began pulling on his breeches. "On the night you were abducted, I tried to follow you to the beach, only I was detained by four very determined cutthroats. They knocked Pansy unconscious, banged me across the head, and slit me

open. Then I spent the next week on my deathbed—
when I wasn't too busy bedding Rosa or Monique."

"Oh, Marco! No wonder you seemed in pain last
night when we . . ."

Christina gazed at him, her heart in her eyes. She
yearned to apologize, but the rage on his face was
terrible to see. How he must hate her for the mean-
spirited things she had said last night! She feared
that an attempt to make amends now would seem
cruelly inadequate and only infuriate him more.

So she remained silent. He pulled on his boots,
shrugged on his shirt, and left the cabin, slamming
the door.

For over an hour, Christina clung to the bunk as
best she could as the ship pitched and rolled, and
rain battered the skylight above her. Her conscience
told her she should get up, dress, and go offer comfort to the British refugees, yet she was too nauseated
by the heaving of the boat to move.

At last, the storm quieted a bit. Marco came back,
drenched and shivering, his teeth rattling. He tossed
her nightgown at her—which, curiously, was quite
dry.

"We seem to have weathered the worst of it," he
muttered, his words ending in a shudder.

Quickly donning the gown, she sprang up from
the bunk. "My God, you are soaked. You will catch
your death!"

"Would you mourn me, wench?" he asked gruffly,
hugging himself in a futile effort to get warm.

"Of course I would! Now get out of those clothes
before you take the ague, you fool!"

"Always trying to undress me, aren't you?" he
grumbled as he began removing his clothing. "I ordered the cook to bring hot water for a bath." He
winked at her lasciviously. "I thought we might
share it."

She rolled her eyes. "How can you even think such indecent thoughts at a time like this?"

"With you, I am always indecent," he drawled.

"True," she conceded.

A rap came at the door then, and Marco gestured to Christina to dash behind the dressing screen. She did so, listening as the door opened, the cook and Marco exchanged a few words, and then the man left.

"The coast is clear, darling," he called out.

She emerged, wondering at his odd state of mind, for the storm had definitely put him in a belligerent mood. Her eyes widened as she viewed his nakedness. Next to him was the huge pitcher of steaming water the cook had left.

"Pull out the tub and fill it up, wench," he muttered, dashing for the bed, then diving under the blanket, shivering.

As much as she felt for him in his misery, her pride was wounded at his ordering her about this way. Why couldn't he simply have asked her to pour his bath? She would have done so eagerly. Instead, he had to act like a big, spoiled tyrant.

She set her jaw in a stubborn line and stormed off behind the screen, dragging out the small tin tub. She tossed Marco a rebellious glance and found that the miscreant was watching her every move in fascination as he lay on the bunk with the wool blanket pulled up to his chin.

It took all the strength in her body to pick up the heavy pitcher. Even as she finally managed to do so, the ship pitched again and water splashed over her from head to toe.

"God's teeth!" she cursed, dropping the pitcher in fury.

Then she heard him laugh.

Her seething gaze swung around to slam into him. She froze as she glimpsed him sitting up in the bunk

and staring at her intently. He looked so glorious un-
clothed, save for the blanket draped at his waist,
with a hazy light from the skylight pouring down
over his golden mane of hair and beautiful, muscled
chest. Why was he staring at her so avidly? She
looked down, at the drenched gown clinging to her
body, and at once understood why.

She wanted to rave at him with anger, but instead
her voice came out a pathetic whine. "See what
you've done?"

"Come here, love."

She stamped her foot. "No."

"Forget the bath. Come warm me properly."

On trembling legs, she crossed the cabin.

His arm snaked out and he pulled her into the
bunk with him. "My, you're so very wet," he teased,
his lips against her cheek.

"You are one to talk."

He chuckled and rent the cloth of her nightgown
from her neck to her waist.

"Marco! Damn it, that was the only nightgown in
the chest of clothing the Spanish pirates gave me."

"The gown is also sopping wet, and separates me
from your hot little body." He pulled the shredded
cloth off her. "Besides, did I not say you would not
need it?"

She groaned.

Tossing the wet linen on the floor, he pulled her
close. "Ah, this is so much better," he murmured, still
shivering as he clutched her close.

She harrumphed. "You mean you are not going to
ravish me again?"

"Is that an invitation?" he taunted, running his fingers through her hair.

"Of course not."

He chuckled. "I do not always have to devour you,
cara."

"You don't?" she asked with feigned amazement.

"Warm me up, and then we shall see ..."

For long moments, they snuggled face-to-face, until he ceased his quivering. Christina hugged him tightly and massaged his strong, tight muscles, savoring the closeness. Marco continued to caress her face and stroke her hair, until his fingers caught in a snarl, pulling a yelp of pain from her.

"Hey, take it easy!" she scolded. "It is not as if I have had you to brush my hair—"

Abruptly, she broke off and stared at him. He was staring back at her, so tenderly.

"Not in so long," she finished in a small voice, and then his mouth took hers.

"I know, *cara*," he whispered afterward. "Not in so very long."

Then he released her and sat up against the headboard.

"What are you doing now?" she asked, bemused.

He reached for his hairbrush on the shelf above the bed. "I am going to brush your hair, of course. Don't tell me you object?"

Her happily glowing eyes bespoke her answer.

Marco pulled Christina's body between his spread thighs, so that her back rested against his chest, and then he began gently brushing her long, shiny locks.

"How does that feel?" he asked.

"Um ... nice." Actually, it felt illicit and wonderful, Christina mused, to sit there with him, both of them totally nude while he ministered to her needs.

"Just nice?" he teased.

"I've never had my hair brushed quite like this before," she admitted breathlessly.

He smiled as he carefully untangled a lock. "I have missed doing this."

She placed her hand on his hard, warm thigh. "I have missed our being friends."

Although he continued the careful brushing, she

felt his thigh muscle go tense beneath her fingertips. "So you do need me after all," he muttered bitterly.

She turned her face up to his. "I have always needed you."

"Have you?" he asked, pinning her with an admonishing look. "Even though my loyalty goes no farther than my breeches?"

She chewed on her lower lip. "That was—perhaps—an unfortunate remark."

His scowl grew formidable. "Only perhaps?"

Her eyes simmered with anger. "Well, how do you think I have felt all these years, watching a constant parade of women troop in and out of your bedroom?"

"A constant parade? Be serious, Christina!"

"I *am* serious!"

His jaw tight, Marco brushed a strand of hair away from her face. "Why do I ever try to explain anything to you?" he muttered to himself. "You will never believe me. Now turn around so I may finish."

"No. First I have a question."

He set down the brush. "Yes?"

Her countenance grew uncertain. "Where are you, Marco?"

"What do you mean?" he asked warily.

"I remember, long ago, when you told me about that place within yourself where you go, where you find contentment."

"I have not lost that place, *cara.*"

"Are you safe from me there?" she asked with a trace of hurt.

For a long moment, he did not answer, an intent frown sculpting his face. At last he touched the firm line of her jaw and murmured ironically, "I doubt I am safe from you anywhere."

Her chin came up. "But you don't need me, do you? That is what you told me before the Renaldis came."

He sighed and reached out to stroke her face. "I was only trying to do right by you, *cara*."

"Were you? You told me you wanted me—but not to marry."

Her bitter words needled his conscience. "I never meant to hurt you, Christina." *Even though you have hurt me terribly with your own mistrust and your cruel accusations*, he added to himself in anguish.

"But the fact remains that you want me only to satisfy your physical needs," she accused.

"No, that is not true." He smiled. "In truth, you are very hard to resist, *cara*—so brave, so full of life and spirit and passion."

"Am I?"

He smiled wistfully. "Think of what it has been like for me to watch you grow up, to love you as a friend, and then, one day, to realize that you are a grown, ravishing woman—and that you want me."

"How did that make you feel?" she asked eagerly.

"Frightened," he admitted ruefully.

"Very?"

"Very."

"And now?"

A shuttered look crossed his eyes. "Now it pains me that you have had to endure the dark, evil side of this world. Now I long to see your smile again."

"Do you?"

"*Sì.*"

Longing to lighten the emotional mood, Marco ran his index finger teasingly over Christina's lower lip until, at last, she broke into a grin—and also sank her teeth into his fingertip.

"Ouch!" he cried with mock outrage. "I requested a smile—not an assault on my person!"

"It always gives me pleasure to attack you," she crooned.

"Shameless hoyden." He grabbed her shoulders and firmly turned her. "Now, sit still, wench, and let me finish, before I throw you across my knees and use the brush on your bottom to teach you some manners."

She giggled and took his large hands, placing them over her breasts. "I am your captive, my lord."

Marco shuddered. The feel of her tight nipples against his rough palms was too much for him. He leaned over to nibble at her delectable throat. By the time he could think to pick up the brush again, her hair had gained many new tangles.

The remainder of their voyage was pleasant, filled with many hours of making love. While Marco and Christina avoided provoking each other, neither did they resolve the impasse between them.

In the day and a half before they reached Charles Town, Christina made friends with the British refugees, particularly the women and children. While all of the adults seemed aware that Marco and Christina were occupying the same cabin without benefit of marriage, no word of criticism was ever directed their way. Indeed, all of the refugees seemed profoundly grateful to Marco for saving their lives and taking them to safety.

With one of the British women in particular, Anne Simmons, Christina became close. Anne was one of the lucky ones—she, her small child, and her husband had all been spared when Carlos sacked the *Odyssey.* While Anne's husband helped out at the helm, the two women sat together on the fo'c'sle hatch and chatted for hours. Christina soon fell in love with Anne's son, Billy, who often cuddled in her lap. Sometimes Marco would stride by and grin at her as she held the child. At those moments, she would have given her eyeteeth to know what he was thinking.

On the afternoon when they approached the South Carolina coast, Marco stopped by the hatch with a deck of cards. Choosing Billy as his partner, he challenged the women to a game of whist. The four gathered about the hatch and played several hands. Anne and Christina laughed when Marco brazenly cheated, helping Billy sort his cards and whispering instructions in his ear. Anne's husband came by once and cheered the men on. Christina's heart was warmed as she watched Marco patiently answer the boy's questions. Anne leaned over toward Christina and whispered, "He's such a fine man, your Captain Glaviano."

Watching Marco show the boy how to deal, Christina had to agree.

Not surprisingly, the men won every hand. After four games, Marco made their excuses and grabbed Christina's hand, pulling her belowdecks to his cabin.

Once they were inside with the door closed, he turned to her and said devilishly, "Now I want my reward for winning."

"Your reward for winning?" she cried, outraged. "You cheated at every hand, you rogue!"

He laughed. "I demand my prize, nonetheless."

"What prize, you reprobate?"

Christina was expecting something appropriately depraved, and could not have been more surprised when Marco turned to pick up a small plate from his desk. He extended the dish, which was filled with fruits and cheeses, toward her.

"I want you to eat all of this," he commanded.

"All of *that*? You must be jesting."

His expression was solemn as he shook his head. "Not at all, *cara*. I have been watching you over the last couple of days. You still are not eating enough, and you are far too thin."

"If I eat all of that, I shall retch."

"It is not that much," he coaxed, advancing toward her with a winsome grin. "I insist that you take better care of yourself. Lie down on the bunk and I shall feed you."

"No."

"No?" His eyes danced with laughter. "You are quite a scrawny little mite to be waving your fist at a giant. If you wish to defy me, woman, you must first put more flesh on those bones. Right now I could blow on you and knock you over."

"Oh, you are impossible."

Laughing, he pushed her toward the bunk. Seconds later, she was lying on her back, laughing, with the plate balanced on her bosom. Marco was dangling a bit of cheese over her tightly shut lips.

"Eat, *cara*."

"No, I'm not hungry," she gritted between clenched teeth.

"If you finish everything on the plate," he offered, "I shall reward you."

She feigned nonchalance. "*That* again."

"*That* again?" He was outraged. "You mean you have become bored with my lovemaking?"

"Not bored." She curled her arms around his neck. "But very spoiled."

He was staring at her sternly and trying to insinuate the bit of cheese between her tight lips. "You think I can no longer shock you? Surprise you?"

Her white teeth grabbed the chunk and she gazed up at him raptly. "Shock me. Then surprise me."

He shook his head. "Oh, no. Not until this plate is clean."

She pouted.

"I shall make you very glad you did it, Christina."

"Very glad?" she asked meaningfully.

"*Very*."

She gorged herself.

Afterward, Christina was groaning with more than passion as Marco set aside the empty plate, then began raising her skirts and moving himself down her body.

"Marco, if you lie on my belly right now, I shall explode," she moaned.

"I am not planning to lie on your belly."

His comment intrigued her all the more. She watched, wide-eyed, as he gathered her skirts around her waist and spread her thighs. He caressed her swath of silken hair and roved his gaze over her hungrily.

"So pretty," he murmured.

"Marco!"

Leaning over, he parted her, then stroked her with his tongue in the barest whisper of a caress.

Christina went insane, and for a moment they struggled frantically as he tried to control her wildly writhing hips. Yet soon he succeeded in pinning her down.

"It's useless to fight me, *cara*," he murmured wickedly. "You have had your feast—now I will have mine."

He did. Afterward, when she was still breathing in ragged gasps and trembling violently, he pulled her into his arms.

"Did I reward you sufficiently?" he asked huskily.

She nodded. "You shocked me even more than that."

"Shall I refill your plate?"

"Only if you want me to die of ecstasy."

He chuckled, then drew back to stare searchingly at her beautiful face, her bright eyes.

"Where are you, Christina?" he murmured intently.

"Floating on a cloud."

"Are you safe from me there?"

"No! Never!" she cried, kissing him passionately.

"Oh, *cara, cara*," he murmured.

"I love you," she whispered.

She expected him to take her then, with great devouring strokes, but instead he touched her emotions and her heart when he pulled her close and buried his lips in her hair, cherishing her.

That evening, when *La Spada* finally slipped into the bay and tipped her sails toward the Charles Town peninsula, Christina stood on deck at the railing. Anne Simmons joined her there.

The kindly matron touched the girl's hand. "My dear," she began, "I do not mean to be prying into your affairs, but I have discussed you with William, and we both want you to know that you are welcome to disembark with us at Charles Town—and to stay with us at our home there for as long as you please."

Christina felt both surprised and touched. "Why, thank you, Anne. You are most kind."

Anne squeezed her hand. "Just let us know your decision before we reach the harbor."

"I certainly will," Christina replied.

As Anne slipped away, Christina stared out at the marsh grasses and palmettos of the barrier islands they were passing. Her heart was filled with a strange melancholy. Charles Town had once been her home, yet the areas they were passing were alien to her now. Did she really belong anywhere, or to anyone? She laughed ruefully to herself. Marco considered that she belonged in his bed, and in some ways, they had drawn closer over the past couple of days. Yet he had never claimed her for his own, his bride. He had never told her he loved her, and as far as she knew, he still planned to turn her over to Vittorio when they returned to Isola del Mare. In a sense, then, Charles Town was as much her home as the island was.

With a heavy heart, she went off to find him. She located him in their cabin, sitting at his desk and por-ing over a chart. Anguish rent her anew as she remembered their beautiful afternoon in his bunk—

Yes, there had been tenderness, closeness. But there were still no words of love, no commitment.

She went to him and touched his arm. "Marco?"

He turned, caught her in his arms, and pressed his face to her bosom. "Yes, my love?"

"We need to talk."

"Yes?" He stared up at her, and the beauty of his bright blue eyes almost crushed her resolve.

She cleared her throat. "Anne Simmons has invited me to stay with her and her family in Charles Town. I have thought it over and I think . . . I feel it might be best for all concerned."

She had thought he would be relieved, yet she could not have been more wrong. His arms went rigid around her, and his tender expression gave way to one of suspicion, then of anger.

"Do you mean to say, *cara*, that after all we have been through, all we have shared, you are planning to leave me?" he asked in a voice so low, it sent a shiver through her.

Trying not to betray her fear, she broke away from him. "Well, what of you? What are you planning to do with me? Besides the obvious, that is!"

He lunged to his feet. "The obvious? Is that how you categorize what we have shared?"

"I do not mean to denigrate what we have shared. But it is not the same as having a future together!"

"A future?" he repeated ruefully. "I think that decision is in your hands, Christina. You have brought us to this impasse."

"What do you mean by that?" she cried, exasperated.

"If you do not know, then I cannot make you understand," he said stubbornly, crossing his arms over his chest.

Her eyes beseeched the heavens. "Oh, you are maddening. I am going to go to Charles Town."

Now he was livid, grabbing her arm. "Just a minute, you little brat!"

"How dare you call me a brat!"

"Why shouldn't I have the privilege? I am the very man who made you one, aren't I?"

"Oh!" She was seething.

"Christina, I've taught you many things, haven't I?"

"Indeed, yes!" she sneered.

"I've spoiled you, and I've tolerated your headstrong, hoydenish ways."

"I have been forced to tolerate *you!*" she felt compelled to point out.

His eyes took on a hard, dangerous glint. "But I've never taught you what *no* means, have I?"

His words were frightening her, and she began backing away.

"Well, have I?" he demanded.

She made a dash for the door, but he caught her and shoved her against it.

He was shouting now. "No, Christina, you may not leave me! Do you hear me? No, no, no!"

She was speechless.

"Well?" he demanded. "Do you understand?"

"I—I understand," she stammered at last.

"Splendid," he yelled.

He turned on his heel and stormed back to his desk, sitting down, slamming open his journal, overturning his inkwell, then cursing violently.

She crossed the cabin and stood behind him for a long moment. At last she dared to reach out and touch his rigid shoulder.

A moment later, she was grabbed and pulled down into his lap.

THIRTY-THREE

As if a portent of things to come, the morning they returned to Isola del Mare dawned misty, overcast, and cold. As soon as the lookout in the crow's nest spotted the island through the fog and called down, "Land ho!" the men on deck swarmed around striking the sails and tying them down, while Claudio carefully maneuvered the craft through the shoals and reefs leading to the harbor.

Marco joined Christina at the railing, and the two exchanged tense smiles. Christina mused that the past few days of their voyage had been idyllic, between the hours they had spent making love and the interludes when Marco had again fed Christina fruits and cheeses in bed until she felt half nauseated. He had noted every small physical change in her, delighting in the new color that had bloomed in her cheeks, and in the fact that her ribs no longer stood out quite so prominently. If only he would try as hard to bridge the emotional gap that still yawned between them, she thought sadly. While both of them had savored their time together, Marco had still made no mention of a future they could share.

He was staring at the gray shawl she wore draped over the shoulders of her burgundy broadcloth dress. "Are you cold, *cara?*" he asked solicitously. "There is a chill in the air this morning."

She shrugged. "I am all right." Tossing him a look of challenge, she added, "Besides, we will be home any minute now, won't we?"

"That is true." Staring off at the rolling terrain of Isola del Mare, now shrouded by choking mists, he added, "There is something I must tell you before we dock."

"Yes?"

He paused for a moment, gathering his thoughts as *La Spada* coasted into the inlet of the harbor. Noting that the schooner George Hollingsworth had chartered was still tied up at the wharf, he released a heavy breath and said, "One of the main reasons I let Carlos go is because he admitted to me the name of the man who had hired him to kill you."

Christina's eyes went wide. "Someone hired Carlos to kill me?"

Marco nodded grimly. "That is why all those ruffians kept popping up on the island. They were after you all along, *cara.*"

"My God! Who would do such a thing?"

"Your guardian, Charles Rutgers."

"My guardian!" she cried, stunned. "You must be jesting."

"I am afraid not, *cara.*"

"But why would Charles Rutgers want me dead?"

"I must assume he has designs on your fortune."

"But—how could he steal my fortune?"

Marco thoughtfully stroked his jaw. "I have no idea what exact provisions your parents left for you,

Christina. But I suppose it is entirely possible that if you were out of the way, Rutgers could claim your inheritance for himself."

"Why, the scoundrel!" she declared. "In truth, I never really knew Magistrate Rutgers that well, but my poor departed parents must roll about in their graves to know that he so abused their faith in him."

"*Sì*," Marco concurred. "When you think about it, it all makes sense. For instance, why did Rutgers show so little regard for your safety in the first place, sending you and Hesper off to live on Edisto Island? He is a powerful man in Charles Town, as you know, a magistrate of His Majesty's court. With you dead, who would challenge him for claiming your legacy, even if he did not honor all the legal niceties?"

"Oh, Marco." Trembling, she fell into his arms. "Why did you not tell me this on the night you rescued me?"

"You had been through an ordeal, *cara*. Why should I have further tortured you with the knowledge that the man your parents had trusted with your life had betrayed you? Besides, as you may recall, we were involved in a very heated argument involving other matters."

She pulled back slightly. "What will we do?"

He tenderly brushed a wisp of hair from her brow, but his eyes held a murderous resolve. "After we dock, I will kill him."

Christina was aghast. "Marco! Kill a magistrate of the King's court? Why, you could end up with a bounty on your head!"

He shrugged. "We are among friends. Who on the island would betray me?"

"But when Rutgers doesn't return to Charles Town, won't they come searching for him?" She paused for a moment, then snapped her fingers. "I know! Let me kill him!"

"You?" He grinned. "My, but you're a bloodthirsty wench, aren't you?"

"Better me than you. After all, I . . ." Her voice faltered, then she rushed on. "That is, if I am going off to Venice—"

Abruptly, he grabbed her chin and tilted it upward, forcing her to face his stern visage. "Are you?"

She was about to reply when they were both jolted as *La Spada*'s hull scraped against the wharf.

"We will talk about this later," Marco muttered.

In another moment, as they disembarked down the plank, Marco clutched Christina's hand, and she could not help but smile at him. Perhaps they would soon resolve things. Had he not twice become angered when she had mentioned leaving him?

However, as they headed into the woods along the trail, Don Giovanni came rushing toward them, and Marco abruptly dropped her hand. Something inside Christina went cold. So much for his settling things between them. She felt utterly forsaken.

"Marco! Christina!" Don Giovanni cried. "Thank God both of you have been safely returned to us!"

The effusive Italian hugged and kissed them both, then drew back to look them over. To Marco, he said, "So you managed to rescue the girl from the Spanish pirates! I do hope she was not—er—"

"She is unharmed," Marco put in tightly.

"Very good!" Don Giovanni beamed from ear to ear. "Now we must return to the house and inform the others—"

Marco held up a hand. "A moment, my friend. I am afraid there will be a very distasteful matter I must attend to back at the house. You see, the Spanish pirate Carlos informed me that Christina's guardian, Charles Rutgers, hired him to murder her—and now I am, of course, honor-bound to call out the villain."

"Dio mio!" Don Giovanni uttered, his eyes wild as he crossed himself. "This is terrible!"

"Sì. Perhaps when we reach the house, you had best take the others off somewhere—"

"But you do not understand, my boy."

"Understand what?"

"Rutgers has already left. Soon after you sailed, a British warship passed through the islands, and Rutgers flagged it down and impelled the captain to give him passage back to Charles Town."

"Damnation!" Marco swore. "So the coward has fled?"

"Unfortunately, yes." Don Giovanni's shrewd gaze focused on Christina. "But why ever would a magistrate of the British court want to kill this lovely young lady?"

"I suspect that, as Christina's guardian, Rutgers has designs on her fortune," Marco related grimly.

Don Giovanni paled. "Then we must all go to Charles Town at once to put a stop to his thievery!"

Marco's gaze narrowed on his old friend. "Are you not losing sight of the fact that Christina is safe and sound? Is not her well-being much more important than the fate of her inheritance?"

"Oh, of course! Of course!" Don Giovanni hastily agreed. "The rest will be resolved in good time, I am sure. Let us return to the house now and celebrate her return—as well as her imminent marriage to my son!"

He wrapped an arm around each of their waists and towed them both toward the house. Christina could not believe Marco was simply letting his old friend assume that she and Vittorio would still wed.

About fifty yards from the house, Pansy leapt out of the bushes to greet them. "Pansy!" Marco cried exultantly, kneeling down and petting the sleek black cheetah, who affectionately licked his face.

"Is she all right now?" Christina asked, stroking Pansy's flank.

Marco felt the cat's head and nodded. "Her wound is completely healed."

"Oh, that one is a holy terror and most anxious for your return, my boy," Don Giovanni put in. "Why, one day recently, the crafty cat dragged in a boar's carcass during luncheon. I do swear that Donna Flora and my daughters still have not recovered from the calamity."

The three chuckled and continued on to the house. But as they joined the others in the salon, Christina found that the expected "joyous reunion" was surprisingly subdued. Vittorio greeted her with a stiff curtsy bordering on indifference, pecking her cheek and then turning away. Donna Flora and her daughters were somewhat less restrained, all three hugging Christina briefly and murmuring platitudes. Only George Hollingsworth greeted his stepniece with true warmth, springing up to embrace her affectionately. "My dear, our prayers have been answered!" he cried, and then proceeded to ask many questions concerning her well-being.

During the luncheon that followed, Marco launched into a long monologue regarding their adventure, informing one and all of Charles Rutgers's perfidy, of how it was a wonder Christina had not been killed, and expressing his own frustration that Rutgers had already slipped away, doubtless having ascertained that his dastardly deeds would soon be discovered. Marco prudently omitted from his account the fact that he and Christina had spent the voyage home as lovers.

Christina suffered through the meal while battling a maelstrom of emotion over Marco's apparent abandonment of her. Once Marco had finished his discourse, Don Giovanni started babbling about how he planned to leave with his family and Christina two days hence, and Marco made no move to correct him. This confused and hurt Christina all the more. And there were other strange undercurrents of tension in the room that she could not begin to comprehend. Vittorio kept exchanging heated glances with the serving girl Antonio. Jovita kept tossing burning glances toward Giuseppe.

Marco kept directing fervid glances toward Christina, and again she had no idea of any possible message being sent. But she was ready to strangle him for forsaking her to the Renaldis.

Later that day, as rain began to pour outside, Christina barged in on him in his office. "So, do you just plan to give me to the Renaldis, Marco?" she demanded.

He glanced up at her from his desk, his features displaying surprise and bemusement. "Do I?"

"That is certainly how it sounded at luncheon."

He stood up to confront her implacably. "If you wish to stay here, Christina, then you are going to have to say the words."

"What words? That I want to stay?"

He shook his head. "The words you should have said to me on the night I rescued you. You should know what they are by now."

Totally exasperated, she stamped her foot. "Oh, you are driving me to Bedlam!" Having spent her temper, she became uncertain, twisting her fingers together. "What do you want me to say, Marco? Have I not already told you that I love you?"

He gazed back at her for a moment, and she could have sworn she saw his stony facade cracking just a bit. "That is a good beginning," he replied with a catch in his voice. "But it is not enough."

This enraged her. No man rubbed her nose in her own feelings! No man told her that her love was not enough! She charged past him toward the door, shoving him out of her way. "Oh, you insensitive brute! I give up trying to understand you! Sometimes I hate you, Marco Glaviano!"

She ran outside into the rain, and mumbling a curse, Marco tore after her. He shivered as the cold droplets pelted his body. He could barely see her ahead of him in the dense greenery.

"Christina!" he shouted. "Dammit, come back here before you catch your death!"

"What do you care? Leave me alone!" she cried, tearing off down the trail into the jungle.

"Christina, you wayward brat! You never do have sense enough to come in out of the rain!"

Marco hurried after her, skillfully keeping his balance on the slippery trail and dodging the myriad mangrove roots that snaked across the path. He finally caught up with her, grabbing her around her slender waist, only to have her pelt him with her fists and shriek obscenities. It struck him how comical they must look, both of them struggling in the rain and bellowing like lunatics. He hefted her over his shoulder and she kicked and screamed. He swatted her smartly on the behind and chuckled at her spirit. She was begging to be tumbled and bedded—and suddenly, he was in a most obliging mood. Indeed, he was eager for the impasse between them to end—in more ways than one. He was looking around for a secluded spot in the foliage when they abruptly collided with another person.

Marco hastily set Christina down, and both of them staggered as they confronted a white-faced, drenched Vittorio, who stood there making an absurd attempt at dignity amid a soaked wig and a veritable flood sluicing from the corners of his tricorn hat.

For a moment, neither Marco nor Christina could speak. Vittorio's outraged gaze darted from one to the other. Then, uttering a sound of contempt, he charged on.

Christina called, "Vittorio, wait—"

She tried to detain him, only to have her words curtailed as Marco again seized her and swung her up over his shoulder.

"Marco, stop it!" She beat on his back, but he might have been made of wood for all he took note. "What is Vittorio bound to think?"

"To hell with what he thinks!"

"At luncheon you cared what he thought!"

"At luncheon I was waiting for you to make your move."

"*What* move? Dammit, Marco, won't you at least let me go after him, explain—"

"No!"

"Not *no* again!"

He laughed and bore her into the trees, his spirits soaring as he spotted a familiar, abandoned hut. Ducking down at the low entrance, he carried her inside and set her on her feet, restraining her by the wrist and glancing around. While droplets of rain and sprays of smoky sunlight pierced the thatched roof, the structure provided adequate shelter from the storm, and the sight of the canvas hammock stretched across one corner set his imagination soaring to new and devilish heights.

She seemed to read his thoughts. "Oh, no, you don't, Marco Glaviano! You keep doing this to me, and afterward, our problem will still not be solved."

"One problem shortly will," he retorted wickedly. Indeed, when he spotted a long strip of rag on the floor, the sinful possibilities hardened his loins to an unbearable arousal.

He grabbed the rag and quickly, intently, tied one of Christina's wrists to each end.

"What are you doing now?"

"Making you my love slave," came his unabashed reply.

Her eyes went wide as he pulled her toward the

hammock, tugging her by her bound wrists. "Marco Glaviano, you fiend! You are not bedding me *there!* That canvas looks ready to fall apart, and the hammock is so narrow!"

"A tight squeeze?" he replied with a depraved smile. "Precisely what I have in mind."

Without further ceremony, he lay down on the hammock and pulled her on top of him in a straddle. For a moment, they swung wildly, then he steadied their weights with his foot. Gripping the cloth that bound her wrists, he looped the center section behind his neck, effectively binding her to him.

"Kiss me," he murmured, pulling her toward him.

"No."

"Yes."

She did.

Afterward, even Christina was laughing, and feeling shockingly aroused by Marco's brazen shenanigans. She tugged on the cloth and teased, "You know, I could choke you like this. Indeed, I have been thinking all afternoon of how I would love to throttle you."

"Ah, but that is what makes the game so enjoyable," he taunted back as he stroked her breasts through her wet gown. He began purposefully unbuttoning her bodice. "You are my love slave, but I must also trust you with my neck."

"Trust *me* not to strangle you?"

He laughed heartily as he began pulling up her skirts and freeing his own erection. "Mount my mast, m'lady, and strangle away."

Giggling, she obliged, only to have her chuckles end in a frenzied gasp of pleasure as she sank herself onto him.

"Still hate me?" he murmured.

Her smile was full of love, but her womanly sheath was wicked and tight. "I'm strangling you, aren't I?"

"God, yes," came his tortured reply. He pushed her

legs wider apart until her feet were braced on the dirt floor. He felt her fingernails dig into his shoulders and stared up at her face, so bright with passion, so frantic with arousal. "Now swing, *cara*."

"Swing? Which way?"

"*Every* way."

"Oh, Marco."

Before the afternoon ended, they rocked wildly in every imaginable way—and even invented a few new ones.

So he would not receive his apology. It no longer seemed such a tragedy. He had *her*, didn't he, and wasn't she worth more than any apology? Couldn't he tie her to his bed every day for a year and devour her without mercy until he soothed his own pride? No, he would use the hammock—a more fitting torture device, he decided.

These were Marco's thoughts as he sat with the others at dinner. It was high time to end this impasse with Christina. Certainly the girl had hurt him, but she was obviously too stubborn to realize how grievously she had wounded him. He had hinted and hinted, done everything but say the words for her, and he had gotten nowhere. Enough.

Besides, after quiet reflection and prayer, he realized now that he had acted much too proud in this, placing his own outraged vanity above their future lives together. Pride was surely the deadliest of all sins, throwing up barriers to the love and closeness *il Dio* would have them share.

Thus it no longer seemed to matter so much that she had never said those magical words: "I'm sorry." When they had loved each other so gloriously in the smoky hut this afternoon, he had realized that "I love you" definitely sufficed. He smiled at the memory, his fingers tightening on his fork as he recalled her cries of pleasure and his own wild groans of ecstasy.

Afterward, they had returned to the house, drenched and bedraggled, and it had been a miracle that they had not been discovered.

Now he only wanted to put an end to the pretense. He wanted her as his wife, in his arms, in his bed, sharing his life, bearing his children. And he was tired of hearing Don Giovanni drone on about taking her to Venice. She was *his*, by damn! It was high time he set the others straight.

"Don Giovanni," he said sternly.

Interrupted in mid-sentence, Don Giovanni regarded Marco quizzically. "Yes, my friend?"

Marco stared at Christina, then back at Don Giovanni. "Now that Christina is safely back with us, and her betrayer, Charles Rutgers, has been exposed, I have an announcement to make concerning her."

"Yes?"

Marco had his mouth poised to speak when, all at once, Vittorio popped up and said to his father sanctimoniously, "I, too, have an announcement to make regarding Christina."

Don Giovanni glanced confusedly from his friend to his son. "Yes, my son?"

Vittorio regarded Christina with icy contempt. "I refuse to marry Christina. She was taken off by pirates, and doubtless despoiled"—he paused to stare at Marco, who appeared ready to leap over the table and murder him, then rushed on—"and furthermore, the girl is having an unnatural relationship with her *uncle.*"

At this pronouncement, Don Giovanni was rendered wild-eyed and speechless. Donna Flora's head pitched wildly; she moaned, then slipped to the floor in a swoon. After a confused moment, Don Giovanni bent over to retrieve his fallen wife.

Christina bolted to her feet to confront Vittorio. "Marco is not my uncle. He is the man I love."

Marco grinned idiotically at Christina.

"B-but, my son," Don Giovanni exclaimed as he pulled the half-comatose Donna Flora back into her seat and waved a hand in front of her face, "you must marry Christina! The contract has been made!"

Vittorio gestured toward Antonia, who had been standing in the shadows. As the serving girl came forward eagerly, he wrapped a protective arm around her and announced, "I am going to marry Antonia. She is obedient and devout, as a wife should be. She comes from a humble upbringing, and puts on no vain airs. Besides"—he colored, then drew himself up with pride—"she is going to have my child."

In the wake of this revelation, Donna Flora's eyes rolled back in her head and she collapsed again, this time unnoticed by her flabbergasted husband.

Don Giovanni glanced in horror from Vittorio to Antonia. "This serving girl is *what?*"

"She is carrying my child, Father."

"*Dio mio!*" Taking note of his wife at last, Don Giovanni bent over to rescue her again.

Now Jovita popped up. "I have a confession to make, too, Papa!" Staring at Giuseppe, she burst into tears. "I have sinned terribly! I am going to have the priest's baby!"

Giuseppe grinned idiotically at Jovita.

Don Giovanni was settling Donna Flora into her chair when this new proclamation prompted him to abandon her and make a dive for Giuseppe's throat. Donna Flora crumpled once more, hitting the floor with a thud.

Marco sprang up to defend Giuseppe, who was being enthusiastically strangled by a red-faced and violently cursing Don Giovanni. Grabbing the Venetian's hands, he cried, "It is all right, my friend.

For heaven's sake, restrain yourself! Giuseppe is not a priest."

"*What?*" Don Giovanni cried, glancing from Giuseppe, who was grinning wanly, to Marco.

"Giuseppe is not a priest," Marco repeated. "I guess, in all the confusion, we forgot to tell you."

Don Giovanni released Giuseppe, who began coughing and sputtering for air. As Jovita went to his aid, her father stared in perplexity at the couple. "But if he is not a priest, how can they marry?"

"You are confused, my friend," Marco said, chuckling. "Think about it for a moment. You cannot have it both ways."

"Both ways?"

Don Giovanni was still scowling over this when George Hollingsworth spoke up. "I should be happy to marry any couples who are of such a mind."

Don Giovanni dismissed the offer with a sneer. "Anglican," he muttered. To Marco, he added in exasperation, "What has happened to everyone? All this sin! All these babies—"

"It is the tropics," Marco assured him. "The climate drives everyone mad."

"But the contract," he insisted.

"Forget the contract," Marco said. He winked at Christina. "I have decided to keep the girl."

"Keep her?" Don Giovanni said. "Mary, Joseph, and Jesus! Have you gone mad as well, my boy? Does that mean what I think it does?"

"It does."

Donna Flora was just crawling onto her chair when this new declaration sent her tumbling over, chair and all.

Marco was unprepared when Christina charged across the room to confront him. "I am a woman, not a prize, Marco Glaviano! I have feelings and a will of my own! *No man* decides to keep me—especially not an arrogant cad like you!"

She stormed out of the room, leaving Marco to curse his frustration.

Tossing a resigned glance at his insensible wife, Don Giovanni went off to pour himself a very large brandy.

THIRTY-FOUR

BEFORE DAWN THE FOLLOWING MORNING, CHRISTINA awakened feeling violently nauseated. After spending several miserable moments retching at the basin, she crawled back into bed and shivered in the coldness.

Perhaps she had taken some malady when she had cavorted in the rain with Marco yesterday. Funny, but she had felt queasy several times during the voyage home, too, but had dismissed her symptoms as seasickness—

Suddenly, she sat up as she recalled a couple of the peasant women mentioning similar complaints. No, she had not been seasick, nor was she otherwise ill— her monthly time was overdue, and she was going to have Marco's child.

A fierce joy flooded her and she touched her stomach in wonder. Her first instinct was to rush to Marco and share her news. Then she remembered his arrogant words at dinner last night—that he would "keep" her now. Perhaps she had been a fool ever to think that Marco Glaviano could commit himself to any one woman. He obviously wanted her as a mistress now—and she would never settle for less than a husband. In a sense, though, she could almost understand his reluctance to wed her, since she had already given herself to him without benefit of marriage. She ground her jaw as she remembered him calling her his love slave, his prize. Never once had he indicated that he thought of her as a wife. And how would he feel about the child? Would he want to give up his freebooting ways and become a husband—much less, a father? Didn't her baby deserve much better than that?

Feeling despondent, Christina dressed and went out to sit in the garden as the dawn was breaking. She was surprised when momentarily, George Hollingsworth appeared to join her, already dressed in his somber black suit and round hat.

"Good morning, my dear," he said, sitting down beside her. "You are up and about early."

"So are you."

He nodded. "I like to arise early to say my prayers and read my Bible."

"That is commendable."

His expression grew thoughtful. "Christina, I am glad to have caught you alone. Actually, I plan to leave today, and I would like to invite you to come with me back to England."

"To England?"

"Yes. I would like to help you make a new life for yourself, away from these disreputable privateers."

"I see. That is kind of you, but—"

He held up a hand. "Please, hear me out, dear."

"Very well."

"I do not know what happened to you when you were kidnapped by those depraved Spaniards, nor do I know what has transpired between you and

Marco Glaviano. But I do assure you, my dear, that whatever horrors have befallen you in the past, the Almighty holds you blameless, as do I."

Christina could not help but laugh wryly. "You are very perceptive, and I thank you for your invitation. But the truth is, I am in love with Marco Glaviano, and I think I should stay and work things out with him."

"Oh, my dear!" His expression turned to one of intense pity. "You cannot be thinking of throwing away your life for a man such as that! He will never give you his name. Nor will he forsake his women, or become a suitable father for you children." He patted her hand. "Now, if it is a husband you need, I shall be happy to arrange a suitable match for you back in England, even if there are—er—delicate problems that need to be resolved." He coughed. "Please do not feel ashamed. I am a clergyman, my dear. You can be frank with me."

Christina was stunned at how much her stepuncle had guessed. "You are very generous, but for me to go all the way to England—"

"I tell you what, my dear. Why don't you accompany me back to Charles Town? Don't we need to get in touch with the authorities there, anyway, and see if we cannot put a stop to the heinous activities of your guardian?"

She scowled. "Well, I suppose we should—"

"Come with me that far. Give yourself time to think things through regarding Glaviano, and then if you still don't want to sail with me for England, you can either remain in Charles Town, or, if you insist, I shall arrange your passage back here."

She frowned skeptically. "I am not sure. I think I should speak with Marco first."

He sighed and shook his head fatalistically.

"What is it?"

His sad gaze met hers. "I did not want to have to

mention such a matter again, my dear, but I spotted that Spanish woman—isn't her name Rosa?— slipping into Glaviano's room last night. I would advise you not to consult with that scoundrel at the present time. Indeed, the two of them may still be—"

"You needn't explain further!" she finished, seething. "The bastard! I shall speak with him all right— and if what you say is true, I shall kick his arrogant arse to perdition and back!"

"Christina!" Hollingsworth appeared appalled. "You must control yourself. I insist that you not act in the heat of passion this way—"

"I am going to speak with Marco," she maintained stubbornly. "I—I simply cannot leave with you now."

He sighed. "Very well. It is clear that you are bewitched by this man and determined to remain on this island. But won't you at least see me off at the docks?"

She nodded, feeling badly about her outburst, when George had been so kind to her. "Of course. When will you be ready?"

"As soon as I can eat a brief repast and pack my things."

"I shall be happy to accompany you, then."

A few minutes later, Christina walked with George to the pier where his schooner was tied up. His crewmen were already on board, stowing gear and preparing to set sail. One of them hurried down the gangplank to take George's portmanteau.

Christina extended her hand to George and smiled. "I guess this is goodbye, then."

"I suppose so." Suddenly, George snapped his fingers. "You know, my dear, I almost forgot. There is a jewelry chest of Virginia's that I wanted you to have. It is still in my cabin."

"Oh, I would love to have it."

"Then why don't you come on board with me, and we shall get it."

Christina went with George up the gangplank and onto the deck of the two-masted schooner. As they headed for the companionway, she heard smatterings of French from the crewmen as they prepared to weigh anchor.

Belowdecks, George led her to a cramped but neat cabin. He opened a bureau drawer and pulled out a small, beautiful carved walnut chest. "Here, my dear," he said proudly, extending it to her. "For some reason, Virginia left this behind long ago when she sailed with you and your father for the Colonies."

"Oh, I shall treasure it!" Christina cried, taking the chest.

"There is jewelry inside for you, as well."

"Is there?" Fascinated, Christina set the chest down on the bureau and opened it. "Oh, how lovely!"

"I shall just go have a word with my crew while you examine the contents, and then I shall escort you off the ship."

Christina was too fascinated with the jewelry to really hear George's last comment, or to note him slipping from the room. Captivated, she examined a lovely old pearl necklace, a cameo brooch, a garnet ring.

A moment later, as the chest suddenly skidded to the edge of the bureau, reality crashed in on her. The ship was moving!

Flabbergasted, she left the cabin and hurried back up on deck, only to see that the schooner had slipped away from the pier. She rushed over to George, who stood calmly speaking with his helmsman.

"What in God's name do you think you are doing?" she cried.

He turned, slanting her an apologetic look. "I have decided to take you with me back to England."

"You are carrying me off against my wishes?" she

cried incredulously. "You must have taken leave of your senses!"

He shook his head sadly. "Not at all, my dear. Indeed, quite the opposite is true. Someone must behave sensibly on your behalf, and see to it that you do not make a fool of yourself over this nefarious privateer. As your only remaining male relative, I consider it my bounden duty to assume responsibility for you."

Christina was appalled and exasperated. Never would she have suspected that her stepuncle would pull such a traitorous stunt. "You will take me back to the pier this minute—or I will swim back!"

"You will do no such thing!" George retorted, his face now tight with anger. "You deserve far better than this pirate can give you—and thus, neither I nor my crewmen will allow you to leave this vessel."

Glancing about at the dozen or so husky seamen who stood between her and freedom, Christina was feeling desperate. "Marco will come after me!" she declared.

"Will he?" George countered. "Then let him come see you in Charles Town, and court you properly there. My feeling is that Signore Glaviano will not make an appearance—and that in time, you will see that my action is for the best."

With these words, George turned to converse in French with his helmsman, leaving Christina to seethe in silence. It stunned and infuriated her that George had taken charge of her this way, bearing her away from Isola del Mare against her will. But what gnawed at her most was the possibility that her stepuncle might have spoken the truth. Was it true that Marco would never properly court her, would never give up his other women or marry her? After all, she had a child to consider now—a child who might well grow up bearing the stigma of bastardy.

Oh, if only she could talk with Marco one last

time! Surely George was wrong—surely he would come after her.

Never had she felt so torn.

Moments later, Marco awakened with a splitting headache. Pansy, who he'd let in during the wee hours, stretched and yawned next to him. He scratched the cheetah's head and groaned.

He had been up until well past midnight last night, drinking brandy with Don Giovanni, trying to soothe his old friend's wounded pride and, especially, to convince him to allow his children to marry whomever they pleased. At last he had won the argument and had stumbled off to bed, only to awaken moments later when a woman joined him there. At first he had been overjoyed, thinking that Christina had come to him, and then he had discovered that the female he held was Rosa. He had summarily escorted the saucy wench out through the French doors, with a stern warning that he would throttle her if she dared to disturb him again.

Now, he needed to go find Christina, to admit his love for her, and make plans for their immediate marriage. Perhaps he had erred last night when he had announced so crudely that he was going to "keep" her. Perhaps his mind had been too fascinated by decadent thoughts of tying her to his bed and doing all manner of wicked things to her delectable young body. If she preferred marriage prior to being debauched by him, that would be fine.

He was just getting his thoughts organized when he heard a loud knock at his door. "Come in!" he bellowed.

Marco was stunned to observe a grim-faced Claudio shoving an equally tense Carlos into the room with a pistol at his back. Pansy, picking up on the drama, growled softly next to Marco.

"What is this?" Marco asked, glancing from one man to the other.

"Carlos and his men just brazenly slipped into our harbor," Claudio announced.

"What are you doing here?" Marco demanded of Carlos. "Is your word worthless? Do you not value your own life?"

Carlos grinned sheepishly. "*Amigo*, I am not here to bring you harm. Actually, I have come for the Spanish wench, Rosa. She and I had a little dalliance at Havana recently, and I find that I truly miss her."

Marco laughed humorlessly as he tossed back the covers, stood and pulled on his breeches. "So you are the one who got the wench pregnant."

"Rosa is going to have my child?" Carlos asked with an incredulous smile.

"*Sì*." Marco snapped his fingers at Claudio. "Go fetch the woman. I would like to hear her explain herself."

Carlos appeared bemused. "What must Rosa explain?"

"Why she tried to pass off the child as mine."

"Yours?" Carlos bellowed. Then he paled as Pansy leapt down to the floor and hissed at him.

"Be calm, my friend," Marco warned, reaching down to stroke and soothe the cat. "The *bambino* is definitely yours. Rosa has not been my mistress for many months now—although not for want of her trying. I am sure she only fabricated her claim to make Christina jealous. You are going to have your hands full with that one."

Carlos grinned. "I think I can manage to keep her occupied and out of trouble. I shall keep her in chains, if need be. I have practice in such matters."

"Do you?" As a sudden, painful stab of memory blinded him, Marco crossed the room, and before Carlos could even blink, he smashed his fist into the Spaniard's jaw and knocked him to the floor. Pansy was after her master like a shot, bolting across the room to hover, snarling and spitting, over the downed Spaniard.

"What was that for?" Carlos demanded in an outraged whisper, rubbing his jaw and glancing wildeyed from Marco to the cat.

"That was for the way you treated Christina!"

"But I did not rape her!"

"No, you only treated her like a dog and half starved her, you bloody swine!"

As Pansy continued to growl menacingly, Carlos blinked at his enraged adversary. Cautiously, he stood, backing away from the cat but taking the verbal offensive with Marco. "Why so indignant, my friend? Is it not over between you and the girl? Although I could have sworn from the way you looked at her on my schooner that you were in love with her—"

"I am in love with her," Marco cut in heatedly.

"Then why did you just allow her to leave the harbor with Charles Rutgers, the very man who hired me to kill her?"

As Marco went pale, Claudio slipped back inside the room with Rosa, who smiled tentatively at Carlos then regarded both Marco and Pansy with fear.

Of Claudio, Marco demanded, "What is this nonsense about Christina leaving?"

Claudio nodded. "I saw her leave with your guest, but not until their vessel was already well away from the pier. They sailed past Barnacle Reef just as Carlos's ship was slipping in."

"And you just let Christina leave with Charles Rutgers?" Marco demanded furiously.

Now Claudio's expression went blank. "Charles Rutgers? But boss, she just left with her stepuncle, George Hollingsworth, and I assumed you knew about it."

Marco's gaze swung around to Carlos. "You made a mistake, then?"

"No," Carlos replied adamantly. "I do not care what the man called himself. Christina just left your harbor with the man who hired me to kill her."

"Oh, God," Marco muttered.

Even as he was struggling to digest this news, Rosa abruptly burst into tears. As Marco glanced at her sharply, she cried, "And he is the same man who bribed me to tell Christina that I was carrying your child, Marco. He even paid me to involve Monique. He seemed so pleasant and concerned for Christina. He said he suspected that there was something romantic between the two of you, and that it must be stopped, since you would never make Christina a decent husband."

Rage glittered in Marco's eyes as he approached Rosa. "Did he also impel you to slip into my room last night!"

"Yes!" she admitted miserably. "I did not want to play such a dirty trick on you again, but the Englishman told me that if I did not cooperate, he would tell you of how I had betrayed you, how I had made a fool of you."

"Damn it, woman!" Marco snapped.

"You came to Marco's room last night?" Carlos demanded, turning angrily to Rosa.

"He threw me out!" she sobbed.

"That is beside the point!" Carlos shook a finger at Rosa. "You have some explaining to do, wench. Were you not pregnant with my child, I would take my cat-o'-nine tails to your bottom."

"You are right, I have sinned terribly," Rosa whimpered.

Still glowering, Carlos pulled Rosa into his arms.

Meanwhile, Marco was thrusting his fingers through his hair and muttering, "Damn, I must go after Christina—before it is too late!"

"Let me help," Carlos offered.

Marco was amazed. "Don't tell me that impending fatherhood has at last imbued you with a conscience?"

Carlos sighed, then admitted with surprising humility, "You showed me mercy on the high seas. I owe you, *amigo*."

Marco nodded distractedly. "Suit yourself."

He was dashing off to grab his shirt and his cutlass when Pansy bounded up to him with her leash between her teeth and whined plaintively.

"No, Pansy," Marco scolded. "You may not come along. You will get seasick."

Pansy growled.

"Very well!" he said, taking the leash and placing it about the cat's neck. "Don't cry to me when you are retching your guts out!"

THIRTY-FIVE

An hour later, Christina remained dogged by a very bad feeling as she stood on deck of her stepuncle's schooner. They were now well away from Isola del Mare, and there was still no sign of Marco. She had tried again, several times, to persuade George to take her back to the island, all to no avail. And unfortunately, Hollingsworth was the only person on the craft with whom she could communicate; the skeleton crew spoke mostly their native French language, interspersed with a smattering of English. Only George could effectively communicate with them.

Momentarily, her stepuncle came over to join her, offering her a conciliatory smile. "My dear, I do hope you are not still angry with me. I know I am doing what is right for you."

Christina stared moodily out at sea. "That does not relieve you of your perfidy in taking the decision out of my hands!"

"Believe me, Christina, you will be so much happier with me back in England."

"That remains to be seen."

"Christina, if only you will—"

All at once George broke off as an excited voice called down from the crow's nest, "*Capitaine, une voile.*"

Both Christina and George glanced astern, and Christina's heart surged with joy as she spotted *La Spada* in the distance, making toward them. "Marco!" she cried. "He has come after me!"

George, on the other hand, appeared alarmed, rushing off to consult with the captain. As he returned, the crew sprang into frantic activity, hoisting more sail and bringing the schooner's bow about into the wind.

"What are you doing?" Christina cried. "Trying to outrun *La Spada*? But Marco has come after me! Surely he must love me—"

Abruptly her voice froze as she watched her stepuncle pull out a small but wickedly sharp knife. "A pity that you will never find out for certain, my dear."

She glanced up in horror, her heart thudding as she spotted the gleam of madness in George's eyes. "What do you think you are doing?"

He caught her against him brutally. She was stunned by the strength in his thin body as he held her in a choke hold and pinned the knife to her throat. "What does it look like? I did not want to have to play my hand this soon, my dear, but Glaviano has really given me no choice."

"But your crew—"

"Have been paid very well to keep silent. Believe me, dear girl, they won't come to your rescue."

"But—" Christina's mind was spinning as she tried to hold hysteria at bay. "You *can't* mean to kill me. What possible motive would you have?"

"What motive?" He laughed bitterly. "What else but the fortune that awaits you in Charles Town?"

"Oh, my God! You mean you've conspired with my guardian—"

His cruel laughter interrupted her. "You think I would share what is rightfully mine with another? Your guardian is actually guiltless in this—other than being a rather inept guardian."

"Then it has been you all along—"

"Who has been trying to kill you? Aye. And haven't I been clever? I'm a master of disguise, you see. I fooled all of you, posing as a vicar. I put that charlatan priest of Glaviano's to shame."

"You mean you are not even a vicar?"

"Not at all. I am a barrister's clerk who scrimped and saved for years in order to travel to America again and secure the fortune that I am entitled to. I even fooled the pirate Carlos when I posed as Charles Rutgers and hired him and his gang of cutthroats to kill you."

"But I don't understand. How would my death gain you access to my parents' fortune?"

"You are such a naive child! You mean to tell me you never knew I was next in line in the will?"

She shook her head in horror.

"Not long after your parents died and you disappeared, I came to the colonies and tried to find you, to no avail. At last I gave up, but before returning to England, I retained a solicitor in Charles Town with orders to stay in touch with your guardian." He snorted in disgust. "If only you had remained lost for one more year, we could have had you declared legally dead. But no, you had to surface, didn't you? Unfortunately, your guardian learned of your whereabouts through one of Glaviano's crewmen who landed in his court. I came to Charles Town, hired Carlos to kill you—and the rest you know."

As much as her stepuncle's confession frightened

and unnerved her, Christina's eyes shone with fierce triumph as she spotted *La Spada* gaining on the schooner. "You will never get away with this! Marco is gaining on us."

Hollingsworth tightened the pressure of the knife. "But my dear, by the time he gets here, you will be at the bottom of the sea."

"Then you will have signed your own death warrant," Christina asserted. "For if you kill me, Marco Glaviano will chase you to the ends of the earth until he avenges my death. Do you have any idea how bloodthirsty and vengeful pirates can be? Do you yearn to be keelhauled, or tortured at the mast?"

These words seemed to give George pause. He shouted frantic orders to the crewmen, all the while keeping the knife at her throat.

Despite her current peril, Christina's heart rang with new hope. She knew she had George off-balance and distracted now. All she needed to do was to choose the best moment, when he was truly off guard, to make her move, wrest the knife away from him, and gut him. But she'd better proceed with caution—his knife was razor-sharp and had already nicked her throat. She could not risk being killed— she could not risk any harm coming to Marco's beautiful child.

George's eyes held the frantic quality of a cornered animal as *La Spada* suddenly loomed windward of his vessel, literally knocking the wind out of his sails. The schooner listed as the brigantine slammed her to starboard. Christina and George tottered and her neck suffered another small nick. Still, he managed to hold her in his steely grip. Nonetheless, her spirits soared as she watched Marco leaping over the rails, along with a snarling Pansy on a leash. They were followed by Carlos and a number of Marco's crewmen who stormed the decks of the schooner with knives and cutlasses waving.

Glancing up at George, Christina saw his cheek twitch; his features appeared gripped by a terrible indecision she would soon use to her advantage.

"Stop!" George screamed at the approaching men. "Stop or I will slit the girl's throat as you watch."

The boarding party halted. Marco was in agony as he pulled on Pansy's leash to restrain her and stared at the woman he loved, now caught in the clutches of a lunatic. Then he noted the vengeful gleam in Christina's eyes.

So did Carlos. Never taking his eyes off the man and the girl, he whispered to Marco under his breath, "*Madre de Dios!* She is going to castrate him! Look at her eyes. I am well acquainted with that look of derangement."

Marco handed Pansy's leash to Carlos. "Hang on to her for me."

"*Sì, amigo.*"

Marco's eyes locked with Christina's for another anguished moment as he struggled for the best strategy to free her without causing her injury or death. Then, to his horror, he watched the woman he loved sink her teeth into George's forearm and yank his wrist away from her throat. As Hollingsworth howled in pain and struggled with Christina over the knife, Marco vaulted across the deck and pulled the villain off her. George, with knife still in hand, flailed out at Marco, aiming the dagger for his adversary's belly. Marco adroitly dodged the blow and grabbed Hollingsworth's wrist. With a lethal twist, he shoved the knife deep into George's midsection. Uttering a gasp of pain, Hollingsworth crumpled to the deck and rolled over, his eyes wide open in death.

Marco pulled Christina into his arms. Pansy broke loose and bounded across the deck to join them. The three huddled together joyously.

Then Marco spotted the streaks of blood on

Christina's neck. "*Cara!* My God! Are you all right?" he cried.

"I am fine—I am only scratched," she replied offhandedly, leaning over to pet Pansy. "In fact, you did not have to dispatch George for me. I was prepared to—"

"We saw what you were prepared to do, *cara*," Marco cut in ruefully. "Forgive me for denying you that pleasure, but I had to kill the poor bastard. After all, a man is better off dead than not a man."

"Amen," Carlos added in the background.

Christina had to smile. "I cannot believe it was George all along who was trying to murder me!"

"I know, darling. He posed as your guardian and hired Carlos to kill you. He also bribed Rosa into lying to you about carrying my child, and he even involved Monique in his scheme."

"Oh, Marco! Then you and those women did not—"

"Or course not, *cara*."

Carlos now stepped forward. "I am glad you are all right, Christina."

"You!" she cried with contempt.

All at once, Marco turned very serious. "Do you want me to kill him? Because if you do, I will do it."

She stared at Carlos, struggling intensely as the latter paled by several shades with each second that passed.

"Before you decide," Marco went on gravely, "let me caution you that if I do kill him, you will be leaving a child without a father. You see, Rosa is carrying Carlos's child."

Christina grinned. "Make him marry her, then. Marriage to Rosa will surely comprise a lifetime of hell."

Marco turned to Carlos. "Agreed, my friend?"

He nodded convulsively. "Agreed. And I promise to suffer grievously."

All of them laughed, then further conversation was halted as Marco was compelled to take charge of the problems at hand. He had his crewmen wrap Hollingsworth's corpse in a shroud of sailcloth, weight him down with a cannonball, and heave him over the side. Marco then released the French sailors to return to Charles Town on their schooner, and he, Christina, and the others returned to *La Spada*.

When they were at last under way for home, Marco joined Christina at the railing and took her in his arms. She bit her lip at the reproachful look in his eyes. Pansy lounged nearby, looking exhausted and watching them with a doleful gaze.

"Now, to continue our conversation—" Marco began.

"You are angry at me, aren't you?" she asked.

He gestured toward Pansy. "Do you realize that I had to put up with a seasick cheetah in order to come after you?"

She giggled. "I put you through hell, didn't I?"

He nodded. "Do you have any idea how terribly you frightened me when you left without even discussing it with me?"

"But, Marco, you do not understand," she countered. "I did not simply leave. George persuaded me to see him off at his ship—and then he simply set sail with me on board."

"Oh, *cara*." The anger in his face faded. "Thank God Carlos arrived in time to identify the true villain in all this."

She chewed on her bottom lip. "Then George lied when he told me he saw Rosa slipping into your room last night?"

Marco smiled sheepishly. "Actually, she did come to my room last night." As Christina would have become indignant, he held up a hand. "Let me explain. The truth is, Hollingsworth bribed Rosa again. I threw her out, of course, and were it not for the fact that she is pregnant, I likely would have taken my hand to her backside—which I still may do with you so you will remember never again to scare me this way," he finished in a fit of temper.

Not daunted at all, she stared at him with her heart in her eyes. "I'm going to have your baby."

"Oh, *cara.*" He pressed his face to her hair, and his voice vibrated with emotion. "You have just redeemed yourself. No thrashing."

"You are happy?" she asked with a catch in her voice.

"Very. When did you know?"

"I realized it this morning."

Again he was irate. "But why could you not have trusted me, come to me at once with your news? You never should have gone to the docks with George."

"But I thought you had slept with Rosa—and you have acted so strange, ever since you rescued me!"

"I was waiting for you to apologize."

"You were waiting for *me* to apologize!"

"*Sì.*"

"For what?"

"For what?" He appeared stunned. "For the cruel things you said to me on the night I rescued you! Here I had almost lost my life trying to save you, and you accused me of wenching. *Wenching!*"

"I'm sorry," she muttered, fighting a grin at his wounded expression. "I truly would have apologized then—but you seemed so angry, so unreachable." Abruptly her expression turned suspicious. "Is that why you have acted so terrible to me for weeks?"

"A man has his pride," he maintained stubbornly.

She groaned. "So what do we do now?"

He smiled. "We marry, of course."

"Because of the baby?"

"Because I've wanted to marry you for a very long time now." He grinned. "And I've wanted a baby, too, of course. Perhaps being fat with my child will curb your hoydenish ways a bit."

"What of you?" she countered indignantly. "Will you be willing to give up the sea—and your women? I won't share you, you know."

He caught her face in his hands and spoke fiercely. "Listen to me, now. From the first moment when you claimed me, from the instant your lips touched mine, you have had my heart and I have been with no other woman. There is nothing left for me to give up—not even my heart. For you have it all already. I love you, *cara mia*."

"Oh, Marco. I love you, too."

She stretched on tiptoe to kiss him, and they shared their bliss for a long moment.

"Now we must change the entire atmosphere at our island," he went on soberly. "Bring in a real priest and a real schoolmaster."

Her lips twitched. "You mean that we are all going to become upstanding?"

"Indeed." He touched the tip of her nose. "Of course, the biggest chore will be reforming *you*. Think of all you have put me through! I could never survive going through this again with our children."

She laughed. "Ah, Marco. Just a taste of love, and all at once you are so stern and respectable."

"Ah, but there is one place where I will never be stern—or respectable," he added huskily, pulling her close. "Plan to have many babies, *cara*."

"Oh, I do," she replied, and kissed him.

They headed joyously toward their island in the sun.

EPILOGUE

"**S**HE IS STARING AT ME. WHAT SHOULD I DO?"

Almost two years later, Marco and Christina lay reclined together on the beach. Christina's stomach was large with their second child.

Next to her father, fourteen-month-old Bianca stood in her shirt and diaper, one pudgy hand braced on her father's powerful shoulder. She was an adorable child with a shock of wheat-colored hair, bright blue eyes that perfectly matched her father's, and a sprinkling of freckles across her upturned nose.

"Christina! What should I do?" Marco repeated frantically.

Christina chuckled. "Why is it so terrible that she is staring at you?"

"Well, I do not know," he responded, scratching his jaw and frowning. "Mayhap she thinks I am doing something wrong?"

"You usually are. But you do take being a father

391

far too seriously, Marco. Look at her leaning on you. You need to let her go and force her to walk."

"But she will fall over!" he protested. "She is still a baby, too young to walk!"

"She is not! You have been carrying her around for fourteen months now. What incentive does she have to walk when Papa is there to fetch and carry and spoil her rotten?"

Marco glanced sternly at the baby. "Have I spoiled you, *bambina?*"

Bianca gurgled gleefully.

"See what I mean?" Christina put in. "You will never get her to mind you at this rate."

Marco scowled at the baby. "Bianca, kiss Papa."

Bianco smacked Marco on the mouth and chortled.

He turned imperiously to Christina. "See? She minds me perfectly."

Christina groaned. "Oh, does she? She still will not walk."

Marco carefully removed the baby's fingers from his shoulder. "Bianca, walk! Papa commands it."

The baby stared at him, then fell on her diaper and began good-naturedly digging in the sand.

"See what I mean?" Marco demanded exasperatedly. "She is not ready."

Christina rolled her eyes.

Marco leaned over and gently placed his cheek against his wife's belly. He thought of all the happiness they had known together and his heart filled with joy. He missed his privateering activities not at all. His life was now his family. How blessed he had been—first of all, with Christina's love, and then with Bianca. And now ...

"What do you think, my darling?" he murmured, running his large hand over her belly. "Another girl this time?"

"No, this one is definitely a boy—why, he is a giant already."

"I would not count on a boy," Marco teased.

"Do you have your heart set on another girl?"

He glanced up at her. "My heart is set on whatever you have, *cara*. But we do all seem to be destined to have girls. Remember Don Giovanni's letter that Claudio brought back from St. Kitts? Jovita and Antonia now have two *bambinas* apiece. And Rosa had twins girls—"

"This baby is a boy," Christina cut in vehemently.

Marco grinned, then glanced at Bianca. Horrified, he pulled her fingers out of her mouth. "No, angel, you must not eat the sand. Listen to Papa, please!"

Bianca stared at Marco.

He grinned at the baby. "What do you say, *bambina*? Is Mama to have a boy?"

"Boy!" she gurgled, pulling herself up by her father's arm.

Christina slanted Marco an admonishing glance. "Marco . . ."

"She is not ready to walk, *cara*," he assured her.

"Kiss me, darling, and let her walk."

Heaving a giant sigh, Marco picked up the baby and placed her an arm's length away from him. "Walk, Bianca," he commanded, affecting his sternest tone.

"Kiss me, Marco," Christina repeated.

Releasing Bianca, Marco leaned over to kiss Christina. A split second later, his long arm snaked out to grab the baby, who appeared ready to topple over again.

"Marco! You are impossible."

All at once Pansy came racing down the beach, shrieking stridently as she was harassed by a squawking, flapping Cicero. With a gleeful laugh, Bianca toddled off after the two.

Christina collapsed into giggles.

Marco's expression was stunned. "Why, that devious little minx! She knew how to walk all along!"

"Did I not tell you so?" Christina asked with an air of superiority.

He stared at his wife in horror. "*Dio mio*, she is going to turn out just like you!"

Christina beat on Marco's head with her fists, while he laughed and held her at bay with his forearms. Afterward, she lay back on the sand with a heavy sigh, exhausted by their struggles. She glanced down the beach—Bianca had strayed several yards from them.

"You chase her down, Marco. I am too fat."

"You are adorable—and just the way I like you."

Quickly kissing Christina's lips, Marco sprang up and sprinted off down the beach. The sun outlined the profile of the giant pirate as he scooped his laughing, beloved daughter up into his arms.